COLONIAL COUNTRYSIDE

COLONIAL COUNTRYSIDE

CREATIVE AND HISTORICAL RESPONSES

EDITORS: CORINNE FOWLER,
JEREMY POYNTING

First published in Great Britain in 2024
Peepal Tree Press Ltd
17 King's Avenue
Leeds LS6 1QS
England

ISBN13: 9781845235666

Supported using public funding by
ARTS COUNCIL
ENGLAND

Contents

INTRODUCTION

JEREMY POYNTING

In 2018, the Arts Council of England and Heritage Lottery funded a child-led history and creative writing project called 'Colonial Countryside: National Trust Houses Reinterpreted.' It involved Leicester University, Peepal Tree Press, the National Trust and the spoken word curator, Renaissance One. This three-year project had five elements: working with 100 primary pupils to explore the historical connections of ten country houses to the British Empire; commissioning ten Black and Asian British authors to write about one of the houses in a genre of their choice; assembling a team of expert historians including Miranda Kaufmann, Madge Dresser, Marian Gwyn and Katie Donington to work with both the children and the writers to provide a factual basis for their investigations and imaginative projections; the commissioning of photographs to record the children's experiences by Ingrid Pollard, famed for her explorations of Black British relationships to the countryside; and the production of this anthology which contains the ten creative pieces, each followed by a brief, factual historical essay on the house concerned. The book includes Pollard's photo-essay about the children's involvement with the houses.

The ten National Trust houses featured here – Basildon Park, Buckland Abbey, Calke Abbey, Charlecote Park, Dyrham Park, Kedleston Hall, Penrhyn Castle, Speke Hall, Sudbury Hall, Sutton House and Uppark – reflect the intensity and scale of British colonial and imperial activities over four centuries. From the dawn of the C17th to the mid C20th, the British Empire encompassed Britain's military and naval adventures overseas; its trade in goods and people; the accumulation of individual and family fortunes and the making of the elites who controlled the British economy and political power; the encouragement of colonial settlement and the extensive bureaucracy and military-style policing of colonial rule over millions of subject peoples in Africa, the Americas, the Caribbean, Asia, the Middle and the Far East; and, in its later years, stimulating what the Jamaican poet Louise Bennett called 'colonisation in reverse'[1] in the making of our current multicultural, multiethnic society.

In 1600, the East India Company charter was granted by Queen Elizabeth I. It was permitted to assemble a huge private army, and went on to conquer vast swathes of India, ultimately leading to British imperial rule.[2] In 1660, the Royal African Company (formerly the Company of Royal Adventurers Trading to Africa) was established through a royal charter by Charles II, who granted it a monopoly on slave-trading. This charter gave legitimacy to England's involvement in the slave-trade, and the Royal African Company forced more Africans into chattel slavery than any other slave-trading business.[3] British colonial trade in commodities such as tobacco, sugar, tea, coffee, tropical woods and opium was supported by and stimulated the growth of merchant houses, banks, insurers, political careers, plantation agents and commercial shipping networks.[4] The profits were spent on British country estates, art galleries and artworks, schools, universities and hospitals, roads and railways. Former colonial administrators, East India Company officials and owners of enslaved people became major landowners, which allowed some of them to exert influence as MPs. Meanwhile, many landless rural people were driven from modest self-sufficiency into poorly paid wage labour, because the big estates acquired through imperial wealth quite frequently enclosed what had once been common land. Colonial profits further concentrated the ownership of land, so the current exclusion of British people from access to only 8% of privately owned land can be seen as another legacy of colonialism.[5]

The British Empire's decline was slow (Ireland and Brunei gained their independence in 1921 and 1984 respectively) and the legacies of four hundred years could not and did not end with formal independence – for either colonised or coloniser. In some instances, the last years of colonial rule were marked by intense and violent conflict. This was the case in Ireland, Palestine, Malaysia, Kenya, Aden and Zimbabwe.[6] Even in the Caribbean, where the end of empire was generally peaceful, Britain sent troops to British Guiana in 1953 and imprisoned the leaders of its elected government.[7]

But what happened in the colonial empire is not the subject here. What we (here 'we' refers to Corinne Fowler and myself, as the sharers of ideas and originators of the project and the joint editors of this anthology) wanted to do was to explore how the history of empire and colonialism continues to shape our British present. The centuries-long imperial subjugation of others was justified by beliefs in racial and cultural superiority, ranging from overtly racist ideologies to the paternalism that regarded colonised people as children – as male British legislators regarded women until the Equal Franchise act of 1928 – as though whiteness really was superior. This is still part of a collective inheritance we have to deal with.[8]

Through the process of Brexit, we were aware of a pervasive imperial nostalgia and were concerned by attempts to speak on behalf of 'the nation', as if we all shared the same point of view and had the same material and cultural interests. Specifically, through the visible and much-visited medium of England's country houses we wanted to explore how the long British relationship with the Caribbean and India has shaped us, and how differences of class, gender, ethnicity and sexual identity in turn shaped how that relationship has been experienced.

But it was a particular experience, many years ago, that pointed to what we wanted to achieve. It was a comment made to me at a reception to launch a prize for Black and Asian women writers at Harewood House in Yorkshire. I knew about the property's origins in the 18th century from the profits made by the Lascelles family from their trade in enslaved people, slave-grown sugar and the financing of companies involved in trans-Atlantic trade. The documentation was there in S.D. Smith's 2006 book, *Slavery, Family and Gentry Capitalism in the British Atlantic: The World of the Lascelles, 1648-1834*. This well-researched book was full, as it needed to be, of economic tables and statistical calculations which were unlikely to invite the general reader. Something more was required to explore and communicate the human stories behind the statistics. At Harewood House, there was then (in 2012) no visible evidence of how the house had been financed. During a tour of the building on that occasion, the guide explained that the extensive rebuilding of the house begun in 1840 was the result of 'money coming into the family through marriage'. Nicholas Draper had then recently published his pioneering study *The Price of Emancipation, Slave-Ownership, Compensation and British Society at the End of Slavery* (2010) which documented how owners of enslaved people had been compensated from general revenues for relinquishing their human property (whilst the formerly-enslaved were told they were free, but had to work unpaid for the next six years, virtually an average working lifetime for an enslaved person in the Caribbean at that time).[9] Since Henry Lascelles had received £26,309 in compensation (worth about £3.5M now), the guide's explanation seemed evasive or at best ignorant. Peepal Tree Press had meetings with the Lascelles family, and though, at the time, nothing came directly of discussions we had about ways of acknowledging Harewood's origins, the family nonetheless began its own journey towards telling their part of the story in truthful and imaginative ways. Their guidebooks are now models of historical acknowledgement.

The spark for the Colonial Countryside project came from a quiet remark to me made by Paulette Morris, then working for Peepal Tree, at this launch event. What was needed, she said, was a recognition that what had brought her family to Leeds from Jamaica in the 1950s and what lay behind the splendour of Harewood House, on Leeds's outskirts, was part of the same story. Her family, like many of the descendants of people who had been forcibly transported from Africa and then abandoned in the Caribbean when British investors found other more profitable places for their capital, had emigrated to Britain as a route out of rural poverty or urban insecurity to make better lives. These were decades when unemployment in Jamaica and elsewhere in the Caribbean was regularly around thirty per cent and much employment was seasonal. Jamaica, like so many Caribbean islands, had been held back from development because it was still seen as a place intended to supply sugar and other tropical commodities to European consumers. One consequence of this was that even in the later colonial period, in all the Caribbean islands, educational opportunity was severely rationed, quite explicitly because the majority of the population were intended to remain as unskilled labour. Even in the 1950s, the intake of the Caribbean's 'best' schools, modelled on English grammar schools, came predominantly from the white or lighter brown upper and middle classes, with children of the Black majority massively under-represented.

What Paulette said at the Harewood House event highlighted a connection that many of us had been failing to make. I had read extensively about how plantation slavery and British colonial rule had shaped the Caribbean and about Caribbean peoples' active struggles to define themselves.[10] As a publisher, Peepal Tree Press had long been committed to publishing both Caribbean and Black British writing that reflected on those legacies. I knew about the economic privations that drove Caribbean people to emigrate in the postwar period,[11] the colonial legacies that encouraged some of them to think of the UK as 'the mother country',[12] and their subsequent struggles for social justice in the UK.[13] But even though Eric Williams's *Capitalism and Slavery* had argued, as long ago as 1944, that the trade in sugar and slaves had made a major contribution to British economic development in the 18th and 19th centuries,[14] what I'd never really done was look at the other ways in which the Caribbean (and India) had shaped the making of the UK – an input that began long before the cultural and economic contribution of the post-war 'Windrush' generation. Thanks to the work of the Legacies of British Slave-Ownership project, based at UCL, we are now beginning to understand the extent to which Britain has been shaped by what was a much longer relationship with the Caribbean. Unlike the cotton plantations in the Southern States of America, British-owned sugar plantations were 4,000 miles away, making it too easy to ignore the Caribbean's transformative contribution to the Britain mainland itself. And unlike in the Southern States of the USA, with perhaps the exception of Barbados, there was no white settler culture in the West Indian islands. The white planters in Jamaica were famed for their live-hard, die-young, extreme gluttony and violent sexual predatoriness. Britons went to the Caribbean to make their money from exploiting Black and later Indian labour and then come home with their money. Out of sight, out of mind.

The conversation at Harewood House was something that I shared with Corinne Fowler and she turned this germ of an idea into a practical project that involved the organisations noted above. Corinne expanded the idea by including the plundering activities of the East India Company in India so that the figure of the 'West Indian', the planter/merchant representative of new sugar wealth crossed paths with the East India Company 'Nabob'. Both these figures were significant enough in British culture to generate popular plays about them: Richard Cumberland's *The West Indian* (1771) and Samuel Foote's *The Nabob* (1772). The absence of awareness of the Indian side of this historical connection was all too evident when I visited Powys Castle in mid-Wales (chiefly to enjoy the splendid gardens there), which was once the home of Robert Clive. This was a good many years ago, but I remember how poorly organised the museum was. Cards were hand-written and uninformative and had nothing to say about how controversial a figure Clive had been even in his own day, and nothing that indicated how one of the world's largest Mughal collections had found its way to Powys. The word 'loot' wasn't then mentioned.

We began to look more closely at the range of historical work that threw light on the Caribbean's and India's place in the making of Britain – the flow of wealth, goods and artefacts, people, narratives, cultural influences, ideas and literary writing. It is one of the ironies of British intellectual history that ideas about 'liberty', 'cultivation' and the 'freeborn Englishman' were funded in the eighteenth century by the racial capitalism of the slave trade and slave-grown sugar, as Catherine Hall shows brilliantly in her recent book *Lucky Valley: Edward Long and the History of Racial Capitalism* (2024). It was reading such as this that shaped the ideas about the form this project should take.

From books such as *Legacies of British Slave Ownership* (2014) (and Maxine Berg and Pat Hudson's recent *Slavery, Capitalism and the Industrial Revolution* (2023)), we know much more about the wealth that came back to Britain and how it was invested in land and property, in subsequent industrial development, in buying ennoblement of social status (as Peter Kalu's story about Richard Watt of Speke Hall records) and sometime squandered in spectacular ways, as in William Beckford's Gothic folly of Fonthill Abbey (which collapsed only 18 years after it was built). We know that some of this wealth and landownership persists into the present, such as the holdings of the Conservative M.P. Richard Ernle-Erle Drax, and his continued ownership of the Drax Hall sugar estate in Barbados. One of the writers that Peepal Tree has published, the poet Esther Phillips, grew up in the village next to this estate and is now a prominent voice in the movement for reparations.[15] More recently, we have seen how some of the inheritors of wealth from slave trading and slave-grown sugar have been drawn to write family histories and to offer both real and symbolic tokens of regret, and some institutions have recognised that their status, wealth and cultural power rests in part on the profits of enslaved labour.[16] In books such as *Slavery and the British Country House* (2013), edited by Madge Dresser and Andrew Hann, and Stephanie Barczewski's *Country Houses and the British Empire 1700-1930* (2016) are the beginnings of histories that move from the general to individual houses. Belatedly, this research is finding its way into the guides for some but not all houses and in the labelling of exhibits.

We read work documenting the growth of consumer culture in the 18th century, and the focus on material artefacts as ways of looking at who was involved in their production and exchange and the values that were attached to them. These included goods from the Caribbean such as sugar, rum, mahogany, coffee, tobacco, limes, cotton and indigo. One of the stories in this anthology explores the connections between the cultivated artistry of mahogany furniture in Basildon Park and the brutality surrounding its foresting by enslaved people in Jamaica.

We read work that documents how the slave trade and the sugar industry created the wealth of port cities such as Bristol, Liverpool and Glasgow. This included Madge Dresser's book about Bristol, *Slavery Obscured: The Social History of the Slave Trade in an English Provincial Port c. 1698-c.1833* (2001). It is encouraging that a later edition no longer needs the first part of the title. We read classic books like Sidney Mintz's *Sweetness and Power: The Place of Sugar in Modern History* (1986) which reminded how sugar provided a cheap source of energy for working people (at the cost of their health) in the later 18th and 19th centuries, and how middle-class women boycotted sugar as a form of protest against slavery. In terms of India and the wider empire, we learnt more about the East India Company and about the vital role of produce from the empire in feeding and changing taste in Britain from James Walvin's pioneering *Fruits of Empire: Exotic Produce and British Taste, 1660-1800* (1997). Books such as these made sense of why, amongst the artefacts of Dyrham Park, there are tiles portraying pineapples. We discovered very readable studies concerning the trade in plants from across the empire in diversifying the British garden and creating the whole nursery/ garden centre industry as we know it today, and about the vital activities of Kew Gardens (the Royal Botanic Gardens) in developing plant science across the empire to stimulate plantation-based wealth using the labour of indentured bond-workers from India and China in the rubber plantations of Malaysia, which in turn was vital in making possible the mass motor industry.[17]

We knew Peter Fryer's foundational *Staying Power: The History of Black People in Britain* (1984) and other important books that followed,[18] which focused on the presence of people from Africa, the Caribbean and India in Britain long before Windrush. Miranda Kaufman's *Black Tudors* (2017) documented how far back that presence went. We wanted to work with a vision of the past that recognised that the first Black British writers such as Ignatius Sancho, Olaudah Equiano, Ottobah Cugoana, Mary Prince and others,[19] can still speak to us across time, and that they were engaged with aspects of British society beyond their core messages about the evils of slavery. For example, Olaudah Equiano was an active member of the London Corresponding Society, one of the first radical groups to demand a voice for the vast mass of people without a vote. He lived in the house of Thomas Hardy, a shoemaker who was one of the society's founders and its secretary, who lost his wife in childbirth when she was injured by a church and king mob who invaded his house. Hardy, like other leaders of the LCS – who saw rebellious enslaved people as their allies in their struggle for social justice – was put on trial by the government for treason but acquitted by the jury.

As well as money, people and goods, narratives in many genres flowed back from the Caribbean and India. There are early historical accounts of settlement, with descriptions of new tropical fauna and flora, such as in William Strachey's 'A true reportory of the wracke, and redemption of Sir Thomas Gates Knight; vpon, and from the Ilands of the Bermudas' (1610) (which very probably influenced Shakespeare's writing of the *Tempest*), and Richard Ligon's *A True and Exact History of the Island of Barbadoes* (1657) which weighed up the potential profits and difficulties the island offered the prospective coloniser. At least sixty substantial histories of the Caribbean followed over the next two hundred years, from single island histories to Bryan Edwards five-volume *History, Civil and Commercial, of the British Colonies in the West Indies* (1793, 1819). All these books were published in London. Some provided British readers with seductive accounts of landscapes of tropical plenty and set out to encourage settlers and investors, whilst others, like Edward Long's three-volume *History of Jamaica* (1774, including its account of the 1763 Tacky rebellion) set out to remind the British government and MPs that those who were in the colony creating and sending home wealth needed British military support to survive. Almost without exception, these histories set out to justify white supremacy and the necessity of brutally repressive measures to exact labour from enslaved people to ensure profitable returns on British investments. Only in a much smaller proportion of the writing is it possible to find any element of even ethnographic curiosity about the cultural practices and beliefs of enslaved people. The Gothic novelist, Mathew Gregory 'Monk' Lewis's *Journal of a West India Proprietor Kept during a Residence in the Island of Jamaica* (1833) is one exception. However, the unvarnished truth about the freedom of white owners and managers to indulge their most sadistic desires came not from published books, but from hidden diaries such as those of Thomas Thistlewood, which Trevor Burnard draws on in *Mastery, Tyranny, and Desire: Thomas Thistlewood and His Slaves in the Anglo-Jamaican World* (2004).

We were interested in the legacy of British imaginative writing about the Caribbean and India, beginning with *The Tempest* (c. 1611), which in the relationship between Prospero and Caliban foresees the centuries of clashes between unbridled power and rebellion at the heart of the colonial relationship. It includes Aphra Behn's *Oroonoko* (1688), the multiple versions of the story of Inkle and Yarico first publicised in *The Spectator* by Richard Steele in 1711, Tobias Smollet's 1748 novel *The Adventures of Roderick Random*, which draws on his life as a surgeon in Jamaica, and novels such as Charlotte Smith's *The Story of Henrietta* (1800), a Gothic tale, set in Jamaica, which followed in the genre tradition set by the slave-owning Matthew Lewis, whose novel, *The Monk* (1796), influenced a tradition of Gothic writing that linked the Caribbean and Britain. For instance, stories about 'zombies' fascinated Samuel Taylor Coleridge and Robert Southey and probably influenced the writing of 'The Ancient Mariner'. Wylie Sypher's *Guinea's Captive Kings: British Anti-Slavery Literature of the XVIIIth Century* (1942), a pioneering American study of British literary responses to slavery and the Caribbean, describes many minor works that have long since slipped from view, but which show that the ethical issues around slavery and empire were once much closer to the centre of British culture. In the nineteenth century, there were the racist adventure novels of Captain Marryat that espoused an imperial ideology for younger readers.

As well as the fiction that looked outward, there is also literary writing that looks inward to the consequences of empire on British society. An anthology of poetry about the English country house from the 16th to the 18th century, in which many of the poems touch on the new sources of imperial wealth and the imported artefacts (and people) that came with it, runs to over 400 pages.[20] And, of course, Jane Austen's *Mansfield Park* makes clear its connections to a sugar estate in Antigua where Sir Thomas Bertram goes to deal with 'trouble', though Fanny Price's question about Antigua is met with a deafening silence. It is little commented on, but Charles Dickens's *Dombey and Son* (1848) has a Caribbean dimension when the honest young hero Walter Gay is packed off to Barbados as a punishment for being too kind to Mr. Dombey's despised daughter – though Dickens never tells us whether, as a global merchant house, Dombey and Son engaged in trade in slave-grown sugar. There's Charlotte Bronte's *Jane Eyre* (1847) and the connection it makes between race and madness in the character of the first

Mrs Rochester, the West Indian Creole heiress locked up in the attic, and Emily Bronte's *Wuthering Heights* (1847) where the origins of Heathcliffe in the imperial mixing of races has been suggested in recent films and in Caryl Phillip's novel, *The Lost Child* (2015). We can add Wilkie Collins's *The Moonstone* (1868), whose plot expresses reservations about the benefits of empire, and E.M. Forster's *Howards End* (1910), where the purchase of this country house connects to the profits of the West African Rubber Company – with its echoes of the dreadful cruelties of King Leopold's Congo, via Joseph Conrad's *Heart of Darkness* (1899).

As should be evident from the above, the Colonial Countryside project builds on a wide body of research and publication that has contributed to the necessary re-evaluation of the British colonial and imperial past. One goal of the project was to extend such concerns beyond academia into the public domain, remembering that there were always those who understood the nature of empire, from Dr Johnson who raised a toast in 1777 to the next slave revolt, or the Manchester working men who in 1865 protested the massacre of Jamaican peasants in the aftermath of what became known as the Morant Bay rebellion.[21] Parallel to the Colonial Countryside project, there have been the popular television programmes of David Olusoga, the well-publicised legal case involving the compensation of elderly Kenyans for their torture by British and British-led troops[22] and the embarrassment suffered by British royals over their Caribbean tour in 2022, where they were met by insistent demands for reparations. However, what signalled most clearly that this concern with history had reached wider public attention was when, in 2020, as part of the Black Lives Matter campaign, the statue of the slave trader Edward Colston was consigned to the Bristol docks and thence to a museum.

When we originally defined the project's objectives, there were several goals: that it should focus not just on those who built or purchased British country houses, but on the Black presence connected to those houses; that our schools needed the kind of curriculum that helped make sense of Britain's present-day ethnic and cultural diversity, including for those British children whose heritage included those places which had once been part of the colonial empire; and, perhaps most importantly, we agreed that the best way to open up the past to the present was through the imagination, so creative writing was central to the Colonial Countryside project both in the work of the children and, obviously, in the ten commissions.

As the creative pieces in this book explore, Black people lived in, served in or visited country estates in the seventeenth and eighteenth centuries. Other examples include figures like Dido Belle (1761-1804), the niece of Lord Chief Justice Mansfield; Huang Ya Dong (a Chinese translator painted by Joshua Reynolds in c1776); and the gardener John Ystumllyn (c.1738-1786), an abducted African child who became a horticulturalist in Wales.[23] In much greater numbers there were also the mostly anonymous household servants (whose patronym-less names sometimes appeared in posters advertising rewards for the recapture of 'runaways'). People like these have had to wait to appear in their own person until the writing of stories such as Karen Onojaife's 'Stet', set in and around Charlecote Park, as have the Black children who appear in a significant genre of 18th century painting, as decorative but nameless elements at the edge of the frame, children whose ownership was a symbol of new wealth, whom Seni Seneviratne gives voice to in her sequence of poems in this book.[24] As the historian Laurence Westgaph and others have observed, one of slavery's legacies is that Britain is home to people of African heritage who will never know their original names and places of origin because plantation records imposed the owner's and English names on them.

There were other facts that we wanted the project to engage with. One was that although there have always been British critics of colonialism,[25] most of the original documents on which earlier colonial histories were based had in general been written by those who had vested interests in defending and preserving the system. The owners of enslaved people took great care to deny them the skills of reading and writing (not always with success), so if we ever hear the voices of enslaved people in official documents, we know they had no control over how their voices were recorded. Here, we wanted to give explicit access to Black and British Asian perspectives. Secondly, we were conscious that, whilst a century or so ago there were popular and accessible (if mostly jingoistic and racist) works of fact and fiction aimed at a wide range of British readers, both young and adult,[26] over the past fifty years, writing in Britain about Empire and the colonial past has, until very recently, largely taken specialist academic form. The emergence in the last dozen or so years of novels by James Robertson, Caryl Phillips, Catherine Johnson, Jo Baker, Paterson Joseph and others[27] provided good evidence for our belief that creative writing has the capacity to go beyond historical commentary and explore in sensitive ways the fuller human dimensions of the experiences to be found in the histories of these houses *and* reach a wider range of readers.

As noted, one key goal of the Colonial Countryside project was to contribute to a school curriculum that would help make historical sense of Britain's present-day ethnic and cultural diversity. From the project's inception, the principle of children leading the way was central. As David Olusoga has said, 'if you want a glimpse of the future, go to any infant school',[28] because a significant proportion of those pupils will be of mixed heritage. The schools involved in the project came from Bangor (Wales), Birmingham, Bristol, Derby, Leicester, Liverpool, Plymouth and Reading, some of which were conveniently near the ten National Trust houses. It was at this stage that Renaissance One were involved in setting up the inaugural child-led conference and readings, events with an emphasis on the spoken word – outcomes of the project not contained in these pages but continuing in the learning and confidence of the children who took part.

From the start, the teachers in our ten participating primary schools were astonished at how animated these children were when they looked at copies of seventeenth and eighteenth-century documents – but of course, paper documents and centuries-old handwriting are novelties in their digital world. The commitment to child leadership meant that adult facilitators stood back and watched in awe as participating pupils gave guided tours to adult visitors at Calke Abbey, asked National Trust volunteers about the provenance of colonial objects on display and gave papers at the Colonial Countryside children's conference. They also made passionate speeches at the 2019 British Museum Annual conference arguing for 'relevance' in explaining why their own cultural heritage made them want this history on display in British country houses. One pupil of Indian heritage even initiated a fieldtrip to Tipu Sultan's summer palace in Southern India when she asked her parents to take her there. Afterwards, she reported to a packed auditorium at the British Museum that she had seen a miniature painting of Tipu Sultan at Charlecote Park and wondered why it was there. This led her on a journey into British colonial history where she learned about Tipu Sultan and his struggles against the English and French East India Companies. She said she had noticed that European historians were obsessed with Tipu's struggles with the East India Company, and whereas supporters of Narendra Modi's Hindu nationalism thought of Tipu as a villain because of his Muslim faith, the Muslim curator of the summer palace in Bangalore thought he was a hero for helping to build India's infrastructure, including its silk industry.

In response to the history they encountered, and the Trust properties they visited, the 100 participating pupils produced short personal essays and poems, also co-producing exhibitions with poets and curators on site. One of these poems, displayed at Penrhyn Castle's 'What a World!' exhibition, explored the way in which that property had been built with Jamaican slavery wealth. One poem, a reflection on power and history-telling, about the property owner, Lord Penrhyn, simply read:

He had money
I had history
His money bought my history.[29]

As far as creative writers were concerned, this was a project that stimulated great interest. After a competitive process of application (we had 140 sub-missions), ten writers, nine Black British of various heritages and one Car-ibbean-based author, were selected and commissioned to use their imagina-tions in whatever way they wished in response to one of the ten houses. The variety of approaches more than met our hopes that this was the way to tell the stories. You will find pieces that relate directly to the people involved in the histories of the houses, imaginative inventions of the presence of those who were written out of the historical record, and insightful reflections on the artefacts to be found. Several of the pieces reflect on the feelings of con-temporary Black and Asian British visitors to these properties.

Jacqueline Crooks writes about the ghostly echo of a relationship in India finding its way into the imagined present of Basildon Park, near Reading, an estate which was bought in 1771 and built upon by a former East India Company official, Sir Francis Sykes (who extended the estate by enclosing more land which blocked off footpaths, forcing locals to take the long way round). Ayanna Lloyd Banwo writes about Buckland Abbey, in Devon, once the property of Sir Francis Drake. Her focus is not so much on this celebrated national hero, but on an African, Diego the Maroon (a man formerly enslaved by the Spanish), who accompanied Drake across the globe on his voyages and played a crucial role in his privateering ventures in the New World. Karen Onojaife focuses on the precarious existence of Black servants by writing about a Black page boy in Charlecote Park in Warwickshire in the aftermath of his master's death. Andre Bagoo updates the genre of loco-descriptive poetry in writing about entering Dyrham Park, roughly equidistant from Bath and Bristol, the property of the founding figure of colonial enterprise, William Blathwayt, until his panoramic view is brought up short by the sight of two seventeenth-century African stands given to Blathwayt by his uncle, Thomas Povey. The wooden figures are of two African men kneeling in chains, figures whom contemporary letters refer to as 'two boys'. Mahsuda Snaith writes a series of 'flash fiction' stories about Kedleston Hall, near Derby, which belonged to Nathanial Curzon, the Viceroy of India. Her stories link together images of the Indian past, Kedleston itself and the visit of a contemporary British family of Indian heritage. Maria C. Thomas writes about a school visit to Penrhyn Castle in Bangor, which was built from the proceeds of Jamaican wealth. This sugar wealth was also invested in the family's slate quarries, and the paintings hung in the castle, which are one of the attractions for visitors, were funded by slavery compensation money. Peter Kalu's story about the retired owner of Jamaican plantations, Richard Watt the third, who bought and restored Speke Hall as a way of signalling his rise in social station, expands on another significant use of slavery's profits. The theme of Black servants and enslaved children is featured in a series of poems by Seni Seneviratne, who has spoken about the emotional cost of working on this topic on our Colonial Countryside open access course, called 'Country Houses and the British Empire'.[30] Many houses now in the care of the National Trust are lavishly decorated with Chinese wallpapers, hand-painted in China or produced in Europe, in line with the requirements of wealthy tastes. Hannah Lowe explores the history of these wallpapers in her poetry sequence. Malachi Macintosh writes about a contemporary relationship across the boundaries of race and class, which founders on a visit to the mysterious Calke Abbey in Derbyshire, and the bizarre displays of taxidermy in the glass specimen cases which crowd nearly every room. Perhaps without knowing it, he updates one of the only country house poems written from below the stairs, by the 18th century poet, Mary Leapor (1722-1746), who worked in domestic service. Her poem 'Crumble Hall' is a funny and satirical take on the growing fad for country-house visiting in this period, at the expense of the disparate 'tat' on display. In Crumble Hall,

These Rooms are furnish'd amiably and full:
Old shoes, and Sheep-ticks bred in Stack of Wool;
Grey Dobbin's Gears, and Drenching-Horns enow;
Wheel-spokes – the Irons of a tatter'd Plough.[31]

We think it is rewarding to read these commissioned creative pieces, fiction and poetry, as responses and occasionally as echoes to some of the absences in the earlier British literary response to Caribbean and Indian connections.

Here I want to place on record that the Colonial Countryside project took place within a climate of considerable hostility that began with the response to a separate but related project, and went on to include the publication of Corinne Fowler's own book, *Green Unpleasant Land* (2020). Between 2019-2020, Corinne was commissioned to work with the National Trust to explore the colonial connections of their properties. In this role, she co-authored the National Trust's 'Interim Report on the Connections between Colonialism and Properties now in the Care of the National Trust, Including Links with Historic Slavery'. This report, an audit of published, peer-reviewed research on National Trust houses, was the organisation's first formal venture into the colonial history of its properties. It found that a third of National Trust properties had substantial connections to the British Empire, with proprietors who were colonial administrators, slave-owners or East India Company officials. The involvement of such an important national institution in making these connections set alarm bells ringing in sections of parliament and the press. As Corinne and the National Trust were rapidly to discover, taking this knowledge into a public arena outside academia, provoked the wrath of those who preferred that Britain's colonial past remain unstirred, or at least spoken about in more celebratory terms than the historical evidence would warrant. Heavyweight journalists such as Simon Heffer and Charles Moore (ennobled by Boris Johnson as Baron Moore of Etchingham) wrote inflammatory articles in the *Telegraph*, *Mail* and *Express* to abuse the mainly female authors of the National Trust report in overtly misogynist terms. After the *Mail* became involved, Corinne herself began receiving threats of personal violence, which continued for a year after the publication of her own book, *Green Unpleasant Land* (2020).[32]

The suggestion was that this was just new-fangled "wokeism", but as I've suggested above, what was being released into the public sphere was far from new. From the 1960s onwards, particularly with the growth of Caribbean historiography stimulated by the founding of the University of the West Indies, and Indian history in various Indian universities (from the 1950s and earlier), and postcolonial work in North America and the UK, there was a wealth of research into the nature of British economic, political and cultural relations with the Caribbean islands and Guyana, of British rule in India, and of the struggles of colonised peoples to achieve independence. But if a great deal was published, it was primarily in university presses.

The project also evidently created alarm in government quarters, when leading figures from the Conservative Common Sense[33] Group of MPs and Peers – a group that evidently had the ear of the then Minister for Culture, Media and Sport, Oliver Dowden – requested a meeting with Arts Council of England and Heritage Lottery to demand that no more funding be given to the Colonial Countryside project, on the grounds that this was a 'political project', and public money should not be spent on politics. As it happened, all the grant funding had been spent, but it was a salutary warning that the principle of an 'arms-length' relationship between the DCMS and the project's public funders was evidently not sacrosanct. A voluble group of country house owners also objected to colonial history being spoken about, some writing inflammatory articles about it which triggered further hostile responses. A pressure-group called Restore Trust was established, in 2021, initially to dissuade the real National Trust from communicating country houses' colonial connections to its nearly 6 million visitors, but it has so far failed to have any of their nominees elected despite pouring money into their campaigns. Though these critics claimed that disgusted members were leaving the National Trust in droves, the evidence of increasing Trust membership suggests that the vast majority of their members have no problem with the efforts of the National Trust to provide relevant and historically accurate accounts of their properties.

The Common Sense Group (and some government ministers), demanded an end to the rewriting of history. As any well-taught schoolchild knows, there is a difference between 'history' as events in the past (which obviously cannot be changed) and writing historically about past events, where historians have always been in the business of rewriting narratives from the perspective of the changing present, newly found records and from a variety of different perspectives and motivations. It was, indeed, the absurdity of the idea that histories as narratives could be forever fixed in one version and the extraordinary virulence of these attacks that reinforced our sense that the Colonial Countryside project was timely and important.

Why the virulence? One can only assume that a view of the world as it used to be, regarded in some quarters as essential to the preservation of the world as it is, was felt to be under threat. The arguments have taken two forms. There have been some, like Nigel Biggar, who have argued that, on balance, colonialism brought benefits to the countries and territories that were colonised. Biggar's recent book, *Colonialism: A Moral Reckoning* (2023), argues that empire was committed to 'abolishing the slave trade in the name of a Christian conviction of the basic equality of all human beings. It ended endemic inter-tribal warfare, opened local economies to the opportunities of global trade, moderated the impact of inescapable modernisation, established the rule of law and liberal institutions such as a free press, and spent itself in defeating the murderously racist Nazi and Japanese empires in the Second World War.' It is always a give-away when empire loyalists are keen to claim abolition but not the almost three hundred years that preceded it. When you read Michael Taylor's book *The Interest: How the British Establishment Resisted the Abolition of Slavery* (2020), it is hard not to see parallels between the contemporary defenders of the glories of empire and those who fought tooth and nail to prevent the passing of the parliamentary acts abolishing the slave trade (1807) and the subsequent Slavery Abolition Acts of 1833 and 1838 in the face of ethical opposition that had been growing since the 1760s, not least in the poetry of William Cowper (1731-1800), perhaps the most influential English literary articulator of the feelings that animated the abolitionist cause.[34] Biggar's very selective overview was answered by *The Truth About Empire*, a collection of essays by leading experts in British colonial history, which, insisting that rigorous historical evidence really matters, offered forensic critiques of books like Biggar's which set out to defend the colonial project or adopt an ahistorical balance sheet approach to the topic.[35]

The other form of argument has been to admit that bad things happened, that colonial violence and the cruelties of enslavement were unfortunate lapses in a generally benevolent empire by people who were only acting in accordance with the values of their own times and that it is wrong to judge the actions of people in the past by current ethical standards – as though the experience, thoughts and actions of those millions who suffered under and/or resisted imperial conquest in the colonies were irrelevant. It is an argument that denies both that past events have present legacies and denies that there were critics at the time of those events who made ethical objections to them and to colonialism in general. It is an argument compellingly overturned by books like Jack P. Greene's *Evaluating Empire and Confronting Colonialism in 18ᵗʰ Century Britain* and Priya Gopal's *Insurgent Empire* (2019) which explores the considerable resistance to empire both in the colonies and, crucially, back in Britain.[36]

Another complaint from the critics of "woke" history is that it is an attempt to make British people ashamed of their past and their whiteness. Andrew Gimpson, a member of the Restore Trust group seeking election (unsuccessfully) to the National Trust board, described one of his goals as ending the promotion of 'a self-hating conception of history'.[37] Some revealing assumptions lie behind that description. They include the idea that there is (or should be) an English nation that has a single, unitary view of the relationship between past and present; that a positive emotional response to the English past should be the norm; and, implicitly, that the English nation is white.[38] Whilst assumptions such as these have long been the staple of English nationalist thought, first arising most prominently in the early twentieth century when those invested in empire began to feel threatened by European and Japanese competition and the stirrings of anticolonialism in subject territories, none of these assumptions stands up to the historical evidence. As soon as we recognise that the relationship of different parts of society (in terms of class, gender and race), to allocations of power, ownership of land, capital and political access, is different, both historically and in the present, the idea of a single view of the past is absurd.

And isn't the idea that most of us should feel either *personal* pride or shame in the activities of British people in the past rather silly? In the period when British MPs were making decisions about the abolition of the slave trade and the emancipation of the enslaved, less than 3% of the UK population had the vote, from which women were entirely excluded. It is true that all Britons benefited indirectly in some measure from the profits of empire and colonialism in the rise in living standards and access to cheaper food, and it is also true that some 6% of the population at the time of emancipation had some interest in slavery compensation, but 94% didn't, and amongst the 6% who did, a very much smaller percentage owned the majority of enslaved people. In sum, any benefits from either transatlantic slavery and the sugar trade, or the East India Company's activities were very unequally allocated. We all live among the consequences of past activities, but the responsibility for them and the rewards that come down from them are by no means evenly shared. What must matter in the present is how the legacies of the past impact on groups of people in different ways. This is something, as noted above, that some individual families and institutions that benefited from the profits of slavery have been recognising in recent years, though others await acknowledgement, such as the Church of England and the royal family which sponsored and profited from the Royal African Company.[39] Nevertheless, though the rewards were and are unevenly shared, what is undeniable is that the economic, social and cultural world all of us live in was made in a significant part by the cruelly exploited labour of enslaved Africans in the West Indian islands and Guyana – an evil extending over three centuries that a few individuals and institutions owning up to can never truly repair.[40]

There is finally the implication that telling the truth about the colonial past is the action of people who hate their country and themselves. Tell that to our great national poet, William Blake, prophet against empire from his earliest to his latest work. In *Jerusalem* (the prophecy written between 1804-1820, not the hymn which is part of the earlier epic, *Milton*), Blake writes of Albion, the fallen hero of the poem who is both England as a place and a people, whose worst side, his spectre, displays the selfish spirit of desire for possession and conquest, both in the long wars with France (largely fought over ownership of Caribbean islands) and the cruelty perpetrated both in Britain and in the Caribbean colonies. Blake's reference to 'Druids' in the quotation below is his shorthand for all forms of repressive state power, the military, the priesthood of 'thou shalt not', and the law which protected the wealthy by punishing even the most minor offences against property with 'the Fatal Tree' of hangings at Tyburn. When Blake reclaims Albion as his own, he acknowledges both his own human flaws of selfishness, and indicates that love of one's country is not incompatible with severe criticism of its misdeeds. As Blake writes in *The Marriage of Heaven and Hell*: 'Opposition is true friendship.'

> Albions Spectre from his Loins
> Tore forth in all the pomp of War!
> Satan his name: in flames of fire
> He stretch'd his Druid Pillars far.
> [...]
> Spectre of Albion! Warlike Fiend!
> In clouds of blood & ruin roll'd:
> I here reclaim thee as my own
> My Selfhood! Satan! arm'd in gold.[41]

This is a book that should have been published three years ago but was sidelined by Covid-19 and the long period of closure of National Trust houses. It emerges into quite a different world from that of the original idea.

Endnotes and suggestions for further reading:

1. Louise Bennett, 'Colonisation in Reverse', in *Jamaica Labrish* (Kingston: Sangster's Bookstores, 1966), 179-180.
2. On the history of the East India Company see William Dalrymple, *The Anarchy: The East India Company, Corporate Violence, and the Pillage of an Empire* (London: Bloomsbury, 2019); on how East India fortunes were invested in land and property in Britain see Margot Finn and Kate Smith eds. *The East India Company at Home 1757-1857* (London: UCL Press, 2017).
3. On the Royal African Company see K.G. Davies, *The Royal African Company* (London: Longman, 1957) and William Pettigrew, *Freedom's Debt: The Royal African Company and the Politics of the Atlantic Slave Trade 1672-1752* (London: UNC Press, 2016). The slave-trader Edward Colston was a member of this company which between 1672 and 1731 transported 187,697 enslaved people on the company's ships.
4. For an excellent account of how imperial trade stimulated innovation in business methods, which in turn stimulated the drive to seek even greater profits, *and* the military and naval force to keep out competitors and subjugate opposition from the colonised, see David Hancock, *Citizens of the World: London Merchants and the Integration of the British Atlantic Community*, 1735-1785 (Cambridge: CUP, 1997) and for an earlier period, Nuala Zahediah, *The Capital and the Colonies* (Cambridge: Cambridge University Press, 2010). For accounts of how other British regions participated see Chris Evans, *Slave Wales. The Welsh and Atlantic Slavery, 1660-1850* (Cardiff: University of Wales Press, 2010).
5. On enclosure see J.M. Neeson, *Commoners: Common Right, Enclosure and Social Change in England, 1700-1820* (Cambridge: Cambridge University Press, 1993); for a contemporary take on the legacies of how so much land came into private hands see Guy Shrubsole, *Who Owns England: How We Lost Our Green and Pleasant Land* (London: William Collins, 2019) and Nick Hayes, *The Book of Trespass* (London: Bloomsbury, 2020).
6. On the end of empire see Caroline Elkins, *Legacy of Violence: A History of the British Empire* (London: Bodley Head, 2022).
7. See Cheddi Jagan, *The West on Trial: My Fight for Guyana's Freedom* (London: Michael Joseph, 1966).
8. See, for instance, Saree Makdisi, *Making England Western: Occidentalism, Race and Imperial Culture* (University of Chicago Press, 2013); James Trafford, *The Empire at Home* (London: Pluto Press, 2021); and Peter Mitchell, *Imperial Nostalgia: How the British Conquered Themselves* (Manchester: Manchester University Press, 2021).
9. See Vincent Brown, *The Reaper's Garden: Death and Power in the World of At-*

lantic Slavery (Harvard University Press, 2008). Brown shows how the population of Jamaica in the 18th century changed almost totally every 7 years because mortality was so high. Orlando Patterson in *The Sociology of Slavery* (1967) estimates that if there had been any more normal pattern of live births and mortality (even such as existed among enslaved people in the American South), Jamaica would have had a Black population five million persons greater than it actually was on the eve of abolition. It was cheaper to import new bodies than rely on any attempts to extend working lives by even the most minimal standards of human welfare. These five million lost lives, just in Jamaica, make transatlantic chattel slavery an evil every bit as real as the Holocaust of 20th century Europe.

10. In the period of slavery see Michael Craton, *Testing the Chains: Resistance to Slavery in the British West Indies* (London: Cornell University Press, 1982) and Vincent Brown, *Tacky's Revolt: The Story of an Atlantic Slave War* (Massachusetts: Belknap Press, 2020). For how enslaved and ex-enslaved people created a Caribbean culture distinct from their colonial masters see Peter A. Roberts, *A Response to Enslavement: Playing their Way to Virtue* (Jamaica: UWI Press, 2018).

11. On the pressures which lay behind emigration, see Ian Patel, *We're Here Because You Were There: Immigration and the End of Empire* (London: Verso, 2021) and Ransford W. Palmer, *In Search of a Better Life: Perspectives on Migration from the Caribbean* (Connecticut: Praeger Publishers, 1990).

12. See Anne Spry Rush, *Bonds of Empire: West Indians and Britishness from Victoria to Decolonization* (Oxford: Oxford University Press, 2011).

13. For a popular history of the postwar arrival in Britain see Mike Phillips and Trevor Phillips, *Windrush: The Irresistible Rise of Multi-Racial Britain* (London: Harper Collins, 1998).

14. A recent update on Eric Williams's thesis is Maxine Berg and Pat Hudson, *Slavery, Capitalism and the Industrial Revolution* (Cambridge: Polity, 2023).

15. Professor Sir Hilary Beckles, vice-chancellor of the University of the West Indies, has calculated that 30,000 enslaved people died on the Drax Hall estates during the period of slavery with lives severely shortened by the culture of brutal ill-treatment.

16. See for instance Alex Renton, *Blood Legacy: Reckoning with a Family's Story of Slavery* (Edinburgh: Canongate, 2021). For a narrative of an author who acknowledges both slavers and enslaved people as her ancestors see Andrea Stuart, *Sugar in the Blood* (London: Portobello Books, 2012).

17. See Patricia Fara, *Sex, Botany & Empire* (London: Icon Books, 2017) and J. Gascoigne, *Science in the Service of Empire: Joseph Banks, the British State and the Uses of Science in the Age of Revolution* (Cambridge: Cambridge University Press, 1998).

18. See for instance Gretchen Girzina, *Black England: Life Before Emancipation* (London: John Murray, 1995) and David Olusoga, *Black and British: A Forgotten History* (London: Pan, 2017).

19. For Ignatius Sancho see Rehahn King, Sukhdev Sandu, James Walvin, Jane Girdham, *Ignatius Sancho: An African Man of Letters* (London: National Portrait Gallery, 1997); ed. Paul Edwards and Polly Rewt, *The Letters of Ignatius Sancho* (Edinburgh: Edinburgh University Press, 1994) and Paterson Joseph's novel

The Secret Diaries of Charles Ignatius Sancho (London: Dialogue Books, 2022); for Olaudah Equiano, see *The Interesting Narrative of the Life of Olaudah Equiano; or, Gustavus Vassa, the African, Written by Himself* (1789) and Vincent Carretta, *Equiano The African: Biography of a Self-Made Man* (Athens: University of Georgia Press, 2005); for Quobna Ottabah Cugoano see his *Thoughts and Sentiments on the Evil of Slavery* ([1787] Penguin Books, 1999); for Mary Prince see *The History of Mary Prince* ([1831] Penguin Books, 2000); for a general survey see ed. Vincent Carretta, *Unchained Voices: An Anthology of Black Authors in the English Speaking World of the 18th Century* (Lexington: University Press of Kentucky, 2004).

20. See Alistair Fowler, *The Country House Poem* (Edinburgh: Edinburgh University Press, 1994). For how a later period of poets celebrated empire see Suvir Kaul, *Poems of Nation: Anthems of Empire: English Verse in the London 18th century* (New Delhi: Oxford University Press, 2000).

21. See Priyamvada Gopal, *Insurgent Empire: AntiColonial Resistance and British Dissent* (London: Verso, 2019), 115-116. For how the suppression of the revolt split the British literary establishment, with Charles Dickens and Lord Alfred Tennyson supporting the murderous governor, see Bernard Semmel, *The Governor Eyre Controversy* (London: McGibbon & Kee, 1962). For the event itself see Gad Heuman, *The Killing Time: the Morant Bay Rebellion in Jamaica* (London: MacMillan, 1994).

22. See Caroline Elkins, *Britain's Gulag: The Brutal End of Empire in Kenya* (London: Bodley Head, 2014).

23. For Dido Belle see Paula Byrne, *The True Story of Dido Belle* (London: William Collins, 2014); for Huang Ya Dong see https://www.nationaltrustcollections.org.uk/object/129924; for John Ystumllyn see Paul Edwards and James Walvin, *Black Personalities in the Era of the Slave Trade* (London: MacMillan, 1983), 218-222.

24. For a background to Seni Seneviratne's sequence see David Dabydeen, *Hogarth's Blacks: Images of Blacks in Eighteenth Century English Art* (Kingston-upon-Thames: Dangeroo Press, 1985).

25. See for instance Jack P. Greene, *Evaluating Empire and Confronting Colonialism in 18th Century Britain* (Cambridge: Cambridge University Press (2013) and Priyamvada Gopal, *Insurgent Empire*.

26. See M. Daphne Kutzer, *Empire's Children: Empire and Imperialism in Classic British Children's Books* (London: Routledge, 2000).

27. See for instance James Robertson, *Joseph Knight* (Fourth Estate, 2003); Caryl Phillips, *The Lost Child* (Oneworld Publications, 2015); Catherine Johnson, *The Curious Tale of the Lady Caraboo* (Corgi, 2015); Jo Baker, *Longbourne* (Knopf, 2013); and Paterson Joseph, *The Secret Diaries of Charles Ignatius Sancho* (Dialogue Books, 2022).

28. David Olusoga, Blue Earth Summit Keynote Lecture, 26 October 2023, available online at: https://www.youtube.com/watch?v=8qEANN-Rnd4.

29. Fatima, aged nine, 2021.

30. Seni Seneviratne, Country Houses and the British Empire, University of Leicester, online course, 2022.

31. For Mary Leapor's "Crumble Hall", see *Poems on Several Occasions vol 2* (London:

J. Roberts, 1751), 111-122. For the growing fad for visiting country houses see Adrian Tinniswood, *The Polite Tourist: A History of Country House Visiting* (London: The National Trust, 1998 and Jocelyn Anderson, *Touring and Publicising England's Country Houses in the Long Eighteenth Century* (London: Bloomsbury Academic, 2018).

32. See the Hacked Off website for Corinne Fowler's very restrained account of the abuse and threats she received, sufficient to require police monitoring: https://hackinginquiry.org/public-debate-is-important-waves-of-press-and-political-attacks-damage-it/.

33. The "Commonsense" group might (or might not) be amused by a letter from an ardent planter opponent of the movement for abolition in 1792, who wrote: "We have Mr Pitt, Mr Fox & Mr Burke the great Orators against us, but we flatter ourselves that Common Sense is with us." (Quoted in Catherine Hall, *Lucky Valley: Edward Long and the History of Racial Capitalism*), p. 428).

34. For Cowper's important anti-slavery poems, among a rich collection of poems by others, see ed. James G. Basker, *Amazing Grace: An Anthology of Poems About Slavery 1660-1810* (Newhaven and London: Yale University Press, 2002).

35. See Alan Lester, ed., *The Truth About Empire: Real Histories of British Colonialism* (London: Hurst, 2024).

36. See endnote 25 above.

37. Andrew Gimpson: https://conservativehome.com/2023/11/14/andrew-gimson-why-i-stood-for-election-to-the-national-trusts-council-and-what-can-be-learned-from-the-results/.

38. It might be objected that there are prominent African and Asian-British members of the Conservative Party, some in or formerly in Government, who promote a view not dissimilar to Gimpson's. Anyone who has studied the history of colonial empire will recognise that there were always members of the local elites who for their own advantage embraced empire as an institution and espoused ideas about the superiority of British culture as a way of distinguishing themselves from the mass of the people. V.S. Naipaul portrays a classic of this type (which, ironically, he himself in part parodied/became) in his novel, *The Mystic Masseur*, where Ganesh Ramsumair, one-time Hindu mystic and anti-colonial politician, transforms himself into Sir G. Ramsay Muir, the besuited lover of all things British. Naipaul recognised that such figures often adopt extreme versions of this posture.

39. On the case for reparations see Hilary McD. Beckles, *Britain's Black Debt: Reparations for Caribbean Slavery and Native Genocide* (Barbados, UWI Press, 2014.)

40. For a profound discussion of just how irreparable the four hundred years of Caribbean slavery are, in terms of its genocidal impact, the centuries of bodily and psychological suffering and their continuing consequences in the deeply unequal social structures of the region, read David Scott's *Irreparable Evil: An Essay in Moral and Reparatory History* (New York: Columbia University Press, 2024). Scott does not abandon the case for calling for attempts to rectify historical wrongs, but wants us to see an enormity which is beyond repair.

41. William Blake, *Jerusalem: The Emanation of the Giant Albion*, Plate 27, (New Jersey: Princeton University Press, 1998), 171.

BUCKLAND ABBEY

Buckland Abbey, Devon
©National Trust Images/Mel Peters

Plaster statue of Sir Francis Drake (1540 - 1596) by Sir Joseph Boehm
(1834-1890) in the Lifetimes Gallery at Buckland Abbey, Devon
©National Trust Images/Chris Lacey

AYANNA LLOYD BANWO

DIEGO

'Ships at a distance have every man's wish on board.'
– *Their Eyes Were Watching God*, Zora Neale Hurston

When the sea calls his name, he slips out of quarters and keeps to the dark. He is quiet. Fast too. It's a talent that has served him well over the years and only the dead notice as he crouches low and cuts through the bush. He has only a moment, and if he were to reach it in time the sea would open for him. But when he gets to the coast, breath heavy, heart racing and skin dripping with sweat, there is no road, no escape, nothing but the moonlight lighting a path on the water.

He wakes from the dream, the third one this week, and stares into the darkness.

The sea road stays on his mind for days as he slips in and out of the rooms where he serves meals and readies his master's fine clothing for the day. For weeks now the air in Nombre de Dios has been full of whispers, the tension sharp like the edge of a blade against his pulse. *El Draque. Inglaterra. Bastardo. Sea Dog. Pirate.* He knows the names by heart. Can't help but hear as they whisper to each other, confer behind closed doors even talk openly because they never think he can make sense of the business of great men talking. He gathers their words like jewels and places them in his pockets, measures the skies and the stars, marks the days on the wooden stump outside his quarters and waits.

Days pass and the whispers become a roar. The wind changes, the stars align, and he knows the night he has been hoping for is here. When the sea calls again, he runs to the coast. The sand crunches under his feet, the night glistens, the beach curves like the new moon and there, the light shows them plain: ships making their way inland, silent as breath. And the flags, just as the whispers said: White and Red, The Cross, Inglaterra. The moon rises higher and casts a silver road on the sea.

The map of events unfolds quickly in his head – the risk, the gamble, the reward – and he flings himself into the open air. He runs toward the shore waving his arms to make sure he is seen. A bullet flies past him, then another. He can see the men on the pinnaces now, smaller boats that surround the ship, muskets raised all trained on him. And still he runs. They would not hit him, not today. Not now that the road has opened for him.

'Captain Drake!' His arms are spread wide so they could see he is not armed. 'Do you belong to Captain Drake?' By now it is clear that no forces come with him, that he alone runs toward them in the moonlight. The shots pause but the men do not lower their guns. He can just barely make them out now and he slows down, stops. The men are poised to disembark. One holds his hand up high, signalling to the ships behind to wait, not to fire.

'Who are you? Who sent you?' The man leading the closest boat calls out.

'No one but almighty God –' he bends his back, lowers his head, keeps his hands raised '– to warn you. Do not attack this night!'

Musket fire answers. He ducks but does not run. 'If you shoot me tonight the cost will be your lives!' He flings his voice into the sea and holds his ground. He does not need them to believe him; just to wait, consider. He does not dare look away or even flinch. Slowly the muskets lower. He drops his hands and keeps them loose at his sides, palms out just in case, and walks toward the boats.

'Send for your Captain! I have important information for him. Without me you will all be slaughtered. But take me aboard and you will return to England with more silver than you could ever imagine.'

He can make out their faces by the moonlight. Hard men – he has always known how to read souls – but tired, fuelled only by the promise of wealth and the frenzy of the battle that awaits them. Two men drag him to the boat. As soon as his feet touch the surf his body relaxes a little, but he holds himself steady, taut. Not yet. Not until he has seen the Captain.

They row out to the ship, the *Pasha*. He has heard the name amongst the whispers in the town. The Governor and his men speak of it like it is a spirit, a rumour. The pinnace floats into the air alongside the larger ship, pulled up to the deck by thick, moss-covered ropes. He feels the ascent in his bones, remembers the dark, the stench of bodies, the cries of the dying and then the tiny light at the top of the hold growing larger and larger as they ascended. Then the cold open air, the deck, the chains, a sky full of stars and a moon round and fat, the sea blue-black like death. He breathes deep. Steady. Wait.

They stumble onto the deck, the sails still in the soft dark. But the ship that should hum with activity is quiet with just a few men scattered about, waiting.

'Where is your captain?' Has he missed his chance? Is he too late?

'Our captain leads the attack.'

'You must send word! They know you are coming. Nombre de Dios is defended. What you want, what you really want, you will not find in the city under this moon.'

He scans their faces. Who is in charge, who's face should he focus on? They seem lost without their leader. One finally answers, 'How do you know this?'

'I hear things. Things I am not supposed to. Things that are useful. They say your Captain has been sent by the devil to torment the world. Tonight, God sends me to you.'

He knows he has them now, but the dance is delicate. 'Listen to everything I say and do exactly as I tell you. Send for your captain. Abandon the attack. When it is all over and you are richer than your wildest dreams, I ask only one thing.'

Someone laughs from the small crowd 'I expect he wants his share of our treasure.'

But the man does not flinch. 'They say that in England every man is free. Take me with you to sea. Take me to England.'

In Nombre de Dios, they call him Diego. He knows no other name. If ever there was another, a true, true name, only the sea and the moon and his blood know it now. A name means nothing when your body is not yours. This one will do as well as any other.

Diego looks at the two men who have been stationed to hold him captive in case he has lied. He is playing a dangerous game. Nombre de Dios is no more defended than it always is but with a little luck… He remembers his dream, the moonlight lighting a path on the water. He just needs them to believe him for long enough to set his plan in motion. When the sea is a locked door and the city only holds cruelty, what else is there to do?

The two men keep their pistols trained on him. They have not lowered them since they let him board the ship.

One sailor is short and stocky. 'You are either very brave or very stupid.'

'Or a liar.' This one is tall and glares at Diego as if taking his measure.

'Then he'd be very stupid, wouldn't he?'

The sky has begun to lighten. It has been hours since the moon began to move across the sky. It would not be long now until they returned.

Diego looks up at him from his position on the deck, tied to the mast. 'And you? Are you a brave man?'

The man's face changes from suspicion to anger and then becomes thoughtful. 'Only the rich can afford bravery. The most the rest of us can hope for is someone brave to follow, hope their fate covers ours as well.'

'And hope we go home with more money than when we left, eh,' the taller man smirks, his eyes glinting with the promise.

'Home?' The stocky man looks past them both, 'Better the bottom of the sea.'

His answer hangs between them until the seagulls began squawking in the early morning light.

It is hours before the pinnaces cut through the surf as the men return and the ship comes alive with crew members raising the boats, the sail. The men pour onto the deck. The stocky sailor who holds him captive draws himself to attention and the tall one pulls Diego to his feet.

The crowd parts to reveal a man with hair like flame, two men aiding him, blood streaming from his leg. Diego doesn't need to ask. The way the others move for the man to pass, the ease with which he holds himself amongst them, even injured, the crackle of energy in the air as he approaches; it is not just fear, it is something else that he has never before seen among men. Diego holds his breath. Did it work? Could he have been right? Or would the entire enterprise collapse before he even manages to set sail? He is not surprised that the man is wounded; this is no paper captain who sends men to carry out actions on his behalf. He would be in the thick of battle and any risk there was to be taken, he would take it too.

Large chests emerge from the smaller boat, passed from one man to the other, and are unloaded onto the deck. But the train stops almost as soon as it begins. One sailor flips a lid open – silver and gold trinkets, goblets, coins. These chests would have filled perhaps one pinnace but no more. Diego keeps his face steady; he is in even more danger now. Carefully, carefully. The captain approaches Diego where he stands bound, his captors holding him fast on either side. The cold iron of a pistol brushes his temple. Even with the men aiding him, he and the captain stand face to face, equal in height and the captain stares the stranger dead in the eye.

'You are the man sent to warn me of the attack.'

'And you are the bastard English pirate.'

The air ripples with the sound of pistols raising again.

'Is that what they call me?' The captain's broad face twitched. 'I quite like it.' The air around eases and they lower their pistols.

The captain steadies himself and stares at Diego. 'You lied to my men'

'I did not.'

'You insisted that the city was defended, that they were ready and waiting for us. Not only was the city barely fortified but the treasure? None! What was there to guard?'

'So, you were shot by a phantom? The trees in Nombre de Dios carry weapons, now?'

The captain grumbled 'I know fortification when I see it. They were no more expecting us than I was expecting you.'

'I did not lie. I told your men not to attack. I told them if you listened to me, you and your men would be wealthier than you could ever have imagined.'

One of the men who has been helping to load the chests onto the deck snorts and gestures at the meagre treasure.

'I did not tell you that you would come by that wealth tonight.'

The captain's pale face reddens. It is not anger. It is something else. Diego looks around at the men – the dusty, ragged clothes that hang off their frames, something almost feral in their eyes. They need a victory badly. An army ready for blood had been unleashed on a sleeping town that was barely a town at all; the only wealth they had come by was in the house of Diego's master, Governor de Palma. At any moment the entire crew could turn on him, an easy target for their frustration.

'What use are you to me?' The captain's frustration crackles. 'I should leave you here to your master's punishment or tie you to the mast and whip you till your flesh comes off in ribbons.'

The men around Diego grumble. He sees some of them nod in agreement. There would be some blood sport for them tonight.

'And return to your Queen with nothing? Months at sea with no reward? Waste the wind and the tide? Crawl up and down this coast with no safe way inland?'

The air stills. The sailors are listening. Diego looks around at them all, his arms still bound by the other two men. 'Every skirmish risks your men and every journey depletes your supplies. This place, this territory belongs to Spain. There is no place for you here —' The crew grumbles and the Captain's face grows even redder '— without allies.'

The sky is almost fully lit now by the rising sun. Any minute, the scant forces in the town would reorganise and make their way to the coast. The captain nods to the men who have been holding him steady and they turn away from Diego, carting the captain away. Diego's legs begin to give way beneath him. He has gambled and lost. Then the captain's voice, 'Bring him to me.'

The ship breaks into a hive of activity once again, every man to his station. The two sailors release the ropes. Diego does not dare rub his wrists to release the blood flow into his hands. He steadies his purchase on the deck. The sails catch the wind and billow out and he feels the first motion of the ship, a small city on the move, sailing away from Nombre de Dios.

The captain's cabin is spare. Weapons hang on the walls and the rest of the room is dominated by a large table with maps and tiny metal objects that Diego has never seen before. No finery, beautiful clothing or rich furnishings.

It fits the man who is already on his feet waiting for him. They look at each other for a while in silence. What tack will the captain take? Being summoned to a white man has never ended well. Best to wait and observe. The captain walks across the room, the slightest limp showing that his injury while not life-threatening is more severe than he wishes to reveal. He returns with a bottle, sets it down on the table and gestures for Diego to join him.

The first swig of the liquor burns. The captain is no stranger to the brew. 'How long have you been in service to the governor?'

'In service?'

'Yes. How long have you served de Palma? Is that where you learned English?'

Service. The term is curious. Inadequate. Service was not what it had been at all. Like negotiation is not the word for what was happening now between him and the captain. They share a bottle, but they stand at opposite ends of a table covered in maps. Just like he had once stood with another what feels like a lifetime ago – plotting by the light of the stars, poring over maps sketched in the earth. 'I have learned many things of use to you. The land. When the rainy season raises the rivers, how to build shelter fast. How to appear and disappear. How to listen and how to be heard.'

The captain laughs 'You are a conjurer then, are you? A shaman? A medicine man?'

'Why do you think your men didn't shoot?' It makes him feel good to see the smile on the captain's face falter a little.

'It was a brave thing you did, to risk coming to the ship.'

'One of your men said the same.'

'And what did you say to him?'

'I asked him if he was a brave man.'

'All of my men are brave.'

Diego takes the bottle again when the captain offers it but does not answer and takes a smaller sip this time.

'Do you not think so? To cross the seas, to throw yourself out into the world without knowing whether you are going to come back, to make yourself masters of the waters and come back victorious, to make a name for yourself that you could not make if you stayed at home? What is that if not bravery?'

'From what I have seen of men, none are brave. Some are foolish, some are cruel, most are desperate, and all have a thing they long for that they keep in a secret place inside themselves. But I have not seen this thing that you call bravery.'

The captain takes another swig 'And what secrets do you hold?'

'My secrets belong to me, but I can tell you the secret of a man you need to find, who can help you. It is a secret I have already told so it no longer mine.'

'Why did you not run to him, then? Why take the risk and run to me?'

'Why did you cross the water? You could have stayed at home.'

The captain pauses and sets the bottle down. 'There was nothing for me there.' He looks toward the maps splayed across the table. 'Not nothing –' the instruments that gleamed – 'Not enough.'

Diego stares at the captain. There is something building in the air between them 'Then you have answered your own question. There is nothing for me here either.'

The *Pasha* rides the open waves and Diego rides with it. If Nombre de Dios is a tiny corridor, then the sea is open road. If Nombre de Dios is a no place, the sea is an everywhere, all the places that are, were and could be. The stars fling themselves across the night sky and he climbs the mast when all is quiet until he feels as though he is close enough to touch them. The stars fall into the sea and float on the surface. When the waves are still, they flash like fireflies. Voices ring out in the night – songs about wives left at home and wives found at ports; of good deaths hoped for and long lives not even dreamed of; of gold and silver buried at sea; of mermaids and krakens; of the edges of the world. And the sea swallows them all. He has never been this long above the hold on a ship, walking unbound, the spray of the sea on his face. He has never been amongst white men without having to make himself smaller.

Sometimes they are out in the open sea and Diego cannot see the land no matter which direction he looks. Other times they follow the curve of the shore, slide into green mouths to find fresh water, refill supplies. He shows them how to hunt, stays the captain's hand as he raises a pistol to shoot. No. There are softer ways, quieter ways. Yes. Good. Ask it for permission. Skin it this way. Cook it this way. Silence the fire this way. Step lightly, softly. They listen and follow where he leads them. They are never at home here as he is, but they get better, walk softer, become a band of strange no-place men, emerge from the mouths and take to the sea again.

A ship makes companions where the land does not. He and the captain have become each other's shadows. He looks to Diego when decisions are to be made and Diego nods quietly or shakes his head, no. He cuts the Captain's hair in his quarters when he meets with the first mate. Shaves his beard – presses the blade against his throat, his hands sure. The Captain pauses before he answers, waits for the quiet pressure of Diego's hands. When he stands over the table and pores over maps, few notice his eyes go to the shadow man in the corner. It is a silent alliance. Together they cut through the ocean quiet as fish.

Ten men set off for shore leaving their ship concealed in a small cove. The captain leans close to Diego as they go, their oars moving them forward, the water lapping at the pinnace, silver splashing in their wake. 'Will they know we are coming?'

Diego thinks of his last encounter with the man they sought. He had barely escaped with his life then and has avoided the secret places in the forest ever since. 'He always knows.'

'Will he join our cause?'

'He knows who you are'

'But will he join us?' the captain's voice rises with irritation. He does not like when answers are not straight lines. 'Will he risk his forces against Spain?'

Diego smirks 'You mean will a king ally himself with a pirate even if that pirate says he has been sent by a queen?' This has become a joke between them, 'Where is this Queen of yours? I'm beginning to think you made her up.'

The captain's laugh rolls over the waters. 'You just worry about your king. Besides, any good king knows that his enemy's enemy is his friend. What kind of ruler would this man be if he did not seize the opportunity for riches when it presents itself just as my queen has done?'

Diego knows that from the safety of his big ship the captain cannot know the truth of tight spaces. But he who has seen men's flesh ripped open by dogs, their heads on spikes, flies gathering at their open mouths... 'For you, this is about money and glory. For us –' He pauses thinking on the word, us. '– for us, it is not so simple.'

The captain's voice grows thoughtful 'So how do we know we can we trust them?'

'How do you know you can trust me?'

'Maybe we should throw you overboard and see this king alone,' the captain grumbles 'You say he knows my name so what use are you to me if you cannot ensure our safe passage? He might shoot you on sight.'

'Ah, Captain. Today I am like your Jesus. The only way to the man you seek is through me.'

They wade thigh-deep through fast running rivers that course through the forest, watched by creatures that lie in wait for a man to fall from exhaustion or misstep. The smell of green is thick and close, the buzz of insects unceasing. As much as they had learned from Diego on earlier excursions, the captain's men are still louder than wild hogs.

'How much further?'

'Go ahead! Shout louder. I hope they shoot you. One less to feed.'

'When he dies can I take his boots?'

Diego doesn't bother to silence them. No silence is the world could conceal their approach.

They arrive at a fork in the path and Diego halts the party. To the others it looks like any other they have been down before, but he is not them. He lowers his blade to the ground, spreads his hands wide and a thin, wiry man walks out of thin air, his own pistol raised. The sailors cry out and raise their weapons. Diego wills them steady – Do not fire. Hold. Steady. Wait. Then the captain's voice emerges as he steps out from within their midst. 'You are outnumbered, sir,' he shouts, 'Hold your fire. We seek only friendship.' His own pistol is still raised. 'I do not want to have my men shoot you.'

Only Diego sees the slight smile on the thin man's face before another deep voice rings out from the higher ground to his right. 'I think it is you who are outnumbered' The voice pierces Diego to his bones in the same way it did the first time he heard it. King Pedro stands before them, tall and broad as an old tree, as though he has always been there, part of the forest itself.

The sailors behind Diego shuffle, wrong-footed again and aim their weapons to the newcomer but King Pedro's voice does not waver. 'It would be wise to tell your men to surrender, Captain Drake.' Pedro looks to his right with the slightest inclination of his head and then to his left. Suddenly Diego can see them – dozens of men and women in the trees, concealed in the undergrowth, in the distance on the rise of the forested path, with pistols and machetes all trained on their small party. 'You are in the outskirts of Vallano. This is free land. Here, we have guns too.'

They are led single file through the bush. There are no pleasantries or formalities and the captain catches Diego's eye, looking furious. What did he think? That they were about to bow and scrape to him because he was the notorious Captain Drake?

They arrive at what Diego recognises as an outer camp. There are quarters built from wood, areas for cooking where fires have been extinguished the evening before. They would not be taken to the heart of the village – not yet. Not unless Pedro and the captain come to terms.

Diego stands at the edges and watches the dance play out. Gifts are unloaded and presented to Pedro's commanders. The men examine the goods – iron, supplies, muskets. Then the captain and Pedro leave the group and enter Pedro's quarters to converse alone leaving the rest to watch each other and wait. The whole thing is a farce; they are play-acting at being guests as if one wrong move, one signal from Pedro would not get them all killed on the spot. Kings are kings after all and at that moment all the men – African and English, sailor and soldier – wait at the pleasure of the men they follow.

Diego looks around at the guards. Faces he recognises and others he does not. There are gaps in their ranks, and he can hear what they do not say when they look at him: We see you. We know your name. We do not forget. The bush does not forget.

After what feels like hours, the leaders emerge from quarters. Pedro throws his voice out to the camp, 'Our guests remain with us tonight.' Diego can see the amusement in Pedro's eyes when he says 'guests' but the captain's eyes reveal little. Diego cannot tell whether the conversation has been a complete success, but it is enough that none of them will die today.

The light has dimmed during the time that they have been waiting and the quiet is broken by the squawk of parrots flying west for the evening and the chatter of monkeys in the distance. The men begin unloading the rest of their provisions and set up camp. Soldiers and sailors begin moving as a tentative unit in halting English, broken Spanish and the language of gesture and that is universal. Supplies are shared and before long there is meat turning on a spit above a fire and bottles emerge from supply stores. The glow of the fire barely distinguishes the men of the forest from the men of the sea. Diego steps away from the bonfire, the smell of game and liquor riding the air. The guards have forgotten him, it seems or perhaps the tentative peace has extended even to him until daybreak. He scans the group for the captain and sees him talking animatedly to his second mate and examining a machete handed to him by one of Pedro's soldiers. He looks up as though he feels eyes on him, but Diego has already become shadow again and melts out of the glow of the fire and into the thick dark of the forest.

The leaders emerge from quarters. Pedro throws his voice out to the camp, 'Our guests remain with us tonight.' The Captain's eyes reveal little. He looks at Diego but does not nod. He cannot tell whether the conversation has been a complete success, but it is enough that it seems none of them will die today.

The light has dimmed during the time that they have been waiting and the quiet that prevailed is broken with the squawk of parrots flying west and the chatter of monkeys in the distance. The men immediately begin unloading the rest of their provisions and set up camp. Soldiers and sailors begin moving as a tentative unit – halting English, broken Spanish and the language of gesture. Supplies are shared and before long there is meat turning on a spit above a fire and bottles emerge from supply stores. Only the glow of the fire distinguishes the men of the forest and the men of the sea. Diego steps away from the bonfire, the smell of game and liquor riding the air, feeling as though he belonged with neither. The guards have forgotten him it seems or perhaps the tentative peace has extended even to him until daybreak. He scans the group for the Captain and sees him talking animatedly to his second mate and examining a machete handed to him by one of Pedro's soldiers. He looks up as though he feels eyes on him, but Diego has already become shadow again and melts out of the glow of the fire and into the thick dark of the forest.

Pedro is waiting for him as he knew he would be, and he finds him only by the light of his ebony pipe. They sit next to each other on an overturned log. Pedro takes a deep draw and then passes the pipe to Diego. The smoke does not relax him but puts him even more on the alert.

'I thought the next time I saw you would be the day one of my men brought me your head'

'Me too.'

The night sings around them. He can hear the insects moving beneath the earth, the trees talking to one another, the sound of a waterfall in the distance.

'I could slit your throat right here and your captain would be able to do nothing. Not one of the men out there could save you.'

'You could. But I could do the same. I learned from you.'

'You wouldn't even make it as far as to draw the blade in your boot. And if by some slim chance you did –' Pedro nodded into the darkness '– you would never leave this spot.'

Diego scanned the dark and saw what he had not when he first sat down: men in the bush, watching them.

'They wouldn't need much convincing. I think Angelo, Baptista and Veracruz are most anxious to do it. Maria Estella would feed your entrails to her dogs. We lost good men that day, but they lost friends, brothers, lovers'

'I lost brothers too, Pedro.'

'But you were not there.' Sudden anger rolls off of him heating the darkness. 'You were not there when de Palma's men came in the night, when they took the children. You were not there to hear the screams of the women that we could not protect. You were not there when we had to move and rebuild after they burned the houses and the stores. You were not there to smell the flesh of those they burned so we could not bury them. You did not have to see the heads that they left hanging from the trees. You were away and safe. You chose them over your brothers and sisters in the bush.'

Diego looks up into the darkness. He can imagine the guards' bodies tightening, waiting for even the smallest sign, feel them reaching for the machetes that hung from their hips.

Diego slowly lifts his shirt and turns his back to Pedro. 'Feel.'

Pedro's rough hands fumble toward him in the dark and trace the tree of ridged flesh on Diego's back. A swift intake of breath, a pause and he stops. 'As if they had not done worse to any one of these men here. You think there is anyone here that has been left untouched? How many have run, not once, not twice, but again and again, never stopping searching for this place? You know, like everyone who comes here knows that there is one code: Keep us secret, keep us safe. Never tell.'

Diego pulled his shirt down and then faced Pedro. He took Pedro's hand and placed it on his collarbone. Jagged. Bones that should lie flat are as rugged as the terrain that leads into Nombre de Dios. Diego moved his right shoulder forward and Pedro felt that too. The way the entire frame of Diego's collarbone and shoulder seemed to shift, grind. He moved Pedro's hand lower to the grooves in his side, round and ragged holes that have been filled in with too little soil.

'There are others that you cannot touch.'

Pedro sighs and the forest sighs with him. There are some things that men cannot say.

'Tell me about your Captain.'

'He is not my Captain.'

'Is he not? He speaks of you as if you are his man through and through.'

Diego thinks of the last few weeks on the ship. 'He is strange. There is nothing that separates him from his men, but they follow him without question. I have also seen him be cruel as the sea. He will whip a man for disloyalty, but he keeps a holy man on board. We had just come through a storm. It seemed like it came not from the sky but from the sea itself. The waves rose up and darkened the world with its foam. We could not tell where the sky ended, and the sea began. The men fought with the rigging and held the sail true and we thought we would all meet our end. But the captain, he steered the way and laughed into the storm. He was like a storm himself and chided the men for their lack of heart. When the storm ended he had the holy man pour some water on my head and read from his book. Captain said I was a Christian now. That I sailed with them and was under his protection and God's. I have seen him attack the Spanish ships without mercy, kill every Spaniard aboard and set every slave free. Some have travelled with us and then leave to make their way whenever we make port.'

'He sounds like a mad man.'

Diego smiled in the dark. 'He might be. But he might be the only man who hates the Spanish as much as you do. And he has weapons and more soldiers and more ships. He says he has been sent by his queen. He has come for the mule train and will not leave until he has taken it.'

'Hmm' Pedro mused in the dark. 'And what does he want from us other than our lives laid down in service of his fight?'

'His fight is your fight, no?'

Pedro chuckled. 'We might share an enemy, but we do not share the same fight.'

Diego nods. 'No, we do not.' Sitting in the dark with Pedro, even with all that had passed between them, they are still in perfect accord. 'Then let this be just one of the many battles to come. How many times have we burned whole towns as distractions? Taken supplies that we did not need?

How much treasure have we sunk to the bottom of rivers, treasure that is of no use to us?

'I suppose he'll want that too, the treasure.'

'Yes.'

Diego could almost hear the wheels turning in Pedro's head – the swift calculations, the assessment of supplies, the men that would be lost, the territory that might be gained, how many he might be able to free, the possibility of one day mounting de Palma's head on a stake.

'Well he can dive to the bottoms of the five great rivers for it if he wants to. The rains are already here.'

Diego thought of the captain that he had come to know but still did not quite understand and laughed softly in the dark, 'He might do just that.'

And so, there is an alliance and they are a small army on the move. Word has spread. Messengers faster than even Diego are sent to other settlements ruled by other kings and queens – El Draque will fight with us. Yes, Pedro is with him. Yes. From Rio Guana to Cartagena, the word spreads. They set sail again to return after the rains and at every port more gather to join them. French pirates, Portuguese captives, runaways without kings. Under the night sky they exchange stories of where they have been, how they escaped. They watch Diego with suspicion and curiosity. Who is this man so close to the captain? A slave? A free man? He receives his wages like the rest of the sailors and his boots are strong and good. Diego marks their faces.

One of the newcomers draws Diego's eye. He is slight, barely a man. Keeps to himself as he goes about his work on the ship, cleans his weapons, sharpens his blades and keeps his eyes on the ocean. There is something about him that bothers Diego, but it is as if the boy wears a shroud around his spirit that he cannot penetrate.

'When did the boy get here?' He asks de Santos, a man they liberated from a Spanish prison ship a few weeks earlier. 'Was he on your ship?'

'Maybe. I think he is called Manuel' de Santos shrugs 'So many come and go. I lose track with the tides.' He looks at Diego slyly. 'You should know. I hear you are the captain's secret hand. You know everything that happens on this ship, no?'

'I am nobody, my friend. Just a sailor like you.'

'That's not what I hear.'

'Well,' Diego shrugs 'Your ears belong to you.'

De Santos laughs and they continue to lime the deck 'So how did you get here?'

'On board the *Pasha*?'

'No, the moon! Yes, the *Pasha*.'

'I was captured like you.'

'Ah my brother' de Santos shakes his head 'Better to be here, no? The Spanish have no heart. No blood beats in their veins except to the drums of war.'

Diego shrugs. 'All the ships are the same. How does a man distinguish between his captors?'

De Santos looks at him again, considering his words, 'Perhaps my ears do not belong to me after all.'

They continue their work, but Diego feels eyes other watching him. These do not have the weight of the captain's whose stare is a hammer, insistent and impatient. These are soft and questioning and make the hair stand on the back of his neck. He searches the deck. The boy. The eyes that stare at him across the deck are a deep, soft brown. Then they disappear amidst the other faces.

Later, the night sky is deep and starless, and Diego stands on the deck alone. The bulk of the men are below where there will be song and stories well into the night. The closer they get back to Nombre de Dios, the more he begins to feel anxious. Would the alliance hold? Would Pedro change his mind? Alliances shift during war and Diego has no doubt that this is war, a war that he would not see the end of. Despite what the captain might think, in the short term, he needs Pedro far more than Pedro needs him and Pedro knows it. The dry season might bring a change of heart and despite all his schemes and plots, Diego might end his days in Nombre de Dios.

'You did not tell that man the truth.'

Diego nearly jumps out of his skin. It is the boy. 'It has been a long time since someone approached me without me knowing it.' He does not bother to hide how startled he is. Anyone who could sneak up on him would be able to tell anyway.

'Then you're losing your touch, old man.'

'Old man…?' The prickle at the back of his neck grows and he turns slowly and searches the planes of the boy's face. No, it was not possible.

'Then again,' the boy smiles, 'I always could.'

Diego's eyes widen and a lump grows in his throat. He remembers a small girl, fierce as a fire ants, with laughter like a waterfall. She refused to stay with the women and instead watched the soldiers train, followed along with their drills, sparred with the air. By the time she was ten she could handle a dagger like an extension of her own hand. 'It can't be… you're not… Maribel?'

'Manuel? Maribel? What difference does a name make?'

Diego looks up and down the deck frantically. There is no one close, thank God. 'How? God, why?'

'First, tell me why you lied to that man.'

'Why do you think I lied?'

'Do you think when I was a girl that I watched you all because you were nice to look at? You were taught to be shadows and you learned from the best. I learned from you.'

'How did you get here? Do you know where this ship sails? What we face?'

A cloud passes blocking the moonlight and Manuel's face is hidden in shadow 'That night. The raid. I was one of the children who was taken.'

Diego felt a pang in his gut like a tiny knife burrowing in his inside

'Most of us were born in Vallano. We did not know the life you all knew. Many of us did not survive. Few of us ran. I was one of them. I was lucky. I found a ship, then another and another. I became Manuel. When I heard that there was an English ship, and a captain who had allied with Pedro I knew I had to be on it.'

'Maribel, it is not safe for you here, do you know what these men would... I don't think I can protect you here'

'My name is Manuel.' Eyes sharp and flashing. 'And I don't need anyone to protect me.'

'This is not Vallano, there is no Pedro here to keep the peace.'

'Where do think I have been all these years since you saw me last? I have seen things even you would not believe, old man.'

They lapse into silence, thinking of the places they had been, the roads they have travelled.

'I lied because it is the way. Pretend to be one thing while being another. Be useful. Never show them your true face.' Diego turns to look at Manuel 'Like you.'

'This is my true face'

The person that stands before him is no different from any other sailor on the ship, any of the other black and brown and pale faces that he has seen as they passed through so many ports and it suddenly feels silly to hold on to the memory of the girl he once knew. 'Yes. You are right. It suits you.'

Manuel's voice softens and he turns to Diego again. For a moment he is the child Diego knew. 'Are you not tired of living in the shadows? I want to go home, to stay. I want to see my mother again. I do not know if she is even alive. Don't you want that too? Isn't that why you are here?'

Diego shakes his head. Manuel could not know, too young to understand. 'England. When this is done, I am going to England.'

'England? Why? If we fight and keep fighting, we can be free right here.'

'And always worry about raids? About being captured again? To be always at war? Is that being free?'

'And you think you can be free there over the water? That your captain will protect you when you live among strangers? Stay with us, Diego. Home is Vallano. Home is where we are.'

He does not know how to respond so he says nothing. They stand together and watch the ocean until the sun begins to peep over the horizon.

'I am not an old man, you know.' Diego grumbles.

Manuel laughs softly. 'If you say so, old man'

The green coast rises out of the ocean in the distance.

The two factions meet again like old enemies who have shed each other's blood and called it square. There is no need for subterfuge, no need for stealth. And now the captain' shadow has a shadow. Manuel orbits Diego, though few notice him. To all else he is nothing more than a boy, one of the many captured from Spanish vessels, come aboard at ports, come to seek the captain. But the closer they get to their goal the more worried Diego becomes. Why had it not occurred to him to remain in Vallano? To even broach the subject with Pedro? Suppose once the alliance was over the Captain betrayed him and left him in these islands to be recaptured? And what of England? He thought of Manuel's words. Could there be a home for him in that strange place across the waters? All his plans seem shot full of holes, all because of the words of a child half his age.

The trek across the isthmus to Panama City takes weeks but feels like months and much of it uphill. They learn from Pedro's men how to build better shelters. Shoes become as valuable as food and fresh water. Men die and are briefly mourned before their boots are passed to other men whose own boots have become worn out by the terrain. The colder it gets, even the captain has trouble keeping the men's spirits afloat. They have left a man behind who had not paid enough attention to his feet. Once they cut off the right one there was nothing to be done but leave him. They lose two more to the fever. The leader who Diego has seen command the waves during a storm and steer the ship to safety seems to have lost something of himself and the men flag right along with their leader.

'You know what your problem is, El Draque?' Pedro falls in step with Diego and the Captain as his men lead the way through the dense forest 'You think the world is what you can see from the deck of a ship.' Pedro mutters a few words to one of his soldiers nearby and motions Diego and the Captain to follow him away from the trail. Diego catches Manuel's eye and waves him on to continue with the party.

'Don't worry,' Pedro calls 'We will catch up with them.'

It is a trail that even Diego does not know, thicker and more overgrown than the more worn path they had been travelling. Here the trees are old, older than anything Diego has ever seen, with trunks that span the width of several large men. Pedro stops them at one. Diego looks up and his gaze keeps going. It is as though the tree goes all way into the sky and never ends. They begin the climb, losing purchase on the trunk and finding it again, sliding down and pushing each other up. Pedro slows down for their benefit, 'It will be worth it!' he shouts down.

'Not if I fall and break my neck,' the captain grumbles.

But Diego has begun to feel a fluttering in his chest the higher they go, the sure knowledge that something was about to permanently change whenever they get to the top.

Eventually, the canopy thins. The boughs spread out and they perch on a large branch as wide as the log he and Pedro sat in on the first night in the camp. And there it is. The Atlantic glittering; the sky soft and pink. For a moment there is no Captain, no Pedro, no ships and no England. There is just here and now and the open sea that continues forever. What direction did the ship that brought him when he was still a young boy come from? If he stares hard enough and keeps quiet enough, could he sense its path? Remember with some still part of him the way home?

Pedro's voice interrupts 'Now turn. This way.'

They shuffle on the bough. Turn to face the other way.

'There,' he points.

Another sea. As though the mountain they had climbed and the tree they now sit on split the world in two. Its sky is darker, its water a deeper blue, an almost impenetrable forest of its own.

The captain looks as though someone has hit him in the face. 'The Pacific' he whispers. He turns to Diego, the excitement opening to include him. 'Give me life to sail just once an English ship on that sea'. And Diego sees it all right there and then, the whole rest of his life on the sea with the captain, poring over maps, helping him carve the world into pieces. England suddenly seems a distant foggy land, a place not as real as the sea, not nearly as real as sitting with Pedro and the captain on the highest point in the world, looking at two oceans open before them. Manuel's voice drifts across his mind for a second, 'Stay. Home is Vallano. Home is where we are,' but he pushes the boy's words away.

When they descend and rejoin their men, the captain is again the force he was on the ship in the storm, without doubt, without fatigue as if he is lit by some inner fire. Word reaches the camp that the mule train will approach Nombre de Dios by daybreak and the men set up positions on both sides of the road to lie in wait. The bush conceals them, and they pass the night without fires so not to alert any scouts who may suspect their presence.

For the first time, the captain does not seek Diego's counsel and so he and Pedro wait out the night together.

'I fear your captain has received a gift that I did not mean to give.'

Diego tries to grasp again the euphoria he felt when they first stared at the two oceans, but it has been replaced by a disquiet he cannot name. Pedro's voice is low but where Diego feels uncertainty Pedro sounds assured as if he has seen their fates and accepted them. 'I wanted to show him the sea. But he sees only roads.'

'Roads are not a bad thing. The world is a big place, Pedro. I never knew how big.'

'Hmm.' Pedro does not respond but Diego knows that he has not convinced him of anything. He hasn't even convinced himself. They lie awake and listen to the sounds of the bush.

'Pedro?'

'Hmm'

'If I die tomorrow and you do not, I want you to promise me something.'

Pedro bristles. The scab of broken promises between them had not quite healed but Diego takes his silence for grudging assent.

'There is a boy who travels with us, Manuel. The one with the knives.'

'I have seen him. Fast.'

'Look out for him and make sure he gets to Vallano.'

'Why?'

'His is not my story to tell. But take him with you. Promise me.'

'You have my word.'

They fall into silence and wait for dawn.

The sound of bells breaks open the morning. In the distance, they hear the clip-clop of hooves, the shuffle of feet, the sound of men's voices. The bells grow louder and louder and then there: grey mules laden, the bells around their necks ringing out into the silence. Diego begins counting and gets to 50 before giving up. There must be at least 100 mules each heavy with treasure. He waits, still and silent. Pedro blows the abeng and wakes the forest; they descend on the train. They are bodies in motion, the smoke of gunfire, the wet sounds of blades penetrating flesh, the cries of pain as men fall. Diego loses sight of Pedro, of Manuel of even the captain. The mules begin a stampede. A glimpse of a man trapped beneath hooves; the slick blood on his hands as he buries his blade into another's neck; a chest explodes with gunfire. He cannot tell whether the man trampled underfoot is one of theirs. He cannot tell whether the man he has stabbed is dead or just fallen. There is scant time to think of Manuel, whether he has survived, whether his hands are still as fast as they used to be.

The ambush is short and bloody. By the time the smoke clears, and the cries become whimpers, Diego is shocked at how much they had outnumbered their quarry. No more than 40 armed men – many dead, others now held captive. They had lost men too. De Santos' face stares up at him from the dirt road, some of Pedro's guards that he does not recognise have also fallen. Diego searches the faces of the dead for Manuel but can find him neither amongst the dead nor the living. He looks down at his bloody, torn hands and stands still amidst the whoops of the men around him.

'Diego!' Captain's voice breaks through. His face is joyous and his hands are deep within one of the mule's bags. He pulls them out and they are filled with silver glinting in the early morning light.

The next few hours are a feeding frenzy; even if each man was himself a mule there is no way they could carry everything they have taken. Men fill pockets and provision bags, and the captain and Pedro's second-in-command direct the division and transportation of the booty. Pedro redirects the mules for use in Vallano and gathers his dead. They head back to the to the shelters they had built together in a general state of excitement with a solemn undercurrent of mourning. The remains of the fires they used to cook the night before are ground into the dirt. Diego hopes that the place continues to stand, a perfect vantage point to see the camino below. He wonders what other rebellions will be planned here, what other alliances will be made.

'The men call it Fort Diego, after you.' Manuel's eyes peep at him under the brim of a hat pulled low. He cleans a dagger before sticking it in its sheath.

'Make some noise when you walk.' Diego grumbles but cannot hide the smile that spreads across his face and his pleasure at having left a mark in this place.

'Glad to see you're still alive, old man.'

'No gladder than I.'

Together they stand at the outskirts of the camp and watch the captain and Pedro grasp hands and part. The mules that will head to Vallano are laden, but Pedro is holding a large curved blade, encrusted with jewels from the stores of silver, testing its edge with his thumb. Whatever life it had before, it looked at home in Pedro's large hands. Diego thinks of that blade curved around de Palma's neck and smiles.

'You can still stay you know.' Manuel has been looking at him. 'It is not too late. Come back with us.'

Diego shakes his head. 'I think this is enough. It is enough. You go. Pedro is expecting you.'

'Does he expect Maribel or Manuel?'

Diego looks up at Pedro again, at the men who follow him 'He expects a fighter.'

'I hope we meet again, brother.'

By the time Diego turns back to reply, the boy has disappeared.

As they prepare for the trek back to their ship. Diego looks around once more and catches Pedro's eye. He raises a hand and Pedro nods. Then he catches one last glimpse of Manuel's back as he falls into step with Pedro's men. He does not turn around and all the shadow men melt into the bush.

It is Sunday when they sail into Plymouth. The sky is cloudy, the water is grey slate and the low, rolling hills are shades of green that Diego has never seen before. Diego can see the port up ahead. As they get closer the tiny dots become people. It looks as though the whole town has been awaiting their arrival. The men's spirits are high. They return home with more money than they have ever dreamed of possessing, and the ship is loaded with the treasure promised to the English queen.

The captain comes to stand beside him. 'Home, Diego. This is home. I saw it all last night in a dream, just the way it would be. I will have a grand estate with servants, more rooms than you could ever imagine, fame, glory, a legacy that will last long after I am dead.'

Diego gazes at the coastline, a pale green curve with no rugged edges, a grey sky. 'And what of me?'

'You are a free man here Diego. I promised you that. You will be with me and your name will be sung to the rooftops! Everyone will know of the alliance between the people of Vallano and Captain Drake, an alliance that changed everything. You will be a hero! Children will say the names of Drake, Pedro and Diego until the end of the world.'

Diego can hear the shouting, the singing, the flap of the sail being tacked, the anchor being lowered. The sound that he could only have imagined when he saw the crowds in the distance gathered at the dock becomes a roar.

'Do you remember that day, Captain? When Pedro took us to the top of the tree and showed us the Pacific? The world divided into two, the day clean and new and perfect. How high up, how small we were and how big the sea?'

But the captain can no longer hear him. The ship has docked, and Captain Drake has stepped forward into the roar of the crowd. The clouds roll back, and the sun sets his hair on fire.

BUCKLAND ABBEY: THE HISTORICAL BACKGROUND TO DIEGO

CASSANDER L. SMITH
University of Alabama, USA

The historical archives are full of Diegos, Black Africans who appear as marginal figures in textual documents about European encounters with the early Americas. Quite often they show up as snippets of information, one or two lines that describe how they performed some service for the main figure in the document. They convey knowledge, serve as mediators between parties, perform menial tasks, navigate vessels, take up arms. Sometimes they appear in the text to flesh out the landscape, to help the writer establish a sense of place. In many instances, they function as a collective, a body of enslaved people, perhaps, who serve at the will of enslavers. In some instances, they are free Africans who find themselves in the Americas by means other than enslavement. Some historians, for example, argue that the first Africans might have arrived in the British American colonies in the early seventeenth century as indentured servants. They carry names like Pedro, Maria, Elizabeth, Caesar, and Scipio, in addition to Diego. This is on the rare occasion when they are referred to by name. And it's a first name, hardly ever one derived from an ancestor.

Given the general nature of Black African representations in early British Atlantic texts, the story of Diego in Panama, in the year 1572 or 1573, is truly exceptional. His interactions with Sir Francis Drake, later of Buckland Abbey, were so fundamental to Drake's efforts to raid Spanish gold on the isthmus that Drake accounted for his presence with more than a passing interest in the narrative he produced about that raid. Drake first set sail for the Panama isthmus in 1571, for reconnaissance, then returned a year later with a plan to sack the Spanish colony of Nombre de Dios, a port town on the northeast edge of the isthmus. The town was a crucial way-station for transporting gold, silver and other valuables farmed out of mines mainly in Peru. Annually, the Spanish would convey its pillaged valuables by boat up the coast from Peru to Panama City on the southwest corner of the isthmus. From there, the valuables would be transferred to caravans of mules that would travel by land to Nombre de Dios. Once there, the valuables would be stashed in storehouses until the Spanish treasure fleet arrived, a heavily armed and guarded caravan of ships. That fleet travelled to ports through the Spanish-controlled Atlantic to collect cargoes and transport them back to Spain.

Drake's idea was that he would attack Nombre de Dios during the window which opened up after the mule-train had deposited its riches in the storehouses at Nombre de Dios and before the arrival of the Treasure Fleet to collect the deposits. Things didn't go exactly as planned. During the attack on Nombre de Dios, Drake was gravely wounded by gunshot, which rendered him incapacitated. In the absence of his leadership, Drake's men aborted the attack. Ever persistent, Drake modified the plan. Instead of ransacking Nombre de Dios, he would attempt a tougher feat by directly attacking the mule-train as it crossed the isthmus. Although this required him to hide out in the region for the better part of a year, the plan worked. In April of 1573, he attacked a mule-train right outside Nombre de Dios. Importantly, the effort required that he collaborate with a band of Cimarrones who populated the isthmus. Cimarrones, also called maroons in other parts of the Caribbean, were formerly enslaved Black Africans who'd run away from their Spanish enslavers and built settlements, or palenques, in the jungles of Panama. At the time of Drake's raid, they were technically enslaved fugitives. But they claimed their freedom and often staged attacks on the Spanish to free other enslaved people, to get resources or to vex the Spanish. Led by a man named Pedro, the group of Cimarrones who collaborated with Drake provided the future owner of Buckland Abbey with valuable knowledge about how to attack Spanish mule-trains, which the Cimarrones had done on multiple occasions. They scouted for Drake and led the English through the jungle to reach the mule-trains. They provided the English with food, clothing, and shelter. A common enmity of Spain fuelled this collaboration with the idea that *the enemy of my enemy is my friend.*

As a result of the partnership, the English walked away from the raid with two ships full of precious minerals and other cargo stolen from the mule-trains. Apparently, the Cimarrones told Drake they did not covet the silver and gold seized by the English. They, in fact, claimed that whenever they raided Spanish cargoes, they dumped the loot in the river. Instead, according to Drake, they sought steel, which Drake supplied to them by breaking down the pinnaces, or boats for navigating shallow waters, that he had brought along for the expedition. By all accounts, the collaboration was successful, so much so that subsequent English privateers and adventurers sought to replicate it.

Enriched by this venture, Drake bought Buckland Abbey in 1581.

When he returned to Panama in the year of his death, in 1596, he expected a warm reception from the Cimarrones, but found, upon his return to the isthmus, that the Cimarrones had struck a new alliance with the Spanish. Together they repelled Drake.

In 1626, Drake's nephew, of the same name, published the narrative of his Panama deeds and titled it *Sir Francis Drake Revived*. Appearing some thirty years after the elder Drake's death, the nephew intended the narrative to galvanize what he called an 'effeminate' age. He upheld Drake as a brash, bold, swashbuckling paragon of masculinity and valour. He issued a charge to England to imitate his uncle's imperial conquests in the Caribbean for the good of the nation.

Thanks to that narrative, we know about the importance of Black Africans in helping Sir Francis Drake achieve fame, a legacy. Interestingly, the Black figure most vital to his efforts, Diego, wasn't actually a Cimarron. Here is what we can glean about Diego, based on Drake's narrative. Diego was enslaved to a Spanish enslaver in or somewhere near Nombre de Dios at the time of Drake's arrival on the isthmus in 1572. Drake and Diego first met during Drake's initial failed attempt to raid Nombre de Dios. During the attack, Diego encountered a dozen of Drake's men on the beach just outside of town. The men were tasked with guarding the boats. Upon seeing the men and boats, Diego ran toward the crew, somehow understanding them to be part of Drake's forces. The men, seeing Diego advancing in their direction, immediately fired on him, a series of warning shots to dissuade him from coming further. Diego, though, kept running toward the boats and implored them to take him aboard, which they did. Diego apparently wasted no time ingratiating himself to Drake's forces. He informed them about the defences at Nombre de Dios and warned them to abandon the attack because more Spanish troops were due to arrive at any minute, having been deployed days earlier in response to recent Cimarron raids of the town. Drake did not accept Diego's counsel in that instance. They aborted the mission only after Drake collapsed from a gunshot wound. As Drake and his crew retreated, they took Diego along with them. Apparently, Diego sought refuge from his Spanish enslavers. Why did Diego wait for the English to arrive before trying to run away from his enslaver? Why not seek protection with the Cimarrones? According to Drake's account, Diego claimed that the Cimarrones wanted to kill him. Apparently, the Spanish deployed Diego as a mediator with the Cimarrones, and those mediations often ended with the Spanish committing acts of duplicity that also implicated Diego. So, the Cimarrones harboured a resentment toward him and Diego's efforts to find asylum with the English was because he wished to escape from both the Spanish and the Cimarrones.

Although Drake did not heed Diego's counsel on the beach outside of Nombre de Dios, Diego did become a key source of information for Drake. It was Diego, in fact, who recommended that Drake collaborate with the Cimarrones once he devised the plan to attack the mule-trains. What is more, Diego orchestrated the alliance. It was Diego who initially met with the Cimarrones and made the initial introductions. At the end of Drake's year-long escapade, historical records suggest that Diego went back with him to Plymouth in England. This is suggested, for example, by the appearance of a Black African man named Diego who served as valet to Drake during his circumnavigation of the world in 1577. Diego died of complications from a poisoned arrow wound during that global voyage.

Black Africans appearing in the historical archives are what we call mediations, meaning their representation in the text comes through the perspective of others, usually European clergy, explorers, merchants, travel writers, and conquistadores. In this way, Black African images are constructed by the literary imagination of white writers. We see those Black African figures as the writer of the text tells us they were. In this way, we must read with a good deal of circumspection when we encounter these mediated figures in the archives. We should not, however, assume that the representations are wholly beholden to the writer. As the actions of Diego and the Cimarrones suggest, Black Africans were active doers. Their actions in the material world beyond the text inform the literary imaginations of their writing counterparts. In other words, what they do off the page shapes what the writer puts on the page. Given this dynamic, we can read Black African representations in the texts at face value, but we can also question these accounts of their desires and motivations. Take, for example, the following moment from Drake's narrative in which Diego encourages the English to collaborate with the Cimarrones:

> ...the Negroe forementioned [Diego], being examined more fully, confirmed this report of the gold and siluer, with many other intelligences of importance, especially how wee might haue gold and siluer enough if we would, by meanes of the *Symerons*, whome though hee had betrayed diuers times (being vsed thereto by his Masters) so that he knew they would kill him, if they gat him: yet if our Captaine would vndertake his protection, hee durst aduenture his life, because hee knewe our Captaines name was most pretious and highly honored of them.

This passage makes clear why Diego matters. He is the first one to suggest a Cimarron-English alliance. Taking the text at face value, one might determine that Diego's character is subservient to Drake. He serves the role of native informant and refugee. He also appears to be the sycophant, heaping praise on Drake while looking to the privateer for protection. Alternatively, one could easily read this moment more shrewdly, noting those silences, gaps, and inconsistencies that also shape the passage. The most obvious silence involves Diego himself. He does not speak in the passage. Instead, Drake presents his words as summary, which adds a layer of interpretation to his already-mediated representation. There is a gap, too, in terms of Diego's motives. Is he merely seeking refuge with Drake, or does he have some larger ambition? That question resonates especially within the context of the Cimarrones' purported enmity toward Diego. Given that the Cimarrones were hostile toward Diego, one could surmise that Diego was motivated, in part, by an effort to improve his relationship with the Cimarrones by providing them additional resources – in the form of English manpower and weapons – to attack the Spanish. If one were to read the moment from Diego's perspective, his actions are less syco-phantic and more strategic. Read in this light he might be seen to employ Drake as a tool to curry favour with the Cimarrones. He tells Drake what he thinks Drake wants to hear to make him amenable to accepting Diego's recommendations. The question remains, though, what did Diego want with Cimarron favour? We cannot know the answer to that question, of course. There are limitations in terms of what these archival representa-tions can tell us about Black lives. Those limitations, though, the ques-tions left by the incompleteness of the archives, are important reminders that people of African descent actively engaged with their environments in early Atlantic spaces. We can trace Diego's engagement through the gaps and silences in the textual record, and we can imagine his motives and inner life, as they are explored in the story 'Diego'.

CHARLECOTE PARK

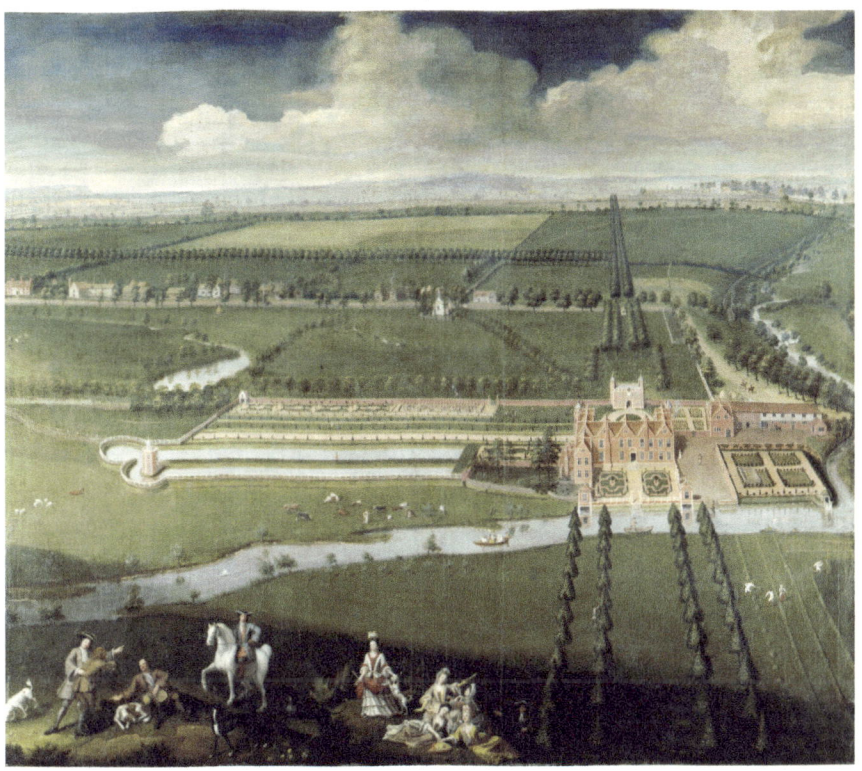

A Bird's-Eye View of Charlecote Park, Warwickshire from the West by British (English) School
©National Trust Images/Derrick E. Witty

Captain Thomas Lucy (c.1655 – 1684) by Sir Godfrey Kneller (Lübeck 1646 - London 1723)
©National Trust Images

KAREN ONOJAIFE

STET

1684

It's the screams that rouse him; high pitched and panicked, rebounding against the flagstones of Charlecote Park at the same time as they slip under his door-frame, rattling his sleepy thoughts.

The first time this happened had been four months prior; shrieks and wails from his mistress the morning Captain Lucy had been carried away by smallpox. Will had listened from his small chamber adjoining her room; her voice distorted by thick, choking sobs, grief unmaking melody.

Better times before. Mornings where he would greet her with a tray of drinking chocolate. No matter the hour, she would always be sitting up ready to greet him, eyes bright and hair rumpled. 'My little monkey,' she would coo, a moniker which Will no longer appreciated but to which he had become accustomed.

Life as Lady Catherine's favoured page, the days mainly slow and sweet as honey. A smart little boy and so there was little taxing to his tasks: dressing her hair, lacing her stays, running messages, or holding her mirror so that she could pass long moments bathing in her own beauty, caught by the soft milk and roses of her face.

But then the Captain had died – so decisively, it had seemed to Will, the man never having been one to go back on a choice once made – and they had all been pitched into a gloom. Lady Catherine no longer cared for her old pursuits, didn't care for Will, or even anyone to dress her in finery or arrange her wig. What was the need when she scarcely took guests, preferring instead to remain abed, languishing in her night things, whatever the hour?

Some of the young housemaids sighed into their laundry baskets when they thought about it; this type of mourning seemed romantic, accompanied as it was by great wealth. But Will had overheard Mrs Manton, the cook, tell Mr Lick, the slaughterman, over a bucket of hare parts, that what ailed the mistress of house was insecurity. Lady Catherine had loved that man, Mrs Manton opined, the way Lady Catherine loved Jesus Christ – in public mainly, and even then, only with much prompting.

Nothing much Will hadn't already reasoned for himself. Perhaps she had loved the Captain, but what gave her air were fine things and high society news – *Precious little of either here in the countryside*, she would sigh, *save for your good self, and tell me, my fine Master Archus, am I really to shake myself into a delight over every lambing season?*

'She needs that baby in her belly to be a boy,' Mrs Manton had continued, 'or else she'll be in a fine pickle.' An heir was needed because, otherwise, Lady Catherine's claim to Charlecote would be as delicate as pie-crust promises, dependent on the whims of the Captain's cousin, which meant that *everyone's* position at Charlecote would be uncertain, because, as all understood, new brooms swept clean.

Then Mr Lick had raised his bushy eyebrows at Mrs Manton meaningfully, causing her to turn round and huff in exasperation upon seeing Will there.

'Will Archus, you will be the death of me with all your creeping about,' she had hissed as she chivvied him from the kitchen, but not before slipping several sugared almonds into his hand.

The Captain had so often been away on this or that campaign, and so while he was gone, Lady Catherine felt cast upon the charity of the Warwickshire gentry, whom she found too provincial for true entertainment. She preferred the comfort of mischievous letters from her London friends, of which she had many, and so how a Mr Fitzroy had come to distinguish himself, Will no longer recalled. Something perhaps in the tilt of her smile upon the sight of his seal on an envelope.

On evenings warm with candlelight, with the spice of desserts still heavy in the air,

Lady Catherine would read her letters with Will's head in her lap, one lazy hand stroking his hair – *curls like peppercorns!* – she liked to say. Evenings when Will would note how she smelt like lavender at her wrists, and how her stomach was a bump hardening, and he wondered if one day she would prefer the feel of her own son's hair, silk beneath her fingers, if she would look upon her milk-and-roses boy as if he had swallowed stars, and tell him that he was such a fine, perfect thing.

But the baby – a boy after all – had come too early, half formed, then fully dead, hastening after a father it had never known. Two months ago that had happened, marking the second time Will had been snatched from sleep by Lady Catherine's wails.

This morning marks the third time he has been stirred by screams, and so he does not immediately leap from the comfort of his featherbed. Instead, he allows himself a few more seconds to lie in ignorance of the specifics of whatever fresh calamity has visited the house. The reprieve is brief. Moll, one of the housemaids, bursts into his room, her eyes wide, her face red.

'Will,' she cries, wringing her hands, 'Lady Catherine is gone!'

He stares at Moll blankly. But he had attended to his mistress only last night? She had not wanted to talk but kept searching for his gaze in the mirror while he brushed her hair, the weight of it cooling his hands like water. How could it be that she was now dead?

'Not dead!' Moll says, though Will is scarcely aware that he had even spoken. 'Worse!' she adds. 'She has run away, Will! Absconded with many of the Lucy heirlooms! Oh, and she has taken Miss Elizabeth, of course. It seems,' and here Moll's voice quivers, 'she has attached herself to the Duke of Northumberland.'

'Mr Fitzroy?' Will stutters.

'No, the man on the moon,' Moll hisses as she advances into the room, hands on her hips, 'of course Mr Fitzroy! So now Charlecote will pass to Sir Davenport and no doubt we shall all be ruined. And Croft is on the warpath, so I would look out if I were you.'

'Me? What do I have to do with it?' he cries, grimacing at the mention of Charlecote's steward. Croft has always glowered at the sight of him, as if Will's very bones offended him somehow but Will had never cared because he had the love of Lady Catherine and if she desired something, then Captain Lucy would see to it and what could Croft do in the face of that? All was different now.

'Well,' Moll says, 'of course he thinks you knew of her plans. Did you?' she asks, her voice lowered conspiratorially.

He ignores her, finally springing from his bed, almost tripping over the hem of his night shirt in his haste to dash past her into Lady Catherine's chamber. The truth is evident the moment he steps inside: her favoured gowns missing from the armoire, her dressing table bare of her rouges and potions, the gold and ivory inlaid hairbrush gone.

'Ach, look at him, he didn't know a hair of it,' Sarah, another maid declares and Will startles, surprised to notice the gaggle of servants in the room.

And, beyond the letters, there had been no secret assignations that Will had been witness to, no obvious impropriety and so what was he meant to have reported, and to whom?

Will believes he is twelve years old or thereabouts – no one has ever been able to confirm – and so he knows that he is too old for the hot tears that are stinging his eyes. He cannot countenance crying in front of these girls, especially while still in his night cap and gown, so he nods at them silently and makes his way back to his room. 'As thick as thieves they were,' he hears Jessie mumble behind him. 'Lady Catherine's favourite.'

'For all the good it's done him,' Moll sniffs. 'She remembered to take her best scents from Paris but the little monkey gets left behind.'

*

For the next few days, Will waits for Lady Catherine to send for him from London.

He dresses in his livery every morning, wearing the silk as armour and he keeps his short coils neatly brushed, for it always pays to stay ready.

No heart for catching tadpoles, jarring ladybirds or holing up in the library even though his time is now utterly his own. He keeps to his room mainly, the days long and empty while the house grinds on around him, without him, as if he were already a ghost.

It's during a sojourn at his window that he sees the tall, rangy figure of Croft, pacing across the jewelled green of the front lawn. Croft pauses and then looks straight up at Will, the ferocity of his bright blue eyes a physical weight that pins Will in place despite the distance. He stares, his craggy face unreadable but Will is not able to mistake the peremptory curl of Croft's gloved white hand; he is being summoned, and so he goes.

Will waits at the scarred oak table while Mrs Manton bustles about; there is no family to cook for, but the servants must still eat. She casts a worried glance at him every time he sighs, eventually dusting flour from her palms and walking over to stand before his slumped figure. She rarely touches him, Will realises. No easy reaches for his person the way Lady Catherine does, or did, as if he were something like a puppy or an umbrella, there to be handled. It disconcerts him now, her way of acting like the amount of space between them is something he might decide.

'You,' she says deliberately when he finally meets her eye, 'are the very best of boys, Will. It's plain that you had no part in all that nasty business. Why, you've been so good for all these years I cannot think of a single reason why Sir Davenport would not keep you on. And…'

Her next words are lost when Croft speaks.

'Mrs Manton,' he says, standing ramrod straight in the kitchen doorway. 'There's many a slip twixt the cup and the lip. It would do us all well to remember that, I think. Will,' he adds, inclining his head towards the despondent boy. 'With me, if you please.'

They end up in the Great Hall, before Captain Lucy's portrait.

Croft waits, his hands clasped behind his back, his head tilted as he considers the painting above them. Will can wait too, is good at it even, casting his gaze towards the stained glass windows. He counts each trio of pikes, the Lucy sigil and he thinks how Lady Catherine once told him that the name Lucy came from a word meaning *'light'*. Right now, he feels dizzy with it, the sun pouring in through every pane of glass.

'Sad times,' Croft says crisply, making Will jump. 'But like a ship, we must adjust our sails. Lady Catherine had… a taste for novelty.' Croft cuts his eyes at Will before he continues. 'Which Captain Lucy, in his wisdom, saw fit to indulge. But Sir Davenport has quite a different outlook from our dearly departed. Do you follow? What I mean is, what are your plans?'

'Plans, sir?'

'Now that you are to move on from here?'

'But I… my intention was to stay.'

'A page with no mistress?'

'If it pleased you, sir,' Will says, 'and Sir Davenport of course, perhaps I might one day be fit to be a footman, and –'

'A footman!' Croft chuckles. 'This isn't Mayfair, boy.'

'But I haven't done anything wrong,' Will says, struggling to keep his voice even as his face grows hot. 'I didn't know anything about Lady Catherine.'

'Whether you did or you did not – '

'But I *didn't*,' Will insists.

'The fact remains that your services are no longer required.'

'By whose say-so?' Will is amazed to hear himself speak so boldly, aware of his heart beating wildly, the pulse heavy in his throat. 'Yours or Sir Davenport's?'

Croft regards Will with a detached air. The boy is still far more child than man, a pot belly stretching the line of his livery coat, and his features round and babyish. But Croft has been to Bristol, Liverpool and London, has seen that boys like Will can grow sturdy like bucks and just as ornery, and what need would they have for such a man at Charlecote?

'You forget yourself, Will,' he says eventually. 'You need not concern yourself with Sir Davenport's words, when mine, as the steward of this house, will do. Your mistress has done you a disservice, I fear, for you have been spoiled and no longer comprehend your place. Surely you understand that she kept you for a pet?' Will simply stares back, a mutinous look on his face.

'In all your trips with her to London,' Croft continues, 'you would have seen all the portraits that her friends displayed – the master or mistress of the house with their little black boy, finely dressed no doubt, but barely in the frame? All trends have their day, I'll grant you, but 'tis a fashionable thing, no more, no less and certainly no indication of meaningful favour, as you now well know, given the circumstances in which you find yourself. You should be grateful that you are being released, instead of just being sold.'

'Sold?' Will says. 'Sir Davenport could no more sell me than he could Moll.'

'*Moll*?' Croft scoffs. 'Moll Flitwick? Come Will, but you and Moll are not the same.'

He crouches down slowly so that he can meet Will's eyes. 'There have been Mantons, Licks, Crofts and Flitwicks serving the Lucys at this very house for the last century. We all can claim Charlecote as a parish while you can claim what exactly?'

'I'm a servant as the rest,' Will insists, digging his nails into the skin of his clenched fists, once again willing himself not to cry.

Croft nods, reaching out to place a large, firm hand on Will's shoulder. 'And yet which other servant in this house has ever been obliged to wear a collar of silver about their neck?' He gestures to the portrait, where Will's likeness lingers to the side, partially obscured by the Captain's horse.

*

Will crouches in the hayloft above the stables and considers his soft hands.

He should be making plans he knows, but his mind keeps snagging on useless things: the echoed groans of the bucks in autumn, or the shedding of their summer skins, leaving their antlers bloody with velvet; moments of hide and go seek with the other servant boys when their betters were able to spare them; all those early mornings when he would creep outside and gulp deep breaths of air, his footsteps disturbing the dew as he walked and watched the mist rise from the silvery twist of the Avon.

Fool, he thinks. How was it that he hadn't come to realise until now that his presence here had always been conditional? Based on whim to hear Croft tell it, based on *fancy.*

He thinks of the sly smile on the old man's face when he had mentioned the collar and even now Will feels hot prickles of shame at his throat, though he had not been asked to wear the thing for months now; *an ornament for special occasions* they had told him; *feast days, weddings or when a famous man comes to paint your likeness.*

Will knew that Captain Lucy had fetched him from a place called Tangiers. He also knew, because Lady Catherine had told him, that he was what some called an Aethiop, or a Moor and that many such as he were found in a place called Africa but the idea was too large and too slippery to fix in his mind.

His memories of life before Charlecote were as thin as smoke, with his first tongue, his first name even, long since lost to him. He had seen others like him in London, though not exactly many; a footman here, a glimpse of a cook there, a handful of scullery maids and, once, a luxuriantly dressed lady-in-waiting, a sheen of pearls strung like a poem around the dark brown of her wrist and an emerald pin stuck fast into the dense coils of her hair.

But London might as well be the moon from Charlecote. He had no money or means, and most likely only beggary there to greet him even if he somehow managed the journey. Besides, it was too loud, too wicked a place for a quiet one like him, a boy who loved the green, lemony sprig of bread and cheese buds on his tongue.

Will drifts between sleep and wakefulness, dreaming of familiar fields while he huddles against scratchy bales of hay, only distantly aware of the snuffles and whinnies of the drowsy horses in the stalls beneath him.

Then, Mrs Manton's voice.

His eyes blink open. Through the stable window, across the gloom, he sees the bob of her flickering candle as she crosses the yard.

'Will,' she calls out, drawing her shawl tighter across her nightgown. 'Will, 'tis not the end of things, you'll see. If we put our heads together – you, Mr Lick and me – I'm sure we will be able to fashion something or other. Will? Please come out. A spot of food and a lot of sleep and mark me, things will look much brighter in the morning.'

He has his doubts. A near lifetime of sugared promises from Lady Catherine had led him here – placeless – and right now Will doesn't feel he has any more trust in him to spare.

He has heard tales of other servants at other houses turned out for one thing or another – the endings almost always bad. This one disappeared to Bristol, that one just disappeared, then that boy sacked from Bramblebourne, fetching up in a ditch two weeks later, eyes white, throat cut.

He wonders what Lady Catherine is doing right now. Perhaps eating marzipan in a room full of golden mirrors with her little girl in her lap, and Will doesn't hate them, not exactly (*a baby*, the thought flares, *she lost a baby*) but when he pictures them, he feels an unnamed emotion clench him from head to toe and, for a moment, he watches his hands shake.

My beloved captain thinks me frivolous because I care for fine things, Lady Catherine had told him once. *But every fine thing has a purpose.*

He mumbles the words to himself now in his ramshackle prayers: *May I have a purpose and let me be quick about finding it, let me not have to spend too many nights alone in the dark*, for Will is still child enough to be troubled by such things and this is, after all, a world where dead boys in ditches can be real enough.

'Over here,' he calls out eventually and Mrs Manton turns towards the stables, her face slackening in relief. The next thing he knows, she is standing beneath him, gleaming like a ghost as she reaches up with one hand to beckon him down. 'This will always be your home, Will,' she whispers, biting her lip as if that might be enough to stop him from seeing that she is crying. So is he.

Liar, he thinks, but still, he climbs down.

1690

One morning, on the way to the counting house, Thomas Beauchamp had watched the ground rumble open as if the Devil himself were coming for them all, then in the next moment, Charlestown had been half swept away by the ocean.

Thomas was not a spiritual man but, naturally, the vigour of the experience had left him disposed to mortal reckonings. So, the next morning over breakfast, he had declared to the small boy by the table, grown desultory in his fanning duties, that sugar money could be made well enough from home.

With that, he began his preparations to leave his plantation, Woodbine, to the care of his attorney, Jenkins, and Thomas directed his mind to the quiet green of Oxhill to which he would soon return, with Myrtilla and Rosa in tow.

Myrtilla, or Tilly, as he prefers – such a good-natured girl, blessed by a pleasing figure, bright face and an easy laugh that bubbled like spring water; Jenkins had done well with his purchase of that one. As for Rosa – black as pitch, usually wearing a scowl just as dark and sullenly silent as a grave – well, the best Thomas could say about her was that she played a fine flute and that whatever one's disposition, he supposed they were all God's children.

He fancied that Tilly would make a good companion for his wife, Perletta, who delighted (rather too much, Thomas thought) in being at one with the Beau Monde. Having a dusky lady in waiting would be just the ticket in their sleepy parish, or at least, this is what he had gleaned from Walter Underhill's correspondence, when the man had asked him to fetch a fancy for his own wife, Lady Alice. While Rosa would not have been his first choice, Tilly had desired it and Thomas prided himself on being reasonable over things he did not care about.

Thomas didn't especially like the Underhills, nor the Lucys, the clan into which Alice Underhill had been born. Those two families, fighting between themselves over who got to be the cock of the walk in Warwickshire, but united at least in looking down on him. *Shop keeper*, he knew they called him behind his back, but also to his face, in forced jest. *Grocer. Sugar man.*

Captain Lucy had once told Thomas that he had no interest in that West India business, that it seemed too lowly a trade. *But how then*, Thomas had wanted to ask, *did the good captain imagine that the little Negro boy who once had the run of Charlecote Park been able to come into his possession in the first place.*

And now the Underhills come to ask him favours, they too believing they could benefit from the business and yet somehow still stand apart. *We are all in it*, Thomas felt like saying sometimes. *This country is in it up to the neck. Always a price for progress, just got to make sure you're not the one stuck for the bill.*

But Thomas was, above all, a practical person. It would do no good to openly antagonise those who might yet still prove useful to him, and so he would keep his counsel, he would fetch a girl for Lady Underhill's fancy and, in the meantime, his sugar money would make mountains.

So, then the journey. The girls' eyes shining in delight, both trembling with excitement at the sight of the ship at the dock. Two and a half months from Nevis to London, rolling across the shifting blues of sea and ocean. Thomas dreamed of Nevis but longed for home, the yearning growing stronger as he neared it. He spent his time in his creaky room, working on the accounts, remembering more instructions for Jenkins, and constructing brittle love letters to Perletta, for although she had requested billet-doux, he was suspicious of excessive expressions of emotion.

Tilly and Rosa seemed to live on deck, only reluctantly going down into the hold at his insistence at mealtimes, or to sleep. Once, he had asked Tilly what on earth the pair of them were about, standing in silence, staring out at the diminishing horizon.

Tilly had tried to smile, failed, tried again, and Thomas almost told her to stop. He didn't want to see such a ghoulish pantomime on her pretty face. He hadn't known what to say when she had pointed to the flurry of shadows that slicked along in the ship's wake – a sight he had never noted before – and told him that it was all nothing, they were just looking out once again for the sharks.

1692

Here at Idlicote, she is called Margaret Lucy, at Lady Alice's request.

Before that, she had been Rosa, as she remains still, to Tilly. Before that, Jenny, and in the time before even that, during those long, searing weeks spent marching in the coffle towards an unknown maw of water, she had simply been known as 'girl'. 'Margaret' has learned not to become attached to something as inconsequential as the names these people give her.

Kitty Underhill frowns at her across the dining table as the servants clear away the breakfast things.

'They say that in London, the thing nowadays is to have a Chinaman for the household. Now *those* are rare,' Kitty sighs.

'Now, now, Kitty,' Mr Underhill says distractedly from behind his newspaper. 'A bird in the hand...'

A bird in the hand does what? Margaret thinks, still not used to all these nonsense phrases and the way people here so often speak the opposite of what they really mean, smiling all the while.

'At least a bird might try to talk,' Kitty says, giving Margaret a narrow glare.

'Come, Kitty,' Lady Underhill says. 'What would we do without

Nuestra Senora de las Nieves? She has made us the talk of the town these past two summers.'

Margaret makes her right hand relax, a silver spoon falling onto the linen tablecloth with a gentle thump.

Nuestra Senora de las Nieves. A joke, Margaret had come to realise; a nod to Nevis but also something about the darkness of her skin in contrast to all the fine white fabrics Lady Alice insists she wear.

Margaret has never been quite sure of her purpose at the Underhills; to have a person entirely for show was such a wild, extravagant thing, and yet that seemed to be the way of it.

Long days of nothingness with Kitty and Lady Alice, then countless evenings where she had been brought out as spectacle, draped in fine brocades or lace, with baby's breath seeding her hair, serving as an interlude between the main course and the sweetmeats, where she would play an air or two on the flute. Some of the women would clap with tight faces, and away from their women, some of the men would make stale jokes about wondering where her colour stopped. All the while Margaret slipped away inside to a different place.

Speak, they asked her. She would not.

Dance, they told her. She refused.

Hold your appetite, they counselled, for she had grown so much since arriving here. Once slender limbs thickened, a former scrap of a waist now fat as a moon and still she ate, in secret if she had to, midnight trips to the pantry where she would slather honey onto her tongue straight from the jar.

Love us, they demanded, *and if you can't do that, at least be grateful.* She could do neither even if she wanted to, but she had never wanted to, even though she understood that this was an easier life than her life in the fields back in Nevis.

Because how to love, or be grateful, after everything? That first long journey, chained in a ship's hold, time made meaningless as they roiled across the boiling froth of an ocean. Sometimes, back then, she felt so hollowed out she was certain she had died and everything she did now were the echoes of a ghost. How to love after the rabble of her first auction block, with the clammy poke and press of thick pale fingers in her intimate places, the yammer of words that she couldn't understand? How to love after the nightmares of Woodbine and its cane fields?

The people here spoke often of British America. How they had heard of unchristian things going on at the plantations over there, how those masters were so brutish and rough, yet they didn't ask Margaret about Woodbine. Perhaps they supposed Mister Thomas had given them all plentiful breaks for merriment, dancing and the taking of bread and tea.

So no, she could not love the people here, or even like them, though she supposed she was treated well enough, considering.

The Underhills are always making haste, though it seems to Margaret that they rarely have anything of consequence to do. This morning, they rush from the dining table. Master Underhill has some tenants to harass, and Lady Alice and Kitty need to discuss choices for Kitty's gown for tonight and its capacity to attract any suitable prospects. Another meal at Charlecote Park where, afterwards, Lady Alice will complain for at least thirty minutes that the manor has never been kept as well as when she lived in it, as she does after every visit to her childhood home.

Margaret is just thankful to be left alone for a few moments so she can steal a glance at Mr Underhill's discarded paper. Tilly has been teaching her to read English, or at least trying to – it's slow-going when done in secret. She scans the page full of cramped print, not understanding all the words, but then her eye is caught by one that is familiar – runaway. Another hue-and-cry notice. They mainly write about men and boys, but today's notice is about a woman, whose name they do not bother to provide. 'Very black' they call her, short and thick, her return being worth two guineas. *I wish you wings.*

Margaret feels her hands tremble as she smooths the page, the crackle of possibility leaping up to meet her from every wrinkle. She decides that she will be gone from here by the time of the feast named after the headless man, Saint John.

*

After dinner, and all the lords and ladies are flushed pink with drink and soothed by the weight of venison in their bellies. There have been card games over gossip and talk of trade while Margaret played her flute – *over there, by the candlelight* – Lady Alice had suggested, remarking almost to herself, how it gave Margaret's skin and pearls a deeper lustre.

Tired of chatter and music, they ask Tilly to read. She has been seated in the corner of the room, waiting. When the room's gaze falls upon her, Margaret sees the almost imperceptible preen; Tilly is beautiful and knows it, knows also that for many, the allure of such beauty increases when its owner pretends not to be aware of it.

Tilly, one of Mr Thomas's pretty girls had lived in the big house at Woodbine. Margaret had disliked her then and probably still would have disliked her now, were it not for the fact that it was just the two of them in this quiet corner of the world, and if she didn't have her, then she wouldn't have anybody. Somewhere, over these two years, much had changed.

They hadn't spoken back at Woodbine. Those were the years when Margaret only used her voice for herself, whispering during whatever few snatched moments of solitude, who she was and where she came from.

So, they didn't speak, but Margaret knew her face because Tilly was wherever Mr Thomas was, and she had grown to hate the way Tilly seemed always to be smiling at everything and everyone, as if she didn't know that Woodbine was a graveyard. But likely it was different for Tilly in the house than it was for her and others in the field and that had made Margaret hate her all the more.

But then Margaret had been plucked from the fields for reasons she still didn't understand, placed in the big house and fed and groomed, her wounds healed, allowed to plump out like a hen before a feast day, before being whisked onto that boat with Tilly and Mr Thomas.

Another nightmare journey, when every night Margaret had screamed herself awake from vicious dreams. Tilly had learned to reach over in the dark to place a hand on Margaret's wrist or cheek, letting her thumb move in wide, warm circles until she was soothed. It was during one of those nights that Tilly had dared speak a word in her language and after a pause, Margaret had replied in kind. It had been Tilly's turn to pause, and there'd been a strange timbre to her voice when she'd muttered 'So you do speak', her thumb still light against the curve of Margaret's face.

This was how they discovered that while they were not from the same place, it was close enough that they shared many words. They learnt each other's language over these nights, and now, on the irregular occasions they got to meet alone, they would talk in a rough combination of the two. They shared much of their past lives – before Woodbine, before Nevis, revealing much but not their real names. This was at Margaret's insistence, wanting at least one thing she could preserve for herself.

The people at the dinner table wouldn't understand the Tilly whose mouth so easily shaped sounds they could not recognise or reproduce, the one who took the time to soothe a scared, sullen girl in the rocking dark of a narrow berth, but then Margaret didn't understand *their* Tilly – *this* Tilly, who seemed so eager to perform for their amusement, always so ready to be looked upon.

'That lilt in her voice! Sir Thomas exclaims proudly, as if he himself had kissed the gift of speech into her mouth. 'When she talks, you'd think you were standing at the top of the valley of a morning, the swaying cane fields below and all that cool mountain air rushing down to greet you.'

Margaret tries to keep her gaze blank at his words; how different their recollections of life in Nevis.

Mr Langley is a young man from Tiddington. An heir, Margaret knows, because it is all Kitty and Lady Alice spoke about in the carriage ride over. He has seemed oblivious to Kitty's charms throughout tonight but he's quick to rouse himself in adding to the pile of suggestions as to what Tilly might read.

'Some Shakespeare!' Kitty interrupts, turning her bright eyes towards Mr Langley as she has heard of his love for plays. The table groans when Colonel Lucy starts with that overtired anecdote of Shakespeare poaching on the Charlecote grounds as a boy.

Mr Langley clears his throat and starts again. 'Perhaps some Bible verse?' he offers. His voice is neutral enough but there is something in the amused glances he trades with another young man across the table that makes Margaret's spine straighten.

The table agrees, feeling that verse would be appropriate for both Margaret and Tilly, who no doubt were still suffering from the heathen ways of their formative years, and besides, there was so much of the Bible that was pleasing to the ear, especially when delivered by one who could read well and in such an oddly pleasing scramble of accents.

'Shall we say, Song of Songs?' Mr Langley suggests and, at this, his friend poorly conceals a snigger.

From her corner, Margaret sees that calculations are being made. There is an insult in this somewhere – or, at the very least, some kind of embarrassment, though she cannot glean the nature of it yet. Mr Thomas is considering if he can bear the cost of expressing his instinctive displeasure at this young jackanapes meaning to make a game of Myrtilla, when this same jackanapes is the heir to a towering fortune but with no brains in his head to know what to do with it – in other words, a good man to have in one's pocket.

'Why not?' Mr Thomas eventually demurs, with a wave of his hand.

The women at the table wear pinched looks – *those* verses at *this* occasion, read by *that* person? Impropriety compounded and surely this was but a jape that would be put to bed soon enough.

But someone scrambles for a bible, and then someone else is showing Tilly the right page, and she only flinches for a fraction of a moment before she begins to read about being kissed, about a man's love being better than wine, about how she is very dark but comely. Tilly stumbles over her words then, her eyes searching for Margaret's from across the room but the moment their gaze connects, Tilly's eyes fall away, and she taps a finger against her lower lip once, as if to restrain herself from something.

The sweet grit in her voice seems to capture them all: the gentry frozen at their table, the servants lined against the wall and Margaret still in the corner. Someone will stop it – they must, but when Tilly talks of eating fruit that is sweet to her taste, of course it can only mean the sweetness of God's love and surely it cannot be so bad to be reminded of that, albeit in this unorthodox way.

When Tilly reads of lips like a scarlet thread, Mister Langley bites his own. His gaze only tears away from Tilly at the crashing sound to his left – Kitty has had an accident with her glass. She murmurs her apologies to her host as two serving girls scurry forth to clear the shards away.

'Myrtilla,' Miss Perletta says sharply. 'If you could fetch my shawl from the carriage?'

Tilly nods, places the Bible on her seat and slips from the room.

'Margaret, go and assist,' Lady Alice commands.

In the fetching of a shawl? Margaret allows herself a small, grim smile; how flustered they were now, not even able to artfully conceal their sudden pressing need to be amongst themselves, so that they could parse what they had just allowed to be done to Tilly in that room.

Tilly waits for her on the other side of the door.

'I suppose you imagine I deserved that,' she says, switching from English. Her gaze is fixed straight ahead.

Margaret doesn't answer until they reach the emptiness of the Great Hall. 'It speaks to their character, not yours.'

Tilly halts, as she always does when she is here, in front of the portrait of the Captain and the young Black boy. They can hear the servants elsewhere, but it remains just the two of them in the room. Many of the sconces have gone out and so the hall is part shadow, part moonlight.

'But still. You think I'm too comfortable with their affections.'

'You would call *that*,' Margaret gestures in the direction from where they have just come, 'affection?'

Tilly stares up at the portrait. They had used to imagine stories for the boy; riches and wealth, perhaps a journey back home, wherever that was, his return long awaited and triumphant. Then Tilly had asked after him, and one of the Charlecote servants explained that he'd been turned out years back, leaving all his fancy things behind. Last they'd heard, he'd moved on a couple of villages over, where he'd picked up the trade of baking bread.

Better than dead, Margaret had shrugged, which is the ending she had expected, but

Tilly had been sorrowful, hoping for a better yarn than that. *Something exceptional*, Tilly had said when pressed, and Margaret understood the yearning, but she also felt there was a lot to be said for being allowed to be ordinary and being allowed a full, complete life just the same.

'You mean to run away,' Tilly says bluntly, and Margaret's breath stops in her throat. In the absence of a denial, Tilly presses on. 'You stole a silver teaspoon this evening. I saw you do it. Saw you do it at the last dinner here as well. And you that has the quickest of tongues has nothing now to say? So I'm right. Feathering your nest before taking flight?' Tilly's voice cannot be anything other than sweet, but the grit in it has sharpened.

'You cannot say anything,' Margaret hisses, grabbing Tilly's elbow until the other girl whirls round to face her and shakes her off.

'And why can't I? Why *shouldn't* I?'

Margaret simply stares, baffled that Tilly could even ask such a question. 'When you leave, they will say that I knew of it. They will punish me for it.'

'Tell them you knew nothing'.

Tilly laughs, her face twisted. She brings her left hand up sharply, as if to strike, but Margaret sees she only means to display it, and or rather the space where a little finger used to be. Tilly usually doesn't like to speak of it, only saying it was down to the master before she met Mr Thomas. 'This is what happened the last time I said I knew nothing,' Tilly says. 'And to think, it was even true that time. You know as well as I that the truth of things rarely matters.'

'Another man, another time,' Margaret shrugs, though her chest is tight. 'Aren't you the one always saying that Mr Thomas is not like the rest?'

'Your ways have made you unkind, Rosa'.

'And your ways have made you weak,' Margaret spits, unable to stop herself.

Tilly's hand drops and she steps forward until they are almost touching. She is dressed in green today. Her eyes are burning and her chest heaves as she tries to keep herself quiet. *She is alive like a forest*, Margaret thinks, nonsensically, and then Tilly speaks.

'When they took an axe to my finger, they warned me to smile through it, or else they would take my hand. And when it was done, they bandaged it up and had me dance a reel with the master's son and I smiled through that too. In fact, was the lightest on my feet I'd ever been, but I suppose that is weakness to you, too. You think, through these nightmares, what is not your way can only be wrong.'

'Is it my approval you want?' Margaret would throw her hands in the air but Tilly stays so close. 'Have it. Your way is your way, and my way is mine, and let us just leave the other to it.'

'And let us just leave each other too?'

Margaret halts, the hurt plain on Tilly's face.

'Would you have even told me, had I not guessed? Or would I have simply awoken one day to the news that you were gone?'

They both know the answer, but Margaret imagines that it would be kinder not to say the truth aloud.

'Your loyalties are...'

'Suspect?' Tilly supplies. 'Much like your reasoning. Where do you suppose to go? Do you imagine you can make your way back home?'

Margaret shakes her head. She no longer allows herself to think of that time before everything.

'Bristol then,' Tilly continues. 'Or some similar grubby place. Assuming you don't end up dead, you'll most likely be begging on a roadside. What kind of a life –'

'*Mine,*' Margaret says. 'It would be mine.'

They stare at each other, their silence thickening. Margaret thinks of those nights when Tilly would reach over to hold her hand in the dark as they crossed an ocean. Of the way her heart simmers every time she enters a room to find Tilly there. Of last summer when Tilly had briefly taken to the habit of curling an arm about Margaret's waist while pretending to swoon, saying in English, '*I cannot woo in festival terms*'. After that first time, she had explained what it meant, and Margaret had felt her face grow hot, thinking to herself that she would take whatever terms as long as Tilly made her feelings plain.

Margaret thinks of the time Tilly had caught her glancing at herself in a mirror, and she had challenged her – *I imagine you think me much changed* – referring to her girth, the spread of dark heft, which she treasured and thought beautiful, because she had chosen it and made it so. Tilly had known her before, when they were both slender like reeds. All Tilly had done was shrug, while holding her gaze in the mirror and said, *I think of you* and then Miss Perletta had called her away.

But these were just half-imaginings, not enough to try to build a life on, which is perhaps what Tilly was asking. *Stay here with her where we can only meet according to the whim of our mistresses, and maybe, one day, during a five minute interlude we have to ourselves, she will say something or I will say something, and we can be certain of nothing else but each other until I am sold away, or until Mr Thomas takes it into his head to take Tilly back to Nevis, or whatever other calamity that might befall us because we are not free here, not like this.*

'So, tell me, Rosa, what do you say?'

'Is it really so bad here?' Tilly tries again. '*This* life?'

'Maybe not for you,' Margaret says, and she is not trying to be hurtful, but Tilly's eyes start to glisten.

Tilly draws away, taking with her the scent of amber, orange and jasmine.

'Mr Thomas told me to choose and so I picked you. To come here,' Tilly clarifies when Margaret gives her a quizzical look. 'I am sorry for my part in it. I'm not sure I even knew what it meant – how far they meant to take us, but still, I am sorry. Because I was glad to get away from Woodbine, but glad to have someone – have you with me.'

'Why?' Margaret says eventually. 'We weren't even friends then.'

'Are we friends now, Rosa?' Tilly laughs, a bitter tilt to her mouth as she shakes her head. 'Had to be a young person, he said. Young as me. Healthy. He didn't like that you don't talk but I told him about your music. How you could charm a sound out of anything. You were kind to my mother. She told me how you would gift whatever you had left over. Although knowing you now as I do, they probably weren't even leftovers. How you helped her plant her provision ground, and then again when it was time to harvest. Much more than I could do for her sometimes, despite my place. Mr Thomas, he...'

'I didn't know that was your mother,' is all Margaret can think to say, remembering that frail old woman with trembling hands. She looks hard at Tilly's face until she finds it – a similarity in the heartshaped chin, and the heavy lids over large, dark eyes.

'How would you have known?' Tilly shrugs. 'You don't talk to people. But anyway, it meant something to me. So, the choice was meant to thank you but – well, it was not mine to make. And I know you think about them. That it pains you – the ones we left behind.'

'Don't *you* think about them?'

Tilly pauses for a long time as she considers. 'And if I threw myself away on guilt, would they be any better for it? I think about my mother. Before we left, she said to me, 'just live, daughter. Whatever you need to say, whoever you need to be. Just live'.' Tilly draws herself up to her full height and gives Margaret a considering look. 'And I aim to do so.'

'No matter the means?' Margaret asks, not letting her gaze leave Tilly's.

'No matter the means. Isn't it as you said? Let your way be your way and let my way be mine. Come now,' Tilly adds, switching back to English as she glides towards the main doors. 'We are late in fetching this shawl.'

*

Before Margaret sleeps that night, she buries her stash of stolen silver in a secluded corner of the vegetable garden, just in case. Brought low with worry, she cannot imagine how she will sleep, but somehow she does. She wakes with a start, her skin hot against sweat-dampened sheets, as she thinks of half-remembered dreams of sitting in a garden, one hand wet with honey, the other oily with myrrh, the air thick with the scent of cedar and a soft mouth against her own.

*

It's six weeks before she sees Tilly again; just a glimpse of her face in a carriage window as the Beauchamps head into town. She turns her face from Margaret as if she were something so easily overlooked and Margaret wonders if this means Tilly feels guilty over an imminent betrayal. Or perhaps Tilly is playing at forgetting, trying to erase the very fact of Margaret's face, and what they said or didn't say to each other in the shadows of the great hall, so that afterwards, when they ask her what she knew, she can sound convincing when she says she knew nothing.

She would like to tell Tilly that for all of Mr Thomas's supposed kindness, if Tilly were to die right now he'd still write his name as her master across her headstone. The disturbing thing is that Tilly is sharp enough to know this and yet.

So, instead, Margaret thinks of Tilly's confession, wonders why she'd told her the truth of things and why then. *You did not have to tell me that,* she finds herself saying often to the Tilly of her mind.

"Do you mean I should not have?" imaginary Tilly whispers.

Margaret does not know what she means, and what is the point of all this thinking when she needs to be making plans. Because, despite the risk of it all, despite all that she will lose, the truth remains that she cannot stay.

The days crawl towards midsummer and she reminds herself of certain things.

You do not have to speak.

> GONE away, since Tuesday last, a Black girl of some 17 years of age, well limb'd with strong teeth, named DORCAS. A large scar under her left eye, speaks tolerable English and some Spanish. She is the property of Mr William Poultney. Any person assisting in her return shall receive a reward of two guineas, by applying to Mr Poultney at 136 Harbour Lane.

You do not have to dance.

> A Negro woman who goes by the name of Bertha, about 20 years old, has absented herself from her Mistress's house these past seven days. If Bertha returns to her mistress, Mrs Whelan, she shall be kindly received...

You do not have to hold your appetite.

> JUNO MORRISSON, a Negro woman servant belonging to Colonel Shaw, left her master's service this 18th instant. Whoever can discover and secure her so that she may be had again shall be handsomely rewarded...

You do not have to love them.

> WHEREAS a Black girl, known by the name of Celine, went away last evening from her Master's house clandestinely...

You do not have to be grateful.

*

Croft, the steward at Charlecote has died. They hold a wake and the cook, Mrs Manton, brings a large honey cake to the servant's table. An old man called Mr Lick laughs and says Croft hated all sweet things and Mrs Manton smiles, says the cake is freshly baked, a gift from an old friend who sends the warmest of regards to the dearly departed.

Margaret watches Tilly, who is busy talking to a blushing stable boy, and she wonders if Tilly has heard of Mr Underhill's recent money troubles, how a younger brother of his is getting married and so the family is in urgent need of ready funds. *How bad would it be*, the Underhills have wondered, *to pass Margaret on, of course not by way of ugly sale, but perhaps in gift?*

Something proper by way of a gentleman's agreement, Mr Underhill concluded, and Margaret has overheard that a gentleman would be coming to Idlicote any time before Michaelmas to discuss the terms.

But before then, the feast of Saint John. Back at Charlecote, making merry in the great hall and as she plays her flute, Margaret's eyes keep drifting to the portrait of the little boy. Will, they say his name was. She tries to picture him – he would be an adult now, perhaps a little older than she. A free man or close enough to it, and so she wonders what has kept him around these parts. If it was a choice, there's something in that she cannot quite understand or respect, but maybe that was her trouble as Tilly had said, always too quick to judge. She wonders if he knows of her and Tilly, what he might think of them, what it might mean for the three of them to look on each other's faces.

She remembers all the times they had stood in that hall and tried to conjure Will out of that gilt frame until he was flesh and blood before them, but they had never managed it, the only bodies available to them being their own.

She will never see Charlecote again if she is lucky, its avenue of lime trees leading to all that glowing red brick and golden-tipped turrets, soon to be just a memory. Already Will is more memory than man for most at Charlecote but the fact of him reminded Margaret of a way that there might be a life beyond these grand spaces, however one came to leave them, and she meant to go as far as she could.

Tonight.

As good a time as any; midsummer, so travelling time in the dark will be short, but everyone will be so sore headed and lazy from drink, that they will rouse later than usual in the morning. With luck, it will be some hours before anyone realises that she has gone and by then, she hopes to have found her first hiding place.

Tilly, once again, spends the evening avoiding her gaze and they are never alone, so Margaret doesn't have the chance to – do or say what exactly? Better this perhaps, a quiet leave taking.

Back at the Underhills, she waits until the household has grown heavy with silence, followed by grumbling snores, then she rises. She has practised these steps, moving as silent as a shadow as she collects her necessary things, dons the rough clothes she has pilfered from the laundry these past few months, better garments for travelling in than her useless dresses. She digs up her silver from its hiding place and then she slips from the grounds, her heart swooping all the while, her breath a hard glass sphere in her throat and her stomach churning.

As she goes, she casts up prayers to old gods.

She has perhaps walked but a mile; the air smells of ash, the night is bright with stars and summer warmth is heavy on her skin. The rustle of startled rabbits and deer, the glimmer of fox eyes, a chorus of croaking frogs and every now and then a raucous, faraway cheer – some late-night revellers on their way to or from another midsummer fire.

Margaret tries not let herself think of anything but one foot in front of the other. Tries to soothe herself with inconsequential things like the memory of first time here that she saw snow. Still, everything seems too loud now she is outside: her footsteps and her fears. Her aim is to get to Bristol and figure things out from there. A big enough place to lose oneself in, to have a simple life, to be ordinary.

She just about manages to stifle a scream when she feels a hand brush the nape of her neck. Whirling round, expecting Mr Underhill or one of his men, she is stunned at the sight of Tilly. She cannot help but glance over Tilly's shoulder before returning a wary gaze to the girl. If she had been trailing her for all this while, it would seem she had decided against raising an alarm, but Margaret, remembering their last proper conversation, remains confused.

'Ow!' Tilly hisses at the feel of Margaret's hard pinch to her forearm, before her face falls into a teasing grin. 'You mean to say you dream of me?'

This irritation feels familiar and real enough. Margaret scowls, turns on her heels, begins walking. She keeps her strides long so that Tilly has to walk briskly to keep up. She is dressed impractically, of course, the long dragging hem of her dress already grass stained.

'This is dangerous,' Margaret says.

'Yes,' Tilly agrees.

'Aren't you scared?'

'Terrified,' Tilly confesses.

'You will be a slow walker.'

'But I have other attributes.'

'We will be more easily caught.'

'Good then that we have spent all these years here learning how to hide. Rosa,' she adds, lightly touching Margaret's arm, 'if you really mean for me to stay behind, then say it. Just ask it of me and by my mother, by the stars, I'll do it and say nothing.'

Margaret scowls, a deep ache stealing through her frame. 'You are no longer used to hard things.'

'But I can bear them.'

'It'll begging most likely, Tilly, like you said. Sleeping in hedgerows or hard streets, doing who knows what for meagre coins and starting again to do it over, day after day.'

'So, ask me to stay behind. Tell me.'

'Tell me why you wish to come?'

Tilly laughs and rolls her eyes. 'Rosa. You know the reason.'

'No,' Margaret says slowly as she comes to a halt despite herself. She looks about them quickly; they are still alone. 'You have to say it. I thought that you and Mr Thomas...'

'We don't always have to talk about them,' Tilly says. 'And you already know the reason. But fine,' she adds. 'I came to understand some things about our place here. But there is also... aside from that, I...'

Margaret is stubborn, her feet firmly planted as if they have time to spare. Her tongue feels thick in her mouth, her pulse beating strong in her fingertips. So here it was. This thing they had been tending to for years, feelings growing deep and thick, and so what to call it?

'I don't trust you,' Margaret says. She wonders if Tilly means to make a game of her feelings, leverage for some as yet unknown advantage, but then she also remembers all those nights in the ship, Tilly's hand light against her face. Both things could be true at once.

Tilly nods, her face sombre and unsurprised. 'All these choices,' she says. 'Who can guess what we might now do? As it happens, I'm unsure of you as well but, we shall just have to keep our eyes on one another.'

Margaret just stares, still waiting, unaccustomed to wanting something precious and seeing that thing materialise before her, thread by thread. She has long since stopped believing in good or easy things, but then these are not words she would use for either Tilly or herself.

Tilly tilts her head then and steps closer, her eyes searching for something in

Margaret's face. After a moment, she decides, her voice only trembling once. 'Would you like me to say that I would send your parents gifts of firewood? Bags of cowrie beads or stacks of yam? Have your uncle accept a skin of palm wine from me, or give your family water during the dry seasons? I would do those things if I could. I *have* done those things, so many times over in my imaginings.' *Finally*, Margaret thinks, a breath still caught in her chest.

At only eighteen, they have both already seen and lived too much. The decisions they were taking now would make life harder still and she knows that this is foolish, that she is perhaps making a silly trade, and that one cannot put much stock in desperate starlit declarations, but she cannot turn away from this night. Maybe she has died a thousand times already and so why not tilt at things now, headlong?

'Rosa…' Tilly pauses as Margaret grabs her hand, turns it palm up, brings it to her mouth. A whisper collects against Tilly's skin before Margaret presses her full lips into the centre of Tilly's palm. Then she takes that same hand and presses it to the swell of her chest so that Tilly can feel the rapid thrum of its beating through the coarse fabric of her shirt.

A soft grin lights up Tilly's face. 'Your name?' she guesses. 'Your real name?'

Margaret nods and laughs, startling herself at the sound. Tilly laughs too, her hand still a warm, live thing against Margaret. They have miles to walk before they can rest, and there are so many things to go wrong. She mostly believes they'll be discovered somehow and dragged right back to where they started, but in this moment, she feels drunk on choosing, on being chosen, and the audacity found in the attempt.

'A fine name,' Tilly says, her eyes fixed on the other girl's face. 'It suits you.'

The stars stay bright, the girls are wide awake and now is the time for running. Somewhere, they can hear the hiss of the river and when they turn a corner, emerging from thick woodland to the clear of night green, they will see the Avon twist before them, feel the cool spray of its mist.

*

Their so-called masters look, but never find them.

Catherine Wheatley, Mrs Thomas Lucy, later Duchess of Northumberland (d.1714) by Sir Godfrey Kneller (Lübeck 1646 - London 1723)
©National Trust Images

CHARLECOTE PARK

RUTH LONGONI

Entering the gates of Charlecote Park with its long avenues of trees, park-land and rivers feels like stepping into another time. The rivers Dene and Avon meet here. The Avon flows through the park on to Stratford upon Avon and Charlecote is situated in what was the southern-most part of the old Forest of Arden. Over in West Park are the remains of ridge and furrow agriculture and archaeological remains of buildings that predate the Tudor mansion, completed in 1558. The Lucy family, whose name de-rives from Lucé in Normandy, have lived at Charlecote since the twelfth century. A combination of wealth derived from the land – and the people who worked it – and advantageous marriages enabled the family to hold on to and improve the estate.

A deer park was established, and beautiful fallow deer still roam the park along with Jacob sheep, sent back by 'Batchelor George' Lucy from Portugal when he visited the British ambassador in Lisbon in 1756, dur-ing his Grand Tour.

Continuing down the long avenue, through the archway of the gate-house you come to the Tudor mansion, altered and added to over the centuries. There would once have been a bustle of activity, horses and carriages, servants, gardeners and craftspeople coming and going. Since 1946, Charlecote has been owned and looked after by the National Trust and its dedicated volunteers.

Upon entering the Great Hall, through the porch emblazoned with Queen Elizabeth I's coat of arms celebrating her visit to Charlecote in 1572, you are struck by family portraits on the walls. Immediately oppo-site is that of Sir Thomas Lucy III and his family painted around 1625, taking dessert with seven of their fifteen children. Also there to impress is the Venetian marble red and white floor and the amazing Florentine *pietra dura* (literally hard stone) table made from semi-precious stones. This ta-ble had once belonged to William Beckford, playboy, author and antique collector whose family fortune derived from sugar plantations in Jamaica. When he went bankrupt and was forced to sell the contents of Fonthill

Abbey in Wiltshire, George Hammond Lucy was one of the most enthusiastic buyers, acquiring many other items of ceramics and furniture.

Charlecote is full of precious items ranging from the ancient Greek vases in the Library and the elaborately carved, locally made, oak buffet in the Dining Room, to the furniture made on the Coromandel coast of India. In the drawing room is a ceremonial Indian sword captured in the uprising of 1857 and there are miniatures of two Indian princes, Tipu Sultan, the ruler of Mysore who died in 1799 defending his palace at Seringapatam from the English East India Company and Nana Sahib, who fought against the British in the Indian conflict of 1857.

Family links and global connections reflect the events that took place during Charlecote's long history, at home and abroad. Above the doorway leading to the staircase in the Great Hall hang two full-length portraits painted by Godfrey Kneller in 1680 of Captain Thomas Lucy (c.1655-84) and his wife, Catherine Wheatley (d.1714). Captain Lucy is wearing the uniform of the Household Guards. Holding his horse and almost fading into obscurity at the edge of the painting is a Black page boy wearing a metal collar of the type worn by enslaved people, on which the name of their 'owner' was commonly engraved. At this period, wealthy people often kept young Black boys as status symbols and they frequently appeared in portraits of the time.[1] Catherine Wheatley, meanwhile, was depicted as a society beauty. She too had a Black page who would serve her chocolate, then still newly fashionable as a drink.[2] We do not know their names or what happened to them as adults. Until the Somerset ruling of 1772, when they reached adulthood, many of these, especially men, were transported to the West Indies where they could be re-enslaved.

These portraits, together with a growing interest in the presence and history of Black people in the British countryside, and acknowledgement that this is part of all our history, has led to research which attempts to piece together information about their lives. Karen Onojaife's story is a fictionalised account that refers to known historical records and aims to breathe life into those whose lives we know so little about.

What do we know about the people in the portraits?

Captain Thomas Lucy, the son of Richard Lucy who served in Oliver Cromwell's parliament of nominees, inherited Charlecote in 1677. The turmoil, bloodshed and constitutional changes of the Civil War were over and Charles II, the restored monarch, was on the throne. Theatres, taverns and racecourses were reopened and puritan morality was overthrown.

Captain Lucy marked a break with the Puritan past of his father. At Charlecote, he lived the life of the upper gentry, taking on responsibilities as a JP and MP. He was a member of the so-called Cavalier Parliament which met at Oxford; there he lodged at Christchurch where the king was housed and he appears to have been quite close to the king. His military career appears to have begun with his procurement of a captaincy under Aubrey de Vere, Lord Oxford, in the Household Guard, a small standing army that the king kept for his personal protection. He was aged around 25 at the time.[3]

Captain Lucy served in the Anglo-Dutch wars of the 1670s, outcome of the colonial and commercial rivalry between the British and the Dutch. There are also records in the Warwickshire County Record Office that Thomas Lucy received two commissions as a lieutenant in the Garrison of Tangier between the years 1681 and 1684 but it is uncertain if he took up these posts, given reports of his other activities at the time.[4]

In 1683 he carried a message to the King offering the borough's support on the discovery of the Rye House Plot to assassinate both Charles and his brother James. For this he was rewarded with two leases of land in Stratford upon Avon, for an old servant.[5]

Back at Charlecote he busied himself making improvements to the gardens by installing a Dutch water garden with canals and elaborate parterres, fashionable at the time. This led to him being summoned in 1682 at the Easter Quarter sessions for stopping the current of the River Avon, causing flooding around Barford. He died at Charlecote of smallpox in 1684 leaving Catherine Wheatley a widow with one daughter, Elizabeth, born in their London House, and aged thirteen when he died.

In his will he referred to his dear wife being with child and that if the child were to be a boy, he would inherit the estate. Provision was made for Catherine of all the household goods, including jewellery for her lifetime and to be guardian of the coming child provided she bring him up in the Protestant religion. The child, sadly, died at birth and Catherine left Charlecote for London, continuing to receive large sums of money from the agent of the estate until she remarried. This occurred a year later in 1685 when she married the man who was to become First Duke of Northumberland. She predeceased her husband and died in 1714 and was buried in the family vault in Westminster Abbey. Davenport Lucy inherited Charlecote.

Much less is known about the Black people who arrived in Britain as the result of the transatlantic slave trade and plantation agriculture in the West Indies. However, records in local archives in Warwickshire do attest to their presence.

In Warwickshire, the Oxhill parish register of 1690 records the baptism of a enslaved woman named Margaret Lucy, belonging to Lady Underhill. Alice, Lady Underhill was the third daughter of Sir Thomas Lucy III and was married to Sir William Underhill of Idlicote. There was also Myrtilla, a young girl from Nevis in the Leeward Islands, who was brought as an enslaved person to the parish of Oxhill. She died at a young age in 1705 and her grave stands on the south eastern side of Oxhill Church. Thomas Beauchamp, a sugar planter, is listed as her 'owner'. Thomas Beauchamp is believed to have married one of the twin daughters of the rector of Oxhill, Nicolas Meese. He may have given or sold Margaret Lucy to Lady Underhill.[6] The parish records also note the baptism on 29th December 1700 of Will Archus, described as 'an adult male black.' Could he be the boy in the portrait with Captain Lucy as Karen Onojaife's story suggests? We shall probably never know.

Thirty-five years later there is a record in the Charlecote Parish register of a Black child of about six years old christened Philip Lucy. Despite various attempts, we know virtually nothing about him or what happened to him, nor if he was related to Will Archus. It was normal to include the names of the parents in the register but this was not done. It is possible that he was in the service of Frances, the widow of the Reverend William Lucy and her nephew Thomas Lucy who ran Charlecote after the death of Colonel George Lucy in 1721.[7]

Links with the slave trade and plantation slavery were not uncommon. At nearby Guy's Cliffe the Greatheed family accumulated their wealth from their many slaves on the island of St Kitts where they owned sugar plantations purchased towards the end of the 17th century.[8]

Endnotes:

1. Pictured but Unknown: Black histories in UCL Art Collections, Gemma Romain, January 2012.
2. *Charlecote Park, The National Trust Guidebook* (ISBN 978-84350-142-9.)
3. *Charlecote and the Lucys*, Alice Fairfax Lucy (London, Victor Gollanz), p. 157.
4. Appointment by Sir Percy Kirke, Captain-General of HM Forces in Africa and Governor of the Garrison and City of Tangier between 28th December 1681 – 1683, as Lieutenant to a Company of which Edward Hastings, Esq.., was Captain. Appointment by George Legge, Lord Baron of Dartmouth, Captain-General of HM Forces in Africa, Governor of the City etc. of Tangier 1683-84 as Lieutenant of a Company of Foot in the Regiment commanded by Colonel Charles Trelawny, Warwickshire's Past Unlocked: Collection Browser 00307 – Lucy Family of Charlecote.
5. *Charlecote and the Lucys*, Alice Fairfax Lucy (Victor Gollancz), p. 157
6. Church of St Lawrence, see Anne Hale, *Oxhill, A Short History*.
7. See also *Whose Story?* National Trust, 2007 and see Jim Layton, *Black People in Warwickshire's Past*, The Educational Development Service, Leamington, Warwickshire.

8. See Terry Roberts, *Further Recollections of a Country Mansion* (Nuneaton: J.T.M., 2014).

Further reading:
Miranda Kaufman, *Black Tudors* (London: One World, 2017).
Peter Fryer, *Staying Power* (London: Pluto Press, 1984).
David Olusoga, *Black and British* (London: Pan Books, 2016).

DYRHAM PARK

A long view across the park to the east front at Dyrham Park, South Gloucestershire
©National Trust Images/James Dobson

William Blathwayt (1649-1717) by Michael Dahl (Stockholm 1656/9 –
London 1743)
© National Trust

ANDRE BAGOO

LITANY FOR TWO BOYS AT DYRHAM PARK

After the house in which a pair of wooden stands,
shaped in the guise of two shackled
slaves, sits in a drawing room.

Share this with me. First, his offices: Secretary of the Lords
of Trade, Under-Secretary of State in the Home Office, Secretary
at War, Clerk in Ordinary of the Privy Council, acting
Secretary of State, Member of Parliament for Bath, Member of
Parliament for Newtown, member of the Board of Trade, and
the post he held for four decades until his death, Surveyor
and Auditor General of Plantation Revenues. Again. Surveyor
and Auditor General of Plantation Revenues – a dry,
bureaucratic title. Surveyor and Auditor General of
Plantation Revenues. Surveyor and Auditor General of
Plantation Revenues. Share this with me. His property – his
wife, whose house became his upon marriage, Mary, pictured
in a portrait sitting in front a giant ornament, her eyes
drifting to the village to the west, her dress the colour of
the deer outside. She bore him four children; three survived.
She died in her fifth year of marriage. Perhaps this is why William
Blathwayt rebuilt her Tudor house, perhaps he'd heard of
the Taj Mahal rising in one of the colonies to the East,
perhaps he diverted his tears to the garden to the south – the statue of
Neptune, the sphinx, the canal, the jet d'eau, the waves in a
line descending from step to step, roaring like billows in a
raging sea. Perhaps. Share this with me. The entry from
the east, the avenue ruled with lime trees that leads to empty
mist, the chestnut trees, the deer whose velvet antlers harden
into bone, antlers with their own tragic history, remembering

injury, furling around the same pain every year. Dyrham.
Dirham. Deorham. The limestone ashlar, the coursed rubble
at north and south elevations, the slate and lead roofs,
the west front of the central block with projecting wings,
the kitchen, the great hall and dining room, the 3:9:3 windows,
the bays to each side set forward, the moulded architraves
with sills, the central round-headed door with double pilaster
to each side and Gothic intersecting glazing bars, the floating
cornice with the Horatian inscription *His utere mecum*,
roughly translated as: *Share this with me*. The moulded
plinth, the heavy cornice, the long and short quoins with V-
joints, the balustrade with dies and fluted urns with ball
finials, the small outer pilasters surmounted by a lead figure
of Mercury, the central doorway with Doric columns,
the double panelled doors, the upper panel with carved festoon,
the richly carved cornice, the segmental pediment
surmounted by a large eagle, the paired columns,
the pulvinated frieze, the hood moulds. Share this with me.
The way the back of the house feels like the front of the house,
the way stories are retold, the way times will change for you too,
dear boys. Share this with me. The lacquer cabinets imported
from China, the glazed book presses, the Dutch Bible, the six
volumes of Grose's *Antiquities of England*, the copy of Sewell's
Large English and Dutch Dictionary, of Errand's *Fortification
demonstre*, the thick treaty by Mazarin, the *Lexicon* by
Scapula, Salmon's *English Herbal*, Clarendon's *History of
the Rebellion*, the *Manual on Water-Works*, Evelyn's translation
of *The Complete Gardener*, *A Treatise on Cider* by Worlidge, *Den
Nederlantsen Hovenier*. Share them. The white Italian marble,
the Flemish oak in the great hall, the black walnut staircase,
to the west, made of wood imported from Virginia, panels
grained to match, the thirty-two steps to the room where you
are in shackles, the two of you – two nameless phantoms, two
wooden slaves like sculptures by Luise Kimme, a white gaze
falling like wine-coloured light upon histories ossified: two
worlds, one of slaves, another of rulers, brought together by
these vessels, tea stands that look like horcruxes and two
little boys (or are they girls?) are trapped and will never
escape, fate as rigid as a carved relief, Peter Minshall's two-
dimensional Pegasus on Carnival Tuesday, a play, a joke,
puppetry and exquisite ventriloquism. Stop and share the red
cedar staircase, to the east, rising to the full height of

the building, treads of Virginian walnut, the pine, the cypress
from the colonies. With me. The Chinese and Indian drapes,
the half a dozen closets, the map of the British Isles,
the stamped leather hangings from Spain, gilded, painted
and embossed with cherubs, flowers and fruit, the chimney-piece
of red and white Languedoc marble. The brass locks and
hinges on doors pierced and engraved with scrolling – tulips,
daffodils, roses and strawberries. The painting of a peacock,
peahen, crane, flamingo, pelican and fowl in a park,
the painting of a street child mocking an old woman, the *trompe
l'oeil* in a silver frame showing a tiled corridor leading to
three rooms, the painting of a cocoa house I don't recognise,
have never stood in. The state bed with crimson and yellow
satin, bought in case of a visit by the Queen. Share me. Share
my body. The tea-table from Java or possibly Vietnam,
the blind balustrades placed by a mason beneath the wrong
window, the Delft tulip pyramids, the Delft cups, the Delft
urns, the Delft tiles showing Chinese fruit trees. The manna
ash trees, the strawberry trees, the seven son flower trees,
the maidenhair trees, the black mulberry, the dogwood,
the katsura that smells of burnt toffee in the late afternoon,
the shrubs along the paths that lead away from the house
to the south where, in the far distance, the Sarsen stones
of Stonehenge rise awaiting sunlight, and daisies grow like
minor characters in myths. Share this story. Of walls
plastered in pale colours, walls now being stripped to reveal
their dark tones. Of the trees from Italy in the heated
orangery with the heavy paired Tuscan columns, the round-
headed double-glass doors with voussoirs alternately
vermiculated. Of the moment I think of another orangery, one
to the north of Brussels near King Leopold's African Museum.
Of when I remember the story of how the Belgians severed
the hands of slaves, then invented a new candy: chocolate
severed limbs. Share this with me. The room in which
the volunteer is upset because of the suggestion that all this
wealth is blood money. No evidence of bribes, she says. But
share this: evidence of everything else. A world in which you
are wooden stands, boys, your black heads meant just to
furnish tea as you carry sugar cane in the sun on your backs,
as you hand over your loads to indentured labourers from
India, as you are sold in squares and now nobody wants you
in their stories, their movies, their witty plays about genteel

aristocracy. Blood money. Share this with me. The church to
the north with two gargoyles, where Gylman Ivie, 30, was
baptised, born, according to historians, long before William
Blathwayt lived, a black man who had two children with
Anna Spencer of Dyrham, their daughter Elizabeth baptised
in the church in October 1578, their son Richard in February
1581 but buried two years later in June 1583, like the story of
all the other Black Tudors. *Sii ilkun fun mi.* Share this with
me. The light coming through the windows of the close room
on the upper floor where William Blathwayt worked, through
the window not now a view of the splendid gardens he made
for himself, but a simple hillside, a wall of grass – the land
itself where, centuries ago, blood was spilled in a war with
three kings, where ancient sunlight fell on bruised limbs, and
ancestors learned the outrage of a world in which so much
pain could exist alongside so much opulence. *Sii ilkun fun mi.*
Open the door for me. Share this with me. The small children
today playing on the lawn, the parents with prams who look
at black foreigners suspiciously, the people leisurely
forgetting you both, boys, the people who are now eating
scones with clotted cream and strawberry jam, the people
who have forgotten that everyone here is from somewhere
else. Sometimes the world is sweet but dense. Sometimes we
have to fight hard to work things out. Share this with me. A
plaque that says this house is a memorial to the soldiers who
died in World War II. A plaque that does not say how millions
of black and brown soldiers came from the colonies.
1,440,500 from India, 629,000 from Canada, 413,000 from
Australia, 136,000 from South Africa, 128,500 from New
Zealand, 134,000 from other places, including 10,280 from
the Caribbean: Guyana, Trinidad, St Vincent, Grenada,
Barbados, Jamaica. 185 from the Caribbean were killed, 697
wounded, and 1,071 died due to sickness. Among the dead:
William Smith, Louis Morris, Richard Alick, Charles Dill,
William Fowler, Cyril Jackson, William Thiele, Joseph
Trimingham – their dates of death: September 22, 1914,
December 17, 1914, February 17, 1915, February 17, 1915,
February 17, 1915, February 17, 1915, May 2, 1915, August
9, 1915. Unseen, unmade, their bodies as invisible as Atlantis,
the island larger than Libya and Asia together, a continent,
a confederation of queens and kings of great and marvellous
power holding sway over all other islands. Share this with

me. The moment when, later, a world away, I sit on
the wooden floor of a yoga studio in Trinidad, and light
comes in through a hole in the simple galvanised roof, throwing a
golden coin on the floor, and dust settles like flakes in a
snowglobe and the earth sighs around the still building and
we are all one forest organism and suddenly I smell the burnt
toffee and she tells us, as she smiles, that our practice has
ended. Share this with me. *Namaste.*

© National Trust / Seamus McKenna

Dutch Delftware tile at Dyrham Park depicting Chinese plants, South Gloucestershire.
©National Trust Images/Chris Lacey

DYRHAM PARK

RUPERT GOULDING

There is history of occupation at Dyrham Park from ancient times, but what is best known centres on the late seventeenth century government figure, William Blathwayt. His unique role at the heart of British politics, colonial administration and military organisation made his fortune, and was actively reflected in the house and gardens he created. For today's visitors, encountering Blathwayt's story, home, and possessions make tangible a complex and consequential period in British and global history.

*

The earliest archaeological materials from around Dyrham Park date to at least the Bronze Age, with worked flints and the remains of barrows found nearby. Adjacent to the parkland is Hinton Hill, an Iron Age hill-fort, and within the garden, excavations have found Romano-British pottery and building debris.

In 577 a significant battle was waged around Dyrham; the *Anglo-Saxon Chronicle* recorded how Saxon leaders Cuthwine and Ceawlin defeated Britons Coinmail, Condidan and Farinmail 'at the place that is called Deorham', before capturing the towns of Gloucester, Cirencester and Bath. The battle was a decisive victory for the West Saxons repelling Britons into Wales and Cornwall.[1]

In 972 Dyrham was an estate of Pershore Abbey, Worcestershire and after the Norman conquest, as recorded in the 1086 *Domesday Book*, a land survey of England and parts of Wales, commissioned by William the Conqueror – the estate was transferred to the leading soldier Thurstan fitz Rolf. Through marriage Dyrham Park entered the Russel family, who lived elsewhere, until Sir Maurice (d.1416) moved there after fighting in France and becoming a county sheriff and Justice of the Peace. Dyrham passed again through marriage to Sir William Denys (1470-1530), a courtier and knight of the body for King Henry VIII, who set about enclosing a 250-acre park and enlarged the house in c.1511.

In 1571 Sir William (c.1525-89) and George Wynter (d.1581) purchased Dyrham Park. They were leading naval administrators: Surveyor and Clerk of Ships respectively. Sir William was an active sailor, and a commander against the Spanish Armada of 1588. Both brothers owned ships used for trade, exploration, and privateering, including investing in their colleague Sir John Hawkins' (1532-95) early enslaving voyages, and George advanced £400 in Sir Francis Drake's project to circumnavigate the globe in 1577. His son John Wynter (d.1619) sailed with Drake, captaining their ship *Elizabeth*, and reached the Strait of Magellan before separating from the fleet in violent storms and returning home.

John Wynter inherited Dyrham Park and an inventory of 1601 records a richly furnished house of 22 rooms. John's son Sir George Wynter (d.1638) received a new licence to create a deer park, though it was not enacted in his lifetime. Sir George's son John Wynter (1622-88) was an active Royalist during the English Civil War and consequentially had a period of financial hardship. That situation changed after the Restoration of the monarchy, and during the 1660s the park at Dyrham was re-established in its current location, though the house remained in need of repair.[2]

*

All was to change after John's daughter and sole heir Mary Wynter (1650-91) married William Blathwayt (1649-1717) in the parish church of St Peter's in 1686. During the preceding marriage negotiations William Blathwayt remarked on the 'necessity of building a new house'. Dyrham today is very much his creation. The first works started in late 1691 on a canal for the elaborate gardens, created with input from the foremost designer and plantsman of the period, George London (d.1714) and Henry Wise (1653-1738). Mary Wynter died the same year and never saw the transformation of her ancestral estate. Construction started on the west front of the house the following January under a little-known Huguenot architect Samuel Hauduroy. In 1700 Blathwayt stepped up his ambitions with a new east front by William Talman (1650-1719), Comptroller of the Royal Works.

The house William Blathwayt created embodied his professional standing. As the leading colonial administrator of his age, his North American colleagues willingly sourced luxury walnut and cedar timber to construct staircases and panelling. As Secretary at War to William III his travels and connections across Europe enabled the purchase of Carrara marble, Dutch gilt-leather hangings, paintings and books, and costly fabrics, some of which were Indian textiles imported through the Dutch East India Company.[3]

The decoration of the house was substantially shaped by Blathwayt's uncle Thomas Povey (c.1613-c.1705), from whom he purchased many prized possessions. This included Povey's substantial library, over one hundred paintings, including works by Samuel van Hoogstraten (1627-78) and Bartolomé Esteban Murillo (1617-82), and a Javanese tea-table with an associated pair of stands (used as side tables), made in the form of enslaved young African men.[4]

Thomas Povey raised Blathwayt as his own son, to follow in his career in government and colonial administration. Povey rose to prominence in colonial matters during the Interregnum, when he became close to Lord Protector Oliver Cromwell (1599-1658). He lobbied successfully for a new Council of Trade (1655-57) and then chaired a Council for America (1657-60). He especially championed, and then equipped, the 'Western Design', a term which described an English expedition that supported Cromwell's plans to reduce the power of Catholic Spain and its dominance in the West Indies. The effort resulted in the English conquest of Jamaica in 1655.

In the 1660s, Povey became the Treasurer of Tangier, a north African colony which was part of the dowry of Catherine of Braganza (1638-1705) upon her marriage to King Charles II (1630-85). Povey was also involved in merchant companies, an unsuccessful Nova Scotia Company, and the monopolistic traders of enslaved people, the Royal African Company.[5]

When Blathwayt followed Povey into a colonial career he was the third generation to do so. Two further uncles forged colonial careers abroad – William Povey became Provost Marshall in Barbados, and local factor for Thomas's plantation owning associates; and Richard Povey, the Island Secretary and Steward-General of Stores in Jamaica. Indeed, the three brothers' father, Justinian Povey (d. 1652), was an early colonial administrator as Commissioner of the Caribbee Islands in 1637.

William Blathwayt became the most knowledgeable colonial administrator of his age, described in his lifetime as 'better qualified than anybody'. For over 30 years he was Surveyor and Auditor General of Plantation Revenues, responsible for accounting for and repatriating fees from North America and the Caribbean to the English crown. For over a decade, he was also a member of the Board of Trade. Colonial policy fluctuated over his career, but ultimately moved towards greater crown control. In Blathwayt's own words colonies 'enlarge the Empire and increase the revenues very considerably', where once 'desperate ventures of little importance' they became 'necessary and important members' of the expanding English realm.[6]

Blathwayt influenced colonial policy through his roles, knowledge, and proximity to power, and he reflected this professional status in the house he made, such that Dyrham Park and Blathwayt's story now evidence a consequential period in British and international history. For example, Barbados, after economic stagnation in the 1640s, shifted its focus from low grade tobacco to sugar. By 1660 Barbados produced nearly all the sugar then consumed in England – generating more trade and capital than all other English colonies combined. The population rocketed to over 53,000; most of the island's inhabitants were enslaved Africans, whose lives were brutal and short. This shared history was evident in Dyrham Park through William Blathwayt's display of a substantial perspective painting of Bridgetown, Barbados, showing ships in the harbour and sugar mills across the landscape.[7]

It was a similar narrative in Jamaica: in the 1660s the initial population of colonists was small, around 3,500, with just above 500 enslaved people. Yet by the end of the century the colonist population had barely doubled, while the numbers of transported enslaved Africans had massively expanded to above 50,000, many shipped from West Africa by the Royal African Company. A variety of crops could be grown in Jamaica, but it was sugar production that prevailed. Blathwayt's painting of a Jamaican cacao tree and roasting hut, dating from c.1672, illuminates this story. Chocolate was a luxurious and lucrative commodity; the painting was instructional, showing the stages in the growth and processing of cacao, as an illustration for an accompanying letter. But the crops were failing and ultimately sugar production took over. Yet it is the pictorial omission that is telling – there are no people in the painting, emphasising the invisible history of those many enslaved and transplanted to work in plantations.[8]

Where the enslaved can be unambiguously seen within Dyrham Park is in the form of near life-sized sculptural figures. Two representations of enslaved young African men crouch supporting large dishes intended to hold luxury foodstuffs. Their collars connected to ankle cuffs by chains are unambiguous signifiers, intended then, as they do to this day, to articulate Dyrham Park's connections with places such as Barbados and Jamaica. It is these figures that Andre Bagoo's poem addresses in this book.

*

The entirety of William Blathwayt's pluralist career is manifest in his home and collections. He held multiple government offices at a time of significant change, encompassing political revolution, economic developments, and major European conflict.

In 1683 William Blathwayt purchased the position of Secretary at War, an administrative role reporting to the monarch and their military commanders. His duties were in the running of army logistics: recruiting, paying, disbanding, moving, and accommodating troops. Under both monarchs James II and William III, the army expanded, centralised, and looked to France to learn effective organisation and professionalism.

In 1688, the 'Glorious Revolution' saw leading statesmen invite invasion by William, Prince of Orange (1650-1702). William landed in Torbay in November and marched towards London. James II and his army set out to engage them, reaching Salisbury with Secretary at War Blathwayt in attendance – he issued the consequential notice: 'His Majesty finding the enemy like to remain in their present quarters, and being under some indisposition of health by a frequent bleeding at the nose, has thought fit to order the foot and cannon to march towards London whither his Majesty is going in person in a few days.' This retreat was the turning point, William would march to the capital unopposed to claim the crown, James would flee into exile and *de facto* abdication, and Blathwayt would at some point in early December 1688 switch allegiance to the new monarch.[9]

Blathwayt was twice a Member of Parliament, first for Newtown on the Isle of Wight (1685-87) and then for the city of Bath (1693-1710). After the successful invasion certain conditions were agreed before William and Mary (1662-94) were given the throne, one being their joint rule to legitimise via Mary a Stuart succession, and more significantly, accepting the terms of a Declaration of Rights, which changed the relationship between monarch and Parliament. William III had no quarrel with these demands for he retained his main objective – control of the army. Now the House of Commons had to meet regularly, agree taxes, laws, and could hold the executive (i.e. the monarchy) to account. These developments underpin British parliamentary convention to this day.

In this evolving system Blathwayt had a dual role. As a Member of Parliament, he could brief his peers on what questions to ask, and as an administrator (somewhere between a senior civil-servant and a government minister) he would provide responses and accounts for MPs' concerns. We see this physically manifest at Dyrham in the Acts of Parliament in the library, archival documents, even the surviving desks and cabinets – the tools of bureaucracy and governance.

During the 1690s, William III brought Britain into his conflict with Louis XIV of France (1638-1715). William desired the English throne ultimately to assist his continental ambitions, which while territorial, were also ideological, in countering what he saw as an intolerant, Catholic and expansionist French monarch. To support this war the English army changed radically; it grew from 35,000 troops in 1688 to over 100,000 by 1697, mostly stationed abroad in Flanders. Managing this operation was ultimately Blathwayt's role. The Dyrham collection contains various volumes on military strategy and one handwritten volume of *Establishments*, which lists the army's composition in 1702.[10]

Wars required funding, and so, alongside the significant changes in military organisation during the 1690s, there were fundamental changes in how they were financed. The Bank of England was set up in large part to lend money to William III for his campaigns. Investors accepted lower rates of interest for long term investment security. The evolution of the banknote was an unintended consequence, for they became exchanged instead of the gold deposits they represented. In 1695 the new Bank's Deputy Governor visited the Battle of Namur, a war they were ultimately financing. Blathwayt was standing next to Governor Michael Godfrey (1658-95) when a stray canon ball killed him. Reflections of such conflicts can be seen in Dyrham Park in the paintings depicting other sieges, of La Rochelle and Tangier, and in Blathwayt's pair of pistols.[11]

*

On the western roofline is a lead statue of Mercury, the Roman messenger god, installed in 1703. That year William Blathwayt wrote to his cousin and agent Charles Watkins, 'I have a [statue of] Mercury for ye Front of ye House which will come by land & now I send you the Pedestall that it may be dispatcht in ye setting up of which care must be taken that the Rail and Balister be preserv'd for another plan.' It is also clearly identifiable in an engraving depicting Dyrham Park made by Johannes Kip in 1710.[12]

The statue of Mercury is based on the famous bronzes by Flemish sculptor Giambologna (1529-1608), who created four versions from 1563, each slightly different. The likely maker of Dyrham's was John van Nost (d.1713) who ran a sculpture yard in Haymarket, London, and was the leading supplier of lead garden statuary. He was a principal supplier to King William III at Hampton Court Palace, including designing a fountain featuring Mercury at the summit, though never completed. Nost made a similar Mercury for Melbourne Hall, Derbyshire, between 1704-1710. That statue was set in a fountain designed under the direction of gardener Henry Wise.

Mercury was the messenger god, but additionally patron of learning, eloquence, and commerce. The caduceus, his wand, symbolises peace, through the representation of two calmed fighting snakes. These meanings and associations would have been self-evident to guests of William Blathwayt, who likely shared a classical education, and would have been understood in direct relationship to the relief motto just beneath upon the façade of the house.

The motto is a Latin phrase 'His Utere Mecum' (sometimes translated as 'share this with me'), taken from the Roman poet Horace's 6th epistle to Numicius, in the first book of *Epistles*. They were extracted from the last verse: *Vive, vale! si quid novisti rectius istis, candidus imperti; si non, his utere mecum* which can be translated as 'Farewell and live well: if you know of any precepts better than these, be so candid as to communicate them; if not, partake of these with me.'[13] The words were a shorthand, intended to convey the larger point of the whole poem. Horace muses on what constitutes a good life and encourages Numicius, through calm reflection, to see his life constrained by time and death, and best lived when avoiding any excessive pursuit of virtue, money and possessions, food and drink, politics and power, or even love. His principal message was that true happiness came through moderation in all these things.[14] The motto, together with the statue of Mercury, was intended to suggest Blathwayt's attainment, through moderation, of a life lived well.

*

Dyrham Park has one other significant Caribbean association. Mary Sarah Oates was born of mixed heritage in Jamaica in 1833. She was the daughter of an unmarried plantation manager George Hibbert Oates (1791-1837) and probably, according to George's will, 'Margaret Cross a free woman of Colour'. Little about Mary's childhood is known, but after her father's death she was sent to England to live with her grandmother and aunt in Bath.

In 1876 Mary Oates married an old family friend, the widower Reverend Wynter Thomas Blathwayt (1825-1909), Rector of St Peter's Dyrham. But in 1899 he inherited Dyrham Park from his childless brother, and so the couple moved into the house. Therefore, during the first decade of the twentieth century Dyrham Park was an Anglo-Jamaican household. Mary died in 1925 and is buried in the St Peter's churchyard.

Endnotes:

1. Frank Stenton, *Anglo-Saxon England* (Oxford, 2001), p.29.
2. Neil Stacy, 'The History of Dyrham House' in *Dyrham Park* (London, 1999) pp. 42-44.
3. Rupert Goulding, *Dyrham Park and William Blathwayt* (Swindon, 2017)
4. Gloucestershire Archives D1799/E240.
5. Thomas B. Povey Murison (b 1613/14, d. in or before 1705), colonial entrepreneur and administrator. *Oxford Dictionary of National Biography*. Retrieved 21 Oct from https://www.oxforddnb.com/view/10.1093/ref:odnb/9780198614128.001/ondb-9780198614128-e-22640.
6. Gertrude Jacobsen, *William Blathwayt* (New Haven, 1932).
7. Richard Dunn, *Sugar and Slaves* (New York, 1972).
8. Philip Emanuel and Rupert Goulding "The whole story of the cocoa': Dyrham Park and the painting and planting of chocolate in Jamaica' in *ABC Bulletin*, Autumn 2021, pp. 5-9.
9. Jacobsen op. cit.
10. Tony Claydon and W.A. Speck, *William & Mary* (Oxford, 2007).
11. The Bank of England, History and Functions (1970) p.6.
12. Gloucestershire Archives D1799/E243.
13. Jon Stone, *The Routledge Dictionary of Latin Quotations* (London, 2005), p. 332.
14. Herbert Musurillo, 'A Formula for Happiness: Horace 'Epist.' 1.6 to Numicius' in *The Classical World*, Vol. 67. No. 4 (Feb 1974), pp. 193-204.

SPEKE HALL

A View of the South Front of Speke Hall by John Suker
©National Trust Images

An Unknown Man by British (English) School
©National Trust Images

PETER KALU

RICHARD WATT, WEST-INDIA MERCHANT, OF SPEKE HALL

It was a gloomy winter evening in Speke, the sky heavy with stiffening cloud, the air damp. Wind moaned as it blew across from the River Mersey and hit the crumbling casement windows of Speke Hall. There, inside the drawing room, West India merchant Richard Watt leaned forward in his chair, freshly ferried from Oak Hall with other sticks of furniture. He turned down the sputtering oil lamp that rested on the japanned coffee table and watched the play of shadows made by the lamp across the empty bookcases lining the walls. Then he turned to gaze for a while out of the windows at the oncoming storm, occasionally glancing too into the cold grate of the library's iron fireplace. He sighed. Richard Watt was in repose, and by instruction rather than choice. The instructing doctor, whose orders were strict, was even now fussing around him as he sat, the doctor's voluminous frock coat interrupting his view.

'You are looking quite the Italian gentleman this evening, Mr Watt.'

This much was true. He had chosen for the visit, his first since purchasing the manor, a fitting outfit: a splendid purple coat of Italian filigree, a deep blue waistcoat trimmed in gold brocade, a crisp linen shirt with white ruffle at the throat and ruched sleeve collars, the same deep blue in breeches with buckle at knee, the finest Dutch white hose, and extra-supple, gleaming black, buckle shoes. Atop his head, he retained his favourite chestnut horsehair wig.

'I have premonitions, Doctor. If I am to shuffle off my mortal coil, I intend to greet St Peter in full style, and with all my receipts.'

The doctor scoffed. 'You'll see me off.' He worked around the great man, manoeuvring a joint here, patting a limb there, before bending to inspect his patient's swollen foot.

'It is Indian cotton, that hose. The finest.'

'Indeed, it is,' the doctor concurred, 'and so soft to the touch.'

His household had sent the doctor to the great merchant, having decided he had gone mad to have decamped to Speke from Oak Hill, with hardly a servant to assist. The doctor had arrived post-haste with two assistants. A fire would be made very soon, against Watts' objections. He was well wrapped, and it was the freezing cold, not heat, that eased his old enemy, gout. His bodily foe had inflamed his joints once more, immobilising one of his hands completely, and making giant pustules on one foot.

'We'll have you up and dancing in no time,' the doctor averred, standing up. 'Now what is this about?' The doctor looked at him with kindly eyes. 'Why here? Why now?'

Richard Watt kept quiet and the doctor, used to truculent behaviour, especially among his older patients, spoke on, supplying with a pliant voice and soft manner such nudges as might loosen even the most recalcitrant of tongues. 'All this rushing around, Richard. You will exhaust your considerable powers. Liverpool, nay England herself, has need of men of your calibre; it is your patriotic duty to recuperate and return swiftly to the fray of life.'

'You do not fool me; I am old and gone to seed.'

'Far from it. You have the lungs of a lusty youth. Breathe in once more.'

The doctor resumed his infernal tapping of ribs and flesh. Richard Watt submitted grudgingly. Yet the doctor's prattle had pricked a memory in him. 'I sailed you know. In my youthful prime, I was a supercargo. You know of those?'

'Pray tell.'

'In charge of goods on and off a ship. Sailing with it from port to port, keeping observation on all.'

'You know shipping like no other, which is no mean feat in this Liverpool.'

'Crossing seas. All kinds of seas, from somnolent to boiling, and all kinds of cargo. The seas have hidden dangers and sudden pleasures. To catch a fair current and avoid the rocks. The Bight of Benin. Cuba. The French privateers. The battles I faced. I rode the waves then, climbed up into the bird's nest to sight land. Called down to the coxswain. 'Land ho!''

'A man of action you were. You hear the troubles of Toulouse? Our fleet is there, Lord Nelson among them.'

'No. A man of commerce. Those were my best of times, on those ships. Look at me now. A landsman. A clumsy oaf, carting this lost foot.'

'It is gout and will pass as all the other bouts.' The doctor poured a draft of something into a vessel the size of a small shot glass that he had retrieved from his medicinal bag. 'Here, this will set about it. Drink it down in one gulp.'

Richard Watt complied. It tasted foul, but didn't all medicine? His mind returned to his ships and the cargoes they'd carried. "*Caveat emptor*,' I told my nephew, 'let the buyer beware, or empty will be both your pockets and mine.' And did he listen?'

'The sins of youth are infinite.' The doctor concurred. He manoeuvred round to his patient's other side and pulled out his shirt, the better to press his head to the man's rib cage and listen for rattles. All seemed fine. Next the eyes. They were curdled. An excess of bile or blood. 'I see your eyelids sliding. Forty winks, Richard, will do you good. You'll wake up fresh as a daisy.'

'The daisies will know me yet,' Richard Watt muttered, but shook the thought off. 'I feel sound, and yet, doctor, I get these Lilliputian hallucinations. Tiny goblins running around at my feet. Strange, joyless sprites, sometimes cursing, sometimes sneering, plucking at my hose and skin. Small, slight creatures, all set on tormenting me.'

'Set no store by them. There may be a small damage to the brain, either from over-excitement or it is simply endogenous. Some temporary physical aberration most often causes these things. You are not going mad. Your brain is an organ like any other. Let it heal. Rest. Here is another tincture.'

'What is it?'

'Laudanum.'

'Expensive?'

The doctor shrugged. 'Mix it with a few drops of rum, or whisky if that is your preference. It will help you relax. Let the god of dreams embrace you, Richard, usher you to warmer climes.

It was not cold, but a creeping, ineffable abjection had stolen into his mind and now sat there, squat. He was here in his Liverpool manor house only by dint of duty. A man of substance had to have his monuments, he had been told, if he wished for posterity to smile upon him, for children in future times to say his name with awe. Speke Hall had the requisite grandeur. Of all the manors he had run a finger along, Speke alone had been the right price and span and view. The thrill of water was across there, in the glimmer that was the River Mersey, winking along. He had told all his captains, board efficiently, check all lists, set sail, tack, then swing out for the Irish sea, through the Bay of Biscay and strike for the Atlantic Ocean. There, the captain should let his vessel rip. A fourteen-gun brig in full sail was a sight to behold, skimming fathomless depths, the howl of wood racing on water, the creak of stretching ropes, the joyful song of aching canvas, the deep murmuring of cargo in the hold, the chase of birds above. All this, and money to be made at journey's end. A monkey with an abacus would know that if expenditure outweighed income, the journey would be ruinous. The thrill of that chase to profit almost matched the wild ride through crashing waves.

'Your pulse is racing.'

'Memories,' Richard Watt murmured to the doctor, 'they plague me like flies.'

The doctor's soft feet finally pattered away. The night had darkened and through the windows of Speke Hall only an impenetrable, rolling gloom could be seen. The wind had kicked up again and the assault on the Hall began. He heard the crash of tree limbs, the cry of glass panes working loose from their lead fastenings in a torment of shrieking gusts. His mind was thrown back a decade and more ago. The West Indies knew better than England how to do storms, and two hurricanes had been sent across Westmoreland, one quick on the heels of the other, the last a terror of magnitude greater even than the French Revolution. He remembered that fateful night, on his estate, George's Plain. He had railed against the storm as devastation befell them. Uprooted trees split and broken, the boiling house toppled over, all the cane flattened, the serried ranks of plantain trees uprooted and the Indian corn fields destroyed. He had run through the estate, finding a mule fallen on the cart track, its legs skyward, the bodies of drowned slaves in piles by the log store. A cane rat tugging at a dead snake. Hogsheads strewn all over, split open, the smithy down too, gaping. A Negro woman crying by a molasses barrel, her dead baby in her lap. The boiling house spun out, crushed, its walls reduced to lumber and a flock of fowl running around the whipping yard. A man, minus an arm, in a daze by a fetlock-smashed, groaning bullock.

The island's doctors were rumoured to be galloping around Westmoreland, their surgeon's saws unsheathed, amputating limb after crushed limb. Cutting arms in one estate, legs in another, and mortally injured slaves despatched *in situ,* out of mercy, by axe to the throat, bullets being in short supply and their report, the doctors said, tending to make the surviving slaves nervous. No building on his estate remained upright. A running total of costs swept through Richard Watt's mind. He had been joined by John Arkwright, his chief overseer and faithful friend, and they crossed George's Plains to survey the devastation. A year's effort laid to waste as the cane had been pushed through a thresher, and the wages of his overseers still to pay, livestock, grain all gone. For the slaves, starvation beckoned. Without the plantain and Indian corn crops, with the breadfruits ruined, it required external relief to feed them, and no such relief was possible: a hundred vessels in Kingston docks alone were wrecked.

His wig blown off, his chemise ripped from his back, Richard Watt urged all hands to save what they could — of machine, beast and man. He knew his losses were high, perhaps irrecoverably so. He felt despair. Who would stay to make money from a land as hostile as this? Who would break bone, tear flesh and ruin eyesight poring over deeds in all the long, swelling year of this remorseless, unforgiving land? This storm was not a punch to the solar plexus, it was his guts being spilt.

There was a sudden pause in the winds and, in a moment of bitter irony, he heard larks singing in the air, flitting gaily though the madness. And why not? This was good for them, seed strewn everywhere, grain stores burst open and ready to be plucked by bird and beast alike. Hobbes' words were never truer. Life was nasty, brutish and short. When man takes on nature, there was only ever one winner. He feared he was looking at his utter ruin.

'Come away, man, come away; you have done all you can!' It was Arkwright the overseer, at his side, imploring, tugging.

'The losses,' Watt muttered, 'the losses. We are staring ruin in the face.'

'Get this on, he has no further use of it. And this.'

Arkwright had tugged off a jacket and shirt from some man, fallen into a ditch with a poleaxe through his face, his brains spilt across it.

'Is it not unseemly thus to –'

'Shush. You'll die of fever otherwise, and he has no further need. Now, let us find shelter, and fast. I fear these winds are not yet done.'

Braced together, the two men set off across the debris-strewn fields to find sanctuary. They stumbled upon a track that led to a hollow. A double line of deep-rooted, stiff trees broke the wind at the hollow's start, and beyond the trees, the lights of an inn beckoned.

'Let us put up at this tavern!' Arkwright shouted across, even though his companion was right beside him.

'But I am without wig and this is not my jacket. Nobody will recognise me.'

'Is it not good once in a while to travel *incognito*?'

'I curse your Latin,' was Richard Watt's retort, but he followed.

They went inside to find the inn full of commotion: the wounded and the dying, all strewn across its tables, and a rough drinking clientele wedged in there too. Anarchy was in the air. Richard Watt backed away. 'This looks more like a Port Royal bar than a Kingston gentleman's club.'

'Step on, step on, the beer's as wet.'

They had tankards filled and found a corner of a table to gather their wits and strength. It was the first time Richard Watt had been in a low tavern in Westmoreland. He watched and listened with wonder at the parade of venality and importunity. It was the world of his youth, a world long forgotten, and his eyebrows darted up and down at the goings-on. After a while, he picked up on the conversation at his elbow between two well-tanked rogues, and was piqued by its theme, the goodness or otherwise of Westmoreland planter, Richard Watt. A doughty man – some forty years of age and with a whiskery face, carbuncled nose and rotted teeth – was expectorating on his companion, a short, sallow, light brown youth of smallpoxed skin, dressed in considerable finery for someone so young and coloured. Manumitted, Watt assumed, and wanting everyone to know.

'Watt? What the devil!' the green-teethed foul mouth opined.

'I beg to differ. Good crops. And his estate never lost any slaves to beatings.

He has run his plantation with fine judgement.'

'Fine judgement be damned,' the older fellow riposted. 'And his nephew, what a type. His nephew had this cargo ship sailing for Gold Coast as bedecked as the pleasure palaces of Paris! He employed a captain useless with a spyglass, terrible at trigonometry, incompetent at cartography, eyes too weak to see the stars, but excellent at the fandango! A captain to end all captains — and all crew and all cargo. But the finest pair of heels ever trod tarred boards. Watt? Numbskull nephew, I say, and numbskull man!'

Richard Watt sat there quietly absorbing this, part-amused, part horrified. His companion, Arkwright, asked with a silent lift of the head, if he should intervene. Watt shook his head. Nevertheless, seeing how distressed the merchant had become at the foul tirade, Arkwright leaned across to the raconteur and tapped him on the sleeve.

'Enough.'

The raconteur whipped round swiftly and placed his nose close to Arkwright's. 'No, there's more.'

'Let him speak,' Richard Watt intervened. 'Every man has a right to his tongue.'

'And speak I shall.'

The teller looked around, his lower lip jutting out, daring anyone to stop him.

Nobody beyond his table paid him any mind: all had matters of more import to be concerned with than these ramblings.

The speaker reprised his theme. 'That nephew. I was on the ship; it cannot be denied. He recruited double crew and each crew on double rations. In Bonny, he took on two Nile crocodiles, placed them in the hold. The crocs ate three slaves a week, and all the length of the voyage, the ship lurched from port to starboard as the slaves ran out the beasts' way. The hull when that ship finally docked at Kingston Port was awash with blood, half the slaves bleeding or gobbled to death, but two fat, healthy crocs proudly delivered. What a nephew! Factor that, Richard Watt! Cheers to the hurricane! However high a man rises, yet God may bring him low!'

Arkwright leaned across again and this time gripped the sleeve of the man's shirt. 'Enough. Desist.'

'He is in his cups, he forgets his self,' his youthful companion said.

The storyteller, rather enjoying the fuss of the two anxious strangers, bellowed out the beginnings of a new episode. 'He had this Sambo sweetheart! Watt! Whither! Wherefore! Wait! Who would guess! He had this Sambo sweetheart!'

'Oh no!' This time it was Richard Watt himself who interrupted, lunging across at the man, who swung expertly away.

Again, the man's young companion did his utmost to mitigate, resting a placating hand on Richard Watt's shoulder. 'My friend Jim, here, is lush and frisky. Pay him no mind. Set a watch on him, he will shortly be kissing the floor. Yesterday the Pope. Today, Richard Watt. Tomorrow, King George. None are free from his barbs. It is his jest; he means no harm. And he generally has no audience.'

Richard Watt sighed, but he decided to endure the discomfort. He was intrigued. Never had he heard the general population's thoughts on his activities; and this new twist startled him; despite himself, he would know more.

The storyteller worked his neighbouring table audience, eyes wide, teeth bared. 'Oh yes, his Sambo mistress. And he did love her greatly, giving her many goatish embraces through the gaps twixt the finery in which he clothed her for parading up and down the town. None was loved so ardently, night and day, as his Sambo wench. So enrapt was he by this fragrant Negro-lady, he took his swelling mistress to England, there to give birth to his son who is being educated even now, at Eton, no less!'

Arkwright stood. He pointed over at the drunkard with his sinewy whip in his hand. 'There is no sin or shame in bedding a slave. And you, sir, are a blockhead to think it. She went away with him on the *Betty*. That is all. Say more and I will ram this fist through your rotten teeth.'

'Correct,' the man roared concerning the first point, but seemingly oblivious to the physical threat made with the second, he leaned forward, right into Arkwright's face as he spoke on: 'And she never came back. She took her freedom in both hands and ran into the English hills with it, that's what. Leaving the lovesick, priapic, sable-stroking Watt at his Liverpool docks in tears. There's no fool as an old fool! Good on that dusky slave! Let's drink to her, I say!'

That was enough for Richard Watt. He pushed Arkwright away, shoved across the tavern table and grabbed the drunkard by the throat. 'One more insult and…'

A hot pain shot through Watt's nether regions.

'Unhand me, you dolt,' the green-toothed man whispered, 'or I will squeeze your sweetmeats, Sir, till the juices run.'

Richard Watt did the prudent thing, and released the man's throat. In turn, the storyteller released all he held, sat down, picked up his tankard and swallowed hard. Then he looked up at the fuming merchant. 'You'd best be along. You hear those howls? Those are my dogs. They bay only for fresh Negro blood and have scented something new. You don't have the essence of Negro in your blood, do you, good Sir?'

Richard Watt would have lunged again, but Arkwright had his arm. 'Leave it, Sir, leave it,' his overseer counselled, ''I've known many such men as he, and he is not worth the knuckle burn.'

Watt slumped. He eyed once more the bloody mayhem around him and saw how little interest anyone had paid to their altercation. Arkwright was right. He was reading too much into it. 'Let us leave here,' he ordered, 'the worst of the storm has passed.'

'Good judgement. Be of good cheer. Even despite this storm, your wealth is unsurpassable. You are rich beyond dreams and will remain so.'

Outside, the wind had indeed abated. Richard Watt walked on, with Arkwright at his side. Yet the tavern bard's words were deep under his skin and he could not let them go. 'You heard him? The temerity. The licence.'

'An idiot and his tales.'

'No, no, no. *Vox pop, vox dei.* The people's voice is the voice of God. Never dismiss rumour, Arkwright. Even if wrong-headed, it carries weight; a man must guard his honour.'

'Very well. Should I go back in there and thrash him?'

'No, what has been said has been said. The cat is out the bag.'

'How do you mean?'

'I must do something about it. Something more general and public.'

'Reputation is a fickle thing, unworthy of the chase in my humble opinion. But if you needs must shore it up, then voyage to England. The time is right. Perhaps this storm is prophetic. Do good deeds over there, establish foundations, set the story straight. In your position, I would pay no heed to tittle-tattle in a colony. It is in the metropolis that reputations are lost and made.'

That night, finally back at his Kingston residence, Richard Watt was distraught. The devastation of the storm was only half his torment. How could the common people think so badly of him? To portray him as dull, whoring, cruel. Was that really what they thought? He had been an explorer. He'd seized the day, taken risks that others had shirked. He had been bold at times and yet not let vanity overwhelm prudence. He had made his fortune in double quick time, and the right way, as a man of character and honour. Why did those here begrudge his good fortune, then? As a man's handshake was his bond, so his reputation was his calling card: it went with him everywhere.

In the small hours of that day, Richard Watt resolved to quit Jamaica. He would shift to England, as Arkwright had recommended. There, he would deal with his errant nephew once and for all, take back the reins of commerce, and do good works.

'You are sweating, Richard, I think it is the fever.'

Richard Watt started. It was the doctor, accosting him at the neck, loosening his shirt. He was in Speke Hall. It was 1795. Winter. A fire was burning and hot coals bickered in the grate. The doctor removed his wig, loosened his buttons, but then left him unmolested. Richard Watt listened to the coals' complaints, and to the storm as it huffed around Speke Hall, clawing at the roof tiles, testing the timbers. Painful as his dream had been, he wanted to be back into it, traces still floating in his mind. *I have been an explorer. I seized the day. 'Land ho!' I took the risks. I was bold. I made my fortune. 'His Sambo sweetheart,' the laggard of the Westmoreland tavern had called her. Blessing was her true name...*

He became aware of a breathing other than his own, a chair beside him, someone resting there. It annoyed him.

'I thought you had gone.'

'Gone where, on a night such as this? I am afraid you are stuck with me. And perhaps it is well. I can keep an eye on you, you have been twitching, muttering.'

'And must I keep an eye on my wallet?'

The doctor chuckled. 'Not at all. My services are *pro bono* tonight.'

'Then you are welcome company, and the more silent, the more welcome.'

'A touch more of the tincture, perhaps?'

'If you insist.' Perhaps his unusually vivid dream had been caused by the libations the doctor kept pouring him. 'I am seeing ghosts,' he said, suddenly, in a confession more candid than he intended. He chuckled anyway. 'They come high-stepping into my dreams, doctor.'

'All the more reason for a dram.'

'Pour away. But then silence, I pray.'

Richard Watt leaned back into deep reverie. *I made my fortune. I explored the world. In all ways Blessing was well named. I imposed myself upon her in a manly way, and to my proud force she yielded. Blessing was as worthy a discovery of any of James Cook. When she lay with me in Westmoreland, it must make the Royal Observatory hesitate and check their machines because time is eternal in her arms. There is no perfume made by man nor scent of woman that can intoxicate more greatly than she. She was a blessing indeed. On the voyage to Liverpool we had three months unimpeded, tasting her presumptuous lips. That journey had been heaven, unsurpassable, the transport of love.*

Lost between past and present, Richard Watt dreamt on. Strange, fraught images, scents and sounds came to him, fuelled as they were by the surfeit of laudanum and whiskey in his bloodstream, dreams in which he thought he saw Blessing, thought he heard her, thought, strangest of all that, at times, he became her.

*

Words cannot describe the journey we made, only sounds. Song. Drums. When we landed, they threw my brother, Obinna, onto a cart for the dead. They wrote me down as Blessing, a nonsense name. I am Chioma. Sometimes you see a flock of birds fly up in the sky. When one of them stutters and falls, the flock hesitates, circles, then flies on. You wonder what happened to that falling bird. Did it land? Is it still alive? I was sold from plantation to plantation. I was hardly a week on George's Plains estate when he took me. They'd warned me about him: 'Don't enter the house, don't meet his gaze, don't turn your back...' So many don'ts piled up, then brushed away. He placed a hand over my mouth to stop my screams, my repulsion. Trapped in the sheets. Again and again. He was often brutal. I learned to simulate. Never underestimate the strength of a woman or her wiles. I taught him to love me. Yes, I was a traitor to my partner and for this we both wept.

Twice I aborted. Even Quabinna said this can't continue. The last time, he caught the stillborn in his hands as I pushed it from my womb. It had Richard Watt's hair. We buried him and wept. So long as I stayed on the plantation this was my fate. I could try to flee to the hills but, even if I outsprinted the chasing dogs, the Maroons might well send me back to punishment and even death.

So, I suffered him. My love was all surface, but men are shallow, and surface is often all they see. I made him love me, buy me dresses, dream about me. There were others he seized, like me, but he always came back to me. One day, he read me a letter from his sister and asked how he should reply, should he promise money? I told him his heart was too full of numbers where love ought to be. He stared at me. I could see his hands twitching and wondered if he would strike me. 'Speak,' he said finally with a sigh, 'speak on.' I advised him not to write of finance but instead fill the letter with tenderness at the loss of her husband. To show affection, bless her boy who was now the heartbeat of her life, express interest in her friends, pledge undying affection to her and a desire for a warm reunion. He noted it all down; it was as if I were instructing a child. I told him that honey, not arithmetic, is needed to rekindle warmth between siblings. He called me wise, thanked me, penned the letter almost there and then, and read it back to me, then let me go. That night, I could not get the smell of him from my skin, no matter how hard I scrubbed. Neither could I get him out of mind. Ugh! I kept thinking, to hell with his sister. Did I not also have a family? Was I not also a woman? And my child, no kind words there from him, not once, even though he knew, he knew.

I endured. On one occasion, I would not do his bidding and he had me chained and hung up naked in his room, then relented, unchained me, wept at my feet, changed his mind and became furious, had me chained again, beat me, then took me as I stood there in chains on tiptoe. He want-ed me to kiss him as he took his pleasure. I refused, that was all. Something so simple, so small. Yet he begged me. I said, take me to England with you, let me see England and I will yield, not before. In a month we were sailing. August 1771. He enjoyed himself that voyage, and I confess I did yield. I called him foolish names, flattered his wit, his habits of fornication, gave him those little nips and teases I knew he so much enjoyed. I asked him how we would disembark when we arrived at Liverpool and people looked upon us: what story would we tell of ourselves? He chortled and told me not to concern myself with that. You have no story, he told me. In England all eyes will be on me alone. I laughed along, told him how true it was that I had no story, and he took to calling me his little nothing, and when he did, I came to him and made small in his arms. In this way, I made it alive to Liverpool. I had always planned to slip away at the docks there, but then this miracle. I heard at dockside the case of Somerset. The more I heard, the more hope billowed through me; if I could find Somerset and his supporters, then in so far as any African woman could be safe in England, I would be safe with him, with them. So that was where I went. I fled from the Liverpool dock almost as soon as my feet touched land. And through all Richard Watt's hue and cry, his wanted posters, his spies, his reward notices promising huge sums for my recapture, I laid low. Eventually, the judgement of Lord Mansfield was given and published and was in our favour. No one who steps on the shores of England can be a slave. None. I bore Richard Watt's child, and I raised her, while lying low. This is my story, that no-one must know, and no-one should seek to tell. As with his sister, my child is my heartbeat, and protecting her is my life's work. They say Richard Watt has no child. That suits us. If no-one finds our story at all, we will be free.

*

The coals were still burning at Speke Hall. Richard Watt slept on as rain lashed the windows; his visions turned back to the Westmoreland storm, the drunken tale in the tavern, the sudden lassitude he'd felt over all of his Jamaica endeavours. He had cut loose, abandoned the cursed isle, packed and shipped himself to Liverpool, Arkwright at his side, to restore his health, sort out his nephew and his financial affairs, and restore any damage to his reputation from tittle tattle. For the first few months, his restorative work had gone well; all things awry were righted, the nephew's debts squared off on good terms, the books balanced, all foolish business loans redeemed. A spring had begun to return to his step. Liverpool once more knew the mettle of Richard Watt.

Arkwright visited one blustery evening, threw a bundle of rags at him in his jocular way, and bade him come with him, incognito once more, for, Arkwright claimed, he would enjoy the chance discovery he, Arkwright, had made.

Richard Watt dressed in the bundle of clothes Arkwright had brought him. They were those of a man of humble status, a plain cotton shirt and the faded breeches of an old tar. Then Arkwright steered him, wigless, along several streets of fine merchant houses then off a harbour road and up some stone stairs into a well-appointed drinking club.

'Sit,' Arkwright ordered. He beckoned for a waiter to order their drinks and nudged a man leaning back on the next table. The man looked up and a knowing glance was exchanged between them, though nothing was said. Arkwright turned to Richard Watt as the waiter came with two tankards of beer. 'Sup and listen,' he said indicating with a discreet thumb the direction of the adjacent table.

The man leaning back at the next table had a clear complexion, well combed, glossy black hair, and a bass voice that was worthy of an opera singer. That voice now boomed out. 'Yes, but among the finest, I say, the finest of merchants ever lived, is Liverpool's own, the noble Richard Watt.'

Arkwright nudged his merchant friend and winked. 'Hear that?' Then he turned to the stranger. 'Why say you that?' Arkwright called out. 'Merchants are two a penny in this city.'

The smooth-faced man addressed him. 'I am only a man of the people, but I can say this. Richard Watt is pre-eminent for his hard-working attitude, his brave pioneering voyages, his judicious choice of investments, and his voluminous learning. In all aspects of his life, he has been generous, firm but fair, and his continence in matters physical as much as financial, his restraint and dedication to service to others are without parallel. He is Liverpool's Dick Whittington. A poor boy who came to town, began as a lowly driver of horse and chaise and made his fortune with hard work and a sunny disposition. Mark my words, history will say, 'There went a man!''

'Hear, hear, let's drink to Richard Watt,' one of his three table companions called out. 'More drinks, more drinks!'

'Should we join them?' Arkwright asked his old companion, with a nudge and a wink. 'Perhaps we can learn more of this incredible man?'

Richard Watt smiled and in this moment, he loved his friend, John Arkwright more than he had ever loved a man before. He had seen through the artifice; he had caught the nod between the two conspirators earlier, and there had been something stilted in the teller's voice, as if trying hard to remember a script, a script no doubt, that Arkwright had supplied. It was why the teller drew no crowds. A true storyteller, an honest liar, always attracted a natural audience. Richard Watt saw through it, and he felt a quiet glow of pride in this. Yet his good friend was well-meaning, and he was loath to disrupt the charade that, he imagined, had taken some effort to set up. So, he joined them. At length, he interrupted the panegyrics.

'Does anyone else tell stories of this Richard Watt?' he asked the table in general.

'None but me,' boasted the teller.

'Ah, actually, there is one at the docks from time to time,' a new speaker blurted.

Watt felt the thud as Arkwright kicked out under the table, and saw the new speaker grimace, but the man was inebriated and spoke on regardless. 'Yes, he does not so much tell stories as pretend to be Watt himself, dressed in a disguise of rags. He tells good stories from what I've heard.'

'Can you repeat them here?'

'Alas, no,' the man confessed. 'I have only heard rumour of him, I have not actually heard his stories first-hand. He is not hard to find, though. They say every Saturday at the appointed hour, which is just as dusk takes hold, he is there at the docks.'

A few more drinks were had, and the session ended. Arkwright strolled back to Watt's residence, the two arm in arm, a little worse for their cups. 'You see my friend, no need to worry about your reputation,' Arkwright assured him. 'You are famous in Liverpool and for all the right reasons. The only thing you need now is a monument. Then your fame shall be eternal.'

Watt stopped. He took hold of Arkwright's head in both hands and kissed his cheeks. 'You are a good man,' he told him, 'and I am ever grateful. You have a heart as wide as an ocean. Now go rest abed.'

Upon such warm embraces the two men parted. For Richard Watt, the night was not yet over. Instead of retiring, he followed the scent of the sea to the docks and wandered up and down there. If his feet occasionally stumbled, his mind was clear: he was determined to find his impersonator. He did not have to search hard. A small crowd had gathered at the Number Two wharf around a colourful man who wore a hat tricked up with the wooden image of a sailing ship, and a necklace draped over his shoulders that held large, linked, shining gold coins. A set of leg manacles rested to his left on the cobbles and five fake *Onadoo* manillas were heaped in a pile to his right. In front of him stood assorted sailors, gawpers, townfolk and rabble. Richard Watt joined them, standing unostentatiously within the crowd. Yet it seemed he had arrived a moment too late, because the storyteller suddenly exclaimed, 'That's it. And as these scars upon my chest are my witness, I am Richard Watt. And that's my story done and so help me God, all of it true!'

People left, chuckling. Some tossed coins into a small tin, an action which the man rewarded every time with a deep grin. Soon the crowd had dispersed, and Richard Watt found himself alone with his doppelgänger and sat down in front of him.

'You are Richard Watt, am I right?' the man said, after having checked with a swift all-round glance that they were alone.

'How did you know?' Richard Watt replied, startled.

'It is my job to know. We have a certain likeness, would you not say?'

Richard Watt looked over the man's face, his shape, his height. They were no more alike than apple and grapefruit. He shrugged the question off. 'You make a living from my story?'

'And why not?'

'I don't object. But let me provide some further details for you to add.' And Watt gave a succinct outline of how his fortune had risen: by carefully amassing capital, the smart use of interest, applying the golden formulae of factoring, utilising the key powers of attorney when agenting, and the importance of regular, accurate bookkeeping.

'I have been assiduous and observant,' Richard Watt concluded, 'I have a library across at Oak Hall. I have read widely on many subjects, though I wear my knowledge, as my clothes and status this evening, lightly. Please, if you add these things, it would be well. Then you would truly tell my story and…' At this point Richard Watt placed a note of large denomination into the imposter's tin. 'I will not be ungrateful for its inclusion.'

'No,' the teller, remonstrated, 'take your money back. I can't use it. You have no story.'

'What do you mean?' Richard Watt cried, surprised by the brusque dismissal of his suggestions.

The doppelgänger resumed, more gently this time as he had caught a glimpse of the original Watt's discomfort and he had not meant to be unkind. He pressed both his rough hands into Richard Watts' and stared into his eyes earnestly. 'When I said you have no story, by that I meant there is nothing I can use in what you have told me. You are a poor Richard Watt, understand? So take your money. I won't have it. What use can I put it to? My listeners know that I am not Richard Watt. It is for this reason that they come to hear my stories, the adventures. If they thought I was the real Richard Watt, they would stop buying me drinks, and start arriving with petitions. No, I am richer as the impostor, Richard Watt, and I tell a better story for it. You climbed the sail and freed the bird. You swam ten leagues when your ship was capsized. You rescued the slave from plunging seas. You walked tightrope across the chasm. You began a poor coach driver and ended as rich as Nebuchadnezzar, yet cared not one jot for money, embraced the simple life. Far more handsome, noble, dashing, intriguing, outlandish and thoughtful is my Richard Watt. You have nothing for me. You have no story.'

'Surely there is value in my story,' Richard Watt said defensively, 'in my version? It is good and true.'

'We shall have to agree to differ, the imposter said softly, withdrawing his rough hands into his lap. Richard Watt made to rise.

'But wait…' The imposter shook his sleeve and pulled out a bottle. He uncorked it with his teeth then proffered it in a nod of truce. 'Let us drink together. To Richard Watt, whichever is the better version.'

Richard Watt took the bottle and raised it to his lips. He drank and laughed and the impostor Richard joined him laughing; and thus reconciled, they drank to each other.

Next morning, when his friend Arkwright visited, Richard told him of the encounter with the fake Watt. His mood had turned again; he was now despondent in the telling. Arkwright once again consoled him. 'Come, don't be morose. In one thing, the faker was right, your story is not important. Stories don't survive. You need monuments. Like the great pyramid of Cheops. Or the Hanging Gardens of Babylon. 'Behold my might and be impressed!' Inspire wonder. Purchase impressive bricks and mortar and place them in family trust in perpetuity. Buy a stately pile. Those survive. The gossip of thieves, bawds, wharf-lurkers, prostitutes and dancers is soon gone, as a drop in the ocean of stories. Only land and brick are real. A man of substance has to have his monuments if he is to be remembered, if children in the future are to whisper his name in awe.'

The storm at Speke Hall had long expired; dawn was now nudging through the glass window. Richard Watt stirred. He tried to stand, and managed, though with such difficulty that he imagined he had acquired the gait of an angry fowl. He waved away a servant who rose from slumber to help and made it unaided to the East wing. There, sunlight was striking the row of old stained-glass windows, their heraldic tints shining down the proud history of prior owners of the Hall. He would have his own glass up there too, Richard Watt thought, adding to the row, and so ensure this manor told his story. Yes, Speke Hall would be his monument. He had no delusions – he was too old for them. He would never be remembered as the great Ramses I, or II. But he could certainly be remembered as Richard Watt, West-India Merchant, of Speke Hall.

SPEKE HALL:
A CONTESTED HERITAGE

LIVERPOOL BLACK HISTORY RESEARCH GROUP

Described as 'a green oasis on the edge of Liverpool' to National Trust visitors,[1] Speke Hall is a Tudor Manor House which drew approximately a quarter of a million visitors in 2018.

The estate's medieval origins are matched by the pedigree of its first owners, the Norrises, fulfilling the criteria, as Carole Fabricant put it, for the country house as a 'publicly consumable product [...] a way of life one could buy in to [...] if not actually buy'.[2] Houses like Speke Hall, together with their contents long represented the splendour of the nation, encouraging a sense of belonging, of Englishness. Speke Hall featured in mid-twentieth-century primary school history books as a monocultural history – which did not include its links to Asia through the Norris family, or to Caribbean slavery through the Watt family.

The National Trust with its mission – 'For everyone – for ever' – is now questioning the sense of Englishness which country houses once habitually conveyed. Speke Hall epitomises the dilemma facing the National Trust which cares for properties with imperial connections: how is the organisation to represent the colonial histories of such places?

Speke Hall and Slavery

At the time of writing, to the casual visitor, there is nothing to indicate that Speke Hall, in its present form, owes everything to transatlantic slavery.[3] As Anthony Tibbles pointed out, Richard Watt (1724-1796), who bought the estate in 1795, made his fortune 'selling enslaved Africans and the products of their labour, which provided the resources for his descendants to indulge their interests and ultimately the funds which ensured the survival of this major timber-framed building.'[4] Few visitors notice that in a window in the Oak Parlour, the coat of arms belonging to Richard Watt sports three African heads. There is, to date, no attempt to interpret this stained-glass window on site, although since 1996 the guide book has explained its significance. More recently in 2020, Speke's former curator Anthony Tibbles produced a special edition of the guidebook, *Speke Hall and the Watt Family*[5] and in 2021 the website explicitly addressed Speke Hall's colonial connections. The connection, however, does not start with Richard Watt I. Colonialism and slavery was embedded in the history and upkeep of Speke Hall over a period of two hundred years.

The Norris Family: Slavery, India and the development of the infrastructure of Liverpool.

The Norris family held the manor of Speke from 1317, although the Molyneuxs held the nominal overlordship until the end of the sixteenth century. The family had a history of service to the Crown, the county and the town, but support for Catholicism and the Stuarts had proved a barrier to public office during most of the seventeenth century. In 1698, William Norris VI (1658-1702), now MP for Liverpool, was appointed to lead a trade mission to India to the Court of the Mughal Emperor Aurangzeb. Although the mission was unsuccessful, William and his brother Edward (1665-1726) managed to make a private profit from Indian goods they brought home, valued at a massive 87,000 rupees. The mission itself was carried out with great pomp and ceremony and William was created a baronet: he would not enjoy the title for long as he died on the return journey.

His business acumen had been displayed locally when back in 1695 he had combined with MP William Clayton (after 1650-1715) to procure an Act for the creation of the parish of Liverpool. This was a watershed in the town's fortunes and totally changed the complexion of the council, which was now all local and free from outside influence. Within ten years, the majority of the council were engaged in overseas trade, three-quarters of them in the transatlantic trade.[6] A small but close group of merchants, often related by marriage, operated with 'remarkable cohesion'[7] to drive the projects which transformed Liverpool's economic potential. The influence and experience of the Norris family in the capital, was of considerable importance to the success of these ventures.

William and Edward's younger brother Richard (1670-1730) would capitalise on Liverpool's new-found independence in 1707, when plans to create an enclosed dock were discussed: Richard Norris and Thomas Johnson (1664-1728), now Liverpool MPs, introduced the Act to allow them raise funds for the dock in 1709. This dock was to be the first enclosed, commercial wet dock in the world. It could hold 100 ships and, because it was gated, it was not dependent on the tide. This meant that cargo could be loaded and unloaded speedily and safely, and gave Liverpool the edge over its rivals. Norris himself took advantage of the business possibilities by buying land in the area; he also reported on the need for a road which the Council agreed to construct and to organise loans to finance the work. He had already shown an interest in developing the town's infrastructure with a project to make the Mersey navigable up to Warrington in 1698, which had been suggested by Thomas Patten (1662-1726) whose copper manufacture was involved in supplying slave ships with trade goods to buy enslaved Africans.

A pioneer in the development of Liverpool's economy Richard Norris was also one of the city's early slave traders, investing in two voyages of *The Blessing* in 1701 and 1702 while also importing slave produced tobacco and sugar. With an eye to the latest developments, Norris was the first to ship cotton into Liverpool, a material produced at that time by enslaved people in the Caribbean.[8] Cotton grown in the southern United States would later underpin the city's most prosperous period.

Speke Hall's association with transatlantic slavery has always tended to focus on the eighteenth-century story of Richard Watt, but Speke Hall's connections had been global since the end of the seventeenth century. Moreover, the benefits went far beyond the Norris family through business projects and the influence they had via public appointments[9] to impact the development of Liverpool itself and the city's capacity to exploit the opportunities which the slave economy opened up.

The Watt Family

When Richard Watt bought Speke Hall and its estate of 2,400 acres in 1795, for £73,500, he had been involved in the slave economy for at least forty years. That year his company Watt and Walker secured a record 5,278 hogsheads – large barrels – of sugar, which amounted to over ten percent of Liverpool's total sugar imports, and 1071 puncheons of rum, also made by enslaved people on plantations.[10] Two years previously, Richard Watt had purchased the 450 ton *Princess Royal* which carried 549 enslaved Africans from Bonny to Jamaica.[11] One year later he died, leaving a thriving business which was, and remained, one of Liverpool's leading sugar importers into the 1810s. He also left over £200,000 in bequests, the Speke Hall and Bishop Burton estates, Oak Hill house in Old Swan and other properties in Liverpool, as well as George's Plain plantation in Westmorland, Jamaica – at 2,700 acres, one of the island's largest estates – and the proceeds from the lease of two other Westmorland estates, Cornwall and

Black Morass, which continued for a number of years after his death.

His fortune was entirely the result of activities covering every sector of the slave economy, from slave-trading, to selling enslaved people to plantation owners, to owning his own plantations, managing others' plantations and running his import business. Having started out in life with relatively little money[12], he left his fortune and slave-related enterprises to his family and their descendants, who would profit further from compensation in 1835 to the tune of £9167.3.5. for the loss of enslaved labour as property following the 1833 Slavery Abolition Act.[13] Richard Watt also endowed his family with privileged status reflected in the properties he had bought, no doubt with that intention: Bishop Burton and Speke Hall came with manorial rights. His descendants became country gentlemen gifted not only with status but the leisure to pursue their interests, which in the case of his nephew Richard Walker (1760-1801) involved buying and refurbishing of Mitchelgrove, a castellated mansion and estate in Sussex, for £115,000. In the case of Richard Watt III (1786-1855) inherited slavery wealth allowed him to pursue a lifelong passion for horse racing. The final Watt owner of Speke Hall, Adelaide Watt (1857-1921), continued to profit from investments made with the 1835 slavery compensation and from income from George's Plain. Jamaica. This income allowed her to endow the Anglican Cathedral and in acknowledging the role her ancestor, Richard Watt I, had played in creating the wealth she enjoyed, she had a memorial inscribed in his name placed next to the cathedral.[14]

The history of the Watts' slaving and slavery-related enterprises is crucial to understanding Speke Hall's story and a dedicated on-site exhibition could draw from numerous sources. Liverpool Record Office holds a record of a bill of sale of two enslaved Africans to Richard Watt, from 1751. There is a notice of the sale of enslaved Africans by Richard Watt and Alexander Allardyce from the *Royal Gazette* of Jamaica, 12 June 1779.[15] St Nicholas Church records show John Dobson, baptised on the 8th March in 1772, was a Black servant to Richard Watt.[16] There is no shortage of evidence, which also includes a revealing copy letter book 1778 -1782[17] covering cargoes Watt had shipped, incredible profits made in his slave factoring partnership with Alexander Allerdyce,[18] the management of his own and two other plantations, Montpelier and Rileys, as well as the operation of his Liverpool trading house in Hanover Street, founded in 1769, on his brief return to Liverpool. Acting as agent for the Montpelier plantation, in particular, his letters to John Rose Ellis could be contextualised by a prizewinning work published by Barry Higman on Montpelier itself,[19] including an archaeological survey which has allowed some reconstruction of life on the plantation. This could be combined with the slave register information available for the Watts' George's Plain estate from 1817,[20] all excellent material for a community project, perhaps using the model of Bexley Heath Heritage Trust's treatment of Danson House,[21] which included teachers' resources that provided the history of these slavery connections.[22]

The key exhibit in such an exhibition at Speke Hall would have to be the so-called blackamoor heads' crest on the Watt coat of arms, in the Oak Parlour. At present they provide the sole clue about the house's slavery connections, even though there remains no signage to that effect. It is interesting that the only known research into the significance of the crest argues that it does not refer to the source of Watt's wealth, but that it simply complies with the metaphorical heraldic conventions of its period.[23] However, there are proven cases of the motif being literal. The first-known form of Saracen heads was incorporated from the Aragon flag in the family crest of Peter III of Aragon to commemorate the defeat of the Moors by Peter I in 1086. In Britain, too, a literal motif was included in John Hawkins' coat of arms. John Hawkins (1532-1595) was the naval commander licensed by Elizabeth I to buy and sell enslaved people. Hawkins has the image of an African in the crest at the top of his coat of arms. A hundred years later the Bishop of London, William Juxon (1582-1663), included four African heads in his coat of arms. He also covered the roof beams of the hall in Lambeth Palace with the same motif. He, too, was involved in the slave trade.[24]

Two families held Speke Hall over a period of seven hundred years. For two hundred years the slave economy profited both families and the fabric of the hall itself. The Norris's involvement with transatlantic slavery was pivotal in the development of Liverpool itself, at the point of the city's relatively late entry into the slave trade. The connection of the two families with the house reflects the change taking place across the country where power through ownership of land was giving way to possession of capital – a transformation to some extent made possible by profits from slavery, though as this essay has indicated, some of that wealth was used to buy the 'respectability' that went with manorial titles, a process which is only now beginning to be acknowledged. Using the records of the Watts' estates in Jamaica would be a fitting way to explore further missing links, to discover the consequences of both families' activities for those who were the source of their wealth – enslaved Africans.

Endnotes:

1. National Trust website 06.04.2022
2. Carole Fabricant, 'The Literature of Domestic Tourism and the Public Consumption of private property' in F. Nussbaum and L. Brown (eds) *The*

New Eighteenth Century: Theory, Politics and English Literature (New York and London: Methuen, 1987), p. 261.

3. Anthony Tibbles, 'My Interest Be Your Guide: Richard Watt (1724-1796) Merchant of Liverpool and Kingston Jamaica, *Transactions of the Historic Society of Lancashire and Cheshire,* Vol 166, Issue 1, p.25, hereafter, Tibbles, 2017.

4. Anthony Tibbles, *Speke Hall and the Watt Family* (Author, 2020).

5. We are indebted to the extensive research conducted by Anthony Tibbles as curator at Speke and over the last 40 years.

6. M. Power, *Creating a Port: Liverpool 1695-1715 hslc.org.uk2017, accessed 21.05.2022.*

7. Ibid.

8. Identified in Nigel Hall's *Liverpool Cotton History* https://www.liverpoolcotton.com/merchants.html which cites LRO 920/NOR/r.91.111, 132, 145, 152, 155, 179, 225, 289, 299, 302, 318.

9. William Norris, MP for Liverpool 1698; Richard Norris, Mayor of Liverpool 1700-01, MP for Liverpool 1708-1710; Edward Norris MP for Liverpool 1715-1722.

10. Goods imported at the Port of Liverpool, *Manchester Mercury* 1769- 1796, cited Anthony Tibbles 2017, p. 15.

11. The ship was captured by the French on its second voyage. TSTDB 83235 & 83236

12. The rags to riches version of Watt's lowly origins is probably apocryphal but it is true that before he went to Jamaica he was in unskilled work and likely that an employer noted his aptitude and sent him to evening school.

13. https://www.ucl.ac.uk/lbs/person/view/13160, 26.04.2022

14. Cited Anthony Tibbles, 2017, p. 31. This association with gentility acquired through a fortune made in the slave economy was not rare – it figures in numerous contemporary accounts and letters notably, Christopher Hassel to his mother on entering the slave trade in 1756, refers to a 'genteel livelihood in trade' (Maurice and Eunice Schofield 'A Good Fortune and a Good Wife, HSLC vol.138, (1988) pp 4-17, and the whole concept of slavery and gentility is explored in Simon Gikandi, *Slavery and the Culture of Taste* (Princeton University Press, 2011).

15. Bill of sale 29 October 1751, LRO 920 Wat/1/2/2.

16. St Nicholas Church baptismal records ' 8 March 1772, John Dobson, A Negro youth, servant to Richard Watt, merchant.'

17. LRO 920/Wat/1/2/1

18. In nine months 1775-76 the company bought 4,235 Africans from seventeen ships for £200,000 at a profit of £20,000, cited Anthony Tibbles 2017, p. 28.

19. B.W. Higman, *Montpelier Jamaica: A Plantation Community in Slavery and Freedom 1739-1912* (Jamaica: University of West Indies Press, 1998).

20. https://www.ucl.ac.uk/lbs/person/view/13160

21. Cliff Pereira, Representing the East and West India links to the British country house: the London Borough of Bexley and the wider heritage picture in *Slavery and the Country House*, Madge Dresser and Andrew Hann, eds. (Swindon: English Heritage, 2013), pp 123-13, https://historicengland.org.uk/im-

ages-books/publications/slavery-and-british-country-house/slavery-british-country-house-web/

22. https://hallplace.org.uk/wp-content/uploads/2018/08/Teachers-Complete-Resource-Notes-for-Bexley-The-Slavery-Connection1.pdf

23. https://www.academia.edu/38990935/Speke_Hall_066_Richard_Watt_I_the_arriviste, Graham, Angus.

24. Joseph Jones 'Monumental Inscriptions, Arms & Co: in the Church & Churchyard of St Mary in Lambeth' cited https://boroughphotos.org/lambeth/ accessed 12/10.2022 and https://blogs.kent.ac.uk/history/2020/07/01/the-church-of-england-faces-up-to-britains-imperial-past/

PENRHYN CASTLE

Penrhyn Castle, Gwynedd, Wales. Aerial view of the castle.
©National Trust Images/Roger Richards

Richard Pennant, Lord Penrhyn of Penrhyn, County Louth (1739-1808)
And his dog 'Crab' painted by Henry Thomson RA in the 1790s; at
Penrhyn Castle, Gwynedd
©National Trust Images/John Hammond

MARIA THOMAS

7 6 4

Lewis snapped a Bubbalicious and tongued the gum off his lips. 6G had been stuck on the minibus forever and he needed another P.I.S.S. At the service station Miss Rowe had warned against going crazy but the cokes were on two-for-one, so he'd snuck a second into his rucksack, along with a bumper pack of Haribo and three packs of the Bubbalicious, banned at home after that run-in with his sister's precious Afro. He was down to £3 to spend in the gift shop, but all he wanted was a fridge magnet for his mum. Maybe one with the castle on it. He had to go home with something to show for himself. If there was any cash left over, he'd see if he could stretch to a postcard for poor old Miss Rowe. Maybe one with the quarry on it, so she could kiss it before she went to bed. How it was possible to be so nuts over a massive hole in the ground, Lewis didn't know.

'Attention, please, class.' Miss Rowe was standing at the front of the minibus, holding onto a seat for balance. 'We're almost at Penrhyn. Like I said, we'll do our tour of the castle first, and then we'll check in to our accommodation afterwards. Make sure to put all your rubbish in the bin bag.'

Davith Walker's hand shot up. 'So we're not going to the quarry, Miss?'

'We are, Davith.' Miss Rowe beamed. 'Tomorrow. I can show you where my grandfather worked. Did you know, kids, the slate mining industry in Gwynedd is – '

Lewis yawned and the Bubbalicious leapt out of his mouth and into his lap. It lay there like a neon worm. Miss Rowe was always talking about her family; she knew mad facts about them. Lewis's grandparents came from Jamaica. Nobody was getting there from Cardiff in a musty minibus. His grandfather never spoke about anything back home, like Wales had wiped his memory of it. Jamaica was a bit like a quarry, really; Lewis had to dig to find anything out.

'We'll also learn more about the Great Strike tomorrow, and how badly the quarry workers were treated,' Miss Rowe continued. 'My *great* grandfather was involved in that and it was a terribly – '

Long and boring story. Lewis sucked up the neon worm from his trousers.

Stories came way too easy to some people. Last year the class had completed family trees, and while the likes of Davith Walker had drawn branches galore, Lewis had struggled to make his project look like he even tried. All that digging had not been fun, not that Miss Rowe and her red pen had cared. She could keep her stories. The quarry and the castle were the rubbish parts of the trip anyway. This was his first night away from home by himself and the 6G girls were going to get pranked after lights out, big time. Craig had some good ideas and a pocketful of fake bugs he got from a cracker. He called himself the King of Pranks. Prankster of the Year, 2007.

Lewis rolled his eyes, remembering. He had ideas too. 'Hey,' he said, nudging his friend. 'What about writing on the mirror to freak the girls out? Something creepy.'

Craig was in the window seat, resting his greasy forehead on the glass. 'Yeah. Sure,' he said, distracted. 'I think the castle's around here somewhere.'

The minibus had pulled onto a smaller road, bordered by trees and grass, as green and calm as if they were driving through a big park. Nothing like the city centre noise and hustle that surrounded the castle back home. It was an overcast day in June. The sun kept peeking from behind large dark clouds that looked like people posing. Lewis spotted a cloud-woman twisted as if she was dancing, and a man crouching, holding his hands out. The minibus moved slowly, and Lewis watched the trees cast long shadows on the grass. They looked a little bit human, too. He thought about Cardiff, about his mum's stew chicken waiting on the hob, suddenly wishing he was back there. When Penrhyn Castle came into view, enormous and towering in grey stone, Craig faked a gasp. 'It's like Hogwarts,' he said and laughed.

'Nah,' Lewis replied, feeling a weirdly annoyed and uneasy. 'Hogwarts is cool.'

*

'Building on this version of Penrhyn started around 1820 and took almost twenty years to finish.' In the huge open space of the Great Hall, a castle employee named Rhonda was talking. She was an older lady with short grey hair and a voice that boomed, even as the Hall tried to swallow it. 6G was gathered tight as a choir in front of her, watching as she waved like a conductor at one corner of the room then another. 'Most of the castle is neo-Norman,' she said, 'but you might call the style of the entrance over there Romanesque Revival. And the carvings are inspired by medieval and Celtic sources, although it's rumoured ancient Mediterranean ruins influenced the building, too...'

Lewis hung at the back of the group, shifting his weight from foot to foot, trying to think about anything other than peeing. Laura Whipple turned around twice just to shush him. There was no choice but to pay some kind of attention. Rhonda kept on: 'George Hay Dawkins Pennant brought in a famous architect called Thomas Hopper to design everything. This incredible staircase was the final part of the castle to be completed. It is made of Painswick stone and –'

Lewis zoned out. It was too hard to believe the castle had been someone's home. Apart from the fancy staircase, the whole room was carved out of white stone, which must have been cold, even with the fireplace cut out of the wall like a great yawning mouth. It reminded Lewis of a chilly old church. And the staircase wasn't actually that fancy. It had a red stain on it that had leapt out at Lewis, and his eyesight wasn't that great. He blinked hard and shifted his weight a little faster. Rhonda had moved on to discussing the windows: *by Thomas Willement, the 'Father of Victorian Stained Glass'.* They were pretty enough, but they didn't look like the sort of thing normal people would put in their house. There again, from what Rhonda had said, the Pennants hadn't been normal people; they'd been rich. *Really* rich. Lewis felt his bladder pulse like an alarm. 'Craig,' he whispered and tugged on his friend's jacket. 'I've got to piss *now*. I can't wait.'

'Well, where are the loos?' Craig whispered back.

'Dunno. Let's go look.'

While Miss Rowe and the TAs hung on Rhonda's every word, Lewis and Craig backed slowly away from the huddle, grinning. The trip was suddenly looking more interesting. Lewis was glad he'd convinced his mother; when he told her about it, she'd hesitated at first: 'Trouble follows you like a stink,' she'd said. 'Tell me one good reason why I'm letting you loose overnight?' She'd signed the permission slip only because of the exhibition. The class was going to learn about the quarry stuff, and about the abolition of the slave trade, for its anniversary. 'About slavery? Oh, that's a good lesson,' his mother had said, like she knew anything about it. Maybe she did, but Lewis hadn't asked. He'd jumped straight on the phone with Craig to chat about sticking plastic spiders in Laura Whipple's bed. But now his mind was firmly on the castle. They had been wandering for ten minutes at least, turning corners to find nothing cool, past dead-ends, roped-off rooms, and locked doors. It was tiring, feeling awkward, holding everything in. Penrhyn was so much bigger than either of them, too full of hard surfaces and shadows. The high of sneaking off had faded and now, in its place, was the sickly thought of Miss Rowe telling them off. Lewis felt himself scurrying, like a mouse. 'What if we get lost?' he whispered to Craig as they continued along the dim corridors, searching. 'And nobody finds us? We'll have to stay here forever.'

Craig laughed loudly and the sound bounced off the stone. 'Yeah, like squatters,' he said. 'Nobody else lives here. We could move in!'

*

The bathroom was narrow with no window and a single stall, and a sign that reminded employees to wash their hands. Lewis ran the hot tap for a moment, letting steam bloom up from the sink. Only Craig would know how close he'd come to wetting himself, and how he'd started to panic and sweat over it, the sweat sour and clinging inside his uniform. And Craig knowing was bad enough. He stooped to wet his face, hoping to feel more like himself. Then he thought about washing under his armpits and began to loosen his tie. There was a funny smell in the air, faintly sweet, like candy floss or the hand soap his mother sometimes used, which made him think of her again and feel very far from home. He wanted a shower, a plate of her food, and a spot on the sofa in front of the TV. Lewis sighed and began to undo the top buttons on his shirt. The light, a neon saucer overhead, flickered once. Then it went off. It was completely dark. Craig, of course, Prankster of the Year. 'Hey, cut it out,' Lewis yelled, and the light came right back on. Brighter, it seemed.

'Huh?' Craig said, poking his head round the door.

Lewis didn't reply. '7. 6. 4,' he muttered, reciting the three numbers that had appeared, etched into the steam on the mirror before him. '764.' The steam dissipated and Lewis saw his reflection staring back at him, his own face a little confused and washed out, his brown eyes too dark and wide. He felt an odd warmth creep across his neck. 'Was that you?' He turned to Craig.

'Was what me?'

Lewis groaned. 'That was my idea, anyway, writing on the mirror. Save it for the girls, yeah, Craig? You're such a dick sometimes.'

*

Craig protested his innocence all the way back to the Great Hall, where Miss Rowe was waiting by herself with a scowl and a wagging finger. 'Craig Jones, Lewis Grant,' she said. 'Both of you have won yourselves detention for a week. Well done. What did Rhonda say about wandering off? You held up the whole class.'

'But –' Craig started.

'But nothing. I've got my eye on the pair of you from now on. Do those buttons up Lewis, please.'

Lewis opened his mouth to speak but all he could think was 7, 6, 4.

'Now, come on,' Miss Rowe continued. 'Let's find everyone. They've already headed to the exhibition. Lewis, I thought you'd be interested in this part of the tour. I'm a bit disappointed in you if I'm honest.'

Craig gave Lewis an angry middle finger and jumped obediently to Miss Rowe's side. He was never much good at getting caught, but he did seem especially annoyed this time. Lewis fell in behind the pair of them, eyeing the slate floor. He wasn't interested in the exhibition, not in the slightest, so Miss Rowe could piss off with her disappointment. Those numbers on the mirror would not leave him alone. Why 7, 6, and 4? Craig had pretended he didn't know what they meant, and now Lewis was beginning to feel a tightening, tingling sensation at the nape of his neck, like maybe the numbers weren't Craig's prank after all.

'Hey.' He poked Craig between the shoulder blades. 'Just admit it.'

'I told you, I don't know what you're on about!'

'Both of you. Behave,' Miss Rowe snapped. 'For goodness sake, you're representing the school.'

As the trio neared the staircase, Lewis noticed the stain again. What was once a small red splotch had taken on the shape of a handprint, about the size of his own. Slowing, Lewis reached out and swiped at the stone. 'Miss?' he mumbled, as his fingers came away damp and trembling. 'Miss? Is this blood?'

Miss Rowe threw him a look over her shoulder. 'Whatever is the matter with you today, Lewis?' she said, glancing at his outstretched hand. 'You're fine. You haven't cut yourself. There's absolutely nothing there.'

*

6G hadn't quite made it to the exhibition. They were huddled in a room with a long mahogany dining table, surrounded by paintings of old dead white people. Rhonda was talking and her voice sounded garbled and far away, like she was underwater or wrapped in cotton wool. Lewis could not stop inspecting his hand. He turned it over, again and again, then held it close to his face and sniffed it. He let the tip of his tongue touch it and it tasted of nothing. Whatever the sticky redness had been, it was gone without a trace. It had disappeared the moment he showed it to Miss Rowe. The stain on the staircase had disappeared too and left him wondering whether he was going mad. His elderly neighbour used to see things that weren't there, and she'd been taken into hospital; Lewis hadn't seen Mrs Roberts since. He shoved both his hands into his pockets and cast about for something else to look at. Anything else.

'Now this is Richard Pennant, the first Baron Penrhyn.' Rhonda was pointing up at a painting in a big gilt frame of a man with silver hair curled at the ends like a lawyer's wig. He had black eyes and a stare that drilled into everyone, as if he was wondering what the hell they were all doing in his house. 'He poured lots of money into the estate, investing in the farms and agricultural buildings. He even built roads, churches and schools.'

'And he developed the quarry,' Miss Rowe added. 'Isn't that right, Rhonda?'

'Yes.' She didn't seem to mind Miss Rowe butting in. 'He turned it into one of the biggest producers of slate in the world…'

Lewis closed his eyes. His head felt fuzzy and heavy, and the creeping warmth at his neck had returned. When he took a deep breath, the air he sucked up was sweet, just like before, except this time he was able to taste it.

'Gross,' Laura Whipple hissed at him. 'Stop it, you weirdo.'

Lewis pulled his tongue in quick. As his eyes snapped open, he caught sight of a shadow in the corner, a dark wavering shape covering a part of the wall. 'Craig,' he whispered, but his friend shushed him, and Laura Whipple shot him daggers again; everyone was glued to Rhonda and the portraits, hooked on the stories behind them. The shadow gripped Lewis; it made no sense. It appeared to belong to itself and seemed to grow the longer he stared at it. Spreading like a thick spill. Lewis felt the first twinge of fear ease into something much calmer, a sensation that glowed in his feet as though he had dipped them into a bath. He inched apart from the group and watched the shadow, now large and unmoving. And oddly dense. It could have been a person, or maybe something even grander than that, like a statue in a park. A thing that might like to be looked at or touched. Lewis drew closer to it with his hand out, closer and closer until...

'Lewis Grant, what are you doing now?' Miss Rowe complained. 'Please, join the group and pay attention.'

'But –' Lewis watched the shadow dissolve into the pale light of the room. Miss Rowe had clearly not seen it, nor had the others whose heads whipped back to Rhonda immediately.

'Penrhyn had no sons, so when he died the entire estate passed to his second cousin, George Hay Dawkins.'

'And the sugar plantations,' Miss Rowe added, sombrely.

'Yes.' Rhonda nodded. 'Everything in Jamaica, too.'

Lewis felt the room and all its beady-eyed portraits squashing him like a cheap football. There was something far more sinister about them than the shadow. He wanted it to come back.

'George Hay Dawkins adopted the name Pennant,' Rhonda went on. 'George Hay Dawkins-Pennant —'

Lewis felt his arm go up. 'Miss Rhonda?' he asked, a little surprised to hear himself calling out. 'Is the castle haunted?' It was a stupid question. Of course, Penrhyn was haunted.

'Well, there are stories.' Rhonda rubbed her hands together, her eyes crinkling as she grinned. 'We'll learn more about the ghost of Alice Douglas-Pennant when we head upstairs to see the nursery. Her father supposedly locked her in there when she fell in love with a gardener.'

'Oh no,' Davith Walker moaned and Craig yelled, 'Cool!'

Lewis let his shoulders slump. Of course, people knew Penrhyn was haunted. But the shadow hadn't felt like it belonged to a boring, lovesick ghost. 'Okay,' he said, when Rhonda mentioned a recent sighting of the fourth Lord Penrhyn in a bathrobe. 'Great.' He ploughed his hands deep in his pockets again.

*

The exhibition was housed in a room off a courtyard, near what Rhonda had said were the servant's quarters. A large window threw light onto the stone walls and cobbled floor, so much plainer than the rest of the castle, except for the exhibits. Other schoolchildren had visited and made contributions: drawings of slaves shackled by their necks that stared gloomily from the walls. Lewis felt his own neck chafe inside his shirt collar. While Rhonda spoke, about the plantations the Pennants had owned, about how Richard Pennant had fought against ending slavery, the class lined the room, peering at the displays. Rhonda's voice carried over everyone's heads; the other schoolchildren had recreated scenes. There was an image of a boiling house where splashes of hot sugar ate the slaves' skin like acid, and a big sugar mill that could trap and grind up limbs. Someone had imagined a young slave, a boy, with startled eyes and a mangled and bloodied hand. Lewis stared at a painting of a plantation that looked very calm and orderly, until Laura Whipple nudged him out the way to inspect it herself. He was tired, suddenly heavy with sleep. All he recognised in the painting were the palm trees jutting like spikes out of the landscape; the rest of it looked a bit like the countryside in Wales. Even the name of the place – 'Denbigh' – sounded a bit Welsh. Lewis wondered if he would ever see the real country where his grandfather was born. Palm trees seemed like the only thing he knew about Jamaica for sure. Davith Walker complained about feeling stuffy so a TA pushed the huge wooden doors to the room wide open. Sunlight poured in, making shapes on the cobbles.

'Miss?' Lewis asked, uncomfortable. 'When are we leaving?'

Miss Rowe tutted and shook her head, ignoring the question. Rhonda was saying something about cash: '£14,683 17s 2d was what George Hay Dawkins-Pennant received in compensation from the British government for having to free them. That's over £1.5m in today's money. Which is really quite a lot...'

Lewis hugged himself and scuffed his shoe at a cobble higher than those around it, watching the beams of light wobble and stretch into the courtyard. Rhonda sounded a little strange again, sluggish and drawly this time, like she'd been dipped in syrup. A sunbeam found him and pooled around his feet, warming them. Slowly, the beam of light began to glow, and widen as if into a path. Lewis felt himself take the first step forward along it, only half-hearing Rhonda continue. '...it was an enormous number of slaves, everyone. 764. The compensation helped pay for Penrhyn...'

*

The sunbeam path pulled Lewis along it, gently, like a current. He passed through the courtyard, back towards the main castle, shedding the sleepiness from his limbs and head, feeling lighter, as if he might float away. It was almost lunchtime, and the sun was tropical; as hot a day as any he could remember. His stomach growled and his mouth was dry and sour. Whatever was happening, his body had chosen to give in to it, and his mind had stopped resisting too. All the questions from before had melted away. Whatever was happening, he would find out soon enough. The sunbeam turned to shadow at the door to the castle. The door opened slowly with a long, loud creak.

'Hello?' Lewis called quietly at the threshold. 'Is anyone there?' It seemed necessary and polite to ask, but there was silence. When he stepped into the corridor, he felt that maybe he should take off his shoes. 'Hello?' he asked again, making his way back to the Great Hall with tentative steps. If he'd turned left or right to look at the stone walls, he would've seen the shadow moving along with him, and the bloody handprint appear again, pointing the way.

Then came the noise. Like someone had flipped a switch. It filled Lewis's ears, low at first, a background soup of voices and movement, then sharper, a real cacophony, the closer he crept to the Great Hall. It sounded like a hub of activity, everyone going about their business, like Cardiff city centre on a Saturday afternoon. Music played, a drumbeat and singing, under bright shouts and laughter and chatter. Just before he rounded the corner into the Hall, Lewis paused and took a breath. He wasn't scared; he understood. So, people *did* live in Penrhyn after all. Or the ghosts of real people. He was so ready to meet them. He whispered to himself, smiling, '7. 6. 4.'

THE PENNANTS OF PENRHYN CASTLE: CONNECTING WALES AND SLAVERY

MARIAN GWYN

Jamaica sits right in the heart of the Caribbean. It was a British possession for over 300 years – from 1655 to 1962 – and the Pennants of Penrhyn Castle owned plantations on the island for much of that time. Acquisitive from the start, the Pennants amassed huge amounts of land – eighteen times the average holding – and they owned just under a thousand enslaved people.[1] Rich, ambitious and keen to consolidate their investments, the Pennants sought high political and legislative positions in Jamaican society as they expanded their interests. Edward Pennant became Chief Justice of the island in the early years of the eighteenth century, at a time when Jamaica was embedding extreme forms of punishment for its enslaved population into its legal code.[2]

Like so many of the wealthiest planters, the Pennants became absentees by the early 1700s, leaving behind hurricanes, slave revolts, tropical diseases, and social isolation.[3] They returned to Britain, bringing their fortune with them, removing at a stroke investment on the island beyond what was necessary to keep their plantations functioning.[4] In Britain, their extreme wealth opened doors of opportunity, advantage, and political power. One became Lord Mayor of London, two were ennobled as barons, and their descendants formed marriage and business alliances with some of Britain's most powerful elites.[5]

Knowing full well that power and status were held in the hands of the landowning classes, they acquired one of the oldest landed estates in Wales – Penrhyn, on which they developed what was to become Britain's largest slate quarry, employing thousands, and which dominated the international slate market for a century and a half.[6] To consolidate their position, they built Penrhyn Castle, a massive country residence that still commands the landscape for miles around. Built in the forbidding neo-Norman style, the Pennants not only wanted the castle to impress but to imply a family pedigree as landed nobility they did not necessarily have.[7] The story of the Pennants of Penrhyn Castle underlines how slaving wealth from Africa and the West Indies was reinvested in Britain, benefiting a broad social spectrum.

The Pennants in Jamaica

The first Pennant in Jamaica was Gifford, a descendant of Thomas Pennant, abbot of Basingwerk in Flintshire. A soldier, Gifford had been garrisoned on the island not long after it had become a British colony in 1655, but, taking full advantage of generous land grants, he soon turned to land acquisition, sugar production and slave ownership.[8]

Gifford's son Edward (1672-1736) increased his father's landholdings and became a significant figure in the Jamaican establishment, becoming Chief Justice and a member of the governing council. On his death, the bulk of Edward's estate was divided among his three oldest sons John, Samuel, and Henry. By the 1720-30s, the wealthiest planters left Jamaica for Britain, the Pennants among them, leaving the running of their estates in the hands of agents. By the 1730s all three Pennant brothers, along with their fortune, were settled in Britain.[9]

Unlike many absentees, who maintained a relaxed approach to their distant estates, the Pennants' near-obsessive attention to the administration of their plantations meant that their Jamaican managers knew little peace. The Pennants not only demanded regular reports on their sugar estates, but they also sent detailed instructions on how they were to be run, even though they never returned to the island to see their plantations themselves.

The Pennants in Britain

Their wealth enabled the Pennants to move into British society at the highest level. Of the brothers who returned, Henry became a landowner, while Samuel, a judge, was knighted, becoming Lord Mayor of London in 1749. Neither was able to fully enjoy his position as each died young and without children, leaving their Jamaican estates to their brother John.[10]

John was a successful West India merchant in London and in Liverpool, two major slave-trading ports. While trading in the Atlantic market, he also invested in the salt industry, going into partnership with Colonel Hugh Warburton of Winnington, Cheshire, who, through his wife, owned half of what had been the medieval Penrhyn estate in north Wales. John began buying the remainder of the estate, soon reuniting it under single ownership when his son Richard married Warburton's daughter, Anne Susannah, in 1767.[11]

Penrhyn flourished under Richard Pennant, ennobled as 1st Lord Penrhyn in 1783. Known as an 'improver', he lavished vast amounts of money in developing his Welsh estate, investing in farms, housing, roads, tourism, churches, and schools. Commissioning the society architect Samuel Wyatt, he transformed the old Penrhyn Hall, which dated back to the 15th century, into a much-admired mock-military gothic castle.[12]

Richard was keen to take advantage of the commercial opportunities offered by the estate, and he soon expanded his slate quarry, just five miles from the castle. His family's extensive industrial, commercial and managerial experiences in Jamaica and in England gave him a significant advantage over other slate producers in the area.[13] By the end of the 19th century, Penrhyn Quarry had become one of the world's largest suppliers of roofing slate.[14]

Despite Richard's growing commercial and landed interests in Britain, he remained focused on his Jamaican assets throughout his life – it was not until after Richard's death that profits from Britain outgrew those from Jamaica.[15] While Richard improved the lives of his tenants and employees in Wales, in Jamaica, which he never visited, he was the owner and exploiter of many hundreds of human beings.

Having no children, on his death Richard's assets passed to his second cousin George Hay Dawkins, who, under the requirements of the will, adopted the surname Pennant. George, dissatisfied with Richard's architectural tastes, devoted his energies during the years 1818-1838 to remodelling and expanding Penrhyn Castle to its current monumental form. Thomas Hopper, the castle's architect, also designed the interior, using neo-Norman styling throughout. A combination of enthusiasm and huge amounts of capital ensured a spectacular building. Of the medieval hall, only a small section of spiral staircase can be seen internally.[16] No visible evidence of Richard's house remains.

The use of enslaved labour in the Caribbean was abolished in 1833-34, during George's tenure, and he received £14,683 19s 2d in compensation from the government for the loss of his human chattels (just over £1.75 million today).[17] George's eldest daughter and heir, Juliana, married Edward Gordon Douglas, a Scotsman and captain (later colonel) in the Grenadier Guards. On George's death, Edward inherited his father-in-law's estate and changed the family name to Douglas-Pennant.[18]

Like Richard before him, Edward Gordon Douglas-Pennant was a vigorous improver of his north Wales estate. Flush with compensation money from abolition, he invested widely in his tenanted farms and in a remarkable art collection. This was bought primarily with the advice of a London art dealer and comprises mostly 16th century Venetian and 17th century Dutch and Spanish works, though also included pieces by Rembrandt, Canaletto, and Gainsborough. Many of these still hang on the walls of the castle today.[19]

Eight paintings, however, are different: these are of Jamaica and were acquired later. Six of these are general landscapes but two are of the family plantations, Pennants and Denbigh.[20] These were painted in 1870, outside of the period of colonial slavery, and they represent an idealised image of sugar production. Working conditions, even after slavery, were harsh, requiring large numbers of workers in a heavily industrialised process, and not the bucolic idyll portrayed in these images. After the 1730s, few, if any, of the Pennants ever visited Jamaica and so these would have been the only depictions the family saw of their plantations.[21]

In her journal, Edward's daughter Adela describes him as a shy but hard-working man. He represented Caernarvonshire as MP for 25 years, until he was elevated to the peerage in 1866, becoming the second 1st Lord Penrhyn.[22] Edward's son George Sholto Douglas-Pennant, 2nd Lord Penrhyn, was a man of strong conviction. He had little time for the developing trades union movement, and his single-minded approach to the running of his slate quarry led to a devastating and long-lasting strike between 1900-03.[23] Perhaps because of local bitterness towards the family following this, the 3rd Lord Penrhyn, Edward Sholto Douglas-Pennant (1864-1927) spent little time at Penrhyn. The castle was not left empty, however, as several of his twelve sisters continued to consider it their home.[24]

Hugh Napier (1894-1949) became 4th Lord Penrhyn on his father's death, his older brother Alan having lost his life in the trenches of the Great War.[25] He served as a magistrate and was a keen breeder of Welsh black cattle. Like so many landed estates between the 1920s and 50s, Penrhyn fell into decline; Hugh Napier sold the last of the family's Jamaican plantations, and, on his death, he left his remaining estate to his favourite niece, Lady Janet Pelham, who adopted the surname Douglas Pennant (without the hyphen).[26] In lieu of enormous death duties, Lady Janet handed Penrhyn Castle, along with around 45,000 acres (18,200 ha) of Snowdonia, to the National Trust, which continues to care for the property.[27]

The Pennants and slavery

The Pennants were committed slave-owners, and Richard Pennant, especially, was a powerful figure in the pro-slavery movement. He was chairman of the Committee of West India Merchants, an influential lobbying group for those with commercial interests in the Caribbean.[28] Richard used his position as MP of Liverpool to speak against abolition, arguing that by ending the trade, Britain would destroy a valuable training ground for young seamen. He firmly denied that the transportation of enslaved Africans across the Atlantic was cruel.[29]

In his letters, Richard urged his agents to treat his enslaved labour force well. The reports he received back, however, show clearly that his workers experienced the same high death and illness rates as others in Jamaica; and despite this evidence arriving regularly at his desk, he took no practical action to improve conditions for his workers.[30]

The British slave trade (the purchase of enslaved Africans and their transportation and sale across the Atlantic) was abolished in 1807, the year before Richard Pennant's death. Slavery itself (the use of a coerced, unfree labour force) became illegal in British colonies during George Hay Dawkins Pennant's lifetime.[31] The profitability of the West Indies sugar industry fell sharply at the end of slavery.[32] By this time, however, the Pennants had already invested much of their Jamaican fortune into the development of Penrhyn slate quarry, which soon provided them with even greater prosperity.

The Pennants owned enslaved people from when they first became planters at the end of the seventeenth century through to the abolition of slavery in the 1830s. As one of their agents observes: 'nothing can be done without negroes'.[33] At the height of their productivity, the Pennants owned around one thousand Africans, but they began selling both people and estates by the 1820s. They sold their last estate, Pennants, which was also their first, in 1940, and Penrhyn Quarry was sold to Alfred McAlpine in 1963.[34]

The Pennant legacy

The Pennants had been enjoying profits from their Jamaican estates for over 100 years before they invested in North Wales. When Richard Pennant, 1st Lord Penrhyn, took ownership of Penrhyn estate, he became one of the largest landowners in Wales. Richard's heirs added further to their holdings, purchasing land in the Conwy valley and in Northamptonshire, along with a prestigious house in London. Penrhyn Street in Liverpool is named after Richard, who was a former MP of what was then Britain's principal slaving port.

At their height, the Pennants owned around 70,000 acres of land (28,300 ha), of which around 45,000 (18,200 ha) were in Caernarfonshire (now part of the county of Gwynedd). Their Caernarfonshire estate included nearly 700 tenanted farms and just under 900 workers' houses.[35]

The Pennants invested widely in developing Penrhyn estate, building roads, hotels, schools, villages, and churches. They were major employers in the area, providing jobs for local people as estate workers, tradesmen, foresters, and gamekeepers. The castle alone employed around 50 domestic staff, 10 stable boys and 50 gardeners. Thousands more were employed at the family's industrial sites of Penrhyn slate quarry and Port Penrhyn.[36]

After Richard Pennant developed Penrhyn slate quarry from the 1780s, it quickly grew into a massive enterprise, supplying slates that roofed the growing towns of industrial Britain and prestigious buildings around the globe. The quarry employed just under 3,000 men at its height at the end of the nineteenth century.

Port Penrhyn is located on the Menai Strait at the mouth of the river Cegin. It is a mile from the castle and six miles from Penrhyn quarry. Slates were originally transported to the port by horse and cart. From 1801, horse-drawn wagons were used on an iron narrow gauge railway. Steam engines were brought in for a new narrow-gauge line during the 1870s. The port was an active site, supporting several enterprises, including administrative offices, a foundry, a number of lime kilns and a writing slate factory.

The family's wealth, initially from sugar and latterly from slate, enabled the Pennants to rise to the highest level of British society and to become significant landowners. Penrhyn Castle, a quintessentially British and extremely prominent country house on the north Wales coast, stood at the centre of a large, well-established international operation founded on Atlantic slavery.

Endnotes:

1. Jean Lindsay, 'The Pennants and Jamaica 1665-1808', Caernarvonshire Historical Society Transactions, vol 43, 1982, p. 43. (article, pp 37-82).
2. Edward B Rugemer, *Slave Law and the Politics of Resistance in the Early Atlantic World.* (Cambridge MA: Harvard University Press, 2018) , p. 35-36.
3. Barry W. Higman, *Plantation Jamaica 1750-1850: Capital and Control in a Colonial Economy.* (Kingston: University of West Indies Press, 2008), pp. 17-18.
4. Higman, p. 27-28.
5. Edmond H. Douglas Pennant, *The Pennants of Penrhyn: A Genealogical History of the Pennant Family of Clarendon, Jamaica, and Penrhyn Castle* (Bethesda: Gwasg Ffrancon, 1982), p. 17.
6. David Gwyn, *Welsh Slate: Archaeology and History of an Industry* (Aberystwyth: RCAHMW, 2015), p. 31.
7. Tim Mowl, 'Penrhyn and the Norman Revival', *Penrhyn Castle* (London: National Trust, 1991), p. 89-90.
8. Lindsay, vol 43, pp. 41-43.
9. Douglas Pennant, pp. 13 and 17.
10. Douglas Pennant, p. 17.
11. *Penrhyn Castle* (London: National Trust, 1991), p. 11.
12. John Martin Robinson, *The Wyatts: An Architectural Dynasty.* (Oxford: OUP, 1979), p. 137.
13. M. Gwyn, monograph in preparation.
14. David Gwyn, p. 250.
15. M. Gwyn, monograph in preparation.
16. *Penrhyn Castle*, pp. 19-28.
17. Centre for the Study of the Legacies of British Slavery. UCL, https://www.ucl.ac.uk/lbs/person/view/22227, accessed 12/12/21.

18. *Penrhyn Castle*, p. 31.
19. *Penrhyn Castle*, pp. 36-40.
20. Since this article was written, these two paintings have been replaced with copies. The original art works are now in the possession of the Pennant family.
21. M. Gwyn, monograph in preparation.
22. Two first lords.
23. Merfyn R. Jones, *The North Wales Quarrymen 1874-1922* (Cardiff: University of Wales Press, 1982), pp. 210-266.
24. *Penrhyn Castle*, p. 33.
25. *Penrhyn Castle*, p. 33.
26. Douglas Pennant, pp. 33-34.
27. *Penrhyn Castle*, p. 88.
28. The History of Parliament Online. https://www.history ofparliament on-line.org/volume/1754-1790/member/pennant-richard-1736-1808. Accessed 14/12/21.
29. James W. LoGefro, 'Sir William Dolben and the Cause of Humanity: The Passage of the Slave Trade Regulation Act of 1788', *Eighteenth-Century Studies*. Summer 1973, vol. 6, no. 4, p. 439 (pp. 431-451).
30. David Ewart, Returns for King's Valley estate, Jamaica, 1 January 1807. Bangor University archive, MS Penrhyn 1455.
31. Marika Sherwood, *After Abolition: Britain and the Slave Trade Since 1807* (London: IB Tauris, 2007), p. 1.
32. Selwyn H.H. Carrington,. *The Sugar Industry and the Abolition of the Slave Trade, 1775-1810*. (Gainesville, Fl: University of Florida Press, 2002), p. 37.
33. Lindsay, Part 1, p. 56.
34. M. Gwyn, monograph in production.
35. *Penrhyn Castle*, pp. 83-85.
36. David Gwyn, p. 225.

SUDBURY HALL

AND OTHER HOUSES

The Hon. Anne Howard, Lady Yonge (d.1775) by John Vanderbank the
younger (London 1694 - London 1739)
© National Trust / Robert Thrift

The Belton Conversation Piece by Philippe Mercier (Berlin 1689 ¿
London 1760)
©National Trust Images/John Hammond

SENI SENEVIRATNE

ALL THE CAPTIVE CHILDREN

"…judging by the large number of portraits in which they appear, many of the black pages could not have been more than nine or ten years old."
— Peter Fryer, *Staying Power*, p. 72

Many portraits of aristocrats in the 17th and 18th century include a black child. It was the 'fashion' at the time to have enslaved black children as servants. In effect, this meant that children were bought, sold, renamed and moved from house to house without any regard for their feelings. These 'trafficked' children were included in portraits as representations of the aristocrat's wealth and status and rarely recognised as sitters in their own right. The tendency to marginalise them has largely persisted to this day, as evidenced most clearly by the fact that portrait titles rarely acknowledge their presence.

TEN WAYS OF LOOKING AT A PAINTING

The Hon. Anne Howard, Lady Yonge
(John Vanderbank, 1737)
Sudbury Hall

It hangs above the fireplace
where there used to be a mirror

a white young woman
dressed in black with a feathered hat

a black child of nine or ten
dressed in red with a silver collar

the woman holds a black veil
and an ostrich feather fan

the child is holding the hem
of the woman's dress

the woman is centre-stage
gazing at the spectator

the child stands behind
looking at the woman

the woman has a name
a title and a family tree

the child has lost his name
his family and his freedom

light shining from the window
makes the child barely visible.

ALL THE CAPTIVE CHILDREN

If I'd been 'handcuffed to history' like Rushdie's
midnight's children, instead of shackled to slavery,
if I'd inherited Saleem's gift and could summon
all the captive children, I would gather them here
in the drawing room of Sudbury Hall. Each of us,
hunted down by traders, transported by slave ships,
stripped of our family trees, has been immortalised
in oils, and hung unnamed in numerous stately halls.

I'd ask the boys at Petworth if they feel resentful
of the animals they pose with, since the Seymour's
grant a higher status in their household to the dog
and horse than those who groom and care for them.
The girl at Belton House might disagree and tell us
how it comforts her to hold a lapdog on her knee
while the boy at Sprivers with a silver tray of fruit
complains about its weight in his aching arms.

I'd want the boy from Claydon House (a souvenir
from Guinea, courtesy of the Royal African Company)
to let us know the name he had, before he was abducted
and named Peregrine by an uncle of Lord Verney.
This might move the boy from Saltram House
to tell us how the Admiral he stands beside, is the man
who seized him, took his name, brought him as a trophy
on his ship, dressed him up and named him Jersey,

Each one of us would have the chance to speak
and listen: the barely visible page at Oxburgh Hall,
and the lost boy at Trerice House who are both
shadows of themselves; the child servant at Upton;
the boy with the Duke of Devonshire at Hardwick Hall;
two from Ham House in white silk and pearl earrings;
and the unnamed page at Seaton Delavel whose job
is to hold the arrows for the family's only son and heir.

I'd sit beside the boy from Montacute and discover
how the painter Vanderbank dressed us both in red,
made us hold the hem of a gown for hours, our necks
aching as we followed orders to gaze up at its wearer.

And I'd let the groom at Charlecote know how much
I envy the consolation of a horse nuzzling his head
and soothing the rising panic, as he strains like me
to breathe and swallow inside his metal collar.

IN WHICH THE CAPTIVE CHILDREN
BEGIN TO SPEAK

The Hon. Anne Howard, Lady Yonge
(John Vanderbank, 1737)
Sudbury Hall

When they brought me here, the strange noises
that passed between them were like stones falling
on my head, until I learned to look for meanings.

My name is the one they use for the flimsy things
inside a binding they call leather. They say book
and their eyes look down on marks called words.

I match the sounds they make to things I see
and read their moods in the foreign language
of their faces. But I won't let my tongue curl

and speak them out. Silence is my hiding place.
I have the lock and key. I'll not open the door.
Some pages may offer words. This one is silent.

★

They place me at the edge of the portrait
like an afterthought, an aside, half-hidden
by the hem of a dress, which I must hold

at a particular height so the folds will catch
the light from the window. My neck aches
and the weight of her gown drags at my arms.

She has a boy of her own, I saw him running
past the shaped hedges down to the lake.
I am landlocked, padlocked in a silver collar

while in my head stories of home run amok
as if to taunt me: my mother's hand touching
my forehead, my bare feet pounding the earth.

John Delaval (1756-1775) as an Archer, with a Page by William Bell
(Newcastle-upon-Tyne 1740 - Newcastle-upon-Tyne 1794)
©National Trust Images

Sir Thomas Lucy
(Godfrey Kneller, 1680)
Charlecote Park

Painted a darker shade than the horse I groom,
you might not see me standing in the right hand
corner of this work of art, were it not for the way

the artist has captured the light that is falling on
this silver collar squeezing my neck. Look for
the white in the horse's eye then follow its gaze

until you see the glint of metal that's fastened
so tight that it hurts each time I try to swallow.
Raise your eyes and you'll see the face of a boy

without a name, painted to be barely visible.
I am the groom. They call me blackamoor.
The horse nuzzles my head, her breath is warm.

John Delavel as an Archer, with a Black Page
(William Bell, 1770)
Seaton Delavel Hall

They say I belong to this boy of fourteen
younger than me and smaller, he calls himself
my master. You see that ornate bow he holds,

it's nothing but a prop. Those weak arms of his
have never readied an arrow to shoot, never felt
the force of a pulled bowstring, the heat of a kill.

My arms are strong enough to hold the weight
of these silver-tipped arrows. They are restless
like me, to be let loose and fly, to escape from

this towering baroque castle, and this boy
who thinks he owns me. This boy who looks,
for all his wealth, as if he won't reach twenty.

Mary Elizabeth Davenport with her page
(John Vanderbank, c1730)
Montacute House

Draw a line from the ochre urn on its plinth
down the curve of grey satin tied in the hair
of this pale woman, to where my eyes stare

at the blue velvet of her sleeve, the white lace
of her cuff. These strange buckled shoes pinch
my toes and the red stockings make my legs itch.

I want to scratch but my fingers must hold still
and echo the shape of hers, though they ache
with the weight of her dress. I matter less to her

than the feather in her right hand. The artist
cares only for the powders he mixes with oil
to make the colours he daubs on the canvas.

Mary Lawley, 2ⁿᵈ wife of Sir John Verney
(Lenthall, c1694-1702)
Claydon House

There's fire in my belly, its heat prickles my skin.
Behind this smile they've painted on my face
rising bile makes me retch. I try to swallow

and the metal collar tightens. They gave me a name
which sits on my tongue like dust, no more mine than
this silk draped on my shoulder to catch the angle

of light, the way it catches the folds on her dress.
The captain who bought me for two yards of cloth
threw my own name overboard then stowed me

in his cabin as a souvenir with the rest of his cargo.
Hungry for the taste of fufu, I laid awake each night
listening to men and women wailing below decks.

Belton Conversation Piece
(Philip Mercier c 1726)
Belton House

The day they brought me here, a white powder
was falling from the sky. It landed on my hands
and face, then disappeared and left a chill.

I know their changing seasons now, the way
I've come to know my place. With less status
than the dog on her lap, I push the wheelchair

of the Viscount's invalid wife, dressed in brown
and gold to mirror her gown. She is heavy and
I'm hungry for comfort but no-one speaks to me.

Why look at the clouds? I'm a boy without wings,
no more than a shadow in their grand house
full of cold corridors and even colder hearts.

Mary Helden with her black page
(Charles Phillips, 1739)
Sprivers

The peach on this silver tray smells ripe enough to eat.
I think its juice might quench my thirst. I lean forward
on my right leg as if I'm about to walk out of this picture,

as if I could rip off these strange clothes, run to the fields
and eat until I'm full. The painter snaps orders at me:
as he strokes the dog, 'Hold still, you're dreaming again,

lift the tray higher, turn your head, let your gaze rest
on her pink cheeks.' I stare past her to the red curtain
that is like a cloud of fire. I can dream in the day but

at night, knees pulled up to my chest, I wrap myself
around my empty feelings. I crave touch but no-one
ever lays a hand on me: not in anger or with kindness.

THE OUTRAGEOUS NEGLECT OF AFRICAN FIGURES IN ART HISTORY

PATERSON JOSEPH

This article was first written for Art UK by Paterson Joseph in 2019. In the essay he considers the figure of the Black sitter in British paintings, many of which appear in British country houses. He also discusses the neglect of these figures by art historians over many decades.

If art is part-representation, then portraiture is representation writ large.

Many nations tell their origin stories in these forms, from cave paintings of animals and hunting scenes, to skilfully wrought depictions of momentous battles and the personalities that shaped the national destiny.

In the case of European art, there's a vital colour that's missing from many of these depictions of our national stories. An example from the UK is the outrageous neglect in the identification of the ordinary African-Britons who have been an integral part of this nation's history since Roman Britain days.

It is an act of snow-blindness that continues to this day. This month, the Royal Albert Memorial Museum (RAMM) have kindly ceded to my request, made through Art UK, to re-examine former curator John Madin's suggestion that Allan Ramsay's *Portrait of An African* no longer be bracketed with 'probably Ignatius Sancho'.

Having lived with Charles Ignatius Sancho's story for the last 20 years (and authoring the play *Sancho: An Act of Remembrance),* my outrage on seeing this attribution in the August 2006 edition of *Apollo* magazine being treated as factual, was fierce. My rage was defused somewhat by Art UK's swift response and promise that the bracketed comments, an opinion, would be removed from the portrait on their website, and the collection informed.

But this has thrown up yet more questions for me, in many ways.

Why, for example, do we have hundreds of portraits from the sixteenth century onwards that depict European subjects who are named fully – as well at times as their pet dog or horse – and the black child next to them in these portraits, merely called 'A Negro' or 'and Servant'?

If this is not racism and an objectifying, dehumanising of an entire ethnicity, I cannot define it at all. I call on the international art community to cease this practice of lazily continuing to objectify children who were not named – for painfully obvious reasons – in the past.

I urge them to make every effort to properly conduct investigations to identify and name these people, at the very least acknowledging their ignorance and willingness to discover their identities. Thus, in some small way, affording them a little dignity in their obscured lives and deaths. If they do not do this, they perpetuate the idea that black people may have contributed to the riches of Europe and America but are in no way worthy of being acknowledged as the human beings they were.

Here, African-Britons have largely been whitewashed from the record of British art history, simply because those charged with recording this history were not minded to include them, with notable exceptions.

Sancho's remarkable story, that he was the first published African-Briton; worked around the Georgian court; became the first black man to receive an obituary in the press; participated in a parliamentary election in 1774 and then, finally, the parliamentary election of 1780 – becoming the first, known, African-British voter to do so – makes him an exciting subject in any age.

Sancho's correspondence with the writer Laurence Sterne was held up as an example to the burgeoning anti-slavery movement of the potential for articulate protest from educated African-Britons. This coverage of a black, British hero makes Charles Ignatius Sancho an exception in history.

However, as we know, exceptions do not make history alone. Wherever I meet art historians, invariably white, handling the long eighteenth century they – near-universally – ignore the less 'notable' black people who were very present in that century and beyond. Why is this?

Racism is not the easy answer, though it clearly plays its part. The main issue is one of interest. If one is not taught that a people matter, then it is left up to that individual to discover this themselves. A rather ad hoc approach to any study in my opinion and subject to falling into negatively-biased ethnic thinking. 'They' are not us; 'they' are not important to 'our' story; 'they' do not matter.

As Hammad Nasar noted in his excellent Art UK article *The bureaucracy of artistic Britishness*: 'As we steel ourselves to navigate a new path through our global relationships in a post-Brexit Britain, it may be worth our while to invest in recognising our expansive histories, and addressing the paucity of cultural stories and collections that allow us to fully imagine an idea of Britain that is capacious enough to embrace all who think of it as home.'

The pitfall of snow-blindness, clearly, lies in our teaching of art history too. If our scholars are being given a skewed, mono-chromed vision/

version of the European art story and, in my opinion, therefore, of European history, then, perhaps inevitably, they are subsequently – from their university days – loudly and confidently in danger of rehashing the same snow-blind view that their own teachers grew up with; forming a vicious, if unintentional, very definitely racially-biased circle.

Black people in portraits of the great and the good do not matter, because they are 'nobodies'. This Euro-biased view of the nation's pictorial story is so prevalent, that it becomes embarrassingly clear that racism is institutionalised in our most prestigious art establishments. How else can this snow-blindness be explained?

I hope that incidences like the recent outrage over the lazy misidentification of Ignatius Sancho will be less prevalent in the future and, more importantly, that these young subjects in European portraiture will become an urgent study of identification by the new generation of art historians.

BASILDON PARK

Victorian Copper Beech in front of the house at Basildon Park, Berkshire
©National Trust Images/James Dobson

JACQUELINE CROOKS

DREAMS ON MY SKIN

The two stories are together because this is a story about the trade routes of empire and how they connected different people and how the artefacts of Basildon Park House connect people across time.

I was drawn to the Sykes' family story of the Indian princess and wanted to imagine who she might have been. I was also fascinated by the slave logging gangs and the trade in mahogany and wanted to draw on this as an alternative to stories of trades we know more about, such as sugar, tea, coffee. It's also a commodity that connects the idea of beauty and admiration with the price that forgotten people paid to enable that beauty.

It was important to include the voices of children, women, and enslaved people in the historical narrative. In particular, I wanted an Indian character and an African-Caribbean character to have their own stories.

I was inspired by the child-led approach of the Colonial Countryside project and having delivered writing workshops with children from Katesgrove Primary School – many of whom had Indian or Caribbean ancestry – so I embedded the children's rights agenda into the story with children at the heart of the story. I also used some of the themes and beautiful lines that the children wrote in the writing workshops at Basildon Park House within the story to meaningfully have children's voices running through the story, connecting them to the past, their ancestors, and Basildon Park House.

There is a family story that Sir Francis Sykes was assisted in his escape from the English factory at Cossimbazar by an Indian princess on the understanding that he would marry her. When he did not, she cursed him with the words 'From the land you came, to the land you shall return.'

(See John Sykes, *The Indian Seal of Sir Francis Sykes: A Tale of Two Families* (UCL Press, 2018)

The festive dining room at Basildon Park, Berkshire
©National Trust Images/Megan Taylor

DREAMS ON MY SKIN

Basildon Park House, 2019
I float into the dining room of your great house. I am silk-soft air. No flesh. No bone. No skin. You would do well to never doubt my mind – it is as strong as ever it was.

It is a dark winter morning. Through the windows I see clumps of limes, beeches and chestnut trees outside in the grounds, strung tight with vines of golden light. They sway and speak of you.

There are school children in the dining room, examining golden griffins, looking up at the coved ceiling of acanthus fronds. Their serious whispered voices are tight navel-strings of sound, pulling me back from the depths.

People come to your great house to find out who you were from the things you once owned. The polished surfaces of mirrors, porcelain, carved mahogany doors, the grain patterned like the silks you used to trade. I have come to see who you really were through the eyes of children.

A tall, slim Caribbean boy is looking at himself in the large mirror on the wall by the door. His African hair is the crown of a tree, the light brown irises of his eyes patterned like the grain of mahogany. The edges of the mirror darken with shadows of the dead. Perhaps he sees this too, because he looks away, walks to the other side of the room, looks out of the open window.

Lamplight glows in this room like our long-ago nights by the river in Cossimbazar, India, when the temples on the riverbank burnished the river gold as it drifted into the Bay of Bengal.

You shut me out of your life two hundred and fifty-eight years ago when you were the Governor of Trade at Cossimbazar. I was the daughter of a Zamindar, landowner – some people called me a princess though we had no royal blood.

I wanted to live in your world. You wanted to live in mine. We ended up not living in the real world.

At last, I am here, inside your great house, on your land.

An Indian girl is standing behind the boundary rope that circles the dining table. She is staring at your chinaware. She is thirteen or four-teen and looks very much like me when I was that age. Hair falling down her back like black silk, fine hairs on her forehead like the trichomes on leaves. She is wearing a pink jacket that seems to be padded with clouds.

I float around her. She smells of damp earth, rain, leaves. I move closer and she pulls her jacket around her and steps over the boundary rope. She traces her finger along the edge of a side-plate. She is looking at my image on the crest of your china where I stand holding out a rose to you.

You loved the rosewater I made for you from my family's rose garden. I scented your pillows and sheets with it so you would dream of me.

Death is better than a flower, the Buddhists say. I know this is true be-cause my dying moments are still unfolding, in cloud forests, beneath the Kala Pani – the black sea.

You must have loved me to put my image at the head of your family crest, on your porcelain. Impossible to be certain with a man like you. I would have preferred to have lived as your wife in this great house.

The Caribbean boy is standing next to the girl who shows him the plate.

'Wonder who she is?' she says. 'I'll ask Mr Vizard or one of the guides.'

'Whoah!' the boy says. 'Woman looks like you.'

'Seriously?'

'The way she's looking, that's you when you seriously want something.'

The girl rolls her eyes, pushes him playfully.

I want to tell them that I am not a ghost. I am a reflection. Floating translucency.

The girl places her palm in the centre of the plate like a doctor feeling for a heartbeat. 'It's like touching water,' she says to the boy. Her voice is nasal, singsong confident, like mine.

'That won't bring her back to life,' the boy says.

'Isn't that why we're here?' the girl says. 'To put life into stale history.'

'Yeah, but we're not ghost hunters!' the boy says. 'We're supposed to find something we connect to.'

'I want something beautiful,' the girl says.

Your great house *is* beautiful but I am not interested in an architec-ture of reverie. Everything is designed in your image: light, dark , secre-tive. From the recessed portico, hidden valley, to the cardamom-green river flowing behind the trees. Remember how we would watch from the shaded balconies of the factory in Cossimbazar as the ships came into port? The air heavy with moisture and heat. Your small boats loaded with goods, their prows carved with mythical creatures.

The Caribbean boy tries to open a drawer in a mahogany side-table, but it is locked.

© National Trust / Christopher
Warleigh-Lack

'What do you think might be inside?' the girl asks.

'Sykes' secrets,' the boy says. 'Maybe a seal, an old map.'

I never found what I was looking for among your papers. You were angry when you discovered that I had been searching through your cabinets, looking at your contracts and seals. I needed to know your dark trails, so I could follow you across the sea, out into the world.

It is raining outside. Monsoon-black clouds are moving closer to the house; tree-root shadows grow and spread in the corners of the room. Some of the children leave to wander around your rooms of bamboo furniture and shells, rooms where the sounds of a dark, distant sea spill from the cracks.

I settle on the mahogany door and feel waves of silver-sleek bodies beneath the shine – others, like me, in the depths.

Two teachers – an Indian woman in a green-gold sari and an English man in a grey, woollen suit – come into the dining room and call the children to lunch downstairs. The man wears gold-rimmed glasses; he squints at his reflection in the darkening mirror.

'Think about what you can't see', he says to the children as they go out.

'Mr Vizard, can we stay and make notes for our stories?' the girl asks.

The teacher agrees.

It is just the three of us in your dining room: the girl, the boy, me. The boy and girl go back to the dining table and step over the boundary rope. There are five chairs on either side of the table and a chair at each end. The girl sits on a chair at the head of the table close to the window, the boy sits at the other end, near the door. She picks up a dinner plate, puts her index finger under my face. Her fingernail is like one of your small diamonds wedged into flesh.

'Maybe I was her in another life,' she says.

'This house is really getting to you, isn't it.' He laughs.

'The walls of old houses have ears and scars,' she says.

I wish I could show the children the scars that were once on my skin. Marks of remembering.

You always wanted to talk about gems, land, battles, taxes, your routes of spreading influence. I see you now, an imprint from long ago, sitting at the head of the table. White-powdered politicians, lords and ladies on either side of it. They smell of wine, orange flower, musk, and amber perfume. You, dressed as a maharaja in purple silk. Indigo eyes, silver hair.

That proud detached way you look at everyone as you tell them about your shipment of mahogany.

'The rotten smell of the wood is still under my nose,' you say.

They laugh.

'The stench of that wood could kill a man, and it probably did.'

They laugh again.

One of the men says you should stick to gold.

'Mahogany is danger and beauty,' you say.

Your guests raise their crystal glasses. 'To Sir Francis Sykes,' they say.

You raise your glass. 'To mahogany,' you say.

The eyes of our guests are bright. They are excited by the idea of intrigues, conspiracies, conflicts and love triangles.

In India, you and I were caught in triangles: the triangle of rivers around the delta of Cossimbazar; the triangular route of your trade across the Atlantic that kept you away from me; the love triangle of you, me, your banian – your secret-keeper. He was your interpreter, bookkeeper, secretary, tending your life like a rose garden. I can smell the rosewater I used to make for you. It takes me back to that long-ago day in Cossimbazar, the day after I put a curse on you. The week before you left India for England where you built this great house of yours. The month after I broke the rules of my people and followed you across the Kala Pani, the forbidden black sea.

*

Cossimbazaar, India, June 1761

Monsoon season is coming to an end. It is a hot day, but the marble house is cool. From the arched window of my room on the third floor, I smell the pungent mud and stagnant water of the Ganges flowing eastwards from the rocky western side of the delta, the timeless current dragging me into the darkness of the sea.

I watch the mahogany ship being loaded with barrels of your saltpetre, cotton, silk. You and your banian must be watching this somewhere near the trade factory, or from among the crowds of merchants, silkworm rearers, cobblers, whispering against the noise of bullock carts and horse-drawn carriages. The dust of saltpetre is on my tongue. Metallic, bitter. It tastes like the pain that is yet to come.

The Bedia woman closes the shutters. 'Everything must be still,' she says. 'Even the air.'

The domed room closes in on me.

'Lie on the floor,' she says. The rosewater scent I have sprinkled is overpowered by the smell of the garlic clove that she is sucking between her teeth. Her gold sari is embroidered with black flowers. Hunched body, small head, gold ring in her broad flat nose. A strange golden bird.

My family had once been poor farmers with two orchards of mango and hogplum trees. Now they trade in silk and live in a palatial house with iron gates, verandas, and rose gardens. Roses are your favourite flower; you say they remind you of your country. I painted the roses for the porcelain you commissioned from China. I decided then to paint roses on my body. Please understand, this was not to please you! I want to change my skin and my destiny as a woman. Mark ownership of my body, wear my dreams on my skin.

I kneel on the floor, naked; watch as the Bedia woman mixes juice from the bhagra plant with the breast milk of a village woman who gave birth to a dead child. 'Be free, take your mind far away,' she says. She unties my long black hair, runs her fingers through it. 'Hair like Kalapani – black sea,' she says. Her voice is hoarse and low.

She pushes me onto the cool marble floor and kneels by my side.

I watch her reflection in the gilt, freestanding mirror. The darkened glass moves with black light. The Bedia woman has come to the palace in secret to tattoo my skin and tell my fortune. But from the moment I saw her standing in the red sandstone doorway I was afraid of what she could see.

She pierces my skin with the rose thorns. The ink flows into my blood, like the sea entering me. I dig my nails into my palms as the pain gets stronger. I feel as if I am being cut in two, different parts me spilling out.

These women are psychics, in tune with earth, trees, birds, sky, sea.

I bat her hand away and sit up. 'Look, too much blood,' I say.

She pushes me back down.

I look into her black eyes. The pain of the thorns going into my skin touches the nerves of my feelings for you, waves of heat that go from heart to head.

Last night you told me you were returning to your land because you were in poor health. You said nothing of your promise that we would be married. I cursed you as I have never cursed before. Now, with the anger and the pain of the thorns inside me, I imagine clawing out your eyes, getting to the network of red roots inside your head, digging deep into your skull to find your thoughts and feelings.

Hours later, the Bedia woman says it is almost done. She chants a mantra to Kali to relieve my pain. I know that now, at dusk, the river will reflect the gold temples, temples that are always empty while the trade factories are full.

I picture the mahogany ship sailing from the port far across the ocean, white sails flapping in cool breezes, curved light reflecting in different directions. My breath is locked tight at the top of my ribs. I feel trapped in the airless room. Acid froths in my throat.

In the mirror, an upwelling of light comes from the depths of reflections and I see an African man. His mouth is open wide in pain. I recognise the pain; it is mine and he is holding it in the back of his throat.

I vomit into the brass bowl by my head where I lie.

'It is almost done.' The 'Bedia woman says. 'Look.'

From my waist to the top of my ribs, my skin is a fabric of bleeding red roses. Identical, stacked in rows like bodies with large heads and bleeding limbs.

'I am burning,' I say.

The Bedia woman sprinkles rosewater on my inflamed skin, then opens the window. 'Pray for the dispossessed,' she says. 'You see them.' She lowers her voice: 'Stay away from the sea.'

I burn with a fever for two weeks, dream myself into the cool of a cloud forest possessed by golden birds. My teeth rattle in my burning mouth. Humming sounds in my head. Impossible to sleep. Impossible to stay awake. I can only fly with the golden birds as death moves inside me, slashing and burning.

I dream the African man. He is sitting in the cloud forest with his back against a tree, sweat on his tattooed face. He is stroking my body with the bark of a tree.

Who are you?

He is pouring a red liquid into my mouth.

Drink, he says.

In the third week my skin bubbles and festers, pus leaks. I am cold-hot-cold, shaking as if possessed. So ill I cannot get out of bed to look through the window. But I know you and the ship have gone.

I dig my fingernails into the scabs that are brown and hard as bark. They leak blood. I feel no more pain. I am still. The African man is leaning against me. I feel his heart.

*

The girl is standing by the window now, writing a poem about me. The boy is stroking the mahogany door. '*This* is it!' he says. 'My connection.' The girl is not listening. He squats, runs his hand up and down the base of the door. His fingers follow the curved lines of light, tracking them back to the point of possession. His irises reflect the swirling grain of the wood.

You were my connection to the world. A man who could take me on journeys of exploration. Yes, you were a man not to be trusted, a man of endless desires, and conceits. You were different with me. I saw the side a woman sees: the vulnerability and fears that shaped you.

'I see patterns like birds, butterflies,' the boy says as he looks into the mahogany door. 'If I keep looking...'

It is raining heavily outside your great house. I feel the sea in my body now, weighing me down. There are heavy juddering sounds of lightning and thunder. I see the African man submerged just below the surface of the mahogany door. For a moment, he and I and the boy are reflected in each other, reflecting the multitudes caught beneath the surface of your possessions. A slipstream just beneath the skin of the wood, flowing deeper into crosscurrents of time, into a fathomless sea. The memory of my last day on earth.

Three months after you left, when my body had healed, I boarded a ship, *The Griffin*, to follow you to England. I was determined you would not shut me out of your life. I knew you would not turn me away.

The ship was loaded with mahogany, turmeric, cowries, saltpetre. 125,000 pieces of chinaware.

I had cursed you to return to the land, but I did not make it to land. There was a storm and the ship was wrecked on the rocks and reefs near one of the small islands close to your country. Sailors, passengers, possessions, sinking towards seabed graves. I did not see the devil in the Kala Pani. I did not see you. The last thing I saw were fragments of bone-white china floating in the depths of the black sea. Bloated black bodies, empty vessels, with the golden light of cloudforests reflected in their glassy eyes.

Jamaica, September 1761
The plantation manager made him a huntsman three years ago because he was the only one of the hundred and eighty-five slaves who could see deep into the green-foaming cloud forest, the only one who could scent mahogany trees the way their mastiffs track runaways.

He is grateful, not for the extra portions of salted mackerel and cod or the cotton clothes, but for the time he is allowed in the cloud forest, scouting alone. He came from a large village with many elders, many brothers and sisters, where everyone lived as one. He resents these people, even himself.

'Tree feels good,' he says. 'Warm.'

He strokes the furrowed bark. It is hurricane season, the air is deathly still, the cloudforest glazed in mist, translucent as the porcelain in the plantation house.

'M'oganwo!' he shouts. Crows fly out of the tree. His voice flies with them, up and beyond the three-tiered green canopy that is many times higher than the decorated ceilings of the Plantation House.

His voice fades. He feels the loneliness in the pit of his stomach.

M'oganwo, king of trees – that is the word in his people's language. People on the island call it mahogany.

He sniffs the bark. A clean, sharp smell of dewy rainforest leaves, limestone. Blood.

He is dizzy from running. He looks up, but the crows have not returned to the tree. There are golden birds hanging upside down from the canopy, like lanterns on a ship at sea.

This is the first time that he and the logging gang have come this far east, far from the plantation, the plantation house, the sea. He is glad to be away from the sea. The memories of interlocking, sweating, rolling bodies. He can no longer bear to be touched. Does not want even the intimacy of talk. He likes the ways of the mahogany trees, their dark, silent self-possession.

He came to these forests with the logging gang a month ago. It took them four weeks to cut their way up the mountains with machetes, axes, and fire. Three white overseers, one sailor, a convict, ten slaves. Apollo and Jein lead oxen loaded with ropes, axes, hoes, and saws. Clendin, Sharper, Nelson and Montague carry provisions of gunger cake, cowpeas, chickens and palm wine. They are far from the coastal woodlands of Buttonwood and Sea Grape.

Most of the time it felt like they were battling against the sea, the dark ferns clotting the forest floor like seaweed; the stinging spray of mosquitoes; the outcrops of white rock; the green wave of bush that seemed to repel them, no matter how fast they chopped against it with sharpened machetes.

He left the camp and the logging gang eight days ago to scout for mahogany.

'How long?' Jacks, the overseer asked as he packed a crocus bag of dried beans and crackers.

He sniffed the air. 'Five days fe go; four fe come back'.

He clawed the insect bites on his neck, scraped off scab and skin with his nails. 'This forest is a b*itch,* Jacks said. 'Scratching the hell outta me.' Jacks is the one who will cross-cut the trees and mark them with the initials of the plantation owner.

'Take Sharper with you,' Jacks said.

Me hunt alone, he said.

Jacks looked to the sky, squinted. Turned his back on him. *'Don't let the forest catch ya.'*

He should have returned to the camp of wooden huts days ago to tell Jacks about this great forest of mahogany he has found. The mood in the camp will be tense now, with nothing to do but sleep through the humid days with white mist weaving between them, closing in tighter and tighter. And the long nights with nothing to do but look at each other across the flickering camp fire with black insects snapping and clicking and stinging.

He is the hunter. He is also the hunted.

The rainy season is a few months away. If they don't get the mahogany out of the rainforest soon they will all drown in mud.

The wind is blowing hard now. The bush is moving. Insects crawling on his skin, biting, sucking his blood. 'Drink,' he tells them. He hears the call of a solitaire, like a flute his father used to play.

He slides to the ground, leans against the tree. The dense branches create a cool dome, like the plantation house. He puts his feet up on a fallen log covered in green velvet moss; feels the blood rush to his head. He will stay here through the night. Whatever is hunting him will soon come.

Tinctures of dark green light seep from the canopy onto his face and he traces his thick fingers across the scarred flesh on his forehead with one hand, feels the patterns of tree bark with the other. 'Mother, father.'

He is a medium between flesh and wood, a medium between the living, the dead and the sea. Images that break through angles of incidence, reflection, and possession.

The managers of the plantation will never come this far into the forest. They are afraid of large bodies of mahogany trees. Yet they do not believe the trees to be living things, that they breathe, have their own markings like the tattoo on his forehead and cheeks.

He remembers the day his face was marked by the artist of his people with sharpened stones and plant juices from the forest. He was six. Surrounded by a sea of dark, shining, smiling faces. Drums, flutes. Dancing.

Marks of belonging and freedom.

Who and what does he belong to now?

He can smell the distant smoke of the logging camp even though he has put sixty, maybe seventy, miles of bush between them, running hard each night, resting in the cool of day beneath great flapping leaves that are like flags marking territory.

He can smell the musk of the men. Their armpits, necks, knees. A salty stench like the sea.

The first time he died he was at sea, lying on his side, tree-root still. Chains at his ankles and wrists. Nails, screws, bolts, iron fittings. The moaning mahogany ship floating through ghost waters. His face turned to the deck, tracking the route by the sickening movements of the ship, the changing tones of wind and sea.

'M'oganwo.'

He died on a ship that sailed from Keta on the Gulf of Guinea, a ship that sailed across the Atlantic to Jamaica.

The white foaming sea is still inside his gut, bloating his stomach so it is impossible to eat the wild hogs that the men in the logging gang roast at night until the skins are black, charred and burning.

'Cook it real good,' Jacks always says to whoever is cooking. 'Dark and crisp, burn it if you have to.'

He will die here. Memories of his lost home seeping from his body like sap onto the sea-dark forest floor.

Any number of things could kill him: snake bite, insect sting, lightning. The thing that is hunting him. He takes his calico shirt off, rubs his shoulder against the bark, moans.

'Hush, hush.' He strokes the tree.

He found these trees three days ago. Around ten thousand feet of mahogany, The size of his village, he thinks. Like his mother, father, grandmother, his people lined up, dark bodies tall, erect, silent, watching him. Waiting for him.

One week on his own, living off wild yams which he roasts in a pit of ashes with the cerasee, pimento, and sarsaparilla that he took from the camp. *This* sweets him.

He unhooks the axe from his leather belt and slides his thumb against the sharpened edge. Slices the skin and leaves a thin trail of blood on his purple-dark skin.

He is the hunter. He is also the hunted. He does not know what is hunting him.

If he brings the logging gang, they will cut this family of *M'oganwo*. They will chain and drag the carcasses thirty miles to the black river. Float them upriver to the sea of sharks and coral reefs and the waiting ships that are loaded with sugar and rum.

He wonders who will carve the mahogany wood into doors with designs of tendrils and blossoms like the vine and flowers that hang from the cloud forest, deep sweeping designs that will bring movement and a strange life back to the dead trees.

He leans his head against the tree. Woman heat. He feels the body of a woman, hot with fever. He is not sure at first whether it is the fever in his own head. But then he sees the strange women sinking into the sea. There are roses painted on her body; her black hair floating behind her turns to ink, darkening the sea. He reaches out to her, but she sinks into the depths of his mind.

He has not held a woman since they brought him to Jamaica. There is no point. The muscles in his body are like rope that is tied. Tied like the crisscrossing routes of ships that bring his people one way from Africa across the Atlantic to Jamaica and another way across the Atlantic with the carcasses of the *M'oganwo*, sailing for England.

Sharper had showed him the routes the day before he left camp. He had made deep marks in the cleared earth with the tip of his machete, showing him where the mahogany went.

'Houses on the other side of the sea, big as the plantation house,' Sharper said.

He strips bark from the tree, boils it until the water turns red. He drinks the blood of the tree. It lights him up from inside.

Tonight, he will become the tree. He will wait for the thing that hunts him. He feels prickles of heat under his skin and his chest floods with acid.

The dark waxy leaves drip the last of the light. There is no breeze now. The orchids, creepers and fungi are still, colourless. Chains of mist circle the trees.

He feels stunted, gnarled and twisted.

He may be asleep, awake, dreaming. He is in the underwater darkness of the hold of the ship. The flooding stench of vomit, shit, tar, rusting iron. His skin warping, cracking in the salty air.

Ghost-grey threads of mist. He cannot move. The thing that hunts him is coming.

His mind is as tangled as the crisscrossing vines that hang from the canopy. The strange golden birds swoop and fly at him.

He hears the solitaire. Or is it the flute of his father. Someone has died. Is it him? Are his family playing the flute for him?

'M'oganwo!' he shouts because no other words from his language will come. Not even the words for Mother, Father, Brother, Sister.

It starts to rain. Cool on his body, like sea spray. The white foam inside him rolls. He feels the heat under his skin spreading; routes of heat branching out across skin, nerves, bone.

The last time he died he was chained again, lying on his front in the small hut. He did not feel the hot iron when it was pressed into his skin. He smelled roses, then iron, then salt and skin. His skin is burned with the monogram of the plantation owner. The triangular bone on the top of his shoulder. He feels the sea inside him, a tidal wave. He is drowning from inside.

He is in the rainforest and the thing that has been hunting him has caught him. A monster wave of sickness and fear thrashing against his ribcage.

He cannot die again.

He gets up, jumps three times into the air, calling out each time, his machete crossed in front of his body. There are no drummers to call his gods but he sounds this in his head. Quick stepping movements, his torso rigid, holding in his mind the thing that hunts him.

He must let it out. He must let it out.

He vomits blood. His blood. The blood of the tree. Froth, bubbling. The Atlantic Sea.

He drops to his knees and holds onto the base of the tree, imagines it to be the feet of his father. He vomits bile until his body feels light, as if there is no more fluid inside him, no bones, no flesh.

He is floating above the cloud forest, seeing himself two days from now, naked, following the vibrations of trees and subterranean water, going deeper into the forest, finding his way into the star-shaped valleys of runaways, an area of bottomless sinkholes. The air a colourful fabric of giant swallowtail butterflies. He will live with Maroons in a settlement they call Mahogany Hall, built around the roots of an old mahogany tree.

He sees himself six months from now with a rebel woman of the Sereer people who once lived in the forests that ran from the Cees escarpment right down to the Cap de Naze on the Atlantic coast. She will tell him that her people do not believe in gods or kings, only in the forest as the divine way.

He sees their son ten years, twenty years, from now. Tall, lean, V-shaped torso, spinning eyes, bush hair spiky as tillandsia.

He sees the last moments of his life in the eyes of his great-great-great-great grandson who, two hundred and sixty-six years from now, is standing in a great house looking into the reflection of a mahogany door, seeing himself as cloud forest memory.

M'oganwo

Anchored to woodland
and forest-bed
I saw myself felled
my limbs ship-shaped
for water's swell
my arms un-draped
no glimmer of squirrel
my tarred veins sea-ready
The tide is calling out my name.

– John Agard

BASILDON PARK:
RE-IMAGINING A SHARED HERITAGE IN AN
HISTORIC HOUSE IN THE 21ST CENTURY

RAJ PAL

Basildon Park was built between 1776-83 for Sir Francis Sykes (1732-1804), a returning East India Company *nabob*. A pejorative term, *nabob* was an English corruption of the Indian title *nawab* during the later Mughal rulers, and it expressed English public contempt for Company returnees. At the time, the *Town and Country Magazine* defined a *nabob* as someone who had 'by art, fraud, cruelty, and imposition, obtained the fortune of an Asiatic prince and returned to England to display his folly and vanity and ambition.'[1] Buying a British country estate was a way of gaining respectability for *nabobs*, for this group of people who were widely derided for the manner in which they had acquired their Indian wealth as well as for the alleged corruption they had introduced into British politics by acquiring Parliamentary influence, commonly by becoming MPs. The East India Company system, a mixture of trade and conquest, enabled young men to travel to India, often as teenagers. Upon their return, these men upset the established social order, spending their Indian wealth and adopting opulent lifestyles that were once exclusively enjoyed by the aristocracy and landed gentry.[2]

Like other men originating from the lower gentry (Lord Clive of India being the most famous), Sir Francis was associated with a line of yeomen farmers who went to India in the service of an increasingly powerful and aggressive East India Company. Francis Sykes had more than one stint in India. Between 1751 and 1760, he worked his way up the ladder of the East India Company civil service. A wheeler-dealer, he amassed a great fortune after making political and financial connections in high places, becoming friends with the Governor-General of Bengal, Warren Hastings. Robert Clive befriended him in England and brought him back to India in 1764 as a member of the Select Committee. Soon afterwards, Sykes served as Resident at the court of the Nawab of Murshidabad, a position of great political power that provided an easy route to riches.

Sir Francis's career in the East India Company enabled him to amass personal profits of at least £250,000 which he used to purchase three properties, including in his native Yorkshire. Now a major landowner, he was accordingly able to obtain a seat in the House of Commons. Needing to be close to the cultural and political centre of London, Sykes – like many other returnee nabobs – wanted to acquire and build a home in the Thames Valley. For this reason, he bought Basildon Park estate and had his house built on it. Proximity to London was important for all kinds of reasons. Landowners who bought their estates with colonial wealth did not merely rely on an income from land rental, but invested their Indian fortune in trade, stocks and shares. London's commercial importance and centrality to propertied Company families explains why so many of them settled in the valley during the second half of the eighteenth century. That is why the area became known as *England's Hindoostan*.[3]

When Sir Francis ordered his house to be built and his grounds to be landscaped, visitors to his four hundred acre estate would have passed through entrance gates topped with stone pineapples, a fruit which Christopher Columbus had introduced to Europe and which became a popular architectural feature during the colonial period. To be able to serve your guests pineapple, grown at great expense in specially built hot houses, was a symbol of great wealth and status. Sir Francis expanded his vast parklands by enclosing the local commons, where people once grazed their cattle and walked along footpaths which were then blocked off.[4] Such details remind us that colonial activities abroad and the subsequent influx of private land sales, impacted on landless Britons who could no longer put their livestock out to pasture, collect firewood, or walk along the footpaths they'd enjoyed for generations.[5]

Whilst in India, Sir Francis met a powerful, well-known local merchant who became his right-hand man. The opportunities offered by international trade and commerce attracted any number of Indian outsiders to Bengal. Among those who sought the stability, security and commercial opportunities that the Company offered were *banias* (loosely, members of the trading caste) who served the British as businessmen, money lenders, managers, accountants and confidants. It was a man called Cantoo Babu (Krishna Kanta Nandy, 1720-94) who fulfilled this role for Sir Francis Sykes. As William Dalrymple explores in his book, *The Anarchy*, it was networks of local agents and financiers like Krishna Kanta Nandy, also known as *Jagat Seths* or world bankers, who unlocked India's financial capital for the East India Company.[6] Indian banias' access to requisite wealth also meant that they could extend a line of credit which expanded the Company's capacity to maintain, arm and support a large professional force that far exceeded any rival Indian power.[7]

Krishna Kanta Nandy helps us to understand in greater detail how the great fortunes of men like Sykes were acquired. Indian figures like him brought to the table intimate cultural knowledge, networks, trading experience and land management skills, allowing men like Sir Sykes to make their fortunes. It was not just *nabobs'* individual genius, luck or hard graft, but *banias'* know-how which allowed men like Sir Sykes to take advantage of the power vacuum in India which had opened up with the decline of the Mughal empire whilst rival European Companies fought to gain commercial and, ultimately, territorial dominance over India. Prominent in the English East India Company victory was the defeat of Nawab Siraj ud-Daulah of Bengal at the 1757 Battle of Plassey, thereby accelerating a process that had been a key part of the local commercial and political landscape since the early years of Company's presence in Bengal and elsewhere in India.

It is worthwhile delving into the role of someone like Krishna Kanta Nandy, also *bania* to Governor-General Warren Hastings, not merely as a personal manager but within the larger context of the English East India Company. As his career shows, Krishna Kanta Nandy exemplifies the type of Indian who was locked in a mutual embrace with a Company which ultimately subjugated India. In a later period, many such individuals also became exceedingly wealthy and personally benefited from Cornwallis' Land Settlement, which helped them to acquire Indian landed estates and attendant titles. In fact, many *banias* who had worked with the Company went on to live gentrified lives in the image of their *nabob* counterparts in Britain.

The relationship between Nandy and Sir Sykes continued long after the latter had returned to England. Nandy was a trusted figure who had once managed the Indian affairs of Sir Francis and kept all his secrets. He even sent barrels of mango chutney from Bengal to Basildon Park.[8] Sir Francis also brought back an Indian servant to Basildon Park, a man at the other end of the social scale who married locally and was named as Thomas Radakissan in the will of Sir Francis who left him a mourning ring and 7 shillings a week for the rest of his life, worth two days' wages every seven days. A National Trust volunteer found that Radakissan stayed in the area. The couples' distant descendants are still living.[9] We know nothing more of Radakissan and, unless new documents are discovered, we will never hear his voice.

Useful though this knowledge is, it poses a critical question: what is the role of colonial country houses like Basildon Park in twenty-first century multi-cultural Britain? In the light of new evidence, we begin to become aware of historical figures from the global majority whose lives were previously ignored. But these emerging narratives clash with established traditions of admiring great houses' grandeur, however qualified this admiration has been by considerations of class inequality and aristocratic intrigue. All that once seemed solid is melting. In their different ways, Indian historical figures challenge the lingering imperialist ideology, which presented British colonial activity as part of largely benign and civilising mission. As more and more colonial histories emerge, historic country houses offer an uneasy escape for those visitors who seek to escape multicultural city life to dwell in an imagined and unchanging English past.

Surveys regularly indicate that minority ethnic groups in the UK feel a sense of alienation from historic houses, which have a long way to go in fully reflecting their global histories. Country houses had come to be seen, throughout the twentieth and early twenty-first centuries, as unsullied by any connection with colonialism or slavery. Yet a place like Basildon Park, with its multicultural hinterlands of Reading and Slough, cannot afford to ignore these audiences, neither financially nor ethically. The story of Basildon Park *is* quintessentially a story of India and the English East India Company: Krishna Kantu Nandy enabled Sir Francis to acquire a portion of the wealth which the British drained away from India, financing the purchase of Basildon Park estate, where Sykes built his grand house and lived in the style of a *nabob* along with his Indian servant, Thomas Radikissan.

Such stories are as relevant to those potential audiences in Reading and Slough as to the history of Basildon Park itself. Telling those stories offers visitors new *Ways of Seeing*[10] as Britain's country houses emerge as part of a shared heritage which binds us across centuries, and which has the potential to make space for diversity in postcolonial Britain. Basildon Park has a good track record of developing offers that enable it to engage with diverse communities. It also benefits from having a visionary leadership and a team committed to looking at ways to expand its visitor base. Basildon Park's global history broadens the pool of knowledge, and this benefits all, helping us to understand what it means to be British in today's multicultural society.

Endnotes:

1. Tilman W. Nechtman, 'Nabobs Revisited: A Cultural History of British Imperialism and the Indian Question in Late-Eighteenth-Century Britain', *History Compass* 4:4, pp.645-667, 2006, p.646.
2. Shashi Tharoor, *Inglorious Empire. What the British Did to India* (London: Penguin, 2016).
3. Margot Finn and Kate Smith, eds., *The East India Company at Home 1757-1857* (London: UCL, 2018).
4. Nick Hayes, *The Book of Trespass* (London: Bloomsbury, 2020), p.23.

5. Corinne Fowler, *Green Unpleasant Land: Creative Responses to Rural England's Colonial Connections* (Leeds: Peepal Tree Press, 2020), p. 42.
6. William Dalrymple, *The Anarchy: The Relentless Rise of the East India Company* (London: Bloomsbury, 2019).
8. Corinne Fowler, *Green Unpleasant Land*, p. 127.
9. The volunteer was Sarah Spink, a genealogist and historian. See also Sally-Ann Huxtable, Corinne Fowler, Kristo Kefalus and Emma Slocombe, eds., 'Interim Report on the Connections Between Colonialism and Properties Now in the Care of the National Trust, Including Links with Historical Slavery', 2020.
10. John Berger, *Ways of Seeing* ([1972] London: Penguin Classics, 2008).

Sir Francis Sykes, 1st Baronet Sykes of Basildon, MP (1732-1804)
© National Trust / Christopher Warleigh-Lack

CHINESE WALLPAPER

UPPARK AND OTHER HOUSES

Section of the Chinese wallpaper at Erddig, Wrexham
© National Trust / Paul Highnam

HANNAH LOWE

CHINESE WALLPAPER

...and the walls finely adorn'd with China paper, the figures of men, women, birds and flowers, the liveliest I ever saw come from that country – John Macky, *A Journey Through England*, 1724

DAZZLING BLUE

And soon I'm telling everyone I meet
about Chinese wallpaper, the butterflies and lotuses,
the parakeets, how there are one hundred and forty
known cases in bedrooms from Truro
to Perthshire, and more to be discovered. I'm raving

about curators and restorers, how China
could pretty much do everything better than us
with regard to cups, saucers, printing, gunpowder,
and yes, wallpaper, and by the way, when I say 'us'
I don't mean me and you.

Now check out these rainbow-tailed birds, I laugh
scrolling through my phone, check out this dazzling blue!
I'm babbling on about tea-clippers, the Silk Road, the Empire,
and some people glaze over while I'm talking
and some nod vigorously and say wow

because I am nodding vigorously and saying wow
and when I tell Arji I'm meant
to be writing Chinese wallpaper poems
but don't know what to write
he deeply empathises, relating my experience

to his experience as poet-in-residence at Wedgewood –
Wedgewood! he sighs, like what could I say
about Wedgewood? So I share a long story
about the Chinese wallpaper at Coutts Bank on the Strand
and a shipwreck on the Java Sea

where the only thing saved from Malayan pirates
was the Chinese wallpaper – that's how much it was worth –
and he says man, this is like your specialist subject
if you were on Mastermind, and I think he's right
but I know a lot about Joni Mitchell too.

UNFURL

*A sort of paper… with such lively colours, that for splendour and vividness we have
nothing in Europe that approaches it…* John Evelyn, diarist, 1664

this is no ordinary
paper mulberry bark
bamboo blue sandal-
wood so heavy & thick
it smells of places you
will never be the hold
of a ship ten months
at sea the rim of a land
you'll never see

& oh the colours are the
colours of your dreams
– wild rooster red &
dragon god green each
bird & vine block-print-
ed painted by hand &
either you're the paper-
hanger just come from
London with your rule
& scissors or else you
are the Lady

& it's your bedcham-
ber where this paper
will be hung with pea-
cocks & gold camellia
you'll see the shadows
in the dark the silhou-
ettes of scholar's rocks
& mountain pines &
nightly when you lay
your head & close your
eyes blue egrets will fly
the walls above the lo-
tus trees

CONSERVERS

My mother loved to decorate, to paper
over last year's walls with Homebase woodchip
and floral borders, then ask the neighbours over
for gin and praise. I used to pick the pips
of wood and pull the paper off in strips,
then peel away a shred of last year's woodchip,
then another, until I found the brick.

Lady Constable wanted a Chinese room
when seeing Brighton Pavilion, the room
where Queen Victoria slept. She papered hers
in birds-and-flowers on powder pink. Although
conservers, later on, found China paper,
from years before, pasted there below.

THE MINES

'Persons of quality and distinction who had taste and all that must have
something foreign and superb'–
The World, 18th Century London newspaper

Anyone who was anyone
had to have a Chinese Room
and Richard Pennant, Lord Penrhyn,
had three

and built his driveway three miles long
so visitors could view
his towers and turrets
from every turn

and set the bragging mouth
of his grand front door
high up on the cliff
so he could stand

and sweep his eyes
across the valleys and roads,
the fields he owned,
the mines

So rich was he –
(six hundred slaves
and three West Indian plantations
that he'd never seen)

he built a bed of slate
they carried from the quarry
especially for the visit
of the Queen

who look one look
and, finding
that the bed
looked like a tomb,

went opening
doors along the corridor
and chose to sleep
in the China room.

Coda:

slave / slate / slave / slate / slave / slate / plantation / valley / plantation /
quarry / sugar / slate / sugar / slate / slave / slate / slave / slate / cane / slate /
cane / slate / sugar / slave / slate / money

UPPARK

It took a fire to find the India paper
at Uppark House. The smoke and heat
unpeeled the English diaper-pattern green
& there below the centuries and blooming bright –
red peonies, two pheasants on a rock,
the knotty branches of a pine.

Did Baronet and Lady Featherstonehaugh
know or care that 'India' meant China?
Had they learnt their Chinese symbols –
pheasants for beauty, peonies for rank?
As though the papermakers knew just how,
if not exactly who, to compliment?

ISSUES AFFECTING THE CONDITIONS OF
CHINESE WALLPAPER

Chinese wallpapers have survived in remarkable numbers… considering their in-
herent fragility and the domestic use of the rooms in which they were hung
– Emile de Bruijn

A fountain pen in the hands of a running child.
Sunlight. Rain. A jilted fiancé. Unspecified stains.

Three centuries of gaslight. Picking the edges.
Lemon. Licking. Wasps. Champagne.

Directly sticking to walls. English winters. A raid
of weevils. A raid of spiders. A zealous maid

with a pail of butter. Squirrels in the attic.
A furious pigeon. A furious daughter.

A snail's slow ooze. Mildew scrubbed away
with rhubarb stew. A kitchen fire. No alarm.

Other unknown forms of harm. Squashed
moths. The Marquis festering, for weeks, in bed.

A swipe of soot. The smashing of plates.
'Touching up' with English paint.

OM

The curator explains the hanging of this paper
which wasn't made for English walls
and arrived from Canton in short fat rolls

and how the paperhanger pruned and snipped
then patch-worked on a lawn
and painted in a sky

but all the time she's talking
my eye is fixed on a scarlet peony
glued high above the bed,

too bright, unmoored
and floating like a blooded jellyfish
and pasted not, she says, to hide a join

but 'to liven up' the scene. It reminds me
of the yoga class this morning,
Luana talking of the yoga mat

as a journal of the body, and yogi's *drishti*
as the focal point to fix the gaze.
When we began to chant

the room was filled
with a perfect ancient-sounding *Om,*
but for the man in front

like a too-red flower slapped to a wall,
obliviously singing,
louder than us all.

THE HANGER

Now the Orient's in fashion, I'm on a roll,
for who but Jonah Button can trim and hang
this paper, which isn't made for English walls
and is as rare at auction as a man
to hang it proper? It's not the skill with scissors
or a brush, but nerves as firm as my opinion
that I'm the best for it in England! What's more,
it takes audacious grace, as once I pinned
a rose I'd plucked from St James hallowed soil
upon my woman's dreary collar; I'll plant
an extra flower here or there – any wall
is much enriched by Button's autograph!
And I'll retire on an income soon –
without the Hanger, there is no China room.

(And if Sir Bondham curses now my rate,
I'll leave him hang his precious India paper,
I'd like to see him balanced up a ladder
with a roller and a bucketful of paste!)

DNA

Down on the Canton docks, I climb **On Christmas Day, I spit into a test tube**
aboard the only ship in port **and later slip it in a plastic envelope to mail away**
and take my chance to sail away **to a post-box in America and wait for 60 days**
and evenings, stand on deck alone **until an email reads Results are in and shows**
to smoke and see **a rainbow map with flags on every continent. My DNA says**
the frigate birds keep vigil in the sky **English, Portuguese, West Coastal African**
half tethered to the tea clipper, half free **Armenian, Ashkenazi Jew and 0.6%**
and watch a hundred other ships criss-cross the Java Sea **of me is unassigned**
We voyage back through centuries to Billingsgate **the fattest pie chart chunk**
where the dockhands haul in crates of porcelain **is not surprisingly Chinese**
and silk and tea **and yet I am surprised. China was the softest voice, a murmur**
and on we sail to the port of Kingston **in the house of mystery where I grew up**
and on again to Limehouse Docks, and there I go **My Chinese grandfather?**
strolling with my weathered case up Pennyfields **He sailed across the world**
past the seamen's boarding house and English-Chinese grill, **and somehow**
the Chinese laundry. And when the cold tugs water from my eye **landed here**
I take my handkerchief to wipe away the salty English tears **he landed here**
then keep on walking, turn the corner into fog and disappear **inside of me.**

THE EMPIRE

And when I came back from Felbrigg Hall[*]
it wasn't the Chinese wallpaper I thought about
though it was sad and beautiful
with its ducks and egrets and magnolia;
not the sweary taxi driver, nor the curator
who didn't seem to know why I was there.
It wasn't the extra pair of socks I bought
in Asda, to fend off the brutal weather
or the social worker who phoned
to talk about my mother
as the car wound the long road from Cromer: no,

it was the two strange figurines
hung high up on the master bedroom wall
with their laughing shiny faces
and clownish clothes –
they were earthquake detectors
from China, circa 1860
and even then, it was my grandfather
I thought of, stepping off a boat from China
to Kingston docks, and my father
stepping off a boat to postwar Liverpool
in his papery suit and gleaming brogues.

[*]The Chinese Wallpaper at Felbrigg Hall is one of the earliest known surviving examples in the UK, hung around 1752.

EMILE DE BRUIJN

CHINESE WALLPAPER:
BETWEEN FICTION AND REALITY

Section of the Chinese wallpaper at Erddig, Wrexham, hung in the 1770s, showing a cock, hen and chicks, symbolising courage and benevolence, and a lily, associated with a long and happy marriage. © National Trust / Paul Highnam

Chinese wallpapers can be found in historic houses across the British Isles: this simple statement touches on the extraordinary cultural impact of those relatively fragile paper wallcoverings that came from the other side of the world. One way to better understand the significance of Chinese wallpaper is to look at it as a hybrid product. It is both Chinese and European, having been made in China using Chinese motifs, techniques and materials, but specifically intended for use in European interiors. It is a form of decorative art, designed as wall decoration, but it was made using the techniques and visual language of Chinese fine art printing and painting. The scenery on Chinese wallpapers is deeply meaningful, reflecting the well-established symbolic meanings and associations of Chinese bird-and-flower and landscape imagery, and yet most of that original significance was lost in translation when the wallpapers came to Europe. These wallpapers have always to some extent been seen as exotic, even though they quickly became integral, domesticated components of high-end European interiors.

How did this shape-shifting and yet remarkably stable product emerge? To answer that we need to go back to the start of large-volume trade between Europe and East Asia, which took off in the early 16th century, when Portuguese ships ventured beyond the Cape of Good Hope into the Pacific. Soon Portuguese merchants were bringing products like spices, tea, porcelain lacquer and silk textiles back to Europe, and from the late 16th century they were joined by the Spanish, who were arriving in East Asia via their colonial settlement in the Philippines.[1] Drawn by the huge profits to be made, Dutch and English merchants also began to sail to East Asia from around 1600, organised in East India Companies, early forms of joint-stock enterprises.[2]

An important reason for the attractiveness of South- and East-Asian goods was that they were made to levels of sophistication that were not available in Europe. Indian chintzes were bright and colourfast, Chinese porcelain was relatively strong, beautifully coloured and subtly decorated and Japanese lacquer was more advanced in finish and decoration than any European painted surfaces.[3] The strong colours, reflective qualities and exuberant decoration of these goods chimed with the sensibilities of 17th-century European baroque design. East Asian lacquer was used as wall panelling, starting in the Dutch Republic in the 1650s and subsequently spreading to England and Germany.[4] European artisans began to produce goods in pseudo-Asian styles, such as tapestries, painted panelling and furniture, chased silver, painted leather hangings and paper wallcoverings, all inspired by the decoration of Asian textiles, porcelain and lacquer.

The Duchess of Lauderdale's Private Closet at Ham House, Richmond upon Thames, decorated in the 1670s with English imitation-lacquer chairs, a Javanese or Vietnamese lacquer table raised on a European-made base and a Chinese porcelain teapot with silver-gilt mounts added in London. ©National Trust Images/John Hammond

It is a fascinating feature of 17th-century European culture that the concept of authenticity as we understand it, in the sense of an object or concept having a provable, exclusive origin in a particular culture, did not yet loom large. Asian objects could be appropriated, taken apart, added to, copied or reinterpreted without significantly losing their desirability and cultural prestige (see illustration above). An English-made object in a pseudo-Asian style could unproblematically project an Asian aura, as long as it conformed to the accepted English notions of Asianness. In this context of cultural fluidity, anything Asian was referred to as 'Indian', while lacquer (or imitation-lacquer) objects were called 'Japan' and porcelain was termed 'China', regardless of its actual origin.

Another 17th- and early-18th-century European trend that influenced the appreciation of Asian objects was the drive to organise society along rational and disciplined lines. The scientific revolution was embedding respect for analytical and evidence-based ways of working and thinking. Civil, military and religious institutions were increasingly organised centrally and systematically, and society as a whole placed more emphasis on 'civilised' qualities such as politeness, restraint and reason.[5] This chimed with the contemporary European perception of China and Japan, partly fed by the admiring books written by Jesuit missionaries, as being well-established, highly sophisticated societies that managed to combine rationality and virtue with technical excellence.[6] So for Europeans to own Asian and pseudo-Asian goods was both materially and intellectually aspirational.

Part of the Chinese wallpaper at Felbrigg Hall, Norfolk, hung in 1752. The scenery was partly woodblock-printed and partly hand-painted. ©National Trust Images/Chris Lacey

Looking at evidence of 'India pictures' mentioned in advertisements in British newspapers and magazines, Chinese prints and paintings on paper seem to have been readily available in cities like London and Dublin in the early years of the 18th century.[7] This period also saw the development of paper wallcoverings in Britain and France, some of which were in pseudo-Asian style. Curiously, pictorial wallpapers produced in China for the European market only seem to have appeared around 1750, from the evidence of the earliest firmly dated surviving examples (see illustration on page 198). Unless substantially earlier examples are still to be identified, it would appear that the 'copy' paradoxically preceded the 'original'. But that surprising sequencing may in fact demonstrate the fundamentally hybrid nature of Chinese export wallpaper, as coming not just out of certain Chinese traditions and capabilities but also out of an at least partly fictional European conception of Asia.

Chinese landscape wallpaper at Blickling Hall, Norfolk, hung c. 1760. ©National Trust Images/Chris Lacey

The imagery on Chinese wallpaper, as it first appeared in Europe as a purpose-made product in the mid-18th century, drew on two longstanding East-Asian pictorial traditions. One of those was the imagery of birds and flowers, which had been a distinct genre in Chinese art since the 10th century. The various birds and flowers acquired symbolic meanings, so that such images could convey complex meanings and associations.[8] The other tradition was landscape imagery, which had an equally long pedigree in Chinese art. Like birds and flowers, Chinese landscapes pictures were partly symbolic, embodying the dynamic harmonies of society, and even of reality itself, in the interaction between mountains and water, high and low, light and dark, smooth and rough.[9] So although both of these genres could be realistic and detailed, they were also thoroughly metaphorical and stylised – or, in other words, fictional.

The earliest surviving Chinese wallpapers in Britain, dating from around 1750, were printed in black ink from carved wooden blocks, with colours added by hand. They may have been made in Suzhou, in the Changjiang (Yangtze) river delta, which was a centre of sophisticated printmaking at that time. From about 1760 Chinese export wallpapers seem to have switched to being fully hand-painted, which may be because in 1757 the Chinese government concentrated all the foreign merchants in the port city of Guangzhou (Canton) in southern China, possibly thereby making products from Suzhou less commercially viable for the westerners.[10]

Set of Chinese paintings on paper used as wall decoration at Erddig, Wrexham, 1770s. ©National Trust / Paul Highnam

In the following decades Chinese wallpapers kept changing, with the painting workshops in Guangzhou adroitly responding to changes in European fashion and demand. The 1770s saw bird-and-flower wallpapers with brightly coloured backgrounds (see illustration on page 195), which may be related to the increasing use of colour in European material culture during the same period, apparent in the bright greens, blues and reds in European costume and porcelain.[11] The same period saw not just the production of landscape wallpapers (see illustration on page 199), but also of the supply of sets of smaller landscape pictures, a ready-made, easily installed adaptation of the 'India pictures' from the beginning of the 18th century (see illustration on page 200). In the 1790s the bird-and-flower wallpapers became in some ways more realistic, by the introduction of features from Chinese gardens such as balustrades, *jardinières* and bird cages. But at the same time they were sometimes also made more stylised and fictional through the deliberate limiting of the colour palette and the creation of a kind of *grisaille* style.

It is striking that, even though the imagery on Chinese wallpapers was only partially understood by European viewers, they tended to be hung in high-status, intimate spaces such as bedrooms, dressing rooms and drawing rooms. This ostensibly exotic decoration was becoming literally domesticated within the setting of aristocratic, upper-class country mansions and town houses. And although there is little documentary evidence of the exact psychological impact of these wallpapers, it seems likely that there was some kind of correlation between the verdant Chinese landscapes indoors and the relatively informal, asymmetrical landscape gardens that were being developed outside.[12] Significantly, where China was used as a deliberate emblem within English landscape gardens, in the form of pavilions, bridges or pagodas, such as at Shugborough, Stourhead and Kew, it was as a signifier of historical continuity, civilisational excellence and moral probity, on a par with classical and gothic garden architecture.[13]

However, the very associations that had hitherto made China and Chinese culture aspirational to Europeans were increasingly seen as problematic towards the end of the 18th century. This was partly connected to changes in manufacturing and consumption patterns, with European producers increasingly being able to supply the sophisticated luxury goods that had previously been exclusive to China.[14] In addition, as European thought placed increasing emphasis on the independent, active, rational subject defining and acting on the passive, objectified 'world out there', China came to be identified with the latter, seen as static, backward and 'other'.[15] This 'sinophobic turn' was accompanied by greater British economic and political assertiveness *vis-à-vis* China, exemplified by Earl Macartney's diplomatic mission to the Chinese court in 1793, which attempted to negotiate greater commercial access for British trade. The failure of those negotiations was one of the factors that led British traders to smuggle opium into China, to balance the cost of the ever-increasing exports of tea to Britain, which in turn led to the First Opium War between Britain and China in 1839–42.[16]

Chinese bird-and-flower wallpaper in the State Bedroom at Penrhyn Castle, Gwynedd, hung in the early 1830s. ©National Trust / Paul Highnam

Despite these changing perceptions of China, Chinese wallpaper continued to be used as a luxury wallcovering in British elite interiors for most of the 19th century. By that time it seems to have become domesticated to such a degree that a country mansion would not be considered complete without a few bedrooms decorated with Chinese wallpaper (see illustration above). There is an interesting parallel with 'willow pattern' glazed earthenware, which was developed by Staffordshire manufacturers in the late 18th century as a British-made version of Chinese blue-and-white porcelain, and which became ubiquitous in 19th-century British interiors.[17] Like the willow pattern, Chinese wallpaper was a product that emerged out of the encounter between two very different cultures on opposite sides of the globe. It is in the thoroughgoing hybridity of Chinese wallpaper, always oscillating between Asia and Europe, domestic and exotic, fictional and real, that we can observe how the perception of objects changes as they move through time and space.

Endnotes:

1. Maxine Berg, *Luxury and Pleasure in Eighteenth-Century Britain* (Oxford: Oxford University Press, 2005), pp. 50-56, 70.
2. Giorgio Riello, *Cotton: The Fabric that Made the Modern World*, Cambridge: Cambridge University Press, 2013, p. 89.
3. Berg, 2005, p.71; Alexandra Palmer, 'Fashioning Chintz: For the West in the Eighteenth Century', in Sarah Fee (ed.), *Cloth that Changed the World: The Art and Fashion of Indian Chintz* (New Haven and London: Yale University Press in association with Royal Ontario Museum, 2019), pp. 136–49, ref. pp.139–140.
4. Daniëlle Kisluk-Grosheide, 'The (Ab)Use of Export Lacquer in Europe', in M. Kühlental (ed.), *Osatasiatische un europäische Lacktechniken* [*East Asian and European Lacquer Techniques*], München: Bayerisches Landesamt and Edition Lipp, 2000, pp. 27–42; ref. p. 27.
5. Charles Taylor, *Sources of the Self: The Making of the Modern Identity* (Cambridge, Massachusetts: Harvard University Press, 1989), pp. 159, 173–4; Charles Taylor, *A Secular Age* (Cambridge, Massachusetts: The Belknap Press of Harvard University Press, 2007), pp. 228–9.
6. Marcia Reed, 'A Perfume is Best from Afar: Publishing China for Europe', in Marcia Reed and Paula Demattè (eds.), *China on Paper: European and Chinese Works from the Late Sixteenth to the Early Nineteenth Century* (Los Angeles: Getty Research Institute, 2007), pp. 9–28; ref. pp. 10–21; Emile de Bruijn, 'Virtual Travel and Virtuous Objects: Chinoiserie and the Country House', in Jon Stobart (ed.), *Travel and the British Country House: Cultures, Critiques and Consumption in the Long Eighteenth Century* (Manchester: Manchester University Press, 2017), pp. 63–85; ref. pp. 65–7.
7. Emile de Bruijn, *Chinese Wallpaper in Britain and Ireland* (London: Philip Wilson Publishers in association with the National Trust, 2017), pp. 33–36.
8. Jessica Rawson, 'Ornament as System: Chinese Bird-and-Flower Design', The Burlington Magazine, vol. 148, no. 1239 (June 2006), pp. 380-89; Shane McCausland, 'Categories of Paintings in China: Genres and Subjects', in Zhang Hongxing (ed.), *Masterpieces of Chinese Painting, 700–1900* (London: Victoria and Albert Museum, 2013), pp. 41-52; ref. pp. 50–51.
9. McCausland 2013, pp. 46–50.
10. Angela Schottenhammer, 'The East Asian Maritime World, c. 1400–1800: Its Fabrics of Power and Dynamics of Exchanges – China and her Neighbours', in Angela Schottenhammer (ed.) *The East Asian Maritime World 1400–1800: Its Fabrics of Power and Dynamics of Exchanges* (Wiesbaden: Harrasowitz Verlag, 2007), pp. 1–86; ref. p. 33.
11. Susan North, *18th-Century Fashion in Detail* (London: Thames and Hudson in association with the Victoria and Albert Museum, 2018), pp. 14–15.

12. One of the few recorded examples of a contemporary response are the comments in the diary of Caroline Powys (*née* Girle, 1738–1817), on seeing the rooms decorated with Chinese wallpapers and pictures at Fawley Court, Buckinghamshire, in 1771, which she described as 'most beautiful', 'prettier than t'is possible to imagine', 'most curious' and installed 'with great taste', see Emily J. Climenson (ed.), *Passages from the diaries of Mrs. Philip Lybbe Powys of Hardwick House, Oxon., A.D. 1756–1808* (London: Longmans, Green, 1899), pp. 146–7.

13. Bruijn, 2017, pp. 71–4.

14. Berg 2005, pp. 80–3.

15. For these trends in European intellectual history, see Taylor 1989, pp. 167–8, 175, 363–4.

16. Stephen R. Platt, *Imperial Twilight: The Opium War and the End of China's Last Golden Age* (New York: Alfred A. Knopf, 2018), pp. xxiii–viii.

17. For the development of the Willow Pattern, see Robert Copeland, *Spode's Willow Pattern and Other Designs after the Chinese* (London: Cassell in association with Studio Vista/Christie's, 1980), pp. 33–44; for its social and cultural significance in Britain, see Elizabeth Hope Chang, *Britain's Chinese Eye: Literature, Empire, and Aesthetics in Nineteenth-Century Europe* (Stanford: Stanford University Press, 2010).

CALKE ABBEY

Mansion view from the meadow at Calke Abbey, Derbyshire
©National Trust Images/Susan Guy

A large oak case with glass sides and front, two dividing bars vertically in front. Contains specimens of taxidermy, not arranged for display and showing the stages of taxidermy creation. Metal bars across the top are used to suspend specimen birds of prey. Several birds of prey stand on perches on the base, with two pelicans and other birds. Solid base.
© National Trust / Andrew McGregor

MALACHI MCINTOSH

IMPERIAL HOMES

The thing that got him worst were the heads. Everywhere: heads. Of what looked like bulls or oxen, cows and stags. Severed and dark-furred, mounted on wall after wall after wall.

Heads. Then cases of dead animals, stuffed birds – cases of them – stacks and stacks of reenactments where real animals, now dead, were posed in glass cases in what he guessed someone a hundred years ago thought were natural scenes. The whole house, floor after floor, filled with corpses from across the world, preserved.

And again, his was the only brown face, dark skin, anywhere, except on the walls, and Edie, next to him, looked around at it all like she was in love.

'It's so great isn't it?'

They met, he and Edie, the way everyone does these days, on an app – his conversation with her at first identical to another he was having at the same time with another girl.

He started, with her and the other, hi, but Edie wrote back first, almost instantly:

hellooo!

She'd go on to tell him later that his message arrived on a night when she was feeling exactly the same as he was, bored with it all – the whole performance, the swiping and tapping, the picture and profile scanning. She had accounts in three places, paid on one site for a membership and hated it, but thought, that night, why not, I'll just match with everybody, reply to the first guy who writes back to me and keep going until he acts like an arsehole.

He tried being funny in their chat, reused old jokes, sent emojis 🙁 🤓 😬 👍 – the last one a long back and forth in his head – brown thumb, yellow thumb, brown thumb, yellow thumb – then gone, and then, after almost two weeks of a few messages between them each day, they met up.

He left his flat with expectations no more or less than they ought to have been. She'd told him almost nothing in their messages, both of them just skimming the surface of things, entertaining each other:

> you live near Stratford??
>
> Shakespeare country?
>
> I knoow can you believe it?

All he got from their exchanges and her profile was that she was pretty – but everyone's good-looking in their profile pictures – blonde, not bottled, about his age, lived close but not too close – all things he asked for from the app: women, mid-to-late thirties, up to 40 miles away.

So his expectations were what they had to be: she'd be much taller or shorter than she said she was; her body would be softer somewhere that the photos didn't show. Her face wouldn't be the same – different without a dipped chin, odd straight on instead of from the left or right, unfamiliar when in motion. Plus something else. Almost all of them had something else – either physical, like chewing a nail or a scar they tried to hide – or something verbal, a phrase they couldn't help but say like *you're joking!*, or *look at you with your*, or *you know what I mean? you know what I mean? you know what I mean?* Or worse:

One woman, her family originally from Tobago, told him, in one of those long pauses that makes you want to look at your phone, and connected to nothing at all, that it was all getting out of control now, all these immigrants, immigrants everywhere.

'You what?' he'd said.

'Immigrants,' she'd said and gestured, with a chin flick, at a group of bulked-up men with tight t-shirts, one wearing stonewashed jeans. 'It's just getting too much. It's just too much,' she said, and in case it wasn't clear, went on to explain.

But Edie wasn't like that at all. He'd arranged to meet her at one of the bars in town he had on rotation for dates, saw her long before she saw him. In person she was, and this was rare, even better-looking than in her pictures, although still different. Wearing white trainers, a sort of boxy grey dress, her hair cut short on the sides where in the pictures it was long, and now grey – grey dyed? She sat with hands folded and looked alright, good actually, the only thing throwing him off after the approach was when she spoke, her voice.

'Helloo!'

She was posh. That's fine, he thought, not a problem. No problem. He sat, triggered his first-date smile. Around them were Thursday night's finest out in heels, shirts fresh-pressed like his was, hair and beards sharpened up, fake tans slapped on; and, in the middle of them, Edie in plimsoles, the long hello.

He fought to keep his surprise from showing as his mind flipped back and saw all the obvious signs from their messages, where she lived. She was posh, he thought. Posh and White.

Not a problem. Still smiling. Definitely easier separately – posh but not White was rare but not too complicated; usually they felt like they had to compensate for the school they went to, the friends they had. Could be a laugh. White but not posh was also fine, familiar. They'd talk to you about the mixed-race boy on their estate; always had a friend or an aunt or a cousin who had a similar relationship, past or present; sometimes it would be clear they had a preference, or they might say casual things about Black guys that you'd correct them on or not, depending on how you were feeling. Could be a laugh, still. But posh and White was new. A part of his interest in this date was the novelty – a girl from the country-side – so this was just something extra, something that could add to it.

'Wow,' he said, 'even better in real life –' his line. She grinned. They talked.

First the usual – trip, trains, weather, *What are you drinking?* – then deeper.

He asked her if she'd ever been to Brum before and she said once or twice but she'd spent most of her life in London.

'Oh yeah? Doing what?'

'I had a shop there.' Her eyes lost focus, stared a little bit over his shoulder. 'But we had to close it.'

'Oh.'

'No! Don't worry, it's fine,' she said, then asked, after a gap, 'So tell me about yourself.'

In her accent it sounded like an interview question, but he was prepped for it, gave her the basics. When he told her he'd been brought up by his grandmother, mainly, she said she'd been brought up solely by her father after her parents had divorced. He went on with his milestones, leaving out anything complicated – went to uni, got a job, bought his own place, now actually *works* for his old uni – here he laughed, always laughed – doing recruitment; not in the field now but managing a team of six. Watching her the whole time, his stresses in the right places, he saw that all the things that usually landed weren't landing – *my own flat* she barely responded to, *first in the family* didn't register, *manager, six,* didn't even make her eyelids flicker.

'And what did you study?'

'At uni? Started off doing History, but it wasn't really a practical subject, so I switched to Business, then an MSc in Management.'

'Oh,' she said.

'That's not good?'

'No, no don't be silly! It's fine. It's great,' she said, and her eyes defocused again, stared over his shoulder at the bar. 'Another?'

He wrote it off after half an hour. Sometimes he could stay on his game well enough to pretend like it wasn't happening, but with Edie it was impossible. Her eyes kept throwing him off. Boredom detectors. Whenever he said something she didn't care about, she looked away, and half the time she was looking away. He was talking about himself too much when you had to make it all about them – but he had to impress her with something, so told her about rising recruitment figures, promotion pathways, how much he loved his team. She finished drinks two and three and kept watching a point past him, smiling in a polite way that said, No, no, probably not.

Then a long pause. Awkward – neither of them with anything to say to each other. She drained her glass, asked if he wanted another.

'Nah I'm alright,' he said, his head blank. 'You?'

'I'm probably fine, too.' She looked at her glass, absent.

He tried, 'So you were saying before, about your shop. Why'd you close it down?'

'What?'

'You said you had a shop, but then – but then?'

She smiled, but not a real smile. A small shake of her head and her hand on her empty glass. 'Just – life.'

'Life?' he said, trying to sound light. 'You can't just say *life*, man. Tell me more.'

The false smile fell and her eyes went beyond him. As he got ready to say *So, it's getting late*, she told him everything.

After graduating, she and her friend Olivia had talked about what they wanted to do. They had a lot of bad ideas but then came up with this shop, just vintage clothes. It was silly but they were excited by it and tried banks first to borrow money but that was hopeless so they went to their parents cap in hand. They ran it together, just under ten years, 'lots of ups and downs.' It was great fun, mostly, but it made less and less real money, especially after the crash. Then Olivia quit, ran off to get married. Edie tried to keep it going alone, but –

She shrugged.

After that she wasn't up to much, went to Kenya for two years with a boyfriend and worked there doing charity, basically aid. They split up and she came back alone to London and tried to work in fashion, briefly, but it was disappointing. Then she left the country to stay with one of her brothers in Australia, then her dad fell ill and she came back home. And the way she said that word, 'home', was different from the way he'd ever heard anyone say it who wasn't on the BBC. Her older brother was nearby, with his family, but she felt guilty being across the world. 'And so,' she said, with a real smile now, 'I came back. Life. Drink?'

'I'm sorry,' he said, as far off-script as she was. 'How's dad now?'

'Fine. Better. Recovering. It was a stroke. He's mobile. Keeps bullying me to get out of the house!'

'One of my aunties had a stroke,' he said, the words just falling out of him, but it didn't matter; this was over before it started. 'Two in row. Just before my grandmother – yeah – It's not easy. Life. I'm sorry about that.'

She watched him. 'I'm sorry too.'

'It's hard,' he said, and felt embarrassed. Too open.

He wrote it off, walked her to the station thinking, well, it was a learning experience. He'd tried to keep the last half of their time together a bit looser, tried to stick to nothing much that mattered – whether it's okay to still watch the X Factor, whether or not Manchester's hype as a great city is really deserved – but he could see her heart wasn't in it and neither was his. The dad, the shop, his family; his fault for letting it run that way – for some reason it had been harder to control than they usually were. Partly the poshness, he thought, when she gave him a half-second one-armed hug at New Street, the poshness was a big part of it, he thought, as she walked to the barriers, turned back and mouthed, 'Sorry'.

He was back on the app the next day, messaging the other girl into the next week. In the middle of trying to arrange to see her, Edie texted him, after midnight:

i can do better than that!

And he thought okay, sure, why not, and wrote back: I hope so!

They met again and it was clear immediately that she'd committed to making it more fun, and it was. No talk about family, no real words about the past. She made her confession about deciding to respond to the first person who contacted her on the app, told him the village she was in was nice but a bit boring and it was depressing to see all the people who'd never left it; said she felt underdressed the first time and this time he could see she'd made more of an effort – tight jeans, vest top, but still the same white trainers – and he said either way she looked better than all the other women in the place.

Why not?

She spoke and relaxed, her vision fixed, and he started cataloguing, listing, like he always did. The grey hair was strange but she looked okay with it, she had an alright sense of humour – the phasing out thing before had a fair enough explanation; she'd been through some things. She was different. And her body – she must exercise, yoga, probably. Then he realised she'd moved on and was telling him he needed to get out more, see the world, even just other parts of the country.

'There's a whole universe outside of Birmingham.'

'You're joking. Is that possible?' He smiled.

'You know what I mean.'

She said her favourite thing was travelling, said she was actually a bit of a history buff, like he was; that's why she liked seeing the world.

'I'm a what?'

'A history buff,' she said. 'A failed history buff. An *aspiring* history buff.'

'Not too sure about that,' he said, but felt the switch in her, in her teasing, decided to play along. 'Expired, more like.'

She laughed, warm, and he thought *Okay*, sat back and shared a story that always worked on dates about the stupidest boy he went to college with, Meshach, a junior Rasta who was obsessed with Black history, who thought he needed to move to Ethiopia to be closer to Zion.

She listened without laughing at the parts where she should have laughed, said there was a lot of truth in it, it is different out there. She said when she was in Africa it had really transformed how she thought about herself and the world, seeing how people lived.

She went on and he thought maybe he shouldn't have told the story, thrown Meshach under the bus like that without thinking how she'd respond, but he let it slide. She'd lived there; he hadn't. His family was from Jamaica and he hadn't been there in decades.

'You need to get out more,' Edie said, finishing. 'I need to take you out … Or somebody should.'

He reorganised himself, set a smirk he'd started working on at about age fifteen. 'I'm happy for that somebody to be you.'

Close enough. She liked it, the date ending with a longer hug, a text message buzzing in his back pocket before he was out of the station: Edie.

Work was busy. One of his cousins had a birthday party, so they just texted back and forth for another few weeks.

For date three they met for dinner, still in his city, and mostly it just flowed. She kept riffing on the history thing, kept calling him a *history buff*, a *budding historian*, a *history professor*, but added in talk about her world – her brother's struggle to find the right school for her niece and nephew, friends who ran businesses, her other brother's life in 'Oz'.

She wanted to know more about him, but after her reaction to Meshach, he didn't know how to frame it. He felt problems swarming, rising ahead of him in all of his stories. He tried to talk about his past in a way that didn't drag him or anybody else down, tried to make it so what happened to him didn't line up with anything he thought she might think. So he said his dad wasn't really around that much, but it was because of mental health issues that people appreciate more these days, said that he saw him regularly though he rarely did; said his mother struggled with her kids until his grandmother stepped in, but that was okay; said they didn't have much but they were never poor – adding his grandmother came from money in Jamaica, even though she hadn't had much of an education. His grandparents were divorced but that was fine – brave of his grandma in that generation. Most of his school friends were in professional jobs. Then he swerved back to say: my grandmother *was* educated, just not formally.

She let him off, then, must have clocked that he was uncomfortable, pivoted back to, 'So, I need the opinion of a history expert…'

He relaxed and she said again that he needed to get out more.

Overall, the third time was his strongest performance. He charmed and she charmed back, even though his head kept flashing the same question in different forms: What does her life have to do with yours?

At the station, before a kiss she lingered for and he took – why not? – he thought she looked like a visitor from another planet – still in her flat-foot white trainers, another shapeless dress, a small canvas rucksack on her back, her hair grey-dyed – it was dye, her roots were brownish blonde – although it looked good on her – and he thought, Shut up, man. Look at her. Look at her body. Even though he couldn't really see it this time. So he said, without really telling himself to say it, that maybe he could come out to visit her in Redditch one day. You know, to see the world.

She laughed wide enough to show her grey fillings. 'It's Henley.'

'Yeah that one.'

II.

He drove out from the city, the miles widening the landscape, then dividing it into tended patches, pruned hedgerows, flattened plots in rectangles in a near infinite grid. Trees held back at the edges of the motorway crashed around him when he turned off into B roads, country lanes, and then to her village with its dropped speed limit.

As he steered the final miles, he imagined a scene where he took Edie home to see his grandmother when she was alive: Edie's eyes on the burgundy couches, the walls packed with posed pictures of generations of family from across the world, the fussy chandelier-style light fixtures, the textured wallpaper, the wooden map of Jamaica on the living room wall, the bigger one, with a clock nailed into it in the kitchen.

He couldn't sustain it – Edie's hair – *Wha she do to her head?* His grandma with her dark freckles scattered across her face. When he saw her waiting for him outside the kind of house he'd never been inside, her long hello still like being thrown into cold water, his stomach flipped.

She promised he'd meet her father in the briefest way possible, then they'd head out to a local pub where the food was perfect, then 'just see what happens'. He knew what that meant. Just the barrier of the father to clear.

At the door to the kind of cottage he'd only seen in paintings or films – fully detached, four floors, a chimney that wasn't a stubby cylinder poking out of the top of a terrace but one built all along the outside. His stomach stayed flipped when she hugged him, even when she said the bottle of whiskey in his hand for her father was a good choice.

Inside, where he expected something pristine, untouched, it was chaos. Instead of high quality, top-of-the-line, all the surfaces swarmed with things: papers, tea cups half drunk, worn throws falling off the furniture, newspaper piles, book stacks, a kitchen sink and counters covered with washing up. He'd gone to the barbers the night before, had spent extra time ironing his clothes in the morning, and now this mess; he was thrown. When Edie turned him into the living room to see the old man, his guts stayed shuffled. The television on Sky News, BREXIT. The old man in front of it was fast asleep.

'Oh my god. I'm so sorry,' she said. 'He was awake when I left.' She stepped towards him, shook him.

The slumped old man stirred, his stubbly cardigan worn.

'Dad?'

'You go on, you go on,' he muttered, in an accent that wasn't Edie's, was rougher.

'You're ridiculous,' she said. 'Say hello properly!'

The old man turned, scanned him and said, 'Hello, hello,' semi-conscious.

'He's so embarrassing,' said Edie, and introduced them – his hand into the old man's dry hand, the grip firm. 'Let's meet properly after the pub. 'Come on.'

As they left, he heard the old man say, 'I don't know what that was.'

And then at the pub, his was the only brown face anywhere, except on the television screen – something he should have expected but hadn't. It made every flick of eye contact feel like a jab against his skin, the bartender's *What can I get for you, mate* too loud, like it was shouted.

Everyone was looking at them. The place was small, she'd said, so maybe most of them knew her, were wondering why her with him. He said something empty to Edie about her dad being nice and the pub being nice and when she went to the bar for round two he asked himself, What's she getting from this? A novelty, probably. Black guy from Birmingham. Maybe she'd had something on the side in Kenya and that's why she and her other boyfriend split up. But no, not that; she just seemed genuinely ... bored? And there were nice things about her – but... He looked around at the people openly watching. They didn't match up.

Just as he was about to make some excuse when she returned about how tired he was, Edie told him that it was amazing he'd come all this way, that she was flattered that he wanted to see where she lived. But it must feel a bit awkward, being here. So I was wondering, maybe we could leave Dad to it. I'll call my brother to check in on him, and we can do something in the evening where you live.

III.

He took her around the city the next day, after breakfast, played on her joke about getting out more. To his campus to show her the development. To where HS2 would cut through in a few years and transform Birmingham forever. To the town centre to show her the rebuilding, the hope in it. They passed people sleeping rough and not even begging, drove out to Hockley where he grew up, to Harborne for coffee, to Moseley for dinner, back home.

The next weekend she took a turn, spent a night at his on the Friday, then gave him an intro to the countryside, finding it impossible that he'd never been camping and didn't want to. They walked for over an hour, stopped to eat a packed lunch of wrapped sandwiches, Edie laughing and telling him he needed better shoes if he wanted to keep up. Spent the rest of the weekend in Birmingham, theatre at the Hippodrome. Then back and forth, weekend to weekend, taking turns.

More pub lunches in small towns where he could, and did, appreciate the calm, the quiet, the light, but couldn't smile straight with all the stares – the constant stares, the extra-niceness, extra volume, everyone staring and trying to guess why she was with him.

She showed him a castle – a castle? – in Hereford. More walking around its grounds, an inside with decorated ceilings, swords and armour on the walls and a scattering of deers' heads hanging as decorations; in one room a whole family of them. Edie had been here as kid, with her father, who loved taking her to these kinds of places.

He'd never been.

'Never?' said Edie.

'Don't think so,' he said, staring at the heads, their glass eyes. 'Why would I?'

The next weekend they had a break. Something to do with her brother's kids. She said he should meet her brother, but it probably wasn't the best time with a group of four year-olds running about the place.

The following weekend in Brum – relaxation, Edie on his laptop browsing websites for more country houses.

'Another day out,' she said grinning. She did that, played.

'I think I've done enough castles.'

'But we've barely scratched the surface! There are some really good ones. Look.'

She turned the screen:

Calke Abbey is an ancient place. In its woods and fields a mantle of settled antiquity sits over all.

The House, a warren a rooms at once impressive and confusing, strode the catwalk of fashion on uneven heels, derided by some and fiddled with by its owners before being allowed to slip into graceful

'No way,' he said.

She left it, but after a shower, she handed him her phone:

Charlecote is a Victorian Home set in a landscaped deer park.

Mary Elizabeth and George Hammond Lucy wanted to make Victorian Charlecote conform to their fashionable idea of 'Merrie England' in the reign of 'Good Queen Bess'. They spared no expense and spent lavishly on

'Edie I'm really not that interested.'

'Don't be silly. You'll love it. I promise. As a history buff –'

'I'm not.'

'You are! You just don't appreciate it yet.'

'I just want to relax,' he said. 'Rest.'

'This is resting. We can walk around the grounds, sit in the café. When dad and I used to – '

'Edie, it's not restful for me.'

She said something about the day, the weather was bright. He knew this conversation was coming, had to come, at some stage.

'I don't really feel like going somewhere and sticking out the whole time,' he said, and faked a yawn, to soften it. 'Let's just relax. Chill out. Do something a bit more energetic.' He used the smirk.

'What do you mean sticking out?' she asked, her eyes squinting like she really couldn't imagine what he was talking about. It made him question what, at the pub near her house, she meant when she said it was awkward.

'Are you joking? It's obvious.'

'What's obvious?'

'You're kidding,' he said and laughed.

She laughed back, shaking her head. 'I honestly don't know what you're talking about!'

He held up his hands, showed both sides, tugged on his cheeks, his skin.

'Oh my god!' Still laughing, 'Oh my god, who cares about that! No one's paying any attention to that –'

'They aren't?'

'No of course not! Don't be so silly. It doesn't matter. Not to me. And I swear this will be good. I swear it. After this last one, if you don't like it, that's it. Honestly. I'll pick the best one.' She typed on the laptop. 'I don't think you stick out by the way.' More typing, her credit card. 'And even if you did there'd be nothing wrong with it. I've lived in Africa, for God's sake!'

They drove there that same day with him in near silence, his head bubbling – *Fucking Africa*; it's different – but his mouth shut because he didn't want to start a thing; they'd gone so long and not had a thing.

'Seriously. You'll love it,' Edie said. 'I've been. You'll love it. You'll love it. You will.'

They parked and he questioned why he was going along with it. But then his list: she was funny, she was pretty, when she played it was nice; and she was different, and difference is a good thing.

What happened with this place, she said on the walk from the car, is that the old owners were these eccentrics who wasted their fortune collecting curios from around the world. The house got too expensive to maintain so they started closing off its rooms, locking up wings, selling their furniture, eventually flogging the collections that made them broke in the first place. Then the house became the museum it now is. It was ruined and rotting when it was sold and now kept that way as a kind of testament to a lost way of life, the great families who once ruled England.

To him it just looked like a massive white block in the middle of a field.

Inside, he could see Edie walking there freely in another time with not much different about her except her clothes, lords taking her hand as she lifted her skirt to step over the threshold. At that time, he'd have to wait outside, or stand at the gates, more like, or be across the ocean chopping sugarcane – maybe worse – and then he remembered, in a snap of recognition, that he'd been here before.

When that came to him, the anger just went.

He'd been here.

He told her in the darkness of the entrance hall, the ceiling inside lower and more cave-like than expected, the space small compared to the size of the house outside, windowless, the walls decorated, as promised, like the castle before, with heads. 'I've been here,' he said, scanning the six or seven heads on the walls. That's what he remembered: this strange first taste, these trophies in a smaller-than-expected space, and he saw Edie, in the white trainers she always wore, look back at him and grin.

'You see? It's mad. It's great.'

Was it a school trip? Not even half-remembered, totally forgotten. 'Déjà vu,' he said.

'History,' said Edie.

She took his hand and together they moved through into a more beaten and time-worn version of what you'd expect from a place like this: other rooms with framed portraits of pale-skinned people in washed-out white clothes, sometimes holding the hands of children who looked like their miniatures. Family crests and columns, a library of unread leather books, porcelain decorations, grand maps, massive globes that the room guides said were wrong because they made England too large.

Everywhere cast shadows, and everywhere there were heads: of boars, of bulls, even an alligator's pimpled skull. In one room, in a glass case piled with fragments of rocks, sat the top half of a human head, skinless, made into cup that one of the staff said was from Tibet: a Tibetan's head.

'We don't know how the family acquired it, or where it's really from. It's one of the many curiosities in this house,' said the tour guide, museum person, whatever they were.

Then more heads, from everywhere, of every kind and type. Deeper into rooms with glass cabinets of dead birds stuffed and posed, their feathers the colour of the ghosts in the paintings. As they went – and there were rooms and rooms – he didn't know what to say, what all this meant. Why keep all this shit?

They sat down for tea and scones in the café. Again no brown faces, not even one. There were children, middle-aged people who in the house proper talked to the staff like they were neighbours or old friends – just chatting, laughing along in rooms filled with corpses, in a museum of dead bodies.

Edie asked him what he thought and he said, 'Yeah, interesting', seeing how at ease she was with it all, like she was everywhere. She sipped coffee and he watched her sliding through this place a hundred years ago. And maybe it was interesting. Had he really been into history, this is what he would have studied – great families, parliament, kings and queens. In one of the rooms, they'd assembled some bed that had to be preserved at the right

temperature or otherwise it would rot; said it was the bed the family probably bought for the king, for the king alone to sleep in, just in case he popped
in. The sheets were all Chinese, Chinese sheets the hot thing at the time,
the guide said, and Edie said, 'They're beautiful' and he thought maybe they
were shipped over in the same crate that had the Tibetan guys's head in it.
What do all these birds on it symbolise? she asked, Is this how big the beds
always were? It was massive, the posts like scaffolding, the mattress several
people wide, and he thought they bought this *just in case* the king visited, in
case someone like Edie visited, while his ancestors would've been sleeping
on the ground. Then he saw Edie inside it, first as she was with him, then
in period dress, then bare-shouldered under the sheets, with him crouched
at her feet – or someone like him – crouched by the bed in chains, then
with his head on the wall and he couldn't shake the image, and the guide
said, 'Fascinating isn't it?' And he said, 'I've seen it before. I've been here.'
   Now Edie said, 'What are you looking at?'

It made an undertow. On the way back Edie kept saying how great it was,
although it was obvious he didn't feel the same. They slept together that
night and he half saw her as she was and half saw them in the king's bed,
saw chains, saw her father and the mess of the country house. Edie's skin
looked too bright and his looked too dark, and it gave him energy but
made him angry and afterwards he felt strange. He got up while she slept
and paced his own immaculate flat and thought *What are you thinking?* Her
underwear lay just inside his bedroom door. It was simple, basic, but his
mind gave it lace, layers, then ballooning fabrics. He thought of the family
that owned the house blowing money on dead birds, and that family and
the one that owned the castle comparing mounted heads. The Tibetan's
head. His head. Edie's. Edie's body.

They went to London. Edie wanted to show him where her shop used to
be. She said sorry about the house. It's clear he didn't like it, which was
fine. But standing out doesn't matter. It really doesn't. Really. Sometimes
it's good a thing.
   He didn't respond to that and when they arrived in Islington, where
her shop had been, he said 'I've been here, I've been here before', but he
wasn't sure why.
   She took him to meet some friends in a part of London he didn't know.
He was dressed in his best, had been to the barber's, was on this new
beard shape he felt was working, while the friends' clothes were mostly
scruffy, clean but not pressed. 'Eeds!' they called out to her and the wom-
en air-kissed, and the men had over-tight handshakes and said *Hello mate!*
too loud and he wanted to go home.

All of them were rich – fine. All of them had the same voice, like the Queen's but softened with swearing or slang that sounded wrong out of their mouths. All of them said *fucking,* constantly. It was so *fucking* hot. Or so *fucking* big. Or It's so *fucking* stupid. Then they left the restaurant for – a bar? A club? – it was both and neither – the bustle of people, the mix of ages and faces like back home – but then they ended up in place with just one other Black guy who looked miserable. He made eye contact with him, looked down.

All night and all day, almost compulsively, he said, 'I've seen this before', or, 'I know this beer', or, 'This reminds me of a place'. At some point he said, 'My grandad loved cricket too.' But no one responded, no one seemed to care.

Later, when he lay next to Edie in bed in her friend's spare room, restless, he watched her breathing and thought about houses.

'Go to sleep,' she said, and stretched a hot arm over him, squashed her face full into his shoulder. 'Close your eyes.'

'Didn't you wonder where they got all those things from?'

'What things?'

'The heads on the wall. There must have been, like, herds in there.'

'Yeah.' Her voice muffled, then just breathing.

'They must have had people set up all over the world going on killing sprees, basically. Then they what, bring them back and sort through for the best ones? How do they pick?' He was only talking to himself, sounded like an idiot. 'They said that at the end there were only three people left in that house. Just three. In all that.'

'Go to sleep.'

They kept seeing each other. He asked her about her father's accent and she told him he was a grammar school boy; his parents didn't come from much. And your mum? he asked, hoping she'd say the same, but Edie just laughed:

'Her!'

More and more he'd slip out of their conversations and into visions: Edie with his grandmother, her father fully awake when he visited.

She wanted him to meet her brother and his kids. There was a birthday party for her old friend Kerry back in London. She asked him if he planned on living in Birmingham forever.

'What's wrong?' she'd say, more often, as he slipped from where they were to somewhere else.

Come and meet Dad properly, my brother, his partner.

Come camping. It's great. It's fun.

'Your friend James,' he said in response. 'The whole time we were out, I was saying to myself that he reminded me of someone.' And he described this Pakistani guy he went to school with, dirt poor, who had nothing in common with her friend James, who looked nothing like James, who sounded nothing like James. He couldn't stop himself.

Edie had some friends in Scotland who invited her to come and stay. She told him she was going and that he could join her, but in a way that sounded like she wasn't so sure. She was gone for five days, didn't really text, and his head cooled with work, other worries, then she called him to say she'd decided, last minute, to fly to Ireland to see some other friends who'd just bought a place. He could come? This time the invite felt genuine, enthusiastic – but he didn't want to, couldn't really afford to, didn't go.

Then she texted, at the end of the week: **Can we talk?**

IV.

There's a story his grandmother always told. The whole time he lived with her, for the entire time she was alive, she kept a Bible by her bedside, and another, fresher one with a ribbon bookmark in her living room. The story, from somewhere in the Gospels, was that a rich man had three slaves. He gives each of them some money. One gets five talents, one gets two talents, another gets one – *to each according to his ability*. The guy that gets five talents invests it, doubles it, and so does the guy who gets two. The one with the single talent buries it in the ground. When it's time for the master to ask what each slave had done with his investment, the two who made a profit get praised, and the one who didn't, makes an excuse: I know you're a harsh man and I didn't want to upset you by losing it. The master gets angry, tells the third slave, and his grandmother always said this word for word, *For to all those who have, more will be given, and they will have an abundance; but from those who have nothing, even what they have will be taken away.*

For his grandmother the moral of the story was simple: work hard and it'll pay off. When his teachers said he was playing up at school – *For to all those who have, more will be given;* if she asked him to fetch something from the kitchen and he dragged his feet – *from those who have nothing, even what they have will be taken away;* and, in the times he did something she felt was worthy, she'd talk about the talents but begin, *Remember Jesus say.*

Remember, he thought, when Edie on the phone told him all the things if he was honest he'd been expecting from the beginning. It had been great, she said, but she felt she needed to make a change. Being up here, seeing old friends, just opened up her eyes. Dad was fine now and recovering and it'd been that way for a while. Her brother was less than two miles away, could cope, always could. And there's only so long you can stifle yourself. It had been great, though, she'd learned a lot, and he was brilliant, but she'd just spoken to her other brother and he said why not come back down, you're not doing anything up there. And he was right. But it had been lovely, really. So eye-opening. And

V.

He did what you do for a while, stalked Edie for a full week after they'd split. On his phone, after work, he found enough pictures she'd posted online to reconstruct her trip. At the airport. On her plane to Sydney. A stop off in Singapore. Then her brother, his daughters, his partner in the harbour with a spray of sea foam in the background, bright white smiles, clear blue skies. All she posted about was how excited she was. All her friends, including the ones he'd met, posted back that it was wonderful and excellent and a great chance for her to finally do something for herself for once.

Then he stopped watching and moved on. There was nothing in it. They were too different. She kept taking him to places where he didn't fit in.

He needed to stick with women more like himself; women who got it, who you didn't need to explain anything to, who knew.

But then he thought about the girl from Tobago, whose family was from Tobago, who his app and the first half of their conversation said was his exact match, but who said there were too many immigrants, immigrants everywhere.

'These Romanians, Bulgarians. They don't have any connection to this country. Our families built this place up. We belong here,' she said. 'We do.' Then she asked him if he knew this guy, Dean, who she knew from school.

And he did.

CALKE ABBEY: A PLACE OF ISOLATION AND CURIOSITY

SARAH LONGAIR

Calke Abbey is a highly unusual National Trust property, its unique character striking the visitors as soon as their exploration of the interior begins. The faded grandeur of the house, retained as it was when left to the Trust, stands in contrast the conventional image of an opulent and manicured 'stately' home. Beneath these peeling wallpapers and apparently cluttered rooms lie a wealth of hidden histories. Since the middle of the nineteenth century, successive generations had left many rooms untouched, leaving their contents frozen in time, exactly as they had been more than one hundred years ago. In contrast to other properties in the Colonial Countryside project, it has few direct links to empire as found elsewhere in landed estates and country houses. Family members in the nineteenth century did not serve in colonial territories as administrators or in the military, and its construction was funded out of wealth acquired locally rather than through imperial trade or slavery. Several of its owners, including the 7th baronet, Sir Henry Harpur (1763 – 1819, who later took the surname Crewe), the 9th Baronet, Sir John Harpur Crewe (1824 – 1886) and his son, Sir Vauncey Harpur Crewe (1846 – 1924), were allegedly reclusive, shunning aristocratic society and preferring to spend their time on the estate. What makes this house so interesting is how the wider world – while rarely ventured into by the inhabitants – seeps into almost every room.

The present house was built in 1702 – 4 for Sir John Harpur, 4th Baronet, incorporating parts of the existing Elizabethan and Jacobean structures. Sir Henry, the 7th Baronet, added the grand south front portico, loggia and balcony in 1806 – 7. The vast collections have been built over many generations, but were particularly enhanced by Sir John (9th Baronet) and Sir Vauncey in the nineteenth century. These two men had an avid interest in the natural world, which led to the acquisition of large quantities of taxidermy including birds, mammals, eggs, butterflies, books, shells and geological specimens. It is these numerous examples of animal bodies and heads with which Malachi McIntosh evocatively opens the *Imperial Homes* short story and which haunt its protagonist's memory after visiting Calke Abbey. In addition to taxidermy and natural history specimens, there are numerous paintings, furniture and artefacts. The book collections are typical of an aristocratic collection, covering a wide range of topics, including architecture and music, as well as law and science, and understandably strong in natural history. The library of Sir John Gardner Crewe, a cousin of the family and regarded by some as the father of British Egyptology, was added in 1875. His collection was stored separately from the main library and has remained in situ since then. These examples give us a picture of how material relating to the wider world came to Calke.

As a historian of the British Empire interested in objects and visual culture, my investigation of the house focused upon its objects and in this short essay I will discuss some of the items which caught my attention and reveal the widespread reach of Britain's empire upon daily life. The extent to which people in Britain engaged with imperial issues has been a topic of debate in academic circles since the 1980s, in particular through the works of John MacKenzie and Bernard Porter. While it is notoriously hard to gauge how Victorian Britons 'felt' about the empire, recent work by scholars focusing upon the material traces of empire within Britain has demonstrated that objects – whether commodities, souvenirs, raw materials or artefacts – were central to how the majority of people in Britain experienced empire in the nineteenth and twentieth centuries.

One of the most outstanding items in the family's collection, and one which speaks vividly of the eighteenth-century British taste for luxurious commodities from 'the east', is known as the State Bed. This object catches Edie's attention in McIntosh's story and prompts the anonymous protagonist to reflect upon why she, as a white woman, felt comfortable surrounded by such objects while he only felt alienation. The Chinese silk hangings, depicting scenes of human figures, animals, dragons and buildings, are in pristine condition as they had lain in packing cases since coming to the house. Family tradition records that this bed was a wedding gift from Queen Caroline, wife of George II, to Lady Caroline Manners when she married Sir Henry Harpur in 1734. The vibrancy of its colours and exquisite embroidery illustrate why such items were so prestigious, bringing an element of the exotic into the bedrooms of the elite.

The natural history collections are the most noticeable and prominent of all objects in Calke Abbey. Sir John and his son Sir Vauncey developed this expansive and wide-ranging array of specimens. Sir John had been particularly devoted to breeding longhorn cattle and Portland sheep, winning prizes at agricultural shows. Howard Colvin, who first wrote the history of Calke Abbey, describes the transformation of Calke: 'Animals, tame or wild, living or dead, were now becoming Calke's principal *raison d'être*.'¹ Sir John's son, Vauncey, from a young age shared this enthusiasm and birds – in particular stuffed examples – became his principal interest. While many of the animals were hunted locally, Sir Vauncey also bought exotic examples to add to the collection. The evidence of his collecting is clear for all to see in almost every room of the house. What is even more staggering is that the current displays represent only half of the original bird collections – the other half were sold after Sir Vauncey's death to pay for death duties. His collection also extended to butterflies and birds' eggs. The so-called Bird Lobby in Calke houses just some of these hundreds of specimens.

Sir Vauncey's passion for observing, shooting and collecting birds led him on a rare venture overseas on an ornithological trip to Egypt in 1869 – 70. A notebook in the Derbyshire archives records his nature notes and a list of the birds he shot on this expedition. He also acquired a selection of Egyptian artefacts, on display in the Saloon. The label in this case describes the items as 'Collection of Egyptian curiositys [sic] brought by me from Egypt and Nubia in 1869 & 70. Vauncey Harpur Crewe. May 5th 1879.' They include what are likely to be contemporary items in the nineteenth century, such as a stringed instrument, jewellery and two daggers, and a metal figurine, similar to a shabti. The case also includes two small crocodile heads, which appear to have been mummified. Such objects were typical of the kinds of material available for British travellers who regularly visited Egypt in the mid to late nineteenth century. The region became the focus of attention across the world in 1869 with the opening of the Suez Canal. Vessels bound for the Indian Ocean and further east no longer had to take the long journey round the Cape of Good Hope, but could cross the Mediterranean and pass through the new canal into the Red Sea. Many more vessels from Europe were therefore bound for Egypt from 1869.

Numerous other items attest to a fascination with the wider world, even though the Harpur Crewe family rarely experienced it at first hand. Particularly notable in the drawing room is a 'costly Chinese pagoda carved in ivory', as described by John Bernard Burke in 1852 in his *Visitation of the Seats and Arms of the Noblemen and Gentlemen*. This intricately carved ivory structure was reportedly a present to Lady Jane Crewe, wife of Sir George Crewe, the 8th Baronet, from a friend in the East India Company. Elsewhere there is an architectural fragment from the Mosque at Fatephur Sikri, a famous Mughal palace outside Agra, an African thumb piano and a Tibetan Buddhist skull cup. These items are found in display cases, crammed full with unusual objects from closer to home, such as a piece of silk from the room from which Mary Queen of Scots's courtier, David

Rizzio, was seized and murdered. Material from the wider world, then, sits alongside more local curiosities.

The library too testifies to an interest in travel writing and the world beyond Calke, including some celebrated volumes, such as John Gould's *The Mammals of Australia*. The globe in the library dates from 1870 so captures a moment in time when the British Empire was steadily growing. All the areas of territory controlled by Britain are coloured red, which was, as well as with pink, typically used from the late eighteenth century for maps and cartographic representations of imperial territory. Canada, Australia, New Zealand and India stand out prominently and visually underline the global reach of the empire. The globe also purports to show 'all the latest information', but also underlines the limits of colonial knowledge. Vast areas of Africa are simply labelled with names of communities, such as 'Zulu tribes here'. Had the globe been made 30 years later, almost all of Africa would be coloured by the possessions of European nations, following the so-called 'Scramble for Africa'.

While no members of the family line of inheritance served overseas, there were relations who did. Georgiana, Lady Harpur Crewe, wife of Sir John, the 19th baronet, inherited several items related to the Battle of Trafalgar in 1805, from her father, Vice-Admiral William Stanhope Badcock (later Lovell). After the capture of the *Santa Trinidada* in the battle, the young Badcock as a midshipman acquired an ornamental gilt dirk (a kind of thrusting dagger), belonging to the Spanish admiral's son. It is housed in a specially crafted wooden box at Calke. The Vice-Admiral's exploits are recorded elsewhere in the house – on display are a painting of the battle by the same artist who illustrated his reminiscences, published in 1837, and a portrait of his brother, General Lovell Benjamin Lovell, similarly a hero of the Napoleonic wars.

As is clear from this discussion, there are traces of empire across the house. Even on the playroom floor lies the skin of a tiger, the hunting and display of which was synonymous with the domination of India. While these elements were amassed, curated and consumed by the Harpur Crewe family, there were also many servants and staff who also engaged with these objects, whether to clean or serve around them. There were usually around twenty five to thirty staff members, and it is quite possible they had more direct links to empire, with family members in the army or navy or serving overseas. Perhaps their lives were more connected to the wider world than the Harpur Crewes. While I have concentrated here on the apparent contradiction of a household of global items amongst a family of reclusives, some members of the family had a more adventurous spirit. Sir Vauncey's daughter Winifred seems to have defied the Harpur Crewe tendency to isolation. Her worldwide travels are recorded on a charming hand-drawn map. She entitled the map: 'Miss Winifred Crewe/ her travels/ France Spain Switzerland Africa Burma India Ceylon/ about 23,000 miles.' She has drawn her extensive route onto the map, highlighting how she saw the empire with her own eyes, unlike many of her forbears who only experienced the world from the environs of Calke Abbey.

Endnote:
1. Howard Colvin, *Calke Abbey, Derbyshire: A Hidden House Revealed* (London: National Trust, 1985), p. 68.

KEDLESTON HALL

Sheep at Kedleston Hall, Derbyshire.
©National Trust Images/Arnhel de Serra

George Nathaniel Curzon, 1st Marquess Curzon of Kedleston, KG, GCIE, PC, MP (1859-1925) in the Robes of Chancellor of Oxford University by Sir Hubert von Herkomer, CVO, RA (Waal 1849 ¿ Budleigh Salterton 1914) ©National Trust Images/John Hammond

Kedleston – The Peacock Dress
©National Trust Images/David Brunetti

MAHSUDA SNAITH

UNEARTHED VOICES:
A FLASH FICTION COLLECTION

1. For ever. For everyone
Object of interest: Kedleston Hall building

Derbyshire 1787
Welcome, dear visitor to Kedleston Hall. I trust you had a good journey?
My name is Mrs Garnet, the housekeeper of this fine establishment and I
shall be your guide today.

How did I gain this post, you ask? I was just about to talk upon that very
matter. It was Baron Scarsdale who hired me, before this great hall was
built. You should have seen the old estate, a shabby little dwelling. As soon
as the Baron inherited it, he was quick to tear it down and begin work on
the magnificent building you see before us.

You are correct, there was once a village here. A medieval parish that
contained cottages, a malthouse and rectory... And villagers, of course. It
was relocated. Quite necessary to improve the view of the property and
create the acres of luscious parkland you see behind us.

Now, let's take a moment to look upon the exterior of this fine hall.
Note the majestic façade with steps winding up like diamonds on a tiara.
Quite the sight, don't you agree?

Yes, it was the young Robert Adam he employed to be architect. You
see, the Baron fancied a Roman touch to his Derbyshire estate and Adam
had just returned from three years study in Rome. My master had the
vision of a building that would rival Chatsworth. Rome reborn in Britain!

What is it you're asking now? ...Funds? I'm sure I am not the right
person to answer such a question. Yes, I believe Baron Scarsdale made a
number of clever investments, a most canny fellow... Very possibly in the
American colonies. Perhaps the East India Company, too. But those really
are the Baron's *personal* matters, don't you agree?

Hello? Wait there! I'm afraid that is not the correct way! Now that I
have caught up, can I respectfully inform you that it is ordinarily the outer

steps we make our entrance through. This is Caesars' Hall... Yes, I suppose we can start from here. Please give me a moment to catch my breath.

Within the niches you will find busts of Roman Emperors... Ah, but I see you are more interested in the columns. Sixteen in total supporting the great hall above... Like servants, you say, supporting the wealthy. Well, I suppose that could be a fair comparison, considering how very grand the Marble Hall is and how honoured the staff are to be working for such fine family... Like subjects of the Empire too? Well, I hardly see the connection there. What is your title again?

I see you are now heading to the Great Staircase which leads us to the Marble Hall. See how well spent the support from below is? Twenty veined alabaster pillars quarried from Ratcliffe-on-Soar and sculpted by hand. A floor of polished Hopton Wood, stone inlaid with white Italian marble and honeysuckle detail.

There you are again, walking on while I am still talking. If I was a less jovial guide, I believe I would reprimand you! Let's pause here at the Saloon for a moment. The dome you see above is directly influenced by the great Pantheon in Rome... No, the Baron has yet to visit Rome himself, yet it does remain a great inspiration.

Now you are entering the State Apartment. Note the gilt sofas, blue damask wallcoverings, mirrors framed by gold palm-tree relief. See how these are replicated upon the bed posts of the grand state bed. Look closer and you will see ostrich feathers bursting out like fountains... Do we own ostriches? How cruel of you to tease me with such questions.

Yes, of course, there are many more things to see. The Music Room, the Library, the Drawing Room... But you do not wish to see them? I must say, my visitors are usually of a more patient calibre than yourself. Remind me of your title...

Now you are truly mocking me! A fortune teller, you say. You shall be asking to see my palm next. But it's not my future you see... Ah, *Kedleston's*. Well, I'm afraid I do find it hard to believe, especially with such a sly grin upon your face. And what, if I am so bold to ask, is it you claim to see? A house in India, modelled upon this one... And a train station too, in Huddersfield of all places! About the boy's future I can believe. I am sure you are right in saying he will change history, the same as his ancestors have done before him.

Let's move on. No, I am afraid I cannot hear any more. Indeed, I am beginning to feel quite unwell... You see other guides in these rooms of the future? Well, I do not wish to contradict you, but they are unlikely to have as much knowledge as myself. One dressed as me you say? I believe you are trying to flatter me but are causing quite the opposite effect.

Let's exit through the hall. Yes, I am sure there is much more for you to say but, as housekeeper, I have many other duties to carry out... Yes, I heard what you foresaw. Open air theatres, celebrations of world festivals and health walks all on Kedleston grounds. Please do mind the steps on the way down... Child historians! What a novel idea. And visitors in their thousands from all classes and races. Indeed.

Please do take care of yourself as you retrieve your coach from the stables. Yes, I am sure to recover after a brief rest. What is that you say? Such an interesting way with words you have...

For ever. For everyone.

Yes, quite poetic. A motto for the future, I'm sure.

2. Waste Not. Want Not

Object of interest: an Indian chess set and a sign in the kitchen

Derbyshire, 1867

He weren't meant to show me. Neither of us had business in the main house that early in the morning. But Sammy is a scamp, smitten on me they say, and told me the polishing of a hundred staff boots could wait.

We balance on the bottom rung of the Kedleston Hall ladder, Sammy the hall boy and me, the between-maid. But there are gains from being so low. Stories drain down to us like the waste I pour down the sluices during slop duties.

*

I followed him into the drawing room, treading softly, as if the floorboards would tattle on us. The room were decked in sailor blue with images of merfolk sculpted on the sofa legs. I looked at a saucy bare-breasted mermaid, painted gold and reclining, as if on leave. Sammy told me how the previous day's visitor, Sir Henry Wilmot, had sat upon her seat. His mulberry coat was decorated with silver badges that stood in a line like us servants waiting for morning inspection. One of them was the Victoria Cross for bravery, given to him for some ruckus between his men and some Indian mutineers.

Sammy had heard none of this himself; the story had drained down to him in pieces from the upper staff. That and how the children had been there for tea with little Georgie sat by his mam's side, eyes round as moons, as he listened to the Captain. Lady Scarsdale dotes something awful on that boy. Getting him fitted in London for velvet suits, putting his hair in corkscrew ringlets. 'Course, Reverend Scarsdale don't approve. He's a thrifty man, wandering round the house removing coal from fires. In our kitchen he' fixed a sign above the fireplace that reads *Waste Not. Want Not.*

We waste nothing, yet still I want.

*

Sammy grinned as he led me to the table with the chess set.

It'd been brought out for the Captain; a gift given to the family from India. The upper staff hadn't cleared it away for fear they'd be scolded for disturbing a half-finished game.

'Marvellous, int it?' said Sammy.

I looked at the hand-painted figures of soldiers with rifles and close-fitting uniforms on ivory squares, natives with spears and loose garments on ebony ones. Along the back, were strange beasts with long noses; elephants, Sammy told me, which was where the ivory came from. On their backs were tall boxes carrying the king and queen, too posh to get their feet dirty.

Sammy was keen as mustard about the cannons, but it was the faces of the soldiers that drew me in. The butler says the British used their 'superior intelligence' to put these Eastern savages back in their cages. But these do not look like savages. These men have calm faces, noble.

The butler is an ass. I believe he'd put me in a cage if he could.

The sound of feet echoed down the corridor. Sammy rushed to the door but I stayed put.

'Come on Tilly!' he hissed.

I looked at the soldiers one last time, then returned to my duties.

*

The next day, Reverend Scarsdale was due to give the sermon for Sunday service. The church is a stone's throw away from staff quarters but we always wait for the family to enter first.

As we stood waiting, I thought of the night before when I'd dreamed of canons and rifles blasting amongst palm trees, elephants charging, men falling blood-soaked to the ground, and then, out of nowhere, a peacock lying dead amongst the wreckage. The peacock I'd seen in the dining room. I served up there once, when there was smallpox amongst the staff. I stood at the back of the room and stared at the mirror fixed to the wall opposite. We'd been told not to look directly at the guests, rather to observe if their wine needed refilling through the mirror. We're meant to be invisible.

I remember, in the reflection, seeing a portrait hanging high above my head. On it was painted a dead deer, head hung over a table edge, and a basin filled with other carcasses – rabbit, swan – the peacock laid across the top. I looked at its fine feathers, colours as vivid as cornflowers. It seemed so cruel to kill something so beautiful and for what? They had plenty meat already.

When the family arrived at the church, we filed in after them. I held my book of *Daily Prayers for Servants*. Mam gave it to me, saying I could work my way up to under-cook, then cook, then lady's maid and perhaps one day housekeeper if I kept my head down and followed its rules. The wage could support the whole family.

I walked to the back pews and watched the governess with her chin lifted as she stood by the children. If only the mistress knew how she treated those poor souls. Withholding food. Tying them to chairs. Marching them to the pleasure grounds with strips of paper fastened to their clothes with *Liar, Sneak, Coward* written across them. She does this to wound the children's pride, but I think it only puffs them up. Each year their power grows while hers wanes. One day, the tales of their mistreatment will be her undoing. Even the innocent can rebel.

When the service was over, I dropped my prayer book on the floor and let the feet of the lower staff trample over it. Perhaps I have the devil in me, for he was a rebel himself, a fallen angel, or so the great book says.

I had dreamed of rebellion. And the rebellion was good.

3. My Name is Kolkata
Object of interest: a sandalwood shrine with brass figures of deities

Namaste! Assalam Alaikum! Sat Shri Akal! Hello!

My name is Kolkata. You may know me by other spellings and monikers – Calcutta, the City of Joy, the once mighty capital of the British Raj – but I remain the same bustling city, inhabited for over two millennia. Observe my streets filled with baby-taxis, mopeds and yellow cabs blasting their horns in a friendly din as ambling pedestrians cross their path. Follow the smell of aloo puchka. Watch as they are freshly fried by the roadside – crispy hollowed-out shells filled with delicately spiced potato and topped with tamarind sauce. Pop one in, let the flavours erupt and shower down upon your tongue! Good, yaar?

Now, with your appetite satisfied, follow me to the Hooghly River, for this is where our story begins.

Many years ago, in this vast and spirited city, there lived a Viceroy called George Nathaniel Curzon. Having visited India four times before his viceroyalty, he had written extensively about its people, though not always graciously. His predecessor was known to visit the homes of Bengali families, his wife dressed in a sari as she sat on the floor eating with her fingers in the traditional way. George, however, preferred to host State Balls, dinners and garden parties within the gated grounds of Government House. As imposing as the Birla Mandir, this fine building was furnished with mahogany, gold, crystal chandeliers and woven rugs, the numerous servants dressed immaculately in duck-white uniforms. With a building modelled on his childhood residence, George felt quite at home.

Yet there were times, between ruling a nation and hosting soirees, that George would take his wife, body guards and escorts, on afternoon drives through my great city. He loved the Maiden Park to the south of his home, was proud of the East India Company's Fort William, had collected funds for the Victoria Memorial to commemorate the passing of his great Queen and was most fond of the rippling waters of the Hooghly River. Once he drove as far as the old neighbourhood of Kalighat, past roadside mosaics of gods that watched him closely with divine eyes, before being stopped by an enthusiastic crowd of locals who swarmed around his carriage. Astonished by the sight of their ruler amongst them, they pressed their palms together as if pleading for alms.

George asked his escort what the locals wanted. The young man, who was new to his role, quickly disappeared into the crowd before returning with a gracious, overeager smile.

'They want you to come and see the shrine of their goddess,' he said.

Of course, his wife, Mary, protested but George knew from his study of Disraeli that the world was divided into the ruling classes and the masses; those who belonged to the first category must make it their duty to humour the second graciously.

When George entered the temple, he was greeted with a reeking stench similar to that of decomposing fish, and when he was ushered to the central shrine, he was faced with a figure so dark and menacing it made his lips quiver. This was Kali, the black skinned deity with three raging eyes, her teeth in a fearsome snarl as a golden tongue hung over her lips. In one of her four hands she held a curved sword, in another the severed head of a moustachioed demon. The demon, the escort explained, represented Ego which needed to be slain by Divine Knowledge in order for a person to attain liberation.

George looked into the fiery eyes of Kali and then upon the marigold garlands hung by worshippers around her neck, and saw something of himself in her. He nodded slowly. The crowd, excited by this reaction, directed George, via a river of hands and gestures, to the southeast of the temple. Here the reeking fish-stench intensified with each step. Men were standing, heads bowed in prayer, in a pool of pale green water, rippling in circles around them.

'They want you to bathe in the holy water,' the escort told George with his overeager smile. 'It will give you great moksha.'

George had heard of moksha, a concept shared amongst the many religions that resided in this city. It was a word for release, enlightenment, liberation. He shook his head, chuckling quietly to himself.

'I am the ruler of the British Raj,' he said. 'I have no need for liberation.'

And so, he left. Back in his barouche to Government House, to his State Balls and garden parties.

But what George Nathaniel Curzon did not know was the goddess Kali had been watching (for, of course, she is always watching). Her appearance may seem fierce to those unfamiliar with her form, but Kali is a goddess of great compassion, the divine protector and the destroyer of all evil. It is her duty to give moksha to her children.

From that day, she observed George as he squabbled with Kitchener, his Commander-in-Chief, and felt his exasperation when he was accused of indifference to the Indian famine. George was heartbroken following the death of Mary and infirm with a lifelong back ailment, and Kali would appear in his restless sleep and offer him her gift. Each time, he would roll away. After he ignored the petitions and protests against the partition of Bengal, the wise and beatific goddess Kali decided to depart.

You cannot give moksha to a person who believes he has it already.

Now, at the end of this story, it is time for me to leave. Please take care as you make your way back through my bustling streets. Visit the shrines, dip in their pools, feel the weight of ego lift from your shoulders as the divine luminosity of knowledge releases you.

Chaalo Aavjo! Allah Hafiz! Sat Shri Akal!

Come back soon.

4. *The Tigress, the Maharaja and the Viceroy*
Object of interest: a tiger skin rug

Once, there was a tigress who knew what lay in the human heart. Each day she would prowl the Gwalior jungles listening to the desires of the locals. Some of them wanted a good harvest, some of them riches, while others were quite content with their lot.

One day, men came to the forest with a buffalo. The tigress narrowed her amber eyes and knew that the buffalo had been given as an offering. But when other men built platforms on the branches of banyan trees, she realised these offerings were not out of respect, but sent by the Maharaja Scindia to fatten up the tigers for a great shikar. He was planning this in honour of a man he called the Viceroy.

She had heard this man's name before from the twittering of green-winged pitta birds. They said there were many jungles preserved for the use of the Viceroy's shikars, where partridges, bison, crocodiles and elephants were hunted. But it was the Royal Bengal tiger that was most prized by the pale sahibs. Their magnificent bodies, with the feet of their hunters planted on their stripes, always made such striking photographs.

The tigress ran through the jungle, roaring her warning to the creatures that lay within. There had been many shikars before but she knew that when man tries to impress he tends to get carried away.

On the day of the Viceroy's hunt, armed soldiers walked through the jungle with drum beaters and barking dogs, making a clamorous noise to drive the animals into the hunter's path.

The tigress crept through the terrain, catching sight of the Viceroy as he lay on his stomach across a platform. His eyes were steely, his nose as sharp as his attention when he spotted her through the barrel of his gun. He shot, his aim good enough to strike but not enough to kill. The tigress stumbled into the jungle with a trail of blood following behind like glistening rubies on a necklace.

The Maharaja, having been alerted to the Viceroy's frustration, followed this trail with his finest hunters. As she felt them approach, the tigress narrowed her amber eyes and spoke to Maharaja Scindia in a language only he could decipher. He raised his hand, ordering the men to stand back.

The Maharaja followed the whispers of the tigress into a cave. The tigress sensed his terror, his heart thudding as hard as the drums of the beaters. When he saw her lying before him, panting from the agony of her wound, he laid down his rifle.

This was when the tigress told him her tale.

Many years before, the tigress, who was queen of this jungle, was cursed by a demon who was jealous of her power. He gave her the knowledge of what lay in a human heart and therefore the whims that would one day destroy her kind. The tigress implored the Maharaja to see past his narrow desires and protect the animals of his lands. If humans continued with their unbridled slaughter, the Royal Bengal tiger would soon become a thing of legend.

Tears rolled down Scindia's cheeks like rain falling down a dry canyon. He confessed his great shame for acting without foresight. But his need to please the Viceroy, who had hunted on the backs of elephants in Cooch Behar, overwhelmed him. He was soon to be wed to a fine princess and knew that to please the British Raj would also please her.

The tigress pondered the Maharaja's dilemma. She decided that, because she was maimed and full of suffering, he could use her body as a gift to the Viceroy, but only if he promised to kill no more tigers for at least one year. He was to cut out the tigress's heart, where the curse had been placed, and thus release her from this lifecycle. However, if this pact was broken, he would be cursed for the rest of his days.

The Maharaja agreed to this pact, cutting out the tigress's heart which he found to be a giant ruby that shone brighter than a blood moon. He placed it into the folds of his boat-shaped hat and vowed to not hunt a tiger for at least another year.

But as soon as he left the cave and saw the great cats of the jungle coming to mourn their queen, the Maharaja's greed muddied his mind. If the Viceroy was pleased with one dead beast, how much greater would his pleasure be when presented with two? He ordered his men to shoot the nearest tiger. As soon as the bullet pierced its heart, the giant ruby fell from the Maharaja's hat, hitting the ground as a lump of stone.

The Maharaja Scindia transported the two tigers to the Viceroy in a carriage drawn by four horses and posed beside him for a photograph, feet placed on the tigress's stripes. He tried to forget the pact he had broken; he had never been a believer in curses.

But then, soon after, the princess he'd been promised broke off their engagement. She wrote to tell Scindia she had met her true love at the Delhi Durbar organised by the same Viceroy he had tried so hard to impress. She later became regent of his rival district, Cooch Behar. When he did marry, the Maharaja Scindia's wife bore him no children and when he finally sired an heir with his second wife, the boy almost died. There were accolades: aide-de-camp to Edward VII, an honorary degree from the University of Cambridge, but the Maharaja was plagued with jealousy and never content with his lot. Was this, though, the result of the curse, or the destiny of a person who cares too much about the thoughts of others?

As for the tigress, she now lies flattened out in an English country house, her amber eyes wide open.

5. The Peacock Dress

> *"Give me the girl that knows a woman's place and does not yearn for trousers. Give me, in fact, Mary,"* George Nathaniel Curzon

Delhi, 1903
Mary stands before the mirror in her chemise and drawers. She has fainted eight times this week and can see the result in her lack of colour, her skin almost as pale as the white cotton.

She pinches her cheek, strokes her brow as the temporary maid wraps her corset in place, threading the laces through the eyelets on the back. She is called Ritu, on loan to Mary at Red Fort because her own maids are sick with fever. Ritu is a jackfruit of a woman, short and round with prickly looks and gestures. Mary has found this with the Indian staff — some so loyal and adoring, others seemingly ungrateful of the work they are given. Ritu yanks at the laces of the corset, knocking the breath out of Mary's small frame. Mary raises a hand. Ritu stops until she nods again. This is the price a woman pays for elegance.

She suspects George, her dear Pappy, is already fully dressed in his Vice-regal robes, each medal pinned meticulously in place. He has organised the last two weeks of the Durbar with his usual exacting attention to detail. What was once a deserted plain has been transformed into a tented city complete with telegraph and telephones, a post office with its own stamp, a light railway, hospital and magistrate's court, as well as a complex sanitation system and electric lights. He has sent his aide, Dr Watts, on regional tours across India in search of the finest crafts – sandalwood vanity boxes, ivory statues, handstitched cloth – to display in the exhibition hall, so that guests can witness the luminous sparkle of the jewel in the Empire's crown.

Ritu drapes a linen petticoat over Mary's head until it drops down to her waist. There is a riot of laughter as Irene runs around Mary's feet. Her ayah chases after her with Baba in her arms, flapping her hand as if shooing off mosquitoes. Irene bumps into the side-table. They all cry out as a jug of water almost tips onto the skirt of Mary's dress. Irene is ushered out of the room, tears welling in her eyes.

Ritu, as if in fear of more calamities, fixes the skirt on next. It is made of champagne-coloured taffeta, lined with densely woven Indian muslin and has a long train edged with silk flowers. But it is the gold thread embroidery that makes the dress dazzle, intricately handstitched to appear like peacock feathers with iridescent beetle wings sewn onto the eye of each plume. This is East meets West, a symbol of the riches that come with Empire.

As Ritu begins fitting the bodice, Mary, feeling lightheaded, holds onto the side-table. The jug tumbles over, liquid cascading like a waterfall and leaving a dark stain on the crimson rug beneath. The doctors have said Mary should be resting; she has barely managed a staircase without fainting of late. If her mother saw her now, she would order her to bed. But Mary must carry on with her duties and uphold her family name. She is, after all, the first American to sit on the Viceroyal seat. She knows others expect her to be brash and opinionated like her sisters who flirt with staff at Government House and bow mockingly at Pappy's feet. So Mary keeps her voice low, only speaking after her husband has spoken and only ever in agreement. A wife's role is vital in this world of politics.

Ritu brings Mary a new glass of water, frowning as if Mary's stumble has inconvenienced her. Mary gulps the water down, pats her mouth with a handkerchief, then stands tall as the bodice, decorated with the same peacock design as the skirt and covered with hanging lace on the upper arms, is firmly attached. She drapes the ruby necklace around her own throat, then places a tiara upon her head.

The door opens; it is Pappy. She can tell from the wrinkle across his forehead that he is troubled. He has already been humiliated by the 9th Lancers and by those Europeans who'd applauded them even after all he'd done to reprimand their abhorrent behaviour with the native cook. Then there was the New York newspaper article declaring that, when the people of India had asked for bread, Curzon had given them a Durbar. And then the King sending his brother in his place for the ceremony had been a hard blow. Yet still, they had been showered with addresses and gifts from across the world and all present had been enthralled by the fireworks displays and the glamorous dances. All this, when her Pappy suffers so badly with his back, a secret he tells no one but her.

Mary pulls on her gloves until they reach her elbows.

'It has been a marvellous two weeks Pappy,' she tells him, 'After tonight, we will be the talk of the globe.'

He looks at her for what seems the first time. The wrinkle melts away.

'My dear Kinkie, I am the most blessed man in the British Raj,' he says.

No one sees this soft side to him. He acts the superior role he thinks is expected of a Viceroy, but in small circles he laughs easily and is charming. This is her real Pappy.

They walk to the State Ballroom and pause behind the doors. The highest-ranking guests are inside, drinking the finest wines of India. Mary and George enter, the electric lights making her dress sparkle as richly as the fireworks of the Durbar. All eyes in the room turn, gazing at her in wonderment.

Her job is done.

6. We Are Not Your Jewel
Object of interest: Miniature portraits of Indian monuments

October 16th 1905
We watched as he walked into the holy river. Behind him boats were moored to poles and women crouched on the steps as they rung out wet saris of saffron orange and lotus pink. When he came back onto the banks of the Ganges, Tagore dressed himself in a plain cotton kurta before collecting his pile of rakhis from the ground. We had our own bundles of the crimson threads clasped in our hands. He nodded at us and we began to tie them to our neighbours' wrists.

He was not what I expected. Out in Dhaka we had heard of the great

Rabindranath Tagore, grandson of a dewan of the East India Company, from a rich family who had lived in palaces, a writer and social activist. I had expected a grander figure, not the slender man before me. His beard was as long as those of the gurus who sat by the river, hair curled at the base of his neck like the unfurling leaves of a fern. Yet I could feel the power in his gentle manner. As my youngest brother Atu told me, it is not brawn that wins a battle, it is knowledge.

After we began our march, Tagore stopped regularly to tie rakhis, here to an elderly woman's wrist, there to a child's. This is our tradition during the festival of Raksha Bandhan, sisters tying threads to their brothers' wrists as a promise of protection. But that day there was a new meaning to the ritual. The raki was Tagore's symbol of unity and would be tied upon the wrists of people of all creeds. This was his peaceful protest against the British declaration in August that Bengal was to be divided by October – two months to shatter a land. The day of the march was the date of that partition. After weeks of boycotting foreign goods, Tagore had told us we should treat that date as a day of mourning. No one would work or light fires in their home. We all kept to this vow with diligence.

As I walked on through the streets, I thought of Atu again. I remembered the day he was chosen to be a cook in an army regiment and his excitement to serve the British. He was always fond of their strange words and bland food. He felt honoured with this new position. So did we.

I was knocked by shoulders as the march grew bigger. Thousands of Muslims, Sikhs and Hindus had come from across Bengal: Calcutta, Dhaka, Sylhet. Crowds lined the street as we began our song of protest written by Tagore himself, a prayer to keep Bengal safe and united. Puffed rice was thrown by women from rooftops, grains falling upon us like the first rain of the monsoon. People blasted conch shells and cheered us on. I watched as Tagore tied a rakhi to a young man's wrist.

I'd never thought that my brother, not just my sisters, would need protection. But how was I to know what would happen to Atu that night? That soldiers of the regiment would return drunk and belligerent, that they would ask him to bring more drink than they could handle? That he would comply until they asked him to provide women for them too and, then, how they beat him mercilessly for his refusal and leave him broken and bleeding on the floor? No brother would be able to predict such horror.

We approached the mosque and Tagore began to enter. The crowd warned him to not overstep his mark. He looked at us nodding softly, like a cow dozing in the sun. We watched as he met the mullahs at the doors. They talked quietly to each other so we could not hear their words.

Of course, my brother's story is not a rare one. There are many beatings on the tea plantations and within the houses of the Raj. But after

Atu's body was found in the morning, his murder was treated so care-lessly by the police that my parents wrote to the Viceroy himself. He was appalled; the matter had been hushed up without his knowledge. He told my father he would go through the correct procedures to see that justice would be done for Atu.

In the end, my brother's name was pulled through the mud. The courts said he was drunk, a thief, another untrustworthy coolie. Perhaps it would have been better if we had said nothing.

Or perhaps, this is what they want us to believe.

Yet still, I viewed the Viceroy as a noble man for his efforts — until he announced the plans for partition, which was when I realised he was a fool. He saw no issue with dividing the Hindu regions from the Mus-lim regions, encouraging the use of Hindi as the national language when Bangla runs through this region like the tributaries that run through its land. Even after the petitions were sent, he ignored them all, not realising the devastation he was about to cause.

We watched the mullahs as they listened to Tagore's words. I held my breath until they placed their hands upon his shoulders and held out their wrists for him to tie the threads. They understood the need for unity in these divisive times. They understood we were stronger together than apart.

A new feeling surged through the crowd as we left the mosque. We were no longer individuals but joined together in one moving body. We continued to sing, continued to tie rakhis, continued with our march of unity. I could not protect Atu anymore, but I would protect these people. We would not be divided.

The British like to describe India as the jewel in their crown. They see us as an ornament, something to own and parade with pride. But we are not an ornament. We are not their jewel.

We are our own people with our own voice.

And we will be heard.

7. *From India's Coral Strand*
Object of interest: A betel nut cutter

1906, The London Fete
This is a strange place they have taken us. We stand on stage in a tent, with British women sitting on seats in front of us, fluttering hand fans at their clammy faces. They wilt like lotus flowers in lakes during dry season.

Of course, I know real heat. I am from Madras! This weather does not bother me or the other ayahs, even wearing these British clothes: stock-ings, drawers, petticoats, hoop skirts, chemise, corset, camisole and bodice. Aye! And that is without the boots, gloves and bonnet! If we were all able to wear the saris, petticoats and blouses set left behind at the Ayah's Home then everyone would feel so much more at ease. I thought this too, back in India, where the memsahibs thought wearing white linen and holding up parasols would stop them from fainting, when still wearing corsets and layers that drowned them. I did not say this, of course; it was not my place.

We stand on the stage in neat lines. The British are always so orderly. The audience mutter between themselves, looking at our dark skin and nose rings as though we are zoo animals. Our matron, Mrs Dunn, stands at the front with her neck stretched tall. She has instructed us that we are representatives not only of the Ayah's Home and its Christian values, but also the Empire. This responsibility feels weighty, like sacks of rice carried on the back of buffalo.

Mrs Dunn sits at the piano, flattens out her skirt and begins playing 'From Greenland's Icy Mountains'. Between prayer services, readings of the Bible and needlework, we have been practising this song as though trying to win a prize. I have sung about Africa's sunny fountains, Ceylon's spicy breezes so often now that the words have lost all flavour. Yet still the line about India's coral strand dries my throat and cracks my voice. Each time I sing these words I see rose-gold beaches and sea the colour of gemstones. Then, my family walking along those shores. Since my husband's death, Amma and the children rely solely on the money that I send them. And then, of course, I think of the other children, the charges I took on for the British family who had hired me for the passage to England. I had wet nursed the baby and busied the older children with card games as I kept the memsahib hydrated with water. This same family, a few days after landing, had thrown me out with nothing but a week's wages.

I stayed in a London lodging house that took all my money. It was riddled with damp and women were sleeping on the floor in such large groups there was no room to roll over. Eventually, when my money ran out, the lodging house threw me onto the streets. The missionaries found me sitting in an alley, a shabby woollen shawl wrapped around my shoulders as I held out my hand for loose change. Aye! The shame of it. They took me to the Ayah's Home where other women from India, Malaya, Jakata, China, had also been abandoned. It was then that I realised I was not alone.

They treat us well in the home, cooking kedgeree and chapatis in the kitchen. They have betel nut cutters, ornate fancy items, that we use to make paan. They give us embroidery lessons and read the newspapers to us while we work. This is how we heard about Viceroy Curzon fleeing to Agra after his resignation, to be near our beloved Taj Mahal. It was said that, after his wife's death, he had a 'breakdown' – a word I had not heard before. Mrs Dunn told us he had returned to England under a dark shadow, receiving no honours or earldom as had become the Viceroy tradition. The other ayahs gossip about this, but I prefer to talk about our most recent trip to Westminster Abbey. Aye! The floor was so polished I could see my reflection upon it!

Don't think me indifferent. It is hard to find comfort in another person's misery when I am battling so much with my own.

I sing of salvation, oh salvation! But when I come to the line about the heathen bowing down to wood and stone, I trip over these words as if they are pebbles. They don't know that at the home I keep a shrine to Ganesh at the back of my linen cupboard. Each day I finish my prayers to Lord Jesus Christ before moving on to my prayers to the elephant-headed god. Surely, a person cannot have too much faith. I wonder if Mrs Dunn will throw me onto the streets if she finds out. This seems to be the British custom.

As we continue to sing, the women before us stop wafting their fans and smile as though they are sitting in pools of cool water. I wonder if this is because they are hearing about the ancient rivers and palmy plains of the Empire that we ayahs are here to represent. Or perhaps it is because they are viewing us no longer as zoo animals but children performing charmingly in a school play.

Or is it because our voices are sweeter than honey and spice?

We finish the final line, singing of the King, creator, redeemer who '... in bliss returns to reign.' We hold the final note a little longer, stretching it a little higher, just as we have been taught. The audience applauds. Mrs Dunn stands and bows with a humble smile that tries not to look too proud. I smile too; the missionaries will receive donations for the home and sell our embroidery to the crowd. This money will help other ayahs like me. I will pray for these women when I finally return home.

Though to which god, I am not quite sure.

8. One Million More Women Than Men: 'No Votes, Thank You'

Black Friday, 18th November, 1910

Today is a day for protest.

We lead the march to the House of Commons singing our battle song as crowds line the street.

By my side is Emmeline Pankhurst, dressed in a full-length fur coat that gathers dust on the hem with each stride. Alongside us are England's first woman doctor and first woman mayor, a headmistress and a physicist. Evelina Haverfield rides behind us on a horse with a riding crop in her hand.

She is our very own Lady Godiva, though perhaps with more clothes.

And then there is me. The papers have given me many titles: Socialite of British high-society, Goddaughter to Queen Victoria, Princess of Lahore. Trouble maker.

I prefer Sophia Duleep Singh.

My first name is pronounced so-fire. My intention is to ignite change.

When we reach St Stephens Gate, the police who have been tailing us suddenly quicken their pace.

...Women have not, as a sex, or a class, the calmness of temperament or the balance of mind... to exercise a weighty judgment in political affairs.

They form a line and close in, forcing us against the railings of the gate. We watch as other officers begin to attack the 300 women who have followed us. They fight back with lioness fury, teeth flashing as they pull men off their horses.

The policeman standing before me starts grabbing my waist as though I am meat in a butcher's shop and he is the butcher.

'Don't touch these ones!' the officer-in-charge bellows. 'Home Secretary's orders!'

Churchill. He would rather we were worn down than arrested. He does not want any martyrs from today's protest.

The policeman removes his hands, exhales a stale, reeking breath against my cheek. I try to push past him but the more we push the more the policemen lean in, crushing our bodies until we can barely breathe. We watch as other officers beat the women in the crowds, swinging their helmets as though they are clubs. I see the protesters being groped about the breasts and their skirts being lifted.

...Political activity will tend to take away woman from her proper sphere and highest duty... maternity.

Bystanders, women and men, pick up the protesters from the ground, walking them to safety and pressing handkerchiefs against their cuts.

Then, Evelina breaks from the line.

From her horse, she whips policemen with her riding crop, knocking some from off their own mounts. We cheer from the gate as we are pushed back so hard we can smell the metal of the bars as they press into our cheeks.

When the police finally jostle Evelina to the ground, she punches an officer in the jaw. She screams fiercely as she is pulled away.

'Next time I'll bring my revolver!'

...The presence of a large female factor... would weaken Great Britain in the esti-mation of foreign Powers... It would be gravely misunderstood and become a source of weakness in India.

I was raised in an English country manor that had parrots, monkeys and jackdaws in the garden. We always knew we were different, but it was only when my sisters and I visited India for the first time that we fully under-stood how. We travelled in disguise to the Delhi Durbar, against Curzon's orders. When we arrived in Lahore to observe the eclipse of the sun, we saw awe in the local people's eyes when they looked upon us. I met with Indian nationalists, each time introduced as 'the Granddaughter of the Lion of Punjab'. I had always known I was a princess but I had never known that, with this title, came power.

Afterwards, I stayed in Punjab to learn the language. The poverty and deprivation I saw was devastating. I have lived a privileged existence, full of balls, fine gowns and high society. But, after India, I could not return to that life. Once you have seen the cracks in a portrait, it is impossible to un-see them.

...Women would then demand the right of becoming M.P's, cabinet ministers, judges...

As the police are distracted by Evelina, they relax the line and I break free. A woman with cuts on her brow is being pushed repeatedly to the ground by an officer, the violence escalating with each thrust. I walk in front of him, standing my ground as though I am made of iron, and demand that he stops. He sees my face; it is quite recognisable, then he runs into the crowd like a startled mouse. But I have already noted his badge number and repeat it over in my mind.

... Those persons ought not to make laws who cannot join in enforcing them. Wom-en cannot become soldiers, sailors or policemen...

I am arrested along with 115 other women.

As I am pushed into the back of a van and taken to the police station, I think of my sisters. Bamba studying to be a doctor in Chicago only for her course to be cancelled with the claim that women are incapable of the intricacies of surgery. I think of Catherine, living with her female lover in Germany. Then I think of my poor mother, neglected by my troubled father as he squandered their riches, left to drink herself to an early grave.

The National League for Opposing Women's Suffrage tells us there are one million more women than men in Great Britain and Ireland. They say this means we will swamp the male vote. But surely if there are more of us, we should have more say.

When they open the doors and I step out of the van with my fellow warriors, I consider Curzon's seventh reason for opposing suffrage.

… If the vote were, granted, it is probable that a very large number of women would not use it at all.

He does not know the heart of a woman. We would never give up so easily.

9. Let Curzon Holde what Curzon Helde
Object of interest: a portrait

March 1925, Kedleston Hall
After examining the servants' uniforms and fingernails, George decides to inspect Kedleston Hall.

The pain in his back is excruciating today, as though the muscles are being slowly pulled apart. He keeps his posture erect (his corrective girdle gives him no choice) walking stiffly past servants who scurry by with lowered eyes. He has kept his reputation of pomposity since Oxford with that blasted Balliol rhyme:

> My name is George Nathaniel Curzon,
> I am a most superior person,
> My cheek is pink, my hair is sleek,
> I dine at Blenheim once a week.

He'd found it amusing back then. Being thought of as superior had its advantages, but when it interfered with his political life, he realised it had its drawbacks too.

George walks along Trophy Corridor, ignoring the sharp pains rising to his ribs. Taxidermied animals line the walls, glass-eyed and inert. He runs his finger along a tank containing birds of prey. It leaves a powdery dust on his fingertip. Standards at Kedleston have dropped since his return. He has repeatedly sent back food (the cooks seem incapable of cooking an egg) and has had to deal with the outright churlishness of the housekeeper when he moved her to the kitchen wing to make way for a smoking room. The footmen he finds particularly intolerable, gadding about on boats on the lake to seduce girls and handing in their notice in impertinent letters written on Gracie's coronated paper. Of course, he has had his own dalliances, but he has always known his priorities.

He stands in front of the stuffed head of a bison. There is a little wooden plaque beneath it stating 'Indian Bison. Shot in Mysore by Lord Curzon. August 1902'. He remembers those days of the big hunts, being taken by princes to shoot tigers on the backs of elephants. In those moments, he had not felt like a mere Viceroy, but a king

A twinge jabs into George's chest as though he has been punched. Strange, he has never felt the pain spread so high. He dismisses it, moving on to the Eastern Museum. There is still work to be done, but what a memorial to the East! Howdah seats, Afghan tables and miniature portraits of Indian monuments upon gold painted boxes. He helped restore so many of these: Red Fort at Delhi, the shrine of Fatehpur Sikri and most treasured of all, the Taj Mahal. Now all his energy goes into renovating Kedleston, electrifying the building his penny-pinching father refused to modernise. Putting in telephones, a lift. When he is gone, they will say Marquis Curzon of Kedleston was a man who respected the past yet headed towards progress.

Or perhaps, he thinks, as a prickly pain stabs into his flesh, they will say other things.

George bows his head and clenches his jaw. He decides fresh air is what he needs and heads out through the doors of Caesar's Hall and over the pebbled drive. He hears the gushing water beneath the arches of the bridge ahead, scans the horizon covered with mature trees that look like tiny sculptures. He reaches the lawn and draws in a deep breath.

The pain eases.

He recalls hearing, as a child, that the Viceroy's residence in Calcutta was a replica of his family home. This fact ignited his ambition to become Viceroy himself and rule in that twin house. After his return from India he taught his daughters ditties to remember it by;

'While the pillars of Government House, Calcutta were lath and plaster, those of Kedleston were pure alabaster.'

His aim was to maintain the flat a's in their Derbyshire accents. He always maintained high standards with his daughters, questioning them over lunch about geography, mathematics, English literature. He believed girls should be taught everything – except politics.

His eyelids flutter as the pain returns. He glances over to the family wing with the knowledge that Cim and Baba are currently visiting. He hasn't spoken to Irene since the emancipation scandal. He imagines she is careering about somewhere, broadcasting how he withheld her mother's inheritance. She wrote to him recently saying things might have been different if there had been warmth and understanding at home. Since the vote, George has seen the reckless confidence of the modern woman. He has no idea how to deal with them.

The other two girls have barely spoken with him since their arrival, spending their time reading and knitting. Last night, he had hinted that life, perhaps, contained things more serious. Cim's face grew scarlet.

'I've been reading Plato's Republic upstairs,' she said. 'Is that serious enough for you, father?'

He doesn't know where his daughters get their arrogance from; their mother was so docile. She lies now in the church he has restored behind the hall. He added a chapel tomb for her, along with a marble effigy. His own vault waits beside her, his coffin already commissioned to be worked from a 200-year-old Kedleston oak embroidered with the Curzon arms and motto: *Let Curzon holde what Curzon helde.*

George smiles at these words, then becomes dizzy. He tries to steady himself, the way he has always steadied himself in life, planting his feet, not wavering. But his vision blurs and, when he turns back to Kedleston Hall, he stumbles sideways. He sees Irene's face, aged eight, eyes round with fear, throat unable to swallow, as he questioned her in Latin.

Coloured lights flash across the hall as George drops to the ground. He hears the deafening outrage of protesters outside Government House. Initially over famine, then over partition.

He tries to push himself back to standing but, when he fails, George rests his head on the dewy grass. All he ever wanted was to better this world. Perhaps, he did not always get it right. He knows he has not been a good man but, looking back, he does not think he has been a very bad one.

George closes his eyes. Kedleston Hall disappears.

10. Take Me to the Eastern Museum.

2019, Derby

For her 80th birthday, Nani wanted to go to the Eastern Museum. Mum didn't know where that was so she asked me to Google it. I don't know why she thought I'd be better than her at this, I'm only twelve.

We sat before mum's ancient laptop. At the top of the search results was 'Eastern Museum of Motor Racing'. Mum looked hopefully at Nani but she shook her head.

Next, came 'East Midlands Aeropark'. Nani shook her head again.

I thought carefully before typing, 'Eastern Museum Derby' which self-corrected to 'Eastern Museum Derby*shire*'. I clicked the first link. Nani's eyes lit up like a fully charged phone.

'Really?' Mum said. 'This is where you want to spend your birthday?'

Nani stroked Mum's arm as if she'd finally understood a complicated maths problem. I snickered into my hand.

★

During the car journey, Nani started telling us English words that originated from India, as well as their definitions. She can be completely random sometimes – wearing socks in summer, singing Hindi songs loudly in the supermarket.

'Bungalow!' Nani cried. 'A one-story house or cottage.'

We arrived at an arched entrance, which was when Mum told me to switch off my tablet, even though I was halfway through a level of Minecraft. It took a million years to drive through the grounds. All I could see was grass and trees and green, green, green.

'Pyjamas!' Nani cried. 'Loose fitting trousers and top worn at night.'

Then, as we approached a little bridge, I saw Kedleston Hall. It was a proper mansion, like one of those places rich housewives own in reality T.V. shows.

When we got inside, the staff asked if we needed any help but Nani was on boost mode and had marched ahead with her walking stick. Mum showed our tickets and began looking at busts of old men sitting in holes carved out in the walls.

'I remember this place,' she said. 'We came here when we were little.'

Her phone began ringing.

'It's your dad,' she said, looking at the screen. 'He's collecting the cake. Take care of Nani, won't you?'

I rolled my eyes but Mum didn't notice because she'd already rushed outside. Then I searched the hall. There were lots of people with white hair, though none of them looked like Nani. I wondered why she'd chosen this place for her birthday. It wasn't like it was connected to *our* family.

If I'd had a choice, I would have chosen a trampoline park.

I saw a flash of Nani's mustard coloured sari disappearing into a large room at the end of the hall. As I ran in after her, I was met by a tiger. Its pale eyes were glassy and round, teeth fixed in a roar that made the skin around its nose ripple.

'Don't worry, beti,' Nani said, leaning on her walking stick. 'It is no longer alive.'

She laughed loudly, as though she'd told a joke. I looked down at the tiger skin rug, its flat body spread out like a pancake that hadn't reached the sides of a pan.

'Pukka!' Nani cried. 'Good, proper, *reliable*.'

She laughed again and my cheeks burned. Seeing as it was her birthday, I stopped myself from rolling my eyes.

I spotted an information sheet that said the room was called 'The Eastern Museum', the place Nani had wanted to visit. It was filled with glass cabinets and fancy furniture. There were wooden statues of Hindu gods and Buddhas, ivory tusks hanging from the wall and Indian jewellery in glass cases.

'Why is this stuff here?' I said.

Nani held a finger up.

'Good question, beti,' she said.

We walked to a case full of walking canes with ornate handles, carved picture frames and sculptures of elephants, all made of ivory. I remembered when I was little, seeing an elephant in a zoo pacing back and forth in an enclosure that was too small for her, butting her head against the cage. Suddenly I felt overwhelmed, like I had become that elephant.

'Hullabaloo!' Nani cried. 'Clamorous noise or disturbance.'

Her smile dropped when she saw my expression.

'Let's sit outside, beti,' she said.

★

When I was little, Nani took care of me whenever I was ill. She would buy Lucozade and feed me Italian biscuits from the cash-and-carry. It was only when we sat on the flower-print sofa in the entrance hall that I realised how much I missed those days. Technology was good for some things, but it couldn't replace spending time with your Nani.

She held my hand and, noticing that I couldn't speak, explained how her grandfather had worked in a place called Government House in India. The building was modelled on the same designs as the house we were sat in. She told me how he'd worked for George Nathaniel Curzon who'd been born and brought up in Kedleston. He was Viceroy of India and had brought back the items to the museum.

I had a hundred questions. What was a Viceroy? What was Government House? Why had George been in India and why had my family worked for him? But then, before I could ask anything, I saw Mum walking towards us.

'There you are!' she said. 'I thought I'd lost you. Where next?'

Nani didn't speak. I could tell she was thinking about her family; her grandfather working in Government House, her own parents separated in India during something called partition. Her shoulders sagged, as if her energy had been drained.

'Why don't we go to the café?' Mum said. 'They've got curry on the menu.'

Nani's eyes lit up, fully charged.

'Curry! An aromatic dish flavoured with spices.'

I laughed. Then Nani laughed. Even Mum laughed. As visitors glanced at us, I forgot to be embarrassed, or confused, or overwhelmed.

This was my family. This place was our history. And the future was full of possibilities.

JOANNA DE GROOT

INDIA, BRITAIN, AND KEDLESTON HALL: A HISTORICAL CONTEXT

A visit to Kedleston Hall offers some interesting contrasts. It is very much a product of the interests and resources of a long established local landed family, the Curzons, employing the skill and talent of an architect, Robert Adam, who played a major role in creating one of the most highly regarded styles in British architecture. Adam's 'neo-classical' architectural and interior designs have become familiar and much reproduced features of town and country houses in Scotland, England, and Ireland, and thus visible parts of distinctive 'British' landscapes and 'heritage'. Kedleston is also associated with British imperial and global history through George Curzon, Viceroy of India 1899-1905 and Foreign Secretary 1919-24. This is most visible in the 'Eastern Museum' which occupies much of the basement floor at Kedleston and contains many of the objects he bought or was given before and during his time as Viceroy.

The rebuilding of Kedleston in the 1760s, used the newly fashionable Adam as designer and was planned to house classical statues collected by its owner, Nathaniel Curzon, while also including exotic elements in its mainly neoclassical design. Very 'English' associations with the wealth and taste of the landed classes are also flavoured by British connections to a global world, which were already well established when Kedleston was designed, built, and furnished. The Greek and Roman themes of the building and its contents were products of travel and collecting by elite British men on the European 'Grand Tour' and the associations which such men made between imperial Rome and the global expansion of British power, wealth, and influence. The large gilded palm tree motifs used in the state bedroom and dressing room recall eighteenth century British contacts with, and exotic images of Asia, Africa, and the Americas.

By the 1760s the British had sizeable trade and political involvements in the Caribbean, the Indian subcontinent, the coast of West Africa, and North America. The labour of enslaved Africans in the West Indies produced the sugar which sweetened cups of tea brought from China by the

East India Company (EIC). Silk imported from India, Italy, or China was worked into the fabrics used for furniture and clothes seen in country houses like Kedleston. Investments in Caribbean plantations and Indian or African trade as well as in land and transport in England sustained the incomes and influence of propertied families. British governments shaped their diplomatic, taxation, and military policies in the light of these global connections. While the Curzons of the eighteenth century did not have the direct links to India, such as underpinned the Clive influence at Powys, or the Child family at Osterley (where Adam also worked) the redesign of Kedleston did reflect global and cosmopolitan aspects of their times.

The 1760s and 1770s, when that redesign was undertaken were a crucial time of transition in British involvements in India. The EIC's need to defend its commercial interests in India politically, diplomatically, and militarily, which increased from the 1740s, onward, intensified their links to governments and politicians. These ranged from government involvement in the EIC finances to military support for warfare in India. During the 1760s the British conquered territory in India and were recognised by the Moghul emperor as rulers with rights to collect taxes, and the next half century saw continued large-scale expansion of the EIC's territorial and governmental power. This was accompanied by greater intervention and control of the EIC by the British government, marked by the Regulating Act of 1772, the India Act of 1784, the 1813 removal of EIC monopolies and the 1833 Charter Act. When, in 1799, Marquess Wellesley the expansionist Governor General of India commissioned a building for Government House in Calcutta, the centre of British power in India, the designs used for the building drew on Adam's designs for Kedleston. British imperial power and involvement in India bonded the British presence there to the culture of UK propertied elites.

This was the framework for growing EIC commercial involvement in China (notably in the opium and tea trades), in the Middle East, and in southeast Asia and the development of new patterns of trade in Indian cotton and opium. Money made by British men in trade and government in India funded the building and decoration of houses in the UK, just as Indian designs were used for Paisley-made shawls and Manchester cottons, and Chinese designs for the pottery used to drink Chinese and later Indian tea. The luxury silks, ivories, and metalware, and the Indian art objects imported to the UK by such men, like the more modest objects brought back by ordinary soldiers, sailors or missionaries, made 'Indian' objects familiar sights in houses, shops, and museums. Children 's history books celebrated British rule and conquests in India, while pantomime characters like Widow Twankey [named for a type of tea], Ali Baba, and Aladdin embedded oriental images in popular culture, as did 'Indian' images and stories in advertising and missionary pamphlets. 'India' became an everyday presence in the lives of people in the UK as well as an exotic, dangerous, appealing, or controversial matter for missionaries, businessmen and officials involved 'over there', and a feature in elite and popular art and writing in the UK.

By the time George Curzon, future Viceroy of India, was born in 1859 the British connection to India was being consolidated in new forms which also maintained long established patterns of British power and wealth in the subcontinent. One outcome of the military conflicts between the British and a range of Indian opponents to their presence in India during 1857-8 was the replacement of EIC rule in India with Crown rule. Like the establishment of railways and telegraph lines, this reinforced direct relationships between the UK and India stimulating the growing presence of businessmen, missionaries, the armed services, and civilian officials, which began in the early nineteenth century. Trade in European manufactures and Indian raw materials, as well as the needs of government, involved the British in India with Indian allies, and subordinates ranging from rural cultivators and landlords or administrators, to local rulers, soldiers, or urban businessmen. Webs of partnership and unequal power linking British to Indians maintained the British presence in India, which was increasingly celebrated in British politics and culture. This presence was depicted as a civilising mission replacing supposedly decadent Indian tyrannies with order and security, and what were seen as backward beliefs and practices with economic cultural and social progress.

For members of the educated and propertied classes and others, India offered opportunities for careers in government and business, and for missionary and professional activity. Over the nineteenth century hundreds of thousands of British people including businessmen and aristocrats, servants and planters, missionaries and soldiers, scholars and engineers, spent periods of varying length in India. Demand for governmental and other kinds of expertise for imperial use in India and elsewhere shaped the secondary and university education available to privileged men, just as the armed services and merchant navy recruited less privileged men for imperial activities. When George Curzon made his way through Eton to Balliol College Oxford and planned his route to the position of Viceroy of India, he might have been the first in his family to take that path, but the path was a well-established one.

Extensive travel in Central Asia, eastern Asia and Iran, on which he wrote books and journalism, and a career as a Conservative politician and junior minister led to Curzon's appointment as Viceroy of India. As an international traveller and as Viceroy, like other British travellers and imperial officials, he acquired a variety of objects produced in what the British called 'the east' ranging from antique lacquer, metalwork and ivory to objects created by craft workers for western visitors. Along with gifts presented to him during his time as Viceroy they formed a collection of some 1300 objects which in Curzon's 1925 will were divided between Kedleston Hall and the Victoria and Albert Museum. Objects from 'the east' connected Curzon's career in India both to the metropolitan splendour of a major London museum, and to his English landed family heritage. Imperial collecting enhanced the presence of 'the east' in the imperial capital while also transforming the Curzon country seat with the establishment of the 'Eastern Museum' on the lower grand floor at Kedleston in 1927.

Interactions between heritage, empire, and the arts shaped Curzon's role in India, where as Viceroy he promoted restoration, conservation and archaeological work on historic sites including the return of panels from the Taj Mahal looted by the British in 1857. Legislation to protect monuments and the revival of the Archaeological Service of India, as well as the establishment of the Imperial Library and the Victoria Memorial Museum in Calcutta gave institutional support to this work. This promotion of Indian heritage acknowledged the significance of the Indian past and cultures, but also asserted imperial power, with claims to government control of religious sites and the removal of images and statues being used in Indian worship to museums. In England, Curzon continued to combine personal and public action on heritage matters supporting protective legislation for ancient buildings, and willing historic properties at Bodiam and Tattershall, which he bought and restored, to the National Trust. Like his creation of the 'eastern' collection at Kedleston such actions proclaimed the important role of the past in shaping and demonstrating imperial and local aspects of 'Britishness'.

Visitors to Kedleston can look over the house and the objects in it and reflect on the shifting and varied links they show between a Derbyshire stately home and estate, its owners and residents, and a wider world. Like the giant gilded tropical palms, Antonio Zucchi's 1777 painting of *The four continents*, set in elegant Adam plasterwork, gives its British neoclassical style a global and cosmopolitan twist. Beyond the presence of a continental European artist and his use of 'classical' style, it brings a wider world into the Kedleston of the 1770s. That world was one where the British were active and influential participants, whether shipping tea from China and Indian textiles to sell on in continental Europe or trading enslaved people across the Atlantic to produce sugar and tobacco for European use. The presence of both imported Chinese porcelain and the Meissen and Derby versions of porcelain at Kedleston allows us to think about how the success of the former in European markets stimulated changes in the design and making of pottery in Europe. The imperial presence of the

EIC in Asia played a role in the rise of new industries in Britain, reshaping textile as well as ceramic production. As noted already, the classical style favoured by English country house builders of the 1770s became one of the styles used to assert the British imperial presence in India with Adams' designs reappearing in Calcutta/Kolkata. In an interactive process Indian motifs appear on shawls woven in Scotland, and 'oriental' scenes on Derby teapots; the British use words from Indian languages [pyjamas, verandas], while British figures enter Indian paintings, and buildings for British use in India combined local and British elements.

The 'Peacock Dress' worn by Mary, George Nathaniel Curzon's wife, for the grand ball which was part of the 1903 celebrations [*durbar*] held in India to mark Edward VII's accession as King-Emperor, now at Kedleston, was the product of similar interactions. The dress fabric was made in a Calcutta workshop, pictured in the *Illustrated London News*, where skilled workers embroidered muslin-lined silk chiffon with metallic thread, the prized Indian craft of *zardozi* (= gold embroidery). Its peacock feather motif was both a feature of Moghul and Persian design and a newly fashionable pattern found in 1890s British designs sold in Liberty's shop in London. The fabric was then sent to the Paris workshop of leading fashion designer Worth to be made up into a ball dress. Embodying the labour of both French and Indian men and women, it was sent back to India for Mary Curzon to wear at the Durbar ball, held in the palace of the former Moghul emperors in Delhi. Indian and European skills, creativity, and effort were blended in her distinctively female display of imperial power and glamour combining Indian with western elements.

This is not a one-off example. Mary Curzon helped the new Queen-Empress Alexandra acquire and use Indian *zardozi* fabrics made up in Paris for her coronation dress, and other elite British women of the period adapted Indian textiles and designs to their clothes. In the 'Eastern Museum' where Mary's dress was displayed we find objects made by Indian craft workers for British customers, like the ivory paintings of particular places in cities where Indians and British had fought in 1857-8 which by Curzon's time were toured by British visitors. British memories of the so-called 'Mutiny' interacted with the activities of Indian workers and traders and with British travel in India. So too trinkets bought by Curzon in Cairo, Isfahan or Istanbul, also in the Museum, linked his career as an 'expert' imperial traveller in 'the east' to the lives of traders and craftworkers in those cities. They also show how British power and influence in India were supported by involvement in other areas of imperial influence or possession, ranging from Egypt and Iran to China and Burma. The silver and lapis lazuli tables given to Curzon by the ruler of Afghanistan mark a history of British-Afghan relations shaped by interests in India going back to the 1780s, and also demonstrate Afghan craft skills and Afghan use of Arabic inscriptions, linking them to transnational Muslim culture.

Returning to the contrasts between Kedleston's very 'English' aspects and its links to India and empire, noted at the start of this piece, it can be suggested that they show a history of interactions rather than contradictions. 'Eastern' porcelain and tea became part of English country house life, just as cosmopolitan and global influences shaped the setting of that life in Nathaniel Curzon's new house of the 1770s. Architectural styles developed for British buildings are used and sometimes blended with Indian styles in building built for the British in India. Careers in government, business, missionary work and other professional activities became opportunities for British men, including those from landed families, as did investment and trade in India. George Nathaniel Curzon's own distinctive and famous high-profile career in India and in UK politics, and its legacy at Kedleston, were embedded in a varied and many-sided history of the British and their imperial involvement in India. These perspectives add an important interest and richness to the pleasure and insight to be gained from visiting Kedleston.

INGRID POLLARD

A PHOTO ESSAY

Dr. Ingrid Pollard works with portrait and landscape photography to interrogate social constructs such as Britishness, race, sexuality, and identity. Working across a remarkable variety of techniques, from photography, printmaking, drawing and installation, to artist books, video, and audio, Pollard's practice combines meticulous research and experimental creative processes to make art that is at once deeply personal and socially engaged, addressing issues that are urgent and relevant today: the human body, race and migration, our relationship with the natural world.

Throughout her career Pollard has documented the English landscape, uncovering hidden and unseen histories and stereotypes. Her work often presents evidence gathered over long periods of research in which she observes and explores a particular place.

Andre Bagoo is a poet and writer, the author of four books of poems including BURN (Shearsman, 2012), *Pitch Lake* (Peepal Tree Press, 2017) and a book of essays, *The Undiscovered Country* (Peepal Tree Press, 2020). *The Undiscovered Country* was winner the non-fiction category of the 2021 OCM Bocas prize for Caribbean Literature. His collection of short stories, *The Dreaming*, came out in 2022 from Peepal Tree Press. He was awarded The Charlotte & Isidor Paiewonsky Prize in 2017 and shortlisted for the Ernest Hemingway Foundation's annual fiction prize in 2020. His work has appeared in journals such as *Almost Island*, *Boston Review*, *Caribbean Review of Books*, *Draconian Switch*, *St Petersburg Review*, and *The Poetry Review*.

Ayanna Lloyd Banwo is a writer from Trinidad & Tobago currently living in London. Her debut novel *When We Were Birds* is an Indie Next Pick, was named one of the UK *Observer*'s Best Debuts of 2022 and won the OCM Bocas prize in 2023. She is a graduate of the University of the West Indies and holds an MA in Creative Writing from the University of East Anglia, where she is now a Creative and Critical Writing PhD student. Her work has been published in *Moko Magazine*, *Small Axe*,

PREE, *Callaloo* and *Anomaly* among others, and shortlisted for Small Axe Literary Competition and the Wasafiri New Writing Prize. She is currently at work on her second novel.

Jacqueline Crooks is a Jamaica-born writer who writes about Caribbean migration and sub-cultures, in particular the supernatural and supranational stories that sustain the diaspora. Her short story collection, *The Ice Migration*, was longlisted for the 2019 Orwell Prize in the Political Fiction category, and she has also been shortlisted for the Asham and Wasafiri New Writing awards. Her story, 'Silver Fish in the Midnight Sea', was shortlisted in the BBC National Short Story Award 2019. Her stories have appeared in *Wasafiri*, *Virago*, *Granta*, and *MsLexia*. Her novel, *Fire Rush*, was published by Jonathan Cape UK and Viking Press in the U.S.A.

She has a degree in Social Policy from Roehampton University of Surrey and an MA in Creative and Life Writing from Goldsmiths University. She runs her own company providing consultancy services to grass-roots charities. She also delivers writing workshops to socially excluded communities, primarily older people, refugees and asylum seekers, and vulnerable young people.

Peter Kalu writes across a number of genres: poetry, short stories, novels, radio and theatre plays, film scripts, TV scripts, song lyrics and flash  fiction. Most of his works unsettle orthodoxies around the concept of race. His novel *Black Star Rising* (X Press 1998) was the first science fiction novel by a Black British author to be published in the UK. He gained his PhD in Creative Writing from Lancaster University in 2019. In 2022 his ninth novel *One Drop* was published by Andersen Press. In 2023 HopeRoad published a new edition of his *Silent Striker*, and he has published several short stories in Comma Press anthologies. Extracts from his psychedelic memoir will be published and podcast by the Royal Literary Fund in 2023.

Hannah Lowe is a poet, memoirist and academic. Her latest book, *The Kids*, a Poetry Book Society 'Choice' for Autumn, won the Costa Poetry Award and the Costa Book of the Year, 2021. Her first poetry collection *Chick* (Bloodaxe, 2013) won the Michael Murphy Memorial Award for Best First Collection. In September 2014, she was named as one of 20 Next Generation poets. She teaches Creative Writing at Brunel University. @hannahlowepoet

 Malachi McIntosh was born in Birmingham, England, but grew up in the United States. He writes fiction and non-fiction and has been published in *Under the Radar, Flash, Broadcast, The Caribbean Review of Books, The Guardian, The Independent,* and Comma Press's *Book of Birmingham.* His stories have been shortlisted for the Galley Beggar short story competition, longlisted for the Guardian/4th Estate BAME prize and commissioned by the National Trust and Lincoln University. His collection of short stories, *Para-*

bles, Fables, Nightmares was published by Emma Press in 2023. He teaches at Oxford University.

Karen Onojaife is a short story writer and novelist. Her work has appeared in publications such as the *Callaloo Literary Journal, Closure: Contemporary Black British Short Stories*, and *The Best of British Fantasy 2019.* She has participated in the Hedgebrook Writers in Residence program.

Seni Seneviratne is a writer of English and Sri Lankan heritage, published by Peepal Tree Press: *Wild Cinnamon and Winter Skin (*2007), *The Heart of It* (2012), *Unknown Soldier* (2019). Her collection, *Unknown Soldier* (2019) is a Poetry Book Society Recommendation, a National Poetry Day Choice and was highly commended in the Forward Poetry Prizes 2020. Her most recent poetry collection is *The Go-Away Bird* (2023). She has collaborated with film-makers, visual artists, musicians and

digital artists. She has co-edited a Bloodaxe anthology of post-independence Tamil, Sinhala and English poetry. www.seniseneviratne.com

Mahsuda Snaith is winner of the *SI Leeds Literary Prize* and *Bristol Short Story Prize.* Her debut novel *The Things We Thought We Knew* was chosen as a World Book Night Book and her second novel *How to Find Home* was read on BBC Radio 4. She was named an 'Observer New Face of Fiction'. Mahsuda has led creative writing workshops in universities, hospitals, schools and in a homeless hostel. Her short story 'The Panther's Tale' is included in *Hag: Forgotten Folktales Retold.*
Find out more at www.mahsudasnaith.com.

Maria Thomas is an award-winning fiction writer. Her work has appeared on BBC Radio 4, in *A Public Space*, *New England Review*, *Wasafiri*, *Masters Review Anthology IV* edited by Roxane Gay, and elsewhere. She is currently a PhD candidate in Creative Writing at Goldsmiths, University of London, where she is working on a novel.

Emile de Bruijn studied Japanese at Leiden University, the Netherlands, and museology at the University of Essex, United Kingdom. He works as Assistant National Curator for the National Trust, focusing on European decorative art and East Asian art. Among his recent publications are *Chinese Wallpaper in Britain and Ireland* (2017) and *Borrowed Landscapes: China and Japan in the Historic Houses and Gardens of Britain and Ireland* (2023).

Rupert Goulding is the National Trust Senior National Curator for Research and the South West. He has written extensively on Dyrham Park, William Blathwayt, and the colonial connections of the Blathwayt family. He is the author of *William Blathwayt and Dyrham Park, Gloucestershire: National Trust Guidebook*.

Joanna de Groot is a Senior Lecturer in history at the University of York. She works on interacting aspects of gender, race and empire, in the Indian subcontinent and the "Middle East", since 1700, and on the history of Iran. She is particularly interested in past understandings and representations of gender, race, and empire, whether elite or popular, and in comparative, and transnational approaches to those topics. She stresses the importance of linking them to peoples' lives and experience and is currently writing a book on the social and cultural history of nineteenth century Iran in its transnational setting.

Marian Gwyn is a heritage consultant, researcher, writer, and educator. Her expertise covers a wide range of heritage specialities, gained from many years' experience in the heritage industry. Her doctorate, gained at Bangor University, explores the challenges faced by heritage organisations in acknowledging the ways in which their sites and artefacts are connected to slavery and empire. She has sat on a number of Welsh Government working groups, advising on Wales and empire, and on embedding diverse histories into the school curriculum. Marian's work challenges traditional presentations of history and she is committed to helping the heritage industry flourish in an increasingly challenging world.

Paterson Joseph is a British actor and writer. He appeared in the RSC productions of *King Lear* and *Love's Labour's Lost*. On television he is best known for his roles in *Casualty* (1997–1998), *Peep Show* (2003–2015), *Green Wing* (2004–2006), *Survivors* (2008–2010), *Boy Meets Girl* (2009), *Law & Order: UK* (2013–2014), *The Leftovers* (2014–15), *Safe House* (2015–

2017), and *Timeless* (2016–2018). His film roles include *The Beach* (2000), *Greenfingers* (2001), *Æon Flux* (2005), *The Other Man* (2008) and *Wonka* (2023). His 2022 debut novel *The Secret Diaries of Charles Ignatius Sancho* won the 2023 Christopher Bland Prize awarded by the Royal Society of Literature. He is the Chancellor of Oxford Brookes University.

Liverpool Black History Research Group (LBHRG) is a collective of community-led researchers investigating and raising awareness of Liverpool's long black presence. The important contribution of people of African descent to Liverpool's development has gone largely unacknowledged and we are committed to revealing this forgotten history. The group is led by local historian and PhD student, Laurence Westgaph. Its purpose is to share historical knowledge and offer instruction in research skills and techniques, providing learning, training and employment opportunities for the people of Liverpool.

Sarah Longair is a Senior Lecturer in the History of Empire at the University of Lincoln. Her research explores the history of the British Empire in East Africa and the Indian Ocean, in particular through material and visual culture, the history of collecting and the creation of museums. She is the author of several books and articles, including *Cracks in the Dome: Fractured Histories of Empire in the Zanzibar Museum, 1897–1965* (2015), *Curating Empire: Museums and the British Imperial Experience* (2013, co-edited with John McAleer) and *History through material culture* (2017, with Leonie Hannan).

Ruth Longoni studied history and sociology at Warwick University; she has an MA in Comparative Labour History, writing on Socialism and Sexual Politics, 1884-1906. She taught in Coventry schools for 22 years where her work included developing multi-cultural and anti-racist education and teaching children speaking English as an additional language. She is a volunteer for the National Trust at Charlecote Park where she participated in the Interim Report on the Connections between Colonialism and Properties now in the care of the National Trust, including Links with Historic Slavery. She lives in Coventry where she works with its peace movement.

Raj Pal is a curator/historian and activist. After a long career of working in the cultural sector in various capacities, he is now a freelance curator/consultant and has worked on projects at the National Trust, English Heritage and other heritage institutions. In 2022, Raj co-curated the hugely successful "Blacklash: No justice, no peace" exhibition at Birmingham museums & art gallery. He is currently leading a team of curators re-displaying the collections as part of an ambitious re-development of The Harris, Preston,0 and also acting as a mentor to two Welsh museums, Conwy Museum Service and y Gaer Museum, Art Gallery & Library, Brecon to explore imaginative ways of engaging with hitherto marginal communities and groups.

Cassander L. Smith is an associate dean of academic affairs for the Honors College and associate professor of English at the University of Alabama, Tuscaloosa. She is the author of *Black Africans in the British Imagination: English Narratives of the Early Atlantic World* (LSU Press, 2016). She also has co-edited two essay volumes, *Early Modern Black Diaspora Studies: A Critical Anthology* (Palgrave Macmillan, 2019) and *Teaching with Tension: Race, Reality, and Resistance in the Classroom* (Northwestern University Press, 2018), which examines the ways in which scholars from a range of disciplines have encountered and addressed obstacles to teaching about race during a Trump regime. Currently, she is working on a monograph, tentatively titled *Race and Respectability in Early Black Atlantic Literature*, which examines the ways in which issues of race and class merge in the emancipation rhetoric of an early black Atlantic.